The Garlic Ballads

MO YAN was born in 1956 and is a native of Shandong, China. The author of several novels including *Red Sorghum* (made into the internationally acclaimed feature film), dozens of novellas, and numerous short stories, he has won virtually every national literary prize and is the most highly praised Chinese writer of his generation.

HOWARD GOLDBLATT is one of the world's leading translators of Chinese literature. He teaches at the University of Notre Dame.

Mo Yan

The Garlic Ballads

Translated from the Chinese
by Howard Goldblatt

Methuen

Published by Methuen 2006

1 3 5 7 9 10 8 6 4 2

This translation first published in Great Britain by Hamish Hamilton 1995
Published in 2006 by Methuen Publishing Ltd
11–12 Buckingham Gate, London SW1E 6LB
www.methuen.co.uk

Methuen Publishing Limited Reg. No. 3543167

This work was originally published in China in different form by
Writers Publishing House, Beijing, 1988. A portion of this book
first appeared in the magazine *October*, no. 1, 1988

A CIP catalogue record for this book is available from the British Library

ISBN 10: 0-413-77531-3
ISBN 13: 978-0-413-77531-3

Printed a 1, Surrey

T
by way of t circulated
in any for ished and
without a ed on the

Northeast Gaomi Township:
I was born there, I grew up there;
Even though there was plenty of misery,
These mournful ballads are for you.

Novelists are forever trying to distance themselves from politics, but the novel itself closes in on politics. Novelists are so concerned with "man's fate" that they tend to lose sight of their own fate. Therein lies their tragedy.

– Josef Stalin

The Garlic Ballads

CHAPTER 1

Pray listen, my fellow villagers, to
Zhang Kou's tale of the mortal world and Paradise!
The nation's founder, Emperor Liu of the Great Han,
Commanded citizens of our county to plant garlic for tribute. . . .

– from a ballad by Zhang Kou, Paradise
County's blind minstrel

1

"Gao Yang!"

The noonday sun beat down fiercely; dusty air carried the stink of rotting garlic after a prolonged dry spell. A flock of indigo crows flew wearily across the sky, casting a shadowy wedge. There had been no time to braid the garlic, which lay in heaps, reeking as it baked in the sun. Gao Yang, whose eyebrows sloped downward at the ends, was squatting alongside a table, holding a bowl of garlic broth and fighting back the waves of nausea rising from his stomach. The urgent shout had come in through his unlatched gate as he was about to take a sip of the broth. He recognized the voice as belonging to the village boss, Gao Jinjiao. Hastily laying down his bowl, he shouted a reply and walked to the door. "Is that you, Uncle Jinjiao? Come on in."

This time the voice was gentler. "Gao Yang, come out here for a minute. I have to talk to you about something."

Knowing the consequences of slighting the village boss, Gao

Yang turned to his blind eight-year-old daughter, who sat frozen at the table like a dark statue, her black, beautiful, sightless eyes opened wide. "Don't touch anything, Xinghua, or you might scald yourself."

Baked earth burned the soles of his feet; the intense heat made his eyes water. With the sun beating down on his bare back, he scraped caked-on dirt from his chest. He heard the cry of his newborn baby on the kang, a brick platform that served as the family's bed, and thought he heard his wife mumble something. Finally, he had a son. It was a comforting thought. The fragrance of new millet drifted up on a southwestern breeze, reminding him that harvest was approaching. Suddenly his heart sank, and a chill worked its way up his spine. He wanted desperately to stop walking, but his legs kept propelling him forward, as the pungent odor of garlic stalks and bulbs made his eyes water. He raised his bare arm to wipe them, confident that he wasn't crying.

He opened the gate. "What is it, Uncle?" he asked. "Ow! . . . Mother—!" Emerald bits streaked past him, like millions of green garlic stalks swirling in the air; something struck his right ankle, a dull, heavy, gut-wrenching blow. Momentarily stunned, he closed his eyes and assumed that the sound he heard was his own scream as he slumped to one side. Another dull thud behind his left knee. He screamed in pain—there was no denying it this time—and pitched forward, winding up on his knees on the stone steps. Dazed, he tried to open his eyes, but the lids were too heavy, and the pungent, garlicky air drew tears. Still, he knew he wasn't crying. He raised his hand to rub his eyes, only to discover that his wrists were snared painfully by something cold and hard; two faint metallic clicks knifed into his brain.

Finally he opened his eyes. Through the film of tears—I'm not crying, he thought—he saw two policemen in white tunics and green pants with red stripes down the legs; they towered over him, pale smudges on their pants and dark stains on their tunics. But what caught his attention were the pistols and the dark nightsticks that hung from wide, cordovan-colored, artificial-leather belts cinching up their tunics. The buckles glinted in the sun. He looked up into the men's expressionless faces, but before he could utter a sound, the man on the left waved a sheet of paper with an official red seal in front of him and said with a slight stammer, "Y-you're under arrest."

That was when he noticed the shiny steel bracelets on his sunburned wrists. They were linked by a slack, heavy, silvery chain that swayed lazily when he raised his hands. A powerful shudder wracked him. The blood flowed sluggishly through his veins, and he felt himself shrinking: his testicles retreated into his body and his guts knotted up. Chilled drops of urine on his thighs informed him that he was peeing his pants, and he tried to hold it back. But the lilting, mournful cries of the blind minstrel Zhang Kou's two-stringed *erhu* reached his ears, and his muscles turned slack and useless; an icy stream of urine ran down his leg, soaked his buttocks, and washed the callused soles of his feet as he knelt. He actually heard it slosh around in his crotch.

The policeman on the left took Gao Yang's arm in his ice-cold hand to help him up. Another slight stammer. "G-get up."

Still dazed, Gao Yang reached for the policeman's arm, but the handcuffs, clanking softly, dug into his flesh and forced him to let go. Fearfully, he held his arms stiffly out in front, as if cupping a precious, fragile object.

"G-get up!" The policeman's order rang out. He struggled to his feet, but was no sooner standing than a searing pain tore through his ankle. He lurched sideways and fell to his hands and knees on the stone steps.

The policemen grabbed him under the arms and picked him up. But his legs were so rubbery that his gangly frame dangled in their grasp like a pendulum. The policeman on his right drove his knee into Gao Yang's tailbone. "Stand up!" he growled. "What happened to the hero who demolished the county offices?"

The comment was lost on Gao Yang, but the rock-hard knee against his tailbone helped him forget the pain in his ankle. With a shudder he planted his feet and stood up. The policemen loosened their grip, and the one with the stammer said softly, "G-get moving, and h-hurry."

His head was swimming, but he remained confident that he wasn't crying, even as hot tears welled up and spilled over to cloud his vision. The handcuffs dug deeply into his wrists each time he was shoved forward, and he suddenly—finally—realized what was happening. He knew he had to find the will to force his stiffened tongue to move: not daring to address his tormentors, he gazed pitifully at Gao Jinjiao, who was cowering beneath an acacia tree, and said, "Uncle, why are they arresting me? I haven't done anything wrong. . . ."

Wails and sobs followed. This time he knew he was crying, even though no tears flowed from his now dry, burning eyes. He must plead his case to the village boss, who had tricked him into coming outside in the first place. But Gao Jinjiao was rocking back and forth, bumping against the tree like a penitent little boy. A muscle on Gao Yang's face twitched. "I haven't done anything, Uncle, why did you trick me like that?" He was shouting. A large bead of sweat on the village boss's forehead refused to roll down. With his yellow teeth bared, he looked like a cornered man about to break and run.

The policeman again drove his knee into Gao Yang's tailbone to get him moving. "Comrade Officer," he protested, turning to look into the man's face, "you've got the wrong man. My name's Gao Yang. I'm not—"

"W-we've got the right man," the stammerer insisted.

"My name's Gao Yang. . . ."

"Gao Yang is who we want!"

"What did I do?"

"At noon on May twenty-eighth you were one of the leaders of a mob that demolished the county offices."

The lights went out as Gao Yang crumpled to the ground. When they picked him up again, he rolled his eyes and said timidly, "You call that a *crime?*"

"That's right—now get moving!"

"But I wasn't alone. Lots of people were involved."

"And we'll catch every last one of them."

He hung his head, wishing he could butt it into the wall and end everything. But he was being held too firmly to squirm free, and he could hear the faint strains of Zhang Kou's moving yet dreary ballad:

> In the tenth year of the Republic
> A hot-blooded young man came out of nowhere
> To hoist the red flag in Paradise County
> And lead the peasants in a protest against unfair taxes.
> Village elders dispatched soldiers to surround them,
> Arrested Gao Dayi and sent him to the executioner's block.
> He went to his death proudly, defiantly,
> For the Communists, like scallions, could not all be felled.

He felt a warmth in his belly as the strength returned to his legs. His lips trembled, and he felt strangely compelled to shout a defiant slogan. But then he turned and stared at the bright red insignia on the policeman's wide-brimmed cap, and lowered his head again, overcome with shame and remorse; letting his arms fall slack in front of him, he followed obediently.

Then he heard a tapping sound behind him and strained to see what it was: his daughter, Xinghua, was walking toward him, tapping the ground with a scarred and scorched bamboo staff that banged crisply against the stone steps and resonated painfully in his heart. He grimaced, as hot tears gushed from his eyes. He was truly crying; there was no denying it now. A scalding liquid stopped up his throat when he tried to speak.

Xinghua was clad only in a pair of red underpants and plastic red shoes whose frayed laces were held together by black thread. Dirt smudged her naked belly and neck. Pale ears beneath a boyish crewcut were pricked up alertly. The scalding blockage in his throat wouldn't go down.

She took high, arching steps—he noticed for the first time what long legs she had—as she crossed the threshold and stood on the stone steps where he had knelt a moment earlier. Her staff was a foot or so taller than she, and he was suddenly and surprisingly aware of how tall she had grown. He tried again to force down the gooey lump in his throat as he gazed at the two shiny black dots in her cinder-streaked face. Her eyes were a dense, demonic black, seemingly with no white at all, and as she cocked her head, a strange expression of mature worldliness settled over her face. She called out to him softly, tentatively, before a scream tore from her throat: "Daddy!"

Moisture gathered in the corners of his mouth. One of the policemen prodded him hesitantly. "C-come on," he said gently, "get moving. They may let you out in a day or two."

Spasms wracked Gao Yang's throat and guts as he stared at the stammering policeman, with his smug, ingratiating look; Gao Yang's teeth parted, and out gushed a stream of white froth streaked with pale-blue threads. He wasted no time, now that his throat was clear: "Xinghua! Go tell Mommy—" His throat closed up again before he could get the rest out.

Gao Jinjiao slinked up to the gate and said, "Go home and tell your mommy that your daddy's been taken away by the police."

Gao Yang watched his daughter drop down on the threshold and rock backward, barely catching herself with a hand on the ground. With the help of her bamboo staff, she stood up again; her mouth was open, as if screaming, though Gao Yang heard nothing but a rumbling noise that might have been far off or could have been right next to him. Another wave of nausea hit him. His daughter looked like a chained monkey being whipped and dragged roughly along, leaping silently but wildly from side to side. Her staff tapped the stone threshold, tapped the rotting wood around it, tapped the hard, dry earth, leaving a track of pale scars in the ground.

His wife's tormented screams from the yard pounded in his ears. "Village Chief Gao," the policeman said, "you lead the way. Let's get out of here." They lifted Gao Yang by the arms, as they would a stubborn, spindly little boy, and dragged him toward the village as fast as their legs would carry them.

2

They dragged him until his heart was racing, until he was gasping for breath and he sweat-stank. To the west of a dark line of acacia trees he saw three buildings with red roofs, but since he seldom ventured beyond the village, he wasn't sure who lived there. They dragged him into the acacia grove, where they stretched and caught their breath. He noticed that their clothes were sweat-soaked under the arms and around the midriff, which earned for them both his respect and his pity.

Gao Jinjiao slipped into the grove. He spoke in whispers. "In the room . . . peeked through the window . . . sprawled across the kang fast asleep . . ."

"H-how should we take him?" the stammering policeman asked his partner. "Have the village chief trick him into coming out? It won't be easy. He used to be a soldier."

Now he knew who they were after. It was Gao Ma; it had to be Gao Ma. He glared at the balding village boss, and would have bitten him if he could.

"No, we'll rush him. We can always bring him down with our prods if need be."

"You don't need me anymore, Officers, so I'll be on my way," Gao Jinjiao said.

"D-don't need you anymore? You have to watch *him*."

He glared at Gao Jinjiao.

"I can't watch him, Officer. If he got away, you'd say it was my fault."

The stammering policeman wiped his sweaty face with his sleeve. "Gao Yang," he said, "you g-going to try to run away?"

Feeling suddenly and perversely defiant, Gao Yang snarled through clenched teeth, "Just you watch me!"

The policeman grinned, revealing two shiny incisors. "D-did you hear that? H-he says he'll take off! The monk can run away, but the temple stays." Removing a ring of keys from his pocket, he fiddled with the handcuffs for a moment. *Snap!* They popped open. He grinned at Gao Yang, who already was rubbing the purple welts on his wrists, a flood of gratitude engulfing him. Once again tears spilled from his eyes. Let them flow, he consoled himself. I am *not* crying.

He gazed into the policeman's face with a look of rapturous anticipation. "Comrade," he said, "does this mean I can go home?"

"Home? We'll send you home all right, just not now."

The policeman signaled his partner, who walked behind Gao Yang and shoved him up against a tree, so hard he banged his nose against the rough bark. Then, before he knew what was happening, his arms were jerked forward until they girded the tree, where the stammering policeman snapped on the cuffs. He was now embracing a tree so big around he couldn't see his hands. He and the tree were one. Enraged by this turn of events, he banged his forehead against the trunk, sending leaves fluttering and cicadas flying, their chilled urine wetting the nape of his neck.

"Didn't you say you were going to r-run away?" the policeman mocked. "Go ahead. P-pull the tree up by its roots and take it with you."

As Gao Yang strained to move, a thorn pricked him in the belly— all the way to his guts, it seemed, since they chose that moment to knot up. To separate himself from it, he had to lean back as far as his arms would allow and let the cuffs dig into his wrists. Then, by arching his back and letting his head droop, he was able to confirm that the blackish-red thorn was no longer stuck in him. White fibers dangled from the tip, and a single drop of blood, also blackish red, oozed from the tiny puncture wound. Now that the crotch of his pants was nearly dry, he noticed the crusty edges of a urine stain that wound around the seat of his pants like a cloud formation. He also saw that his right ankle was swollen and discolored; dead skin had curled back to the edges of the swelling, like transparent sloughed-off snakeskin.

He shifted his body away from the thorn and glared with defensive loathing at the policeman's black leather boots, which shone beneath spattered mud. If they had been wearing cloth shoes, he was thinking, my ankle wouldn't be all puffy. He tried flexing it, but that only sent the bone-crushing pains shooting up his leg. Even as his eyes puddled he reminded himself, Gao Yang, your tears may flow, but you are not crying!

The policemen, one with his pistol drawn, the other holding a black prod, tiptoed up to Gao Ma's yard, where the eastern wall had crumbled until the bricks stood no more than two or three feet high; they could nearly step over it. Inside the yard, a pair of ailanthus "trees of heaven," with droopy leaves, stood at the base of the western wall, creating slivers of shade for a handful of chickens wilting under the scorching sunlight that settled upon piles of rotting garlic like molten silver. Nausea welled up inside Gao Yang. After the price of garlic plummeted the month before, he had begun to associate the long, sleek plants with maggots on a manure pile; the nausea refocused his mind in that direction.

A cracked iron pot lay upside-down beneath the window of one of the red-roofed houses, and he saw the policeman holding the black prod—the one with the stammer—stand on it and crane his neck to see Gao Ma sleeping on his kang. The village boss, Gao Jinjiao, leaned against a tree and bumped it rhythmically with his back. Chickens with mud-encrusted white feathers were squatting in a clump of grass under the blazing sun, stretching out their wings to soak up its energy. "Chicken wings absorbing rays, it'll rain within three days." That was a comforting thought. By craning his neck, Gao Yang caught a glimpse of sky through a fork in the branches. It was bright blue and cloudless; purple rays of sunlight streamed earthward, making the chickens stir and part the grass with their claws. The stammering policeman's partner was right behind him, revolver at the ready, its blue metal glistening. His mouth gaped as he held his breath.

Gao Yang lowered his head, sending drops of cooled sweat sliding down the tree to the ground. The policemen exchanged glances; then the pushing and shoving began: You first. No, you. Gao Yang knew what *that* was all about. Then it was settled, apparently, for the stammering policeman hitched up his belt, and his partner clamped his lips so tightly that Gao Yang saw only a thin, shiny slit in his face. A long, languid fart fanned out under Gao Jinjiao's tree. The policemen tensed like tomcats about to pounce on a mouse.

"Run, Gao Ma, run! It's the police!" The moment the shout left his mouth he felt cold all over and his teeth chattered. It was fear, no mistaking that. Fear and regret. Squeezing his trembling lips shut, he stared straight ahead. The stammering policeman spun around, tripped on the rusty pot, and all but crashed to the ground. His partner, meanwhile, burst into the room, pistol in hand, the stammerer hard on his heels. A crash; then the clang of something hitting a wall.

"Hands up!"

"Put your hands up!"

Gao Yang's eyes were awash with tears. I'm not crying, he reassured himself, I am *not* crying. He could all but see a pair of gleaming bracelets like the ones he had now encircling Gao Ma's powerful wrists. His hands felt puffy and heavy, although he couldn't see around the tree trunk to confirm that. The sensation was one of blood distending the veins until they were about to release geysers of the dark red liquid.

Following a brief but noisy scuffle, the window banged open and a shadowy figure burst through. It was Gao Ma, wearing only a pair of olive-drab underpants. He stumbled over the upturned pot but scrambled back to his feet. The linked actions were clumsy: with his rear end sticking up in the air and his feet and hands clawing at the ground, he looked like a baby that has just learned to crawl.

Gao Yang's lips parted, and from somewhere deep in his cranium he heard a voice, similar to his own yet somehow different, say, You're not laughing, did you know that? You're not.

The rainbow vanished, the sky turned blue-gray, and the sun blazed.

Pow!

The stammering policeman jumped through the window and embedded his booted foot in the overturned pot. He fell to his hands and knees, one foot stuck in the pot, the other resting against it; one hand was empty, the other grasped the black prod. His partner ran out the door, pistol in hand. "Stop right there!" he screamed. "Stop or I'll shoot!" But he didn't shoot, not even when Gao Ma leapt over the crumbling wall and took off running down the lane, sending the sunning chickens scurrying from their grassy redoubts, only to close in behind him like a squawking shadow. The stammering policeman's wide-brimmed cap, dislodged on his way out the window, perched precariously on the sill before landing on its owner's upraised rump, and from there fell to the ground, where it rolled around until the other policeman kicked it ten or fifteen feet as he turned and jumped the wall, leaving his partner to bang on the pot with his prod, filling the air with slivers of metal and loud clangs.

Gao Yang had an unobstructed view of the man extricating his foot from the pot. An isolated image popped into his head: a policeman's leg. The policeman scooped up his cap and jammed it on his head as he followed his partner over the wall.

Gao Ma tore through the acacia grove with such speed that Gao Yang nearly wrenched his neck following Gao Ma's progress as he crashed and thudded his way along blindly, bumping into trees when he glanced over his shoulder; young trees swayed, old ones groaned. Gao Yang was frantic. Can't you make those powerful legs and muscular arms go any faster? Move! They're right behind you!

His anxiety mounted. White and yellow spots shimmered gracefully on Gao Ma's sunburned skin under the mottled shade of acacia trees. His legs seemed lashed together, like a great horse in fetters. He was flailing his arms. Why look back, you dumb bastard? With his bared teeth and long, drawn face, Gao Ma looked just like his namesake, *ma*, the horse.

As he followed his partner through the grove, the stammering policeman limped from his run-in with the pot. Serves you right! The pain in Gao Yang's ankle was excruciating, as if it had separated from its moorings. Serves you right, damn you! The sound of gnashing teeth rose from somewhere deep inside his ears.

"Stop, damn you, stop where you are! One more step and I'll shoot!" the policeman warned for the second time. But still he didn't shoot. Instead he ran from the protection of one tree to another at a crouch, his weapon at the ready. The hunter was beginning to look like the hunted.

The far edge of the acacia grove was bordered by a shoulder-high wall topped by woven millet stalks. Gao Yang twisted himself around the tree just in time to see Gao Ma stymied by the obstacle. His pursuers had their weapons drawn. "Don't move!" Gao Ma pressed up against the wall. Blood seeped through the cracks between his teeth. A steel loop dangled from his right wrist; attached to the other end was its mate, linked by a short chain. They had managed to cuff only one of his wrists.

"Stand right there and don't move! You'll only make things worse by resisting arrest!"

They approached him shoulder to shoulder, the stammering policeman's limp as noticeable as ever.

Gao Yang quaked so violently he set the leaves of the tree in motion. He stopped looking at Gao Ma's face as it faded into the distance. The policemen's white backs, Gao Ma's tanned face, and the black leaves of the acacia trees flattened out and were stamped on the yellow earth.

What happened next took both Gao Yang *and* the policemen by surprise: Gao Ma crouched down, scooped up some dirt, and flung it in their faces. The powdery soil covered them like dust clouds as they instinctively raised their arms to protect their eyes and stumbled backwards, regaining their three-dimensional form. Gao Ma spun around and climbed up onto the wall. Two shots rang out; two puffs of dust rose from the wall. Gao Ma screamed— "Mother!"—and tumbled over to the other side.

Gao Yang screamed, too, and banged his head against the tree trunk. The shrill cries of a little girl emerged from the acacia grove behind Gao Ma's home.

The soil beyond the grove was barren and sandy; after that came a sandbar dotted with red willows, which sloped into a dry riverbed. A second sandbar rose on the other side, fronting a government compound ringed by white poplars, and an asphalt road that led to the county seat.

CHAPTER 2

Paradise County garlic is long and crunchy —
For pork liver or fried mutton forget the onions and ginger:
Planting leeks and selling garlic will make you rich —
You'll have new clothes, new homes, even a new bride. . . .

> — From a ballad sung one summer night in 1986 by
> Zhang Kou, the blind minstrel

1

The garlic stalks had all been sold, and braids of bulbs hung from the eaves. Next came the millet crop, which was spread out to dry before being stored in vats and barrels. The threshing floor in front of Fourth Aunt's home was swept clean by dusk, with stacks of aromatic chaff rising darkly beneath shimmering starlight. June breezes sweeping in from the fields made the lantern flame dance, despite the glass shade, against which green moths banged noisily— *tick tick tick.* No one was paying any attention to this except for Gao Ma. All the others sat or stood or squatted in the lamplight, absorbed by the sight of Zhang Kou, the blind minstrel, on a stool, his high cheekbones illuminated by golden lamplight that transformed his dark, gaunt face.

I'm going to hold her hand tonight, that's all there is to it, Gao Ma resolved with growing excitement. Waves of cool contentment rippled from his body as, out of the corner of his eye, he saw Fourth Aunt's daughter, Jinju, standing no more than three steps from him. As soon as Zhang Kou picks up his *erhu* to sing the first line of his ballad, I'll grab her hand and squeeze it, squeeze each finger. That face, round like a golden-petaled sunflower, is enough to break your heart. Even her ears are golden. She may not be tall, but she's strong as a baby ox. I can't wait any longer; she's twenty already. The heat from her body warms me.

Zhang Kou coughed, and Gao Ma silently moved a step closer to Jinju. Now, like everyone else, he kept his eyes on Zhang Kou.

The fresh aroma of horse manure drifted over from the far edge of the threshing floor, where a chestnut colt galloped noisily, whinnying with spirit. Stars shone brightly in the deep, dark, downy-soft canopy of heaven, beneath which cornstalks, straining to grow tall, stretched and rustled. Everyone was watching Zhang Kou and murmuring unintelligibly from time to time. Zhang Kou sat straight as a board as he fingered his *erhu* with one hand and pulled the horsehair bow with the other, making the two strings sing out with a muffled scratchiness slowly rounding out into crisp, mellow notes that tightened around his listeners' eager hearts. Eyelashes buried in his sunken sockets fluttered, and as he stretched his neck toward his audience, he tilted his head backward as though gazing into the starry night.

Gao Ma edged up so close to Jinju he could hear the faint sound of her breathing and feel the heat of her voluptuous body. His hand moved timidly toward hers, like a pet wanting to nuzzle. Fourth Aunt, perched on a high stool in front of Jinju, coughed. Gao Ma shuddered and jammed his hand into his pants pocket; with an impatient shrug of his shoulders, he stepped out of the ring of light and hid his face in the shadow of someone's head.

Zhang Kou's *erhu* wept, but the sound was soft and gentle, glossy and smooth, like silken strands flowing into his listeners' hearts, driving the accumulated filth ahead of it, and into their muscles and flesh, ridding them of their earthly dust. With eyes glued to Zhang Kou's mouth, they listened as a hoarse yet sonorous lyric flowed from the gaping hole in his face:

"What I'm saying is"—the word "is" soared upward, then settled slowly, languidly, as if it wanted the crowd to follow it from this world into a fantastic realm beckoning to all, asking only that they close their eyes—"what I'm saying is, a breath of fresh air emerged from the Third Plenum of the Central Committee: Citizens of Paradise County will be poor no longer."

His *erhu* never varied from the same simple refrain, and his audience, though enraptured by the music, also quietly laughed at him. The source of their mirth was his gaping mouth, which could accommodate a whole steamed bun. The blind bastard had no idea how big his mouth was. Their tittering appeared not to bother him. When Gao Ma heard Jinju giggle, he pictured a smiling face: lashes fluttering, teeth glistening like rows of polished jade. No longer able to restrain himself, he peeked out of the corner of his eye; but her lashes weren't fluttering, and her teeth were hidden behind compressed lips. Her solemn expression mocked him somehow.

"The county government called on us to plant garlic—the marketing co-op would buy our harvest—one yuan a pound—put it in cold storage—resell at a profit in the spring. . . ." Having grown accustomed to the sight of Zhang Kou's gaping mouth, the crowd forgot its mirthful-ness and listened intently to his ballad.

"The people celebrated when they sold their garlic / Fried some pork, rolled out flatcakes and filled them with green onions / Big Sister Zhang's belly as big as an urn / 'Oh!' she says, 'look at me, I'm pregnant!' . . ." The crowd roared playfully. "Damn you, blind old man!" a woman shouted. A heated fart escaped from Big Sister Li: "Ha, ha," half the women in the audience doubled over laughing.

Jinju was one of them. Damn you, Zhang Kou, do you have to say things like that? Gao Ma swore to himself. When you bend over, your round, tight rear end sticks straight up and I can see the line of your underpants through your thin trousers. That's what happens in the field during the day. Try a tale from *Red Crag*, Zhang Kou. I want to hold your hand, Jinju. I'm twenty-seven already; you're twenty. I want you to be my wife. When you hoe your bean field, I spray my cornfield, my heart sounding like aphids on corn in the dry season. The fields seem endless. Off to the south stands Little Mount Zhou, with its volcanic opening, into which the clouds settle. I ache to talk to you at times like that, but your brothers are always nearby, barefoot and stripped to the waist, their skin burned black by the sun. You are fully dressed, and sweat-soaked. What color are you, Jinju? You are yellow, you are red, you are golden. Yours is the color of gold; you glisten like gold.

Zhang Kou's *erhu* grew more melodious as his voice rose with a tale from *Red Crag*:

> *Jiang Xueqin, out for a stroll,*
> *The police chief swaggers toward her,*
> *A golden watch on his wrist,*
> *His neck a ten-foot garlic stalk.*
> *He crouches as he walks,*
> *He has a Chinese papa and an American mama,*
> *Who joined to produce a living monster.*
> *He leers through slanted eyes,*
> *A pistol held in each hand.*
> *He blocks her way, a sinister laugh,*
> *Heh heh . . .*
> *Pistols pressed up to Big Sister Jiang's breasts.*

She's too good for someone like Liu Shengli. Marrying him would be like planting a flower in a pile of cow dung, or seeing a gorgeous butterfly fall in love with a dung beetle. I'm going to hold her hand. Tonight's the night. He inched closer to her, until he felt their trousers touch. He kept staring at Zhang Kou's mouth—opening and closing, opening and closing—trying to appear calm and composed. Is there no sound coming from that mouth, or is it being drowned out by the din around me? My heart sounds like corn leaves rustling in the wind. And he remembered when he first felt his heart moving toward Jinju, a year earlier.

*

I am lying in the cornfield gazing at clouds being carved up by sharp-edged leaves above me. The clouds vanish, and the sky is clear; the sun-baked ground blisters my back. White sap beads up and dangles from downy filaments, reluctant to fall earthward, like the tears on her lashes . . . millet moves in waves, then is stilled when the wind stops. The ripe stalks bow low as a pair of screeching magpies flies past, one nipping at the other's tail. A curious sparrow follows them, mixing its cries with theirs. The air is pungent with the smell of garlic fresh from the ground.

Jinju is alone in the field, bent over as she cuts down the millet, dropping handful after handful between her legs, where it rustles heavily, hits the ground, and curls upward like a bushy yellow tail. My millet is all bundled and stacked. Emaciated lines of corn trying to see the sun fill the gaps between the stacks, the results of inter-cropping; but the millet bullies the puny cornstalks. Two acres isn't enough for a bachelor like me. I've had my eye on her ever since I was discharged from the army last year. She's no beauty; but then neither am I. Not that she's ugly; but then neither am I. She was just a gangly little girl when I left; now she's so grown up, and so robust. I like robust women. I'll take my millet home this afternoon. My Shanghai-made Diamond-Brand wristwatch, which runs about twenty seconds fast every day, says 11:03. I set it with the radio a few days ago, so it's actually right on eleven. I can take my time getting home.

Gao Ma's sense of pity ran deep as he stood, scythe in hand, secretly watching Jinju, who worked with the same concentration as the magpies chasing one another overhead, followed closely by the solitary sparrow. She didn't know someone was behind her. Gao Ma kept a small cassette player in his pocket, listening to it with ear-phones. The rundown batteries distorted the sound. But it was good music, and that's what counted. A young girl is like a flower. Jinju's back was broad and flat, her hair damp. She was breathing hard.

The good-hearted Gao Ma removed the earphones and lay them against his neck, where the distorted music was still audible. "Jinju," he called out softly. Music coming through the spongy earphone tips vibrated against his throat, making it itch. He reached up and adjusted them.

She straightened up slowly, a blank look on her sweaty, dusty face. She was holding a scythe in her right hand and a bundle of millet in her left. Wordlessly she gazed into the face of Gao Ma, who was mesmerized by the curve of her bosom beneath the pockets of a tattered, faded blue tunic. He said nothing. Jinju tossed down her scythe, split the millet into two bundles, and laid them on the ground. Then she took out a piece of hemp and wrapped up the bundles.

"Jinju, why do you have to do this alone?"

"My brother went to market," she replied softly, wiping her face with her sleeve and pounding her waist with a fist. Sweat had turned her face pale. Wet strands of hair stuck to her temples.

"Cramp in your side?"

She smiled. Faint green stains dotted her front teeth, but the others sparkled. A missing collar button revealed an expanse of soft, white cleavage that unnerved him. The open throat was dotted with tiny red marks from the millet spikes, which had also deposited bits of white powder on her skin.

"Your older brother went to market?" He wished he hadn't said that, since her older brother was a cripple; it was the second brother who normally went to market.

"No," she replied evenly.

"Then he should be out here helping you."

She squinted in the sunlight. He felt sorry for her.

"What time is it, Elder Brother Gao Ma?"

He looked at his watch. "Eleven-fifteen." He quickly added, "But my watch is a little fast."

She sighed softly and looked over at his field of millet. "You're lucky, Elder Brother Gao Ma, you've got only yourself to worry about. Now that you're finished, you can take it easy." She sighed again, then turned and picked up her scythe. "I have to get back to work."

He stood motionless behind her bent figure for a moment. "I'll help you," he said with a sigh.

"Thanks, but I can't let you do that," she said as she straightened up.

He looked her in the eye. "Why not? I don't have anything else to do. Besides, what are neighbors for?"

She lowered her head and muttered, "Well, I could use some help. . . ."

He took the cassette player out of his pocket, switched it off, and laid it on the ground, earphones and all.

"What do you play on that?" she asked.

"Music," he replied, cinching up his belt.

"It must sound nice."

"It's okay, except the batteries are getting low. I'll get some new ones tomorrow, so you can listen to it."

"Not me," she said with a smile. "If I broke it, I couldn't afford to have it fixed."

"It's not *that* fragile," he said. "And it's the simplest thing in the world. Besides, I'd never make you pay."

They began cutting her millet, which rustled loudly. She walked ahead of him, but for every two rows she cut, he managed three; she laid out the bundles, he picked them up.

"Your father's not too old to be out here helping you," he grumbled.

Her scythe stopped in midair. "He has guests today."

The heavy-hearted, mournful tone of her comment did not escape Gao Ma, who dropped the subject and returned to his work. His mood was further soured by the millet brushing against his face and shoulders. "I cut three rows for every two of yours, and you're getting in my way," he snapped.

"Elder Brother Gao Ma," she complained, on the verge of tears, "I'm worn out."

"I should have guessed," he replied. "This is no job for a woman."

"People can endure anything."

"If I had a wife, she'd be home in the kitchen or mending clothes or feeding the chickens. I'd never make her work in the fields."

Jinju looked at him and muttered, "She's a lucky woman, whoever she is."

"Jinju, tell me what the villagers say about me."

"I've never heard them say anything."

"Don't worry—whatever it is, I can take it."

"Well, some of them say . . . don't get mad . . . they say you messed up in the army."

"That's right, I did."

"They say you and a regiment commander's wife . . . he caught the two of you . . ."

Gao Ma sneered. "It wasn't his wife, it was his concubine. And I didn't love her. I hated her—I hated them all."

"You've seen and done so much," she said with a sigh.

"It's not worth a dog's fart," he snarled. Throwing down his scythe, he scooped up some millet and straightened up. Kicking it angrily, he cursed again, "Not worth a dog's fart!"

Her crippled brother limped up about then, as Gao Ma recalled. Though he was not yet forty, his hair was turning white and his face was deeply wrinkled. His left leg, shorter than the right, was rail thin, giving him a pronounced limp.

"Jinju!" he bellowed. "You plan to stay here through lunch?"

Cupping his hand over his eyes, Gao Ma muttered, "Why does your brother treat you like his worst enemy?"

She bit her lip as two large tears slid down her cheeks.

Jinju, I haven't known a moment's peace since you cried that day. I love you, I want to make you my wife. . . . It's been a year already, Jinju, but you avoid me whenever I try to talk to you . . . I want to rescue you from your living hell. Zhang Kou, another dozen lines is all I ask, enough time for me to take her hand . . . even if she screams in front of everyone, even if her mother jumps up and curses or slaps me. No, she won't scream, I know she won't. She's unhappy with the marriage they've arranged for her. It was the day her older brother called out to her, the day I helped her bring in the harvest that her parents signed an agreement with Liu Shengli's grandfather and Cao Wen's parents, stringing three boys and three girls together like so many locusts, a chain with six links, a tawdry way to create new families. She doesn't hate me; she likes me. When we meet, she lowers her head and scoots by, but I can see the tears in her eyes. My heart aches my liver aches my lungs ache my stomach aches my gut aches everything inside me aches. . . . "Commander, hurry, give the order," wailed Zhang Kou. "Send your troops down the mountain . . . save our Big Sister Jiang . . . so many moths have died in the yellow flame of the lantern, our Big Sister Jiang is held captive, the masses fear for her safety. Comrades! We must be cool-headed— if they take our elder sister from us, I'll be the one to grieve. . . . The old lady fires two pistols, her white hair flutters in the wind, tears stream down her face."

Say something, Zhang Kou. Sing, Zhang Kou. "My husband languishes in a prison camp . . . his widow and orphaned daughter carry on the revolution . . ." Zhang Kou, just a couple more lines, two more, and I can take her hand, I can feel the warmth of her body, I can smell the sweat in her armpits. "Making revolution doesn't mean acting rashly. . . . It must be slow and sure, one careful step at a time."

Explosions went off inside his head, and a halo of light swirled until he was encircled by a cloud of many colors. He reached out; his hand seemed to have eyes, or maybe hers had been waiting all along. He gripped it tightly. His eyes were open, but he saw nothing. It was not cold, yet he was shivering; his heart paled.

2

The next night Gao Ma hid behind a stack of chaff on the edge of Jinju's threshing floor, waiting anxiously. It was another starry night, with the slender crescent moon hanging, it seemed, from the tip of a tall tree, its luminous rays weakened by the encircling starlight. A chestnut colt galloped along the edge of the floor, which was bordered on the south by a wide trench whose sloping banks had been planted with indigo bushes. Occasionally the colt galloped into the trench and up the other side, and when it passed through the bushes it set them rustling. The lamps were lit at Jinju's home, where her father—Fourth Uncle Fang—was in the yard talking loudly and being constantly interrupted by Fourth Aunt, Jinju's mother. Gao Ma strained to hear their conversation, but was too far away. A yardful of parakeets—well over a hundred of them—were setting up a deafening racket at the home of the Fangs' neighbor Gao Zhileng. The noise put everyone on edge. Gao Zhileng raised parakeets for profit, of which there was a great deal, and his was the only family in the village that did not rely on garlic for its livelihood.

The shrill squawks of the parakeets grated on the ears, as the chestnut colt, tail swishing rapidly, paced the area, its bright eyes poking holes in the misty darkness. It began nibbling at a pile of chaff, only half-seriously, it appeared, but enough to send the slightly mildewy smell of millet on the wind to Gao Ma, who crept around the stack to inch closer to Jinju's barred gate, through which slivers of light seeped. He couldn't tell what time it was, since his watch didn't have a luminous dial. Around nine, he figured. Just then the clock in Gao Zhileng's home began to chime, and Gao Ma moved far enough away from the parakeet squawks to count the chimes. Nine all together. He'd guessed right. His thoughts drifted back to what had happened the night before and to the movie *Le Rouge et le Noir*, which he had seen in the army: Julien takes Madame de Rênal's hand while he is counting the peals of the church bell.

Gao Ma had squeezed Jinju's hand, and she had squeezed his back. They hadn't let go until Zhang Kou finished his ballad, and then only with great reluctance. In the confusion of all the getting up and going, he whispered, "I'll be waiting for you tomorrow night by the millet chaff. We need to talk."

He wasn't looking at her, didn't even know if she heard him. But the next day he worked so absentmindedly that he frequently dug up seedlings and spared the weeds. The afternoon sun was still high in the sky when he went home, where he trimmed his beard, squeezed a couple of pimples alongside his nose, scraped some of the gunk off his teeth with the scissors, and washed his shaved scalp and neck with toilet soap. After a hurried meal he dug out his seldom-used toothbrush and toothpaste to give his teeth a good brushing.

The parakeets' squawking made him edgy, and each time he strode up to the gate, he meekly turned and headed back. Then the gate creaked, setting off a drumroll in his heart. He thrust his hand into the stack of chaff up to the elbow without feeling a thing. The chestnut colt, suddenly energized, began to gallop, its hooves sending dirt clods thudding into the chaff with scary resonance.

"Where do you think you're going at this late hour?" Fourth Aunt shouted.

"It's not late. It's barely dark out." Just hearing Jinju's voice made him feel slightly guilty.

"I asked you where you're going," Fourth Aunt repeated.

"Down to the riverbank to cool off," Jinju replied with determination.

"Don't be long."

"Don't worry, I won't run away."

Jinju, Jinju, Gao Ma moaned softly, how do you stand it all?

The latch clanged loudly as the gate was pulled shut. From his vantage point beside the chaff, Gao Ma longingly watched her blurred silhouette head north toward the river instead of coming toward him. He managed to keep from running after her, assuming this was a sham for her mother's benefit.

Jinju . . . Jinju . . . He buried his face in the chaff, his eyes dampening. Meanwhile the colt galloped back and forth behind him, and the parakeets squawked. Off to the south, in the stinking, weed-infested reservoir, frogs croaked to one another, the mournful sound falling unpleasantly on the ear.

All this reminded Gao Ma of the night three years earlier when he and the regiment commander's concubine had slipped away together: how the pert-nosed, freckle-faced woman threw herself into his arms, how he held her tight and smelled her heavy body odor. Like holding a wooden log, he embraced her even though he didn't love her. You're despicable, he had cursed himself, pretending to be in love in order to enhance your prospects with her patron. Yet things have a way of evening out, and I paid a heavy price for my hypocrisy.

But it's different with Jinju. I'd die for Jinju, my Jinju.

She walked in the shadow of the wall, skirting the starlit threshing floor, and came toward him. His heart pounded wildly, he began to tremble, his teeth chattered.

She walked around the stack and stopped a few feet from him. "What do you want to talk to me about, Elder Brother Gao Ma?" Her voice quaked.

"Jinju . . ." His lips were so stiff he could barely get the words out. He heard his own heartbeat and a voice that quaked like a woman's. He coughed—it sounded forced and unnatural.

"Don't . . . please don't make any noise," she pleaded anxiously as she backed up several steps.

The colt, feeling mischievous, rubbed its flank against the stack, even extracted some chaff with its lips and flung it to the ground in front of them.

"Not here," he said. "Let's go down to the trench."

"I can't. . . . If you have something to say, hurry up and say it."

"Not here, I said." He walked down the edge of the threshing floor, all the way to the trench. Jinju still hadn't moved. But when he turned to go back for her, she began walking timidly toward him. He threaded his way through the indigo bushes and waited for her at the bottom of the trench, and when she reached the gently sloping side, he took her hand and pulled her to him.

She tried to take her tiny hand, but he cupped it tightly in his and stroked it. "I love you, Jinju," he blurted out. "Marry me!"

"Elder Brother Gao Ma," she replied softly, "you know I've been betrothed so that my brother can get married."

"I know, but I also know it's not what you want."

She loosened his grip with her free hand and liberated its mate. "Yes it is."

"No, it's not. Liu Shengli is a forty-five-year-old man with an infected windpipe. He's too sickly to even carry a load of water. Are you telling me you'd marry coffin pulp like that?"

She whimpered in reply, the sound hanging in the air for a long moment. "What can I do?" she sobbed. "My brother's over thirty . . . a cripple . . . Cao Wenling is only seventeen, and prettier than me. . . ."

"You're not your brother, and you're not required to go to your grave for his sake."

"Elder Brother Gao Ma, it's fate. Go find yourself a good woman. . . . Me . . . next life . . ." Holding her face in her hands, she turned and broke for the indigo bushes. But he grabbed her, making her stumble and fall into his embrace.

He hugged her so tightly he could feel the heat of her soft belly, but when he tried to find her mouth with his, she covered her face with her hands. Undaunted, he began nibbling her earlobe, as fine strands of hair brushed his face. His chill was replaced by hot cinders deep in his heart. She began to squirm, as if tormented by a powerful itch. Suddenly letting her hands drop, she threw her arms around his neck. "Elder Brother Gao Ma, please don't nibble my ear," she begged tearfully. "I can't bear it. . . ." He moved his mouth back to hers and began sucking on her tongue. She groaned, as hot tears welled up and wetted both their faces. A surge of hot air floated up from her stomach, bestowing on Gao Ma the taste of garlic and fresh grass.

His hands moved roughly over her body.

"Elder Brother Gao Ma, not so rough. You're hurting me."

They sat on the slope of the trench in each other's arms, hands roaming freely. Through cracks in the lush indigo covering they caught glimpses of golden starlight in the deep-blue sky. The crescent moon was sinking. An orbiting satellite tore through the Milky Way, and the air was suffused with the distinctive aroma of indigo.

"What do you love about me?" she asked, looking up at him.

"Everything."

The night was cooling off. They talked in hushed tones.

"But you know I'm spoken for," she said with a shiver. "What we're doing, it's wrong, isn't it?"

"No, it's not. We're in love."

"But I'm betrothed."

"You have to register to be legally married."

"Does that mean we can be together?"

"Yes. Just tell your father you won't agree to the wedding."

"No," she protested, tripping over her tongue. "They'd kill me. . . . I've been a burden to them for so long."

"Does that mean you'd rather marry a dying old man?"

"I'm afraid." By now she was weeping. "Mother says she'll take poison if I don't."

"Scare tactics."

"You don't know her."

"I know she's just trying to scare you."

"Wouldn't it be wonderful if you had a younger sister? She could marry my brother and I could be your wife."

Gao Ma sighed and rubbed her chilled shoulder. He was nearly in tears.

"Elder Brother Gao Ma, we can be secret lovers. Then when he dies, we'll get married."

"No!" Gao Ma exploded. He kissed her, and could feel the heat in her belly. A hairy mouth above them touched their heads, as the sound of raspy breathing and the smell of fresh grass settled around their necks. It scared them half to death, until they discovered to their relief that it was only the colt, up to a little mischief.

3

Jinju showed Gao Ma the fateful wedding contract. She had come to his home at noon, a month after their tryst amid the indigo. They had met nearly every night after that first one—in the trench, then later in the fields, hiding in farmland planted with shallots. They watched the progress of full moon and crescent moon, with or without cloud cover; leaves were dusted with silver, insects chirped and screeched, cool dew moistened the dry earth below. She wept and he laughed; he wept and she laughed. The fiery passions of love made the young couple grow haggard, but their eyes glowed and crackled like hot cinders.

Jinju's parents had sent an angry message to Gao Ma: there has never been hostility or rancor between our families, and you have no right to interfere with our arranged marriages.

Jinju burst through the door like a whirlwind and looked anxiously over her shoulder, as if she were being followed. Gao Ma led her over to the kang, where she sat down. "They won't come for us, will they?" she asked in a tremulous voice.

"No," he assured her, handing her a cup of water. But she scarcely moistened her lips before setting the ebony-colored cup down on the table. "Don't worry, no one will come," he reassured her. "And what if they did? We have nothing to be ashamed about."

"I brought it." She removed a folded piece of red paper from her pocket and dropped it onto the table before sprawling out on the kang, burying her face in her arms and bursting into tears.

Gao Ma gently rubbed her back to get her to stop crying; but when he saw it was futile, he unfolded the sheet of red paper, which was covered with black calligraphy:

On the auspicious tenth day of the six month in the year nineteen hundred and eighty-five we betroth the eldest grandson of Liu Jiaqing, **Liu Shengli,** to **Fang Jinju,** daughter of Fang Yunqiu; the second daughter of Cao Jinzhu, **Cao Wenling,** to the eldest son of

Fang Yunqiu, **Fang Yijun**; and the second granddaughter of Liu Jiaqing, **Liu Lanlan,** to the eldest son of Cao Jinzhu, **Cao Wen**. With this agreement, our families are forever linked, even if the rivers run dry and the oceans become deserts. Witness the three principals: Liu Jiaqing, Fang Yunqiu, Cao Jinzhu.

Dark fingerprints were affixed to the paper beside the names of the three men.

Gao Ma refolded the contract and stuffed it into his pocket, then opened a drawer and removed a booklet. "Jinju," he said, "stop crying and listen to the Marriage Law. Section 3 says, 'Arranged marriages, mercenary marriages, and all other types that restrict individual freedom are prohibited.' Then in Section 4 it says, 'Both marriage partners must be willing. Neither they nor any third party may use coercion to force a marriage upon the other party.' That's national policy, which is more important than this lousy piece of paper. You have nothing to worry about."

Jinju sat up and dried her eyes with her sleeve. "What am I supposed to say to my parents?"

"That's easy. You just say, 'Father, Mother, I don't love Liu Shengli and I won't marry him.'"

"You make it sound so easy. Why don't you tell them?"

"Don't think I won't," he replied testily. "Tonight. And if your father and brothers don't like it, we'll settle it like men."

It was a cloudy evening, hot and muggy. Gao Ma wolfed down some leftover rice and walked out onto the sandbar behind his house, still feeling empty inside. The setting sun, like a halved watermelon, lent its red to the scattered clouds on the horizon and the tips of the acacia and willow trees. Since there wasn't a breath of wind, chimney smoke rose like airy pillars, then disintegrated and merged with the residue of other pillars. Doubt crept in: Should he go to her house or not? What could he say when he got there? The dark, menacing faces of the Fang brothers floated before his eyes. So did Jinju's tear-filled eyes. Finally he left the sandbar and headed south. A lane he had always felt was agonizingly long suddenly seemed amazingly short. He had barely started out, and already he was there. Why couldn't it have been longer—much longer?

As he stood in front of Jinju's gate, he felt emptier than ever. Several times he raised his hand to knock, but each time he let it drop. At dusk the parakeets raised a maddening din in Gao Zhileng's yard, as though taunting Gao Ma. The chestnut colt was galloping alongside the threshing floor, a newly attached bell around its neck clanging loudly and drawing loud whinnies from older horses off in the distance; the colt ran like an arrow in flight, trailing a string of peals behind it.

Gao Ma clenched his teeth until he nearly saw stars, then pounded on the gate, which was opened by Fang Yixiang, the impetuous and slightly preposterous second son. "What do *you* want?" he asked with undisguised displeasure.

Gao Ma smiled. "Just a friendly visit," he said, sidestepping Fang Yixiang and walking into the yard. The family was eating dinner outside, surrounded in darkness that made it impossible to see what was on the table. Gao Ma's courage began to desert him. "Just now having dinner?" he asked.

Fourth Uncle merely snorted. "Yes," Fourth Aunt said impassively. "And you?"

Gao Ma said he had already eaten.

Fourth Aunt roughly ordered Jinju to light the lantern.

"What do we need a lantern for?" Fourth Uncle said abusively. "Afraid you'll stuff the food up your nose?"

But Jinju went inside and lit a lantern anyway, then brought it outside and placed it in the center of the table, where Gao Ma noticed a willow basket filled with flatcakes and a bowl of thick bean paste. Garlic was strewn about.

"Are you sure you don't want some?" Fourth Aunt asked.

"I just ate," Gao Ma replied, glancing at Jinju, who sat with her head down, neither eating nor drinking. Fang Yijun and Fang Yixiang, on the other hand, were loading up flatcakes with bean paste and garlic, then rolling them and stuffing them into their mouths with both hands until their cheeks bulged. As he noisily smoked his pipe, Fourth Uncle watched Gao Ma out of the corner of his eye.

Fourth Aunt glared at Jinju. "Why don't you eat instead of sitting there like a block of wood? Are you trying to become an immortal?"

"I'm not hungry."

"I know what's going on in that sneaky mind of yours," Fourth Uncle said, "and you can forget it."

Jinju glanced at Gao Ma before saying in a strong voice, "I won't do it—I won't marry Liu Shengli!"

"Just what I'd expect from a slut like you!" Fourth Uncle cursed as he banged his pipe on the table.

"Who *do* you want to marry?" Fourth Aunt asked her.

"Gao Ma," she said defiantly.

Gao Ma stood up. "Fourth Uncle, Fourth Aunt, the Marriage Law stipulates—"

"Beat the bastard up!" Fourth Uncle cut him off. "He can't come into our home and act like this!"

The two brothers tossed down the food in their hands, picked up their stools, and charged. "Using violence is against the law—it's illegal!" Gao Ma protested as he tried to ward off the blows.

"No one would blame us if we beat you to death!" Fang Yijun countered.

"Gao Ma," Jinju said tearfully, "get away from here!"

His head was bleeding. "Go ahead, beat me if you want. I won't even report you. But you can't stop Jinju and me!"

From her seat across the table, Fourth Aunt picked up a rolling pin and struck Jinju a glancing blow on the forehead. "Doesn't the word 'shame' mean anything to you? You'll kill your own mother."

"Fuck your ancestors, Gao Ma!" Fourth Uncle growled. "I'd kill my daughter before I'd let her marry you!"

Gao Ma wiped some blood off his eyebrows. "You can hit me all you want, Fourth Uncle," he said. "But if you raise a finger against Jinju, I'll report you to the authorities." Fourth Uncle picked up his heavy bronze pipe and hit Jinju hard on the head. With a feeble "Oh" she crumpled to the ground.

"Go report that!" Fourth Uncle said.

As Gao Ma bent down to help her up, Fang Yixiang clubbed him with a stool.

When Gao Ma regained consciousness, he was lying in the lane with a large shape standing over him. It was the chestnut colt. A few stars poked pitifully through the cloud cover. The parakeets in Gao Zhileng's yard shrieked. By lifting one of his arms slowly, he touched the satiny neck of the colt, which nuzzled the back of his hand as its bell tinkled crisply.

The day after the beating, Gao Ma went to the township government compound to see the deputy administrator, who, drunk as a lord, sat on a beat-up sofa, slurping tea. Instead of greeting Gao Ma, he glared at him bleary-eyed.

"Deputy Yang," Gao Ma said, "Fang Yunqiu is violating the Marriage Law by forcing his daughter to marry Liu Shengli. When she protested, he bloodied her head."

The deputy laid his glass on the table beside the sofa. "What's she to you?" he asked snidely.

"She's the woman I'm going to marry," Gao Ma said after hesitating for a moment.

"As I hear it, she's the woman Liu Shengli is going to marry."

"Against her will."

"That's none of your business. I'll look into the matter when *she* comes to see me, but not before."

"Her father won't let her out of the house."

"Out, out, out!" The deputy waved him off as if shooing away a housefly. "I've got better things to do than argue with you."

Before Gao Ma could protest, a hunched-over, middle-aged man walked into the room. His wan complexion contrasted sharply with his purple lips; he looked like a man at death's door. Gao Ma stepped aside and watched him take a bottle of liquor and some canned fish out of a black imitation-leather bag and set them on the table.

"Eighth Uncle," he said, "what's this I hear about an incident involving the Fang family?"

Not deigning to respond to his nephew's comment, the deputy got off his sofa and touched Gao Ma's head. "What happened here?" he asked playfully.

The skin around the wound grew taut, and shooting pains nearly made Gao Ma cry out. There was a ringing in his ears. In a shrill, tinny voice, he said, "I fell . . . banged my head."

"Because somebody hit you?" the deputy asked with a knowing smile.

"No."

"The Fang boys are a couple of useless turds," the deputy continued, no longer smiling. "If it had been me," he said spitefully, "I'd have broken your damned legs and let you crawl home!"

The deputy sprayed Gao Ma with spittle, which he wiped off with his sleeve as the man shoved him out the door and slammed it shut after him. Gao Ma hopped awkwardly on the cement steps, trying to keep his balance, so light-headed he had to lean against the wall to keep the world from spinning. When the faintness finally eased up a bit, he gazed at the green gate; like the opening of a crack in a paste head, his consciousness returned slowly. Something warm and wet slithered into his nasal cavities, then continued down his face. He tried but couldn't hold it back; whatever it was spurted out of his nostrils and entered his mouth. It had a salty, rank taste; and when he lowered his head, he watched the bright red liquid drip onto the pale cement steps.

4

Gao Ma lay dazed on his kang, with no idea how long he had been there or how he had gotten home from the township compound; in fact, all he could recall was fresh blood dripping silently from his nose onto the steps.

Little red pearl drops splashing like fragile cherries—shattering, splashing . . . The sight of those fracturing red pearls comforted Gao Ma. They linked into a string; all the heat in his body was concentrated in one spot, gushing out through his nostrils until a pool of blood formed on the steps. The tip of his tongue, already familiar with the cloying taste, touched his chilled lips, and another crack opened up in his brain; the chestnut colt stood in the township compound before the green gate, where yellow hollyhocks bloomed in lush abundance; it observed him with its moist, crystalline eyes. Gao Ma stumbled toward it and reached out to grab a branch covered with spiny hollyhocks. The sun's rays blazed down, and he felt the heavy flowers dance on top of his head; he tried to look up, but the sunlight stung his eyes. He ripped a hollyhock leaf in half and wadded it into balls, which he stuffed up his nostrils. But the build-up of hot blood swelled his head, and as the salty taste spread through his mouth, he knew the blood was flowing down his throat. All human orifices are connected.

Gao Ma wanted to smash the compound's green gate but didn't have the strength. He assumed that everyone in the township offices—officials, handymen, plumbers, people in charge of women's affairs, family planners, tax collectors, news dispatchers, boozers, meat eaters, tea drinkers, smokers—more than fifty in all, had seen him get tossed out of the compound like a discarded weed or a whipped puppy. He tried to catch his breath as he wiped a bloody hand on the red letters carved into the government office's white signboard.

The young gateman, wearing a plaid shirt, kicked him from behind. "You bastard!" Plaid Shirt railed, although Gao Ma only heard a muffled noise. "Where do you think you're wiping that dog blood of yours? Dumb bastard! Who said you could leave your dog blood here?" After he backed up a step or two to look at the red letters on the wooden signboard, the fires of rage burned in Gao Ma; he aimed a mouthful of bloody saliva at Plaid Shirt, who was agile, wiry—probably a martial-arts practitioner. He sprang out of the way and charged Gao Ma, who worked up another gob of bloody spit and aimed it at the man's long, thin face.

"What are you doing out there, Li Tie?" It was the voice of authority, coming from inside the government compound. Plaid Shirt lowered his arms compliantly.

Gao Ma spat the bloody mess on the ground and walked off without a backward glance at the gatekeeper. With the blue horizon stretched out before him, he moved haltingly down the paved country road; the eyes of an old melon peddler gleamed like phosphorescent lights.

Gao Ma slipped and fell into the gutter, and as he lay amid vines and tendrils, he gazed sadly at the gentle slope of the gutter. Certain he could not walk upright, he dropped to his knees to slink home on all fours, like a dog.

It would be a long, arduous trip; his head, drooping of its own weight, felt as if it might fall off and roll into the gutter. Thorns pricked his hands, and his back felt as if it were being peppered by poison darts.

After negotiating the slope of the gutter, he straightened up. The prickly pains in his back so tormented him that he turned to look behind him, where he saw Plaid Shirt walking up to the gateway with a bucket of water and a rag to clean the blood off the signboard. The roadside melon peddler had his back to Gao Ma, who still carried the image of the old man's phosphorescent eyes. Even in his dazed state, he heard the shrill cry: "Melons—mushy melons. . . ."

The sound stabbed at his heart; all he wanted was to go home and lie quietly on his kang, like a man dead to the world.

Now someone was at the door. He tried to sit up, but his head was too heavy. Straining to open his eyes, he saw the wife of his neighbor, Yu Qiushui, watching him with pity in her eyes.

"Feeling better?" she asked.

He tried to open his mouth, but a rush of bitter liquid stopped up his throat and nose. "You were unconscious for three days," she said.

"You had us scared half to death. Even with your eyes closed you yelled, 'Boys and girls, children on the wall!' and 'The colt! The little colt!' Big Brother Yu called the doctor, who gave you a couple of injections."

He strained to sit up, with the help of Big Brother Yu's wife, who put his filthy comforter behind his back. One look at her face told him she knew everything.

"Thank you, and thank Big Brother Yu." Tears began to flow.

"Crying won't help," she consoled him. "Don't fool yourself into thinking it could ever work between you and Jinju. For now just worry about getting better. I'm going to my folks' house in a few days, and I'll find you someone as good as Jinju."

"What about Jinju?" he asked anxiously.

"They say her family beats her every day. When the Caos and the Lius heard the news, they rushed over to mediate. But as the saying goes, you can't force a melon to be sweet. A happy life is not in Jinju's future."

Suddenly agitated, Gao Ma struggled to climb down off the kang, but she stopped him. "What do you think you're doing?"

"I have to go to Jinju."

"You have to go to your death, you mean. The Caos and Lius are there. If you showed your face, it would be a miracle if they didn't kill you."

"I . . . I'll kill them first!" he shouted shrilly, waving a fist in the air.

"Dear little brother," Yu's wife said sternly, "use your head. Don't think like that. All you'd get for your troubles is a bullet in the head."

Exhausted, he fell back on the kang, tears slipping down his grimy face and into his ears.

"Who cares?" he sobbed. "I have nothing to live for."

"Come now. Don't give up so easily. If you and Jinju have your hearts set on each other, no one can keep you apart forever. This is, after all, a new society, so sooner or later reason will prevail."

"Will you take a message to her?"

"Not until things calm down a bit. Meanwhile, keep your temper in check and concentrate on getting well. Things will get better, don't worry."

CHAPTER 3

The townsfolk planted garlic for family fortune,
Angering the covetous tyrants of hate,
Who sent out hordes of tax collectors
To oppress the masses, bewailing their fate. . . .

> — from a ballad sung in May 1987 by Zhang Kou, the blind
> minstrel, on Blackstone Avenue in the county seat

1

The policemen emerged from the acacia grove dejected and covered with dirt, holding steel-gray pistols in their hands and fanning themselves with their hats. The stammerer's limp had disappeared, but his trousers were ripped from his encounter with the metal pot; the torn cloth flapped like a piece of dead skin as he walked. They circled the tree and stood in front of Gao Yang. Both men had crew cuts. The stammerer, whose hair was coal black, had a head as round as a volleyball, while that of the other man, whose hair was lighter, stuck out front and back, like a bongo drum.

Gao Yang's blind daughter tapped her way through the grove with the bamboo staff; he strained to watch her. When she reached the stand of trees behind Gao Ma's house, she groped along, turning this way and that and wailing, "Daddy . . . Daddy . . . where's my daddy . . . ?"

"Damn it!" the stammering policeman complained. "What's the idea of letting him get away like that?"

"If you'd moved a little quicker, you might have gotten the cuff on his other wrist!" Drumhead shot back. "He couldn't have gotten away with both hands cuffed, could he?"

"It's this one's fault," the stammerer said as he put his hat back on. He reached out and touched Gao Yang's scalp as though to rub it, then gave him a clout.

"Daddy . . . Daddy . . . why don't you answer me?" Xinghua sobbed as she bumped a tree with her staff; when she reached out to touch it, she banged her head on a branch. Her close-cropped hair was parted like a little boy's . . . eyes black as coal . . . the waxen face of the undernourished, like a wilting stalk of garlic . . . naked from the waist up, dressed only in red underpants whose elastic was so far gone they hung loosely on her hips . . . red plastic sandals with broken laces . . . "Daddy . . . Daddy . . . why don't you answer me?" The acacia grove, like a dense cloud, became a dark backdrop for her. Gao Yang yearned to shout to her, but his throat muscles were tied in knots, and no sound emerged. I'm not crying, I'm not crying . . .

The policeman rapped him on the head again, but he didn't feel it; he strained to get free and moaned, their noses detected the translucent, sticky sweat on his body—an eerie, nightmarish stench. It was the stink of suffering. They screwed up their noses, which were filled with the foul air, a dull expression spreading across their faces.

"Daddy . . . Daddy . . . why don't you answer me?"

All right, boys and girls, hold hands, sing, twirl around, see how easy it is, the teacher calls. Xinghua stands in the middle of the road, staff in hand, then gropes her way to the schoolyard gate, where she grasps the metal fence with one hand and her bamboo staff with the other, to listen to the boys and girls sing and dance with their teacher. Chrysanthemums bloom all over the schoolyard. He tries to drag her home, but she struggles to stay put. He screams at her angrily, he kicks her. . . . Daddy, Mommy, hold my hand, hurry, I

want to sing and dance and twirl, see how easy it is! Xinghua
cries yearningly.

Unable to utter a sound, tortured by memory, Gao Yang gnawed
frantically on the bark, which rubbed his lips raw until the tree
was spotted with his blood. But he didn't notice the pain. He
swallowed the bitter mixture of saliva and bark juice, which
brought a remarkable coolness to his throat—his vocal cords
loosened, the knots unraveled. Carefully, oh so carefully, fearful
that his powers of speech might leave him again: "Xinghua,
Daddy's over here . . ." he managed to say before his face was
streaked with tears.

"Now what?" the stammering policeman asked his partner.

"Go back and get a Wanted poster issued," Drumhead said. "He
won't get away!"

"What about the village boss?"

"Slinked off long ago, like a common lout."

"Daddy—I can't find my way out! Come get me out of here—
hurry . . ."

Xinghua was lost in the maze of trees, and the sight of that tiny
spot of red nearly broke Gao Yang's heart. It seemed like only
yesterday that he had kicked that little red behind of hers for no good
reason, sending her sprawling in the middle of the yard, one hand
spread out like a claw that clutched at a dark pile of chicken
droppings. She had picked herself up and cowered against the wall,
her lips trembling as she fought back sobs and tears welling up in her
coal-black eyes. Overcome with remorse, he banged his head against
the tree. "Let me go!" he screamed. "Let me go—"

Drumhead clasped him in a headlock to keep him from hurting
himself while his partner walked around to unlock the manacles.
"G-Gao Yang," the stammerer said, "don't try anything funny."

But as soon as his hands were free, he started to fight—clawing,
kicking, and biting—which left three bloody scratches on the
stammerer's face. As he wrenched free of the headlock and turned to

run toward the tiny spot of red, a light flashed before his eyes, then a shower of green sparks—he dimly noticed something in the policeman's hand giving off eerie green sparks when it touched his chest. Pins pierced his body; he screamed, twitching in agony, then slumped to the ground.

The first thing he noticed upon regaining consciousness was the pair of shiny handcuffs clamped around his wrists and digging deeply into the flesh, nearly cutting to the bone. He was too groggy to recall where he was. The stammering policeman waved the terrifying object in front of him.

"Start walking," he said soberly. "And no fooling around!"

2

Meekly he followed Drumhead up the sandy embankment toward the willow grove. There they turned and trudged across the dry riverbed, where fine sand stung his injured ankle and burned the soles of his feet. He limped along, the stammerer right behind him. Xinghua's wails from the acacia grove were like a magnet that drew his head back to her. The stammerer nudged him with that awful thing, sending chills up his spine. He tucked his neck down between his shoulders; covered with goose bumps, he steeled himself for the rolling thunder of pain he knew was coming. But instead there was only a command: "Keep walking."

As he walked, the image of the thing in the policeman's hand took his mind off his daughter's wails. He realized what it was: one of those electric prods he'd heard whispers about. The chills running up his spine penetrated the marrow of his bones.

After threading their way through another grove of trees, they crossed a second embankment and emerged onto an open field about fifty yards in length, which in turn led to a paved road. The policemen escorted Gao Yang into the township government compound, where Whiskers Zhu, a member of the police substation, rushed out to compliment Drumhead and his stammering partner on their good work.

Hope welled up in Gao Yang's heart at the sight of a familiar face. "Old Zhu," he said, "where are they taking me?"

"Someplace where you won't need ration coupons for food."

"Please tell them to let me go. My wife just had a baby."

"So what? Everyone's treated the same under the law."

Gao Yang hung his head in dejection.

"Are Guo and Zheng back yet?" Drumhead asked.

"Guo's here, but Zheng isn't back yet," Zhu replied.

"Where shall we put the prisoner?" Drumhead asked.

"Lock him up in the office." Zhu turned to lead the way, followed by Gao Yang and his police escort.

The first thing he saw as they shoved him into the station house was a horse-faced young man in manacles curled up on the floor against the wall. He had obviously gotten quite a working-over, for his left eye was black and blue and nearly swollen shut; an icy glare emerged through the slit, while the uninjured right eye was filled with a look of pathetic desperation. Two handsome young policemen were sitting on a slat bench smoking cigarettes.

They pushed Gao Yang down against the wall, next to the horse-faced young man, and as the two of them took each other's measure, the other man curled his lip and nodded meaningfully. Gao Yang was sure he knew the fellow from somewhere, but couldn't remember where. Damn! he lamented. That thing must have fried my brain!

The four policemen were talking: With a son of a bitch like that you have to beat him first and ask questions later. He's in a world of his own, no matter what weird stuff is happening around him. That son of a bitch Gao Ma jumped a wall and got away. You two idiots go back and get out a Wanted poster. Why aren't old Zheng and Song Anni back yet? They had the easiest job. That old lady's got a couple of sons. Here come old Zheng and Song Anni now.

He heard the long, drawn-out weeping of a woman; so, he

noticed, did everyone else in the room. The young policeman named Guo dropped his cigarette to the floor and crushed it with his heel. "To hell with women," he muttered disdainfully. "All they know how to do is cry. It's enough to drive you crazy. Now take our young hero over here—" he pointed to the horse-faced young man with his chin—"you couldn't get a teardrop out of him if you put a razor to his throat."

The horse-faced young man snapped back loudly, "C-c-cry for the likes of you?"

The policemen were speechless for a moment before erupting into laughter. Drumhead turned to his partner. "Say, Kong, old pal, looks like we've g-g-got your brother here!"

That did not sit well with the stammerer. "G-get your old lady, Drum, old p-pal!" he shot back.

The horse-faced young man's speech impediment jogged Gao Yang's memory. He was the young hothead who smashed the county administrator's telephone.

Two police officers—a man and a woman—came into the room, shoving an old woman ahead of them, her hair flying. They had no sooner gotten her to sit on the floor than she began pounding it with her fists and shouting between sobs, "God . . . my God . . . I'm doomed oh my God . . . My own husband how could he do that to me leave me here all alone come down here and take me with you wherever you are oh my God . . ."

The policewoman, barely in her twenties, had short hair, large eyes, and long lashes—a pretty young woman whose oval face was flushed from the heat. "Stop that crying!" she bellowed.

The scowl on her face scared the wits out of Gao Yang, who had never seen such ferocity in a woman before. She wore brown leather shoes with pointed toes and high heels. A holstered pistol hung from her belt. She glowered to show her displeasure at being scrutinized so closely. Gao Yang lowered his head, and by the time he looked up again, a pair of mirror-lens sunglasses hid her eyes from view. She kicked the old woman on the floor. "Still crying, are you? You crafty old bitch, you ancient counter-revolutionary!"

The old woman shrieked. "Ouch! You cruel-hearted girl, you . . . you're hurting me . . ."

One of the young policemen covered his mouth and sniggered. "Say, Song," he teased, "you've gone and hurt her."

The policewoman blushed. She spat at him.

The old woman was still sobbing. "Aunt Fang," Whiskers Zhu said, "keep it down. You have to face the music sooner or later, and crying won't help."

"If you don't stop," the policewoman threatened, "I'll sew your damned mouth shut!"

The old woman looked up and screamed hysterically, "Go ahead, sew it up! You little cunt, no one should be that heartless at your age! Keep it up and you'll have a baby with no asshole!"

As her colleagues roared with laughter, the policewoman walked up to kick the old woman again, but the one called Zheng stopped her.

Gao Yang knew the woman who was crying and making such a fuss—it was Fourth Aunt Fang. She didn't realize that her hands were manacled until she tried to wipe her tear-streaked face, and the sight of the shiny bracelets set her off again.

"Comrades," Zhu piped up, "all this has put you to a lot of trouble. Come have something to eat."

The delivery boy from a local restaurant was riding up to the station house on his bicycle, clutching a food basket with one hand and a bundle of beer bottles with the other, letting the bike steer itself. He screeched to a halt at the gate and jumped off his bike with the food and beer.

"He sure knows how to ride that thing," Zheng said.

Whiskers Zhu turned to greet the delivery boy. "What took you so long?"

"Too many parties today. Five at your township offices alone, plus one at the supply and marketing co-op, one at the bank, and another at the hospital. I've had my hands full here, not to mention the villages down the road."

"Quite a gold mine you've got there," Zhu said.

"For the boss, maybe, but I could run my legs off and he wouldn't give me a cent more than I'm getting now." He opened the food basket, which was filled with meat, fish, and poultry. The tantalizing smells started Gao Yang salivating.

"Put the lid back on till I can tidy up the room," Zhu said.

"Make it quick. I still have to go to Secretary Wang's home in North Village. He called to ask where his order was."

"Find an empty room for the prisoners," Zheng said.

"Where am I supposed to find an empty room?" Zhu asked.

"P-put them in the truck," the stammering policeman suggested.

"Who's responsible if they get away?"

"Handcuff them to a tree," Drumhead said. "That way they'll get some shade, too."

"Get up, all of you!" one of the young policemen ordered the prisoners.

Gao Yang was the first to stand up, followed by the horse-faced young man. Fourth Aunt Fang stayed on the floor and sobbed. "I'm not getting up. If I'm going to die I'll do it with a roof over my head. . . ."

"Mrs. Fang," Zheng said, "if you keep acting like that, we might have to get rough."

"So what?" she shouted. "What will you do, beat me to death?"

"No, I won't beat you to death," Zheng said with a sneer, "but if you refuse to obey orders and create a disturbance, I'm within my rights to use force. You may not know what electricity feels like, but that second son of yours knows well enough."

Zheng took an electric prod out of his belt and waved it in front of her. "If you're not on your feet by the time I count to three, I'll let you have it."

"One . . ."

"Go ahead, let me have it. Pig!"

"Two . . ."

"Go ahead, let me have it!"

"Three!" Zheng shouted as he stuck the prod up under her nose. She shrieked and rolled on the floor before scrambling to her feet.

As the other policemen laughed, the one named Guo pointed to the horse-faced young man. "This son of a bitch is in a world of his own," he said. "Not even an electric shock fazes him."

"You're joking," Zheng said.

"Try it, if you don't believe me."

Zheng pressed the switch of the prod, which spat green sparks of crackling electricity. "I don't believe you," he said, touching the young man's neck.

Not a twitch; just a contemptuous smile.

"That's weird," Zheng marveled. "Maybe it's busted."

"There's one sure way to find out," Guo suggested.

"Impossible," Zheng mumbled, then touched his own neck with it. He shrieked, dropping the prod; holding his head in his hands, he crumpled to the floor.

The other policemen roared with laughter.

"That's what we call testing the law on the lawman," Guo remarked sarcastically.

They walked about fifty paces down the broad compound path, Gao Yang led by the stammering policeman, the horse-faced young man in the custody of one of the young policemen, and Fourth Aunt Fang being dragged along by Zheng and the policewoman. The path led to the county road, which was lined with a couple of dozen tall poplars, each as big around as a tub.

The handcuffs were removed and the prisoners pushed back against the trees, their arms forced back around the trunks so their police escort could snap the handcuffs on. "Ouch! Damn it, you're breaking my arms!" It was Fourth Aunt Fang.

"J-just to be on the safe side," the stammerer said to the policewoman, Song Anni.

Her response was a lazy yawn.

The police all went inside to enjoy their food and beer, now that their prisoners were standing shackled to the trees; but they soon slid slowly down the trunks until they were sitting on the ground, arms wrenched behind them.

3

The shade kept shifting eastward, until the late-afternoon sun shone directly down on the prisoners. Everything turned black for Gao Yang, whose arms felt as if they had floated away, leaving a burning sensation in his shoulders. The horse-faced young man beside him was puking loudly. Gao Yang turned to look at him.

The drooping head at the end of the man's long neck forced his shoulder blades straight up. His chest heaved violently, and there was a sticky, nasty mess on the ground, a mixture of red and white; bottleneck flies were already swarming over from the toilet. Gao Yang jerked his head around, as his stomach lurched and a pocket of air rushed noisily to his throat. His mouth flew open and out gushed a yellow liquid.

The wailing of Fourth Aunt, who was on his left, had soon turned to sobs, and now even they had faded away. Was she dead? Alarmed by this thought, he turned to look. No, she wasn't dead. She was gasping for breath, and if her arms hadn't been pulled so tightly behind her, she would have been sprawled facedown on the ground. One of her shoes had fallen off, revealing a dark, pointed foot stretched out to the side, where ants swarmed over it. Her head wasn't touching the ground, but her white hair was.

I'm not crying, Gao Yang muttered to himself. I'm not.

Summoning all his energy, he got to his feet and pushed his back against the tree trunk as hard as he could, in order to take some of the pressure off his arms. The policewoman, Song Anni, came up to survey the scene. She removed her cap, smoothing her lush black hair, but kept her sunglasses on as she wiped her moist, shiny lips with a handkerchief that quickly covered her mouth as her glance landed on the horse-faced young man's mess. "No problems here?" she asked in a muffled voice.

Gao Yang didn't feel like answering, and Fourth Aunt was incapable of it, so it was up to the horse-faced young man: "No p-problem, even if I f-fuck your old lady!"

Terrified that she was going to hit the young man, Gao Yang spun around to look at him. But the policewoman just turned and walked away, her mouth covered by the handkerchief.

"Worthy brother," Gao Yang said, struggling to get the words out, "don't make things any harder on yourself."

The young man just grinned. His face was as pale as a sheet of paper.

The policewoman returned with Zhu and Zheng in tow. Zhu had a metal pail, Zheng carried three empty beer bottles, and the policewoman held a ladle.

At the tap the water pressure was so strong it made Zhu's pail sing; he filled it to overflowing and carried it away without turning off the water, which sloshed over the bricks and tiles on the ground. The fragrance of fresh water drifted on the air to Gao Yang, who breathed it in deeply. It was almost as if a strange beast in his stomach were calling out: "Water . . . Your Honor . . . be merciful . . . water, please. . . ." Zheng no sooner put one of his bottles under the tap than it was full, froth quickly gathering at the top. He walked up to Gao Yang with three full bottles. "Want some?"

Gao Yang nodded vigorously. He could smell the water, and the sight of Zheng's puffy face filled him with such gratitude he nearly wept.

Zheng held one of the bottles up to Gao Yang, who grabbed the mouth with his teeth and sucked in thirstily, taking a huge slug, some of it taking a wrong turn down his windpipe. He choked so violently his eyes rolled back in his head. Zheng tossed the bottle to the ground and began pounding him on the back. Water shot out of Gao Yang's mouth and nose.

"Slow down," Zheng said. "There's plenty."

Even after polishing off three bottles of water, Gao Yang was still thirsty. His throat was on fire, but he could see by the look of displeasure on Zheng's face that it would be unwise to ask for more.

The horse-faced young man struggled to his feet and was helped to some water by Whiskers Zhu. Gao Yang stared greedily as he drank five bottles. Two more than me, he grumbled inwardly.

Fourth Aunt was probably unconscious, since the policewoman was ladling water over her. Clear when it hit her, the water dripped to the ground a dirty gray. Her short-sleeved jacket, made of mosquito netting and long a stranger to soap and water, regained some of its original whiteness in the dousing. With wet clothes clinging to her back, she looked skeletal, her shoulder blades poking up like sharp crags. Hair stuck to her scalp, from which dirty water dripped to the ground and formed shiny puddles.

The stink rising from her body made Gao Yang's stomach lurch. Maybe, he thought, she's already dead. But just as he shivered from the fearful thought, he saw her white head rise slowly, straining the poor woman's neck to its limit. The water made her hair look thinner than ever, and all he could think of was how much uglier bald women are than bald men. That in turn reminded him of his mother, who was bald when she died, and he nearly wept.

At one time his mother, too, had been a white-haired yet energetic old woman. But that changed halfway through the Cultural Revolution, when her nice white hair was ripped out by poor and lower-middle-class peasants. Maybe she deserved it, since she had married a landlord. Who else could they attack, if not her? A husky, middle-aged member of the Guo family named Qiulang grabbed her by the hair and pushed her head down with all his might. "Bend over, you old silverhead!" he growled. Gao Yang watched from a distance, and the scene was as vivid in his mind now as the day it happened. He could hear his white-haired old mother whimper like a little girl. . . .

Brought to her senses by the dousing, Fourth Aunt twisted her lips around her toothless gums and began to whimper like a little girl. . . .

"Thirsty?" he heard the policewoman ask Fourth Aunt with a hint of tenderness. But instead of replying, she just whimpered. Her voice was hoarse and shrill at the same time, and her sobs lacked the crispness and force of a moment before.

"What happened to all that window-smashing bravado?" the policewoman asked as she dumped another ladleful of cool water over Fourth Aunt's head as a final gesture before picking up the pail of water and walking over to Gao Yang. Unable to see her eyes because of the mirror lenses, he focused his attention on the narrow slit formed by her tightly shut lips. He shuddered, reminded for some reason of a debristled hog. She didn't say a word as she set the pail down, ladled out some water, and splashed it on his chest; involuntarily he tucked his neck between his shoulders and uttered a strange muffled cry. She grinned, her pretty, even teeth sparkling in the light, then scooped out some more water and dumped it over his head. No shudder this time, since he knew it was coming, and after the cool water ran slowly down his back and chest it left gray streaks on his legs. Suddenly revitalized and uncommonly clear-headed, he sensed that the cool water was the greatest source of joy he had ever known. Now as he gazed at the policewoman's lovely mouth, it was with an enormous sense of gratitude.

She doused him only twice before moving on to the horse-faced young man, who stood deathly pale, one eye swollen shut, the other opened wide; his lip curled in a grin for the policewoman's benefit. Insulted by the look, she scooped out a ladleful of water and hurled it into his pallid face with all her might. He, too, tucked his neck down between his shoulders.

"What do you say to that?" she snarled angrily.

He shook his drenched head. "Nice and cool," he replied, still grinning. "Just wonderful."

She scooped out another ladleful and hurled it in his face, not caring where or how forcefully it struck him. "I'll show you nice and cool!" she screeched. "We'll see how wonderful it is!"

"Nice and cool feels good nice and cool feels good . . . !" he was screaming, twisting at the waist, kicking out with both feet, and jerking his head back and forth.

Tossing the ladle to the ground, the policewoman picked up the pail and dumped it over his head. But even that didn't exhaust her anger, so she rapped him several times on the head with the rim of the pail, as if to make sure that every drop of water wound up on him. Then she flipped the pail to the ground and stood in front of him, hands on her hips, her chest heaving.

To Gao Yang, the sound of the pail banging against the young man's head was muffled and wet, and it set his teeth on edge.

The young man, sputtering now, rested his long head—which seemed to swell and turn a mahogany color—against the tree trunk. Gao Yang heard the man's stomach growl and watched his neck stretch forward until the tendons seemed about to pop through the taut skin. Over and over he tried to close his mouth, but couldn't. Then, all of a sudden, it gaped wide, and a gusher of filthy water spewed out, hitting the policewoman full in the chest before she could scramble out of the way.

She shrieked and hopped around. But the horse-faced young man was too busy puking to pay any attention to her chest.

"Okay, Song," Zheng said, looking at his watch. "It's nearly dinner. We'll finish up here after we eat."

Whiskers Zhu picked up the pail and ladle, then fell in behind old Zheng and Song Anni.

4

Gao Yang heard Whiskers Zhu shout into the office phone to speed up delivery of the stuffed dumplings they had ordered, and felt total revulsion; he had to clench his teeth to keep from regurgitating the three badly needed bottles of water he had just finished. The horse-faced young man was still puking, though by now it was just dry heaves. Gao Yang noticed a frothy string of bloody sputum at the corner of his mouth and felt sorry for the sharp-tongued fellow.

The setting sun had lost some of its sting; that and the fact that he had no feeling in his arms instilled in Gao Yang a sense of well-being. A slight breeze rose to cool his scalp, which had been sun-baked, then doused with water until it tingled. All in all, he still felt pretty good—so good, in fact, that he wanted to talk. The horse-faced young man's dry heaves were getting on his nerves, so Gao Yang cocked his head and said, "Say, pal, can't you stop that?"

It had no effect. The heaves just kept coming.

A couple of trucks and a blue minivan were parked at the far end of the township compound, where a boisterous gang of supervised men loaded cartons, cabinets, tables, chairs, stools. Probably helping some official move, he surmised as he became absorbed in the activity. But after a while, the sight of all that stuff was more than he could bear, so he looked away.

Fourth Aunt knelt silently, her hair brushing the ground. When he heard a soft rattle in her throat, he assumed she must be asleep. Another image from the Cultural Revolution flashed before his eyes: his aging mother being vilified on her hands and knees. He shook his head to drive away some bottleneck flies straying from the vile puddle in front of the horse-faced young man. Mother was kneeling on bricks, her arms pulled behind her . . . she rested a hand on the ground to ease the pain, only to have it stepped on by a rough leather boot . . . she screamed . . . fingers bent and twisted so badly she couldn't straighten them out. . . .

"Fourth Aunt," he whispered. "Fourth Aunt . . ."

She grunted softly, in what he took to be a reply.

The restaurant delivery boy rode skillfully up on his bike. This time he carried the food in one hand and steered with the other as he threaded his way between a couple of white poplars, trailing the fragrance of vinegar and garlic.

Gao Yang looked at the sinking sun, whose rays were growing gentler and friendlier by the minute. He knew that the comrade policemen were by then dipping steamed dumplings in the vinegary, garlicky sauce; this held a hidden and frightful significance. When they finish their meal, he reminded himself, they'll come out to put me into a shiny red van and take me . . . where will they take me? Wherever it was, it had to be better than being shackled to a tree, right? But who could say? Actually, it made no difference what happened, as he saw it. "The people's hearts are made of steel, but the Law is a forge." If I'm guilty, there goes my head. Another breeze rose up, rustling the leaves of the poplars and carrying the brays of a distant mule, which chilled the nape of his neck. He forced himself to stop thinking about what might happen.

A woman carrying a bundle stumbled up to the compound gate, where she argued with a young man who wouldn't let her pass. Failing to force her way past him, she took the long way around the poplar grove. Gao Yang watched her approach. It was Jinju, so heavy with child she could barely walk. She was weeping. The bundle in her hands was large and round, the exact shape and size of a human head. But when she got closer, he saw it was only a melon. Not having the heart to look her in the eye, he sighed and lowered his head. Compared with poor Jinju, he had no complaints. People ought to count their blessings.

"Mother . . . Mother . . ." Jinju was so close he could all but touch her. "Mother . . . dear Mother . . . what's wrong?"

I'm not crying, Gao Yang reminded himself, I am not crying, I'm not . . .

Jinju fell to her knees besides Fourth Aunt and cupped the old lady's gray, grimy head. She was sobbing and mumbling like an old woman.

Gao Yang sniffled, closed his eyes, and strained to listen to the shouts of farmers calling their livestock out in the fields. The modulated, rhythmic braying of that mule fell upon his ears. It was the sound he feared most of all, so he looked back at Jinju and Fourth Aunt. The soft orange rays of the sun lit up Fourth Aunt's face framed in Jinju's hands.

"Mother . . . it's all my fault. . . . Mother . . . wake up. . . ."

Fourth Aunt's lids rose slowly, but the whites of her eyes barely showed before the lids closed again, squeezing out a couple of sallow tears, which slid down her cheeks.

Gao Yang watched Fourth Aunt's white, prickly tongue emerge to lick Jinju's forehead, like a bitch bathing her pup or a cow cleaning its calf. At first the sight disgusted him, but he reminded himself that she wouldn't be doing that if her hands were free.

Jinju took the melon out of her bundle, cracked it open with a well-placed thump, then scooped out some reddish pulp and placed it between the lips of Fourth Aunt, who began blubbering like a baby.

Gao Yang's attention was riveted on the melon, the sight of which twisted his guts into knots. Anger rose in him. What about me? he agonized. There's enough to go around.

The horse-faced young man, who had stopped heaving (Gao Yang was too busy watching Jinju to notice), had slid down the trunk that held him captive, until he was sitting in a heap at the base of the tree, his head jerking and his body slumping forward. He seemed to be bowing.

Mother and daughter wailed, obviously revived by the melon they had devoured. This Gao Yang assumed, and he was shocked to see that they hadn't finished even a single wedge. Jinju was cradling her mother's head in her arms and crying so piteously that her entire body shook.

"Dear Jinju . . . my poor baby," wept Fourth Aunt. "I shouldn't have hit you. . . . I won't stand in your way anymore. . . . Go find Gao Ma . . . live happily together. . . ."

Trucks, so loaded down with furniture that they nearly bottomed out, sputtered unsteadily toward them. The police, having finished their meal, emerged in a chatty mood, and when Gao Yang heard their approaching footsteps, his fear returned. A truck creaked and groaned as it drove by, the last slanting rays of sun reflecting sharply off its windshield, behind which sat a red-faced driver.

What happened next Gao Yang would never be able to forget. The roadway was narrow, and the driver probably had a bit too much to drink. Fate would have been kinder to the horse-faced young man if he hadn't had such an elongated head, but a triangular pice of metal jutting out from the heavily loaded vehicle caught him on the forehead and opened up an ugly gash, which showed white for an instant before gushing inky blood. A gasp escaped from his mouth as he slumped further forward; yet even with its extraordinary length, his head stopped short of the ground, since his arms were still held fast around the tree. His blood splattered on the hard-baked roadway in front of him.

The police froze in their tracks.

Old Zheng broke the silence by cursing the red-faced driver with heated fury: "You simple, motherfucking bastard!"

The stammering policeman quickly stripped off his tunic and wrapped it around the young man's head.

CHAPTER 4

Garlic in the black earth, ginger in sandy soil,
Willow branches for baskets, wax reeds for creels,
Green garlic and white garlic to fry fish and meat,
Black garlic and rotten garlic to make a compost heap. . . .

> – from a ballad by Zhang Kou sung to township
> public servants during a garlic glut

1

Fourth Uncle hit Jinju on the head with the red-hot bronze bowl of his pipe. She crumpled to the ground, angered and humiliated. "Brute!" she shrieked, "You hit me!"

"You asked for it!" replied an enraged Fourth Aunt. "You're lucky we don't kill someone as immoral as you!"

"*I'm* immoral? What about you?" Jinju screamed. "You're a pack of thugs—"

"Jinju!" Elder Brother Fang Yijun cut her off sternly. "I won't have you talking to our mother like that!"

After beating Gao Ma to the ground, the Fang brothers stood over him in the flickering lamplight, looming large. Jinju reached up to wipe her burning forehead, and when she pulled back her hand she saw the blood. "Look what you did!" she screeched.

Elder Brother Fang Yijun's silhouette shifted unevenly in the lamplight. "The first rule for a son or daughter," he said, "is to listen to your parents."

Jinju spat defiantly. "I'm not going to listen to them, and I won't be a party to that bogus marriage pact!"

"Her problem is she hasn't been beaten enough," Second Brother Fang Yixiang commented. "She's spoiled."

Jinju picked up a bowl and threw it at him. "Then beat me, you thug, come and beat me!"

"Have you lost your mind?" asked Fourth Uncle, cocking his head. In the kerosene lamplight his face seemed cast in bronze.

"What if I have?" She kicked the table.

Fourth Uncle jumped to his feet like an aging lion, fuming; he reached for his pipe again and swung it wildly at her head, which she protected with her arms, dodging the blow and screaming in terror.

While the Fang brothers' attention was diverted, Gao Ma staggered to his feet. "It's me you want," he said. A chill swept through Jinju's heart as she watched him teeter precariously.

The brothers whirled, the older one struggling to maintain his balance, the younger one standing straight and tall, as Gao Ma rushed forward, straight into a wattle fence, which protested loudly before toppling over, taking him with it. The fence was intended to protect the family's vegetable garden; and later on, whenever Gao Ma relived the episode, he recalled the smell of fresh cucumbers.

"Get him off our property!" Fourth Uncle commanded.

Stepping onto the downed fence, the brothers jerked Gao Ma to his feet and dragged him out to the gate. He was such a big man that the older son was bent nearly double from the strain.

Jinju rolled on the ground, crying pitifully. "Ever since you were a baby," her mother complained, "all you've known how to do is eat and dress up. We spoiled you rotten. Now what do you want from us?"

Jinju heard a thump, followed by the slamming of the front gate, and she knew her brothers had dumped Gao Ma outside. They cast distorted, awful shadows—one long, one short—that filled her with disgust. Her heart contracting, she sat on the toppled fence, where she cried and cried, until her grief and humiliation were submerged in a sense of remorse that started out as a mere trickle but grew into a flood tide. Then, having no more tears to shed, she jumped up in a mad search for something to destroy; unfortunately, she was too lightheaded to stand properly, and collapsed back onto the fence. Her hands thrust into the darkness in front of her, where they touched a thorny vine covered with young cucumbers. In her frenzy, she plucked them off as fast as she could, then tore at the vine, ripping it out of the ground and flinging it at her father as he squatted by the table sucking on his pipe. The vine twisted and writhed in the ring of lamplight, like a dying snake. But instead of hitting her father, it landed on the messy dinner table. He jumped to his feet. Mother climbed to hers.

"You little rebel bastard!" Father shrieked.

"You'll be the death of us. Is that what you want?" Mother complained tearfully.

"Jinju, how could you do that?" Elder Brother asked sternly.

"Beat her!" Second Brother hissed.

"Go ahead, beat me!" she shouted as she climbed unsteadily to her feet and charged Second Brother, who stepped aside and grabbed her by the hair as she passed. Clenching his teeth, he shook her several times before flinging her into the garden, where she crushed or tore or broke everything within reach, screaming at the top of her lungs; when she finished with the cucumbers, she turned her wrath on her own clothing.

"Why did you do that?" Elder Brother complained to Second Brother. "As long as our parents are alive, only they have the right to discipline her. All we can do is reason with her."

Second Brother snorted contemptuously. "I've had all I can take from you," he said. "You got yourself a wife, and now you think you're better than everyone else."

Instead of arguing back, the crippled Elder Brother limped across the wattle fence, bent down, and tried to help his sister up. But his cold hands merely intensified her disgust, and she twisted free of his grip.

"Sister," he implored her after straightening up. "Please do as I say. Get up and stop crying. Our parents are getting old. Starting with dirty diapers and bed-wetting, they raised us to adulthood. The last thing they need now is more heartache."

She was still crying, but her anger had begun to wane.

"It's all my fault. Since I can't get a wife on my own, I have to use my kid sister as a bargaining chip. . . ." He swung his gimp leg back and forth as he spoke, making the wattle under his foot snap and crackle. "I'm worthless. . . ." He suddenly squatted down and began thumping himself on the head with his fists. He was soon crying like a little boy; his pain and despair softened Jinju's heart and turned her wails into sobs.

"Go live your life. I don't need a wife. I'll remain a bachelor until my dying day. . . ."

Mother walked up to him. "Get up, both of you," she said. "What will the neighbors think if they see you fighting like cats and dogs?"

"Get up!" Father echoed her sternly.

The obedient Elder Brother made the wattle snap and crackle as he stood up. "Father, Mother," he said between sobs, "whatever you say."

Jinju stayed awhile longer before climbing to her feet.

By then, Second Brother had gone inside and turned the radio up full blast. An opera singer was shrieking—*wah-wah*.

Elder Brother moved a stool up behind Jinju and laid his hands on her shoulders. "Sit down, Sister. 'Strong winds always cease, and families soon return to peace.' You can't rely on outsiders, but your brothers will always be there for you."

Too weak to stand, she gave in to the gentle pressure of his hands and sat down. So did Father and Mother, he to recommence smoking his pipe, she to ponder a way to bring Jinju around. Meanwhile, Elder Brother went into the house to mix some noodle paste for her injured head. But she pushed him away when he tried to daub it on her.

"Be a good girl," he said, "and let me put some of this on."

"Why are you treating her like that?" Father asked. "She has no sense of shame!"

"Look who's talking," Jinju snapped back.

"Watch that mouth of yours," Mother threatened.

Elder Brother fetched his stool and sat with the others.

A meteor whistled as it sliced through the Milky Way.

"Jinju, remember when you were two, how I took you and your brother fishing in the river? I sat you down on the bank when we got there so he and I could put out the nets, and when I turned around, you were gone. I almost died. But Second Brother yelled, 'There she is!' And when I looked, you were thrashing in the river. So I cast my net and caught you first try. Remember what Second Brother said? 'This time you caught a great big fish!' My leg was fine then. The bone didn't go soft till the next year. . . ." He stopped and sighed, then continued with a self-deprecating laugh: "Nearly twenty years ago that was, and now you're a grown woman."

More sighs.

Jinju listened to the crisp hoofbeats of the chestnut colt as it ran past the gate and down the edge of the threshing floor, and to the squawking of parakeets in Gao Zhileng's yard. She neither wept nor laughed.

Father stood up after knocking his pipe against the sole of his shoe and coughed up some phlegm. "It's bedtime," he said as he walked inside, then emerged with a large brass lock for the gate. *Snap.* He locked it.

2

The Fang compound was humming the following evening. The two sons had carried an octagonal table outside and borrowed four benches from the elementary school. Mother was inside cooking, her wok sizzling. Jinju stayed indoors—hers was the small room off her brothers' bedroom—listening to the racket outside. She hadn't left her room all day, and Elder Brother, who stayed home instead of tending the fields, came in to make small talk every few minutes, it seemed. But she threw the covers over her head and didn't reward him with a single word in reply.

Father and Mother were speaking in hushed tones in the outer room. "They're all wilted and yellow," she said, "and wrapping them in plastic doesn't help."

Jinju smelled garlic.

"You didn't seal them tightly enough," Father said. "They won't get dry or turn yellow if you keep the air out."

"I don't know how the government manages to keep them so nice and green all the way to winter, like they were fresh out of the ground," Mother said.

"Cold storage, that's how. Even in midsummer you have to wear a coat and lined pants in one of those places. How could they fail?"

"Leave it to the government to get things done," Mother said with an admiring sigh.

"As long as they can squeeze us common folk."

The wok sizzled some more, suffusing the house with the smell of garlic.

"Why not have Second Brother go talk to Deputy Yang at the township office?"

"No," Father disagreed. "He might get tired of being asked, and not come at all."

"He'll come. If not for us, at least for his nephew's sake."

"It's not his real nephew," Father said heavily.

Later on, when the lamps were lit, Jinju heard voices in the yard, and from the audible snatches of conversation she could tell that the guests included her future father-in-law, Liu Jiaqing, and Cao Jinzhu, the father of her future sister-in-law, Cao Wenling. Other future family members were present, as was Deputy Yang from the township government. Once the formalities were dispensed with, it was time to start drinking.

Elder Brother walked into Jinju's bedroom with a steamed bun and a plate of garlic-fried pork. "Sister," he said softly, "eat something. Then wash up, change your clothes, and come greet your future in-laws. Your grandfather-in-law is asking about you."

Not a word, not a sound.

"Don't be foolish," he continued in a low voice. "Someone as rich as Mr. Liu surely didn't come empty-handed today."

Not a word, not a sound.

He placed the food on the kang and left dispiritedly. Out in the yard the drinking games had begun, and the party was starting to warm up. Deputy Yang could be heard above the others. Then Jinju heard Mother and Elder Brother whispering in the next room.

"How much is left?" he asked.

"A good half-bottle—seven ounces or more. Is that enough?"

"Far from it. Deputy Yang and old man Liu can polish off a whole bottle by themselves."

"How about borrowing some?"

"At this time of night? Go get an empty bottle. We'll dilute what we have with water and try to make do."

"What if they taste the difference? We'd be laughing-stocks."

"Their taste buds are numb by now. They can't taste a damned thing."

"Still, it doesn't seem right."

"Doesn't seem right? Everywhere you turn these days someone is trying to cheat us out of something. Anyone who doesn't cheat back is a fool. If even the government co-op is dishonest, what's to stop us poor peasants?"

Mother said nothing, and a moment or so later Jinju heard the sound of liquid being poured into a bottle.

"Do we have any DDT?"

"You horrid beast!" Mother tried to keep her voice down. "How can you think such evil thoughts?"

"They say a little DDT makes it taste like real Maotai."

"You'll kill somebody."

"Not a chance. I'll only add a drop, and it's a big bottle. The worst that could happen is it'd rid them of roundworms."

"What about your father?"

"He's too tight-fisted to drink any himself."

Jinju, suddenly agitated, threw back the covers and sat up; she stared at a New Year's wall scroll with a cherubic boy in a red vest holding a large red peach like an offering in his hands.

"Ah, Deputy Yang, Elder Master, Father"—that had to be Cao Jinzhu; the thought sickened her—"try some of this good stuff my brother picked up at the horse market. They say it's a little like Maotai, but since we've never tasted real Maotai, we can't tell."

Cao Jinzhu sniffled a time or two. "Our friend Eighth Uncle is the well-traveled one. If anyone's tried it, he has."

Deputy Yang laughed smugly. "Only a time or two. Once at the home of Party Secretary Geng, and once at Zhang Yunduan's. Eighty yuan a bottle means nothing to someone as rich as Zhang."

"Come on, Eighth Uncle, tell us if it tastes like Maotai," Elder Brother urged.

Jinju heard him smack his lips; he'd taken a drink.

"Well?"

He must have taken another, since she heard him smack his lips again.

"Well, I'll be damned, it does taste a little like Maotai."

"Good stuff," Father said. "Drink up."

The cherubic boy on the wall looked down at Jinju as if he wanted to jump out of the picture.

Liu Jiaqing cleared his throat. "Father of the bride," he said, "I hear the girl has quite a temper."

"She's just a girl," Father said, "who doesn't know what she's doing half the time. She's impetuous, but she'll never get her way as long as there's breath in my body."

"It's not unusual for someone that young to have a mind of her own," Cao Jinzhu said. "Wenling's the same. When she heard that Jinju wanted to terminate the agreement, she caused such a scene at home that her mother and I had to give her a beating."

"Here, Father, let me fill your glass," Elder Brother said.

"No more for me, I've had enough," Cao Jinzhu demurred. "This stuff goes right to my head."

"The good stuff will do that," Deputy Yang said. "But once a girl grows up, you shouldn't be beating her. In our new society it's against the law to beat a girl, even your own daughter."

"To hell with the law!" Cao fired back. "If she doesn't do what she's told, I beat her. Who's going to stop me?"

"You're just being stubborn," Deputy Yang said. "And maybe a tiny bit drunk? If there were only one thing the Communist Party didn't fear, it would be stubborn people like you. It's against the law to beat a person. Now since your daughter is clearly a person, and beating your daughter is by definition beating a person, then beating her is against the law. If you break the law, they haul you away. You watch TV, don't you? When the governor broke the law, they led him away in handcuffs, just like anyone else. You don't mean to imply that you're more important than the governor, do you? You're a smelly piece of garlic, if you ask me."

"So what if I am?" an angered Cao Jinzhu replied—from inside it sounded as if he got noisily to his feet. "If it weren't for all us smelly pieces of garlic, you government bigshots would have to fill your bellies with the northwest wind. It's our taxes that pay your salaries and fill you with good wine and rich food, just so you can think up more ways to bleed us common folk."

"Old Cao"—Deputy Yang was obviously on his feet by now, and probably pointing at Cao Jinzhu with a chopstick—"it sounds like you've got bones to pick with the Communist Party. You're the ones who pay our salaries? Bullshit! We're on the national payroll, and if we lie in the shade all day watching ants climb trees we still get paid. Your garlic could rot until it was nothing but a puddle of goo, and I'd still draw my salary."

"All right," Father interceded, "that's enough. We're family here, so we should support each other, not fight."

"This is a matter of principle," Deputy Yang insisted.

"Will you listen to what an old man has to say?" Liu Jiaqing volunteered. "It's not easy to have family gatherings these days, and since national affairs have little to do with us, why worry about them? Let's concern ourselves with local affairs, like getting drunk."

"Right, drink up!" Elder Brother echoed him. "Have some more wine, Uncle."

"Elder Brother," Deputy Yang said, "I'm warning you two—say, where is your brother?" Elder Brother told him he had gone out. "Anyway, you beat Gao Ma pretty severely."

"They could beat the bastard to death and still not settle accounts!" Father said.

"Fourth Uncle," Deputy Yang continued, "you act like you've lost your mind. I just said it's illegal to beat people."

"He disgraced my family. He's the reason Jinju acted up like she did."

"Interfering with people's wedding plans is nasty business," Liu Jiaqing said.

"Gao Ma lodged a complaint against you," explained Deputy Yang. "I warded him off, but only because we're family. If it had been anyone else, I wouldn't have bothered."

"We're grateful," Elder Brother said.

"You tell your brother he's not to raise a hand against anybody again."

"Eighth Uncle, you know as well as anyone that my brother and I have been honest, law-abiding citizens since childhood. We wouldn't have resorted to violence if he hadn't disgraced us."

"If you must hit someone, go for the buttocks, not the head."

"What do you think, Eighth Uncle? What will he do now?"

"In a case like this . . ."

They lowered their voices, so Jinju went to the window and laid her ear against the paper covering to hear what they were saying.

"Wenling's only seventeen, too young to be registered to marry" Cao Jinzhu said.

"Is there a back door somewhere we can try?"

"Are you asking me to do something improper?"

"Lanlan's only sixteen, that's even worse."

"Wenling's census registration can be changed, but not Lanlan's. We're talking about a different township, and no matter how big my hand is, it can't cover the whole sky. . . ."

"Bring the girl out and let me talk to her," Liu Jiaqing said loudly. His speech was a little slurred.

"Go get her," Father said. His voice, too, was slurred.

Jinju quickly moved away from the window and lay down on the kang, pulling the covers up over her head. Footsteps drew nearer, and as she hid herself in the darkness, she began to quake.

3

The days passed quickly toward the end of the eighth lunar month. Jinju wasn't being watched as closely as before: the gate was no longer locked at night, and she was permitted outside during the day. Elder Brother, who treated her better than ever, even bought her a pair of pigskin shoes, which she merely tossed to the foot of the kang without giving them a second look.

On the morning of the twenty-fifth, Elder Brother said to her, "Instead of spending all day moping around the house, why not come help me pick beans? Second Brother went to help Deputy Yang make briquettes, and I can't manage by myself."

It seemed like a reasonable request, so she picked up her scythe and followed him out the door.

The fields had changed dramatically in the two months since her last visit. Mature, sun-dried kernels of sorghum had turned dark red, the cornsilks had withered, and bean leaves had turned a pale yellow. Under the deep-blue sky the vista seemed endless; Little Mount

Zhou looked like a broken green fan. Birds far from their nests whirred noisily in the sky, a cheerless sound that Jinju found particularly unsettling. She couldn't bear to watch the unnatural movements of Elder Brother as he cut the beans, dragging his game leg behind him. That leg was inextricably linked to her fate, and over the two months of her confinement she had often dreamed it was crushing her; she would awake with a fright, gasping for breath, her eyes filled with tears.

Their bean field abutted Gao Ma's cornfield, which had not yet been harvested. Where are you, Gao Ma? She thought back to the summer before, when a tall, husky Gao Ma strolled over, whistling confidently, to help her with the millet harvest. She could still hear the sound of his voice and see his figure. But the more she dwelled on the past, the more tightly her heart constricted, for she could also hear the thud of stools crashing down on Gao Ma's head, a liquid sound swirling in her ears. She wouldn't have believed her kind and decent Elder Brother capable of such ferocity had she not seen it with her own eyes. "Sit over there if you're afraid this will tire you out," Elder Brother said with a grimace. "I can manage."

Deep lines were etched in the corners of his clouded eyes, which seemed dull and lifeless. Something was hidden behind his expression, she felt, but she couldn't put a name to it. Yet it reminded her of the leg he dragged along the ground. The deformed limb bore the scars of unhappiness and earned him people's pity; but it was hideous, and that earned him their disgust. Her feelings for her brother matched her feelings for his game leg: pity on occasion, disgust the rest of the time. Pity and disgust, an emotional conflict that entangled her.

Gao Ma's cornfield rustled as a breeze swept past, tousling her hair and slipping under her collar to cool her off.

Thoughts of Gao Ma made it both dangerous and necessary for her to look over at his cornfield as it protested uneasily in the breeze: withered tassels and stalks retaining barely a trace of moisture no longer enjoyed the resiliency of their youth, when they had been bent before the wind, their emerald leaves fluttering gracefully like ribbons of satin with each gust to form cool green waves; just thinking about it brought tears to her eyes, for now the wind made the stalks shudder as they stood tall and rigid, their once graceful movements just a memory.

Yellow, withered bean leaves rustled on the plants and flapped around on the ground. When a thorn pricked her finger, she looked down at her hands, which had grown soft in the months since she had last worked. She sighed, without knowing why. Sensing Elder Brother's eyes on her increased both her disgust toward him and a longing for Gao Ma. As her scythe moved mechanically through the bean field, a sandy-colored hare was startled out of its hiding place. No bigger than a fist, with shiny black eyes, it curled into a furry little ball, flattening its ears over its back in fear and remaining motionless. Jinju threw down her scythe and bounded over to the slow-moving animal; squatting down and cupping her hand over it, she felt her heart flood with compassion as she gently pinched one of its ears, which was like a translucent petal. She picked it up carefully so as not to damage the ears; when the soft underbelly lay against her palm, and the tiny animal sniffed her hand in that awkward, timid way that rabbits have, she was deeply moved.

"Get some string and tie it up," said Elder Brother, who had walked up to her. "Maybe you can keep it for a pet."

She felt around in her pocket, hoping to find something, but there was nothing. As she searched the ground, he wordlessly removed a shoelace and tied it around the rabbit's hind leg.

Jinju stared down at the now bare foot attached to Elder Brother's game leg. It was covered with a layer of mud, and shiny as lacquer. He carried the rabbit to the edge of the field and tied it to one of Gao Ma's cornstalks, then cut down a widowed stalk, stripped it, and chewed it for the sweet sap.

Each time Jinju glanced at the rabbit, which was often, she saw it struggling to free itself, straining so hard against the shoestring it looked as if it were trying to separate itself from the ensnared limb in order to escape on the other three. Finally she went over, cut the shoelace, untied the end around the rabbit's leg, and released it. As she watched it hobble off and disappear amid the cornfield's once beautiful, but now distressed, stalks, a vague sense of hope rose inside her. A dark, boundless secret was hidden amid all that corn.

"You have the heart of a Bodhisattva, Sister," Elder Brother said as he walked up. "Your goodness will be rewarded someday."

His garlicky breath sickened her.

She was treated warmly at lunch, probably because everyone had heard of her compassion that morning. During the fall harvest season, when everyone wished he had another pair of hands, they couldn't possibly watch her all the time. So after lunch she went to the well to fetch water. Father and Mother followed her with their eyes, but neither said a word. She returned with two full buckets, dumped them into the water barrel, then went back for more. Instinct told her she had won their trust.

Disappointed that she had not seen Gao Ma, she was, however, greeted by neighbor women at the well, and the peculiar expressions she thought she saw in their eyes vanished when she looked more closely. Maybe I'm imagining things, she thought. On her third trip to the well she ran into the wife of Yu Qiushui, Gao Ma's neighbor, a big woman in her thirties with lofty breasts whose nipples seemed always to be quivering beneath her jacket. As the two women faced each other across the well, Yu Qiushui's wife said, "Gao Ma wants to know if you've had a change of heart."

Her heart nearly stopped. "Has he?" she asked softly.

"No."

"Then neither have I."

"Good for you," Yu Qiushui's wife replied, looking around before tossing a wad of paper to the ground. Jinju quickly bent over as if to draw some water, swept up the note, and stuffed it into her pocket.

That afternoon, when it was time to return to the fields, Jinju begged off, complaining of a sour stomach. Father eyed her suspiciously, but Elder Brother said generously, "Stay home and get some rest."

So she went to her room, bolted the door behind her, and took out the wad of paper (during lunch her preoccupation with the note had made it nearly impossible to keep up a conversation with her parents), which she carefully unfolded with a trembling hand. She could hear herself breathing. When some cold air seeped in through the cracks in the door, she anxiously wadded the paper up again and jerked the door open. The outer room was empty. Then, hearing a rhythmic pounding out in the yard, she tiptoed over to the window, where she saw Mother standing under the radiant autumn sun, pounding ears of grain husks with a glossy purplish mallet. Her net jacket stuck to her sweaty back, and a layer of yellow husks stuck to the jacket.

Finally, it was safe for Jinju to smooth the paper out. She avidly read the handful of printed characters:

Tomorrow afternoon. The cornfield. We'll run away together!

The words, written in ballpoint, were sweat-smudged.

4

More than once she made it as far as the edge of the cornfield, but each time she turned and walked back. Cool autumn winds had removed most of the moisture from the crops, so that Gao Ma's corn rustled noisily and the bean pods in her field had begun to crack and pop. Elder Brother and Father were up ahead, Elder Brother complaining about Eighth Uncle Yang commandeering Second Brother to help make briquettes at the peak of the harvest season. "What are you grumbling about? That's what family is all about—helping one another." Chastised, Elder Brother held his tongue, turning to look at Jinju as if to seek her support.

Father was crawling along on his hands and knees, Elder Brother was hobbling along on his game leg, and the pitiful sight of the two men weakened her resolve to leave. Gao Ma's corn shuddered, it rustled, and she knew he was hiding in there somewhere, anxiously watching her every move. As her longing for him grew, she found it increasingly hard to recall what he looked like; so she concentrated instead on the aroma of indigo and the smell of his body. She decided to help Father and Elder Brother harvest the beans before she ran away.

Throwing herself into her work, she quickly outstripped them both, and by late afternoon had taken in more than the two of them combined. When they neared the final section of the bean field, they stood up and stretched, breathing a collective sigh of relief. Father looked contented. "You've worked hard today," her brother complimented her. "When we get home I'll ask Mother to cook you a couple of eggs."

Sadness kept her from answering. She was already recalling Mother's virtues and some hazy events from her own childhood. My gimpy elder brother carried me piggyback; now he and Father are crawling and hobbling through the field, cutting down beans. The setting sun has lit up the western sky. Their heads glisten. Even the wildwoods are gentle and inviting. There to the north is the village where I've lived for twenty years. Ribbons of chimney smoke mean Mother is cooking dinner. If I run away . . . the thought was unendurable. Off to the east an ox plodded down the road, pulling a cart piled high with beans. "The dog days of summer, sweltering in the sixth month," the driver was singing. "Second Daughter rides her donkey out into the wilderness. . . ."

Sparrows flew by like a dissolving cloud, heading for Gao Ma's corn, which stirred briefly. A tall figure came into view, then just as quickly vanished. She moved toward it but stopped. She was being pulled in opposite directions by equally powerful forces.

Father's voice broke the stalemate: "What are you standing around for? The earlier we finish, the sooner we can go home."

There was no warmth in his voice now, and her resolve

returned in a flash. Throwing down her scythe, she ran toward Gao Ma's cornfield.

"Where do you think you're going?" an unhappy Father yelled.

She kept running.

"You're not going home before we finish, are you?" Elder Brother shouted.

She turned. "I have to pee. You can come along if you don't trust me!" Without another glance at either of them, she darted into the cornfield.

"Jinju." Gao Ma grabbed her around the waist and held her for a moment. "Crouch down," he whispered. "Run like the wind!"

They ran hand in hand down a furrow, heading south as fast as their legs would carry them. Dry corn leaves slapped her in the face, so she closed her eyes and simply ran where the hand led her. Warm tears slid down her cheeks. I'll never come back, she was thinking. The silken thread tying her to home had parted, and there was no turning back. The din set up by dry corn leaves nearly paralyzed her with fear, and she could hear the pounding of her heart.

The cornfield was bordered by a riverbank lined with indigo bushes, and even in her confused state she sensed their unique, intoxicating aroma.

Gao Ma dragged her up onto the riverbank. Instinctively she turned to look back and saw an enormous bronze orb sinking slowly toward the horizon: she saw multihued clouds; she saw an expanse of sunlit fields; and she saw Father and Elder Brother stumbling toward her, brandishing their scythes. Tears gushed from her eyes.

Gao Ma dragged her down the inside slope of the riverbank, but by then she was too weak to stand. The narrow river formed the boundary between two counties—Pale Horse to the south, Paradise to the north. It was called Following Stream. The flow of shallow murky water caused a barely perceptible swaying of reeds at the river's edge as Gao Ma hoisted her onto his back and ran into the water without taking off his shoes or rolling up his pant cuffs. From her piggyback vantage point she heard dry reeds whisper and water splash. She knew the mud was thick and gooey by the way he was panting.

After climbing the opposite bank, they were in Pale Horse County, where a vast marshland spread out before them, planted exclusively with jute. As a late crop, it was still kingfisher green, and still full of life. They felt stranded in the middle of an ocean, and no shore in sight.

With Jinju still perched on his back, Gao Ma dashed into the jute fields. Now they were like two fish in that ocean.

CHAPTER 5

In the eighth month sunflowers face the sun.
If the baby cries, give him to his mother.
Be brave, fellow townsmen, throw out your chests—
If you can't sell your garlic, go see the county administrator....

– from a ballad sung by Zhang Kou, the blind
minstrel, during a garlic glut

1

The police frantically placed the horse-faced young man into a red-and-yellow police wagon. Gao Yang couldn't see his face, but there was blood all over the white tunic wrapped around his head, and more of it dripping to the ground. The unlocked handcuffs dangling from his wrist dragged along the ground as he was lifted into the wagon. A young policeman jumped into the cab to take over for the driver, who stood by ashen-faced, neck scrunched down and arms hanging stiffly at his sides as he quaked in terror. After confiscating his driver's license, the policemen kicked him repeatedly.

"Little Gao, hurry up and get the prisoners loaded," old Zheng shouted. "We'll come back to pick this one up later."

One of the policemen unlocked Gao Yang's handcuffs and ordered him to his feet. As he heard the command and then the click of the lock, his first instinct was to pull his arms forward from around the tree; but they wouldn't answer his bidding, and he was horrified to realize that they might as well not have existed at all. The only sensation was of a heavy weight pressing down on his back. When the policeman moved the limp arms around front with his foot, Gao Yang was relieved to find that they were still attached to his shoulders.

Now that the horse-faced young man was in the police van, the policeman unceremoniously recuffed Gao Yang's hands in front; then he and his partner lifted him to his feet and told him to walk to the van. At that moment he wanted nothing more than to comply with the comrade policemen's request, since they had enough trouble on their hands already. Anything to make their job easier. Which was why the discovery that his legs were no more capable of moving than his arms so disturbed him. He blushed from a profound sense of embarrassment.

They had to drag him to the van. "Get in." He looked up bashfully, trying to speak, but his lips seemed frozen. This time they appeared to appreciate his predicament, for instead of yelling, they lifted him up under his arms; he tried to help by making himself as light as possible when his curled legs left the ground, and the next thing he knew he was lying beside the bloodied young man across the bed of the vehicle.

Another curled-up object was flung into the van. It was Fourth Aunt Fang. He could tell by the way she was groaning that she had banged her hip badly when she landed.

The rear door was latched after two policemen climbed in and sat on side benches. Then the driver started the engine, and off they went. As they drove through the government compound, Gao Yang took a last look at the poplar tree where he had been shackled, and actually felt a tinge of nostalgia. Bathed in late-afternoon sunlight, the trunk had turned deep brown, and the once lush green leaves now looked like a cache of ancient bronze coins. Purplish blood belonging to the horse-faced young man had puddled at the base. The moving van was still parked there, its driver surrounded by a crowd of neatly dressed people who, to all appearances, were making life miserable for him.

Jinju, her belly jutting out in front, stood motionless, a sight that reminded Gao Yang of Fourth Aunt's admonition to go find happiness with Gao Ma. He sighed, for at that moment Gao Ma, who had scaled the wall one step ahead of the police, was a fugitive with handcuffs dangling from one wrist.

As soon as the police wagon was out on the main road, it sped up, and the eerie howl of its siren sent chills up Gao Yang's spine. But he quickly got used to it. Jinju now seemed to be chasing them, but so slowly she all but disappeared from view; and when they negotiated a curve, she and the government compound were gone.

Fourth Aunt was curled up in a corner. Her blurry eyes were open, but what she saw was anyone's guess. Blood from the young man's head dripped onto the floorboards—you could smell it. His body twitched, and his wrapped head lolled back and forth, emitting an occasional puffing noise.

Lying in the speeding police van, Gao Yang felt vaguely motion-sick. He saw swirling dust through cracks in the rear door; trees lining the road fell like dominoes, and fields on both sides spun in slow motion. Other vehicles pulled over when they heard the shriek of the siren, and Gao Yang watched a hounded tractor with an open-air cab crash into a scarred willow tree at the side of the road. Jittery cyclists were left in their dust, making Gao Yang's chest swell with pride. Have you ever gone this fast before? he asked himself. No, never!

2

As they sped along, Gao Yang detected the scent of fresh raw garlic in the young man's blood. Surprised, he breathed in deeply to make sure he wasn't mistaken. No, it was garlic, all right—raw and clean, like bulbs fresh from the ground, a drop of nectar still clinging to the spot where the stalk has snapped.

*

Gao Yang touched the drop of nectar with his tongue, and his taste buds were treated to a cool, sweet taste that relaxed him. He surveyed his three acres of garlic field. It was a good crop, the white tips large and plump, some at a jaunty angle, others straight as a board. The garlic was moist and juicy, with downy sprouts beginning to appear. His pregnant wife was on her hands and knees beside him, yanking garlic out of the ground. Her face was darker than usual, and there were fine lines around her eyes, like veins of spreading rust on a sheet of iron. As she knelt, knees coated with mud, her childhood deformity—a stunted left arm that inconvenienced her in everything she did—made the job harder than it ought to have been. He watched her reach down and pinch the stalks with a pair of new bamboo chopsticks; the effort made her bite her lip each time, and he felt sorry for her. But he needed her help, for he'd heard that the co-op was setting up shop in the county town to buy the garlic crop at slightly over fifty fen a pound, higher than last year's peak price of forty-five. He knew the county had expanded the amount of acreage given over to garlic this year; and with a bumper crop, the earlier you harvested yours, the sooner you could sell it. That was why everyone in the village, women and children included, was out in the fields. But as he looked at his pitiable pregnant wife, he said, "Why not rest awhile?"

"What for?" She raised her sweaty face. "I'm not tired. I just worry the baby might come."

"Already?" he asked anxiously.

"I figure some time in the next couple of days. I hope it waits till the harvest is in, at least."

"Do they always come when they're due?"

"Not always. Xinghua was ten days late."

They turned to look behind them, where their daughter sat obediently at the edge of the field, her sightless eyes opened wide. She was holding a stalk of garlic in one hand and stroking it with the other.

"Careful with that garlic, Xinghua," he said. "Each stalk is worth several fen."

She laid it down and asked, "Are you finished, Daddy?"

"We'd be in trouble if we were," he said with a chuckle. "We wouldn't earn enough to get by."

"We've barely started," her mother answered tersely.

Xinghua reached down to run her hand over the pile of garlic beside her. "Yi!" she exclaimed. "The pile's really getting big. We'll make lots of money."

"I figure we'll bring in over three thousand pounds this year. At fifty fen a pound, that makes fifteen hundred yuan."

"Don't forget the tax," his wife reminded him.

"Oh, right, the tax," Gao Yang muttered. "Not to mention extra-high expenses. Last year fertilizer cost twenty-one yuan a sack. This year it's up to twenty-nine ninety-nine."

"They think it sounds better than thirty," she grumbled.

"The government always deals in odd numbers."

"Money's hardly worth the paper it's printed on these days," his wife complained. "At the beginning of the year you could buy a pound of pork for one-forty, now it's up to one-eighty. Eggs went for one-sixty a handful, and they were big ones. Now it's two yuan, and they're no bigger than apricots."

"Everyone's getting rich. Old Su from the business institute just built a five-room house. I almost died when I heard it cost him fifty-six thousand."

"That kind never has trouble getting money," his wife said. "But people like us, who scratch a living out of the earth, will still be poor thousands of years from now."

"Count your blessings," Gao Yang said. "Think back a few years ago, when we didn't even have enough to eat. The past couple of years we've had good bleached flour for every meal, and our elders never had it that good."

"You come from a landlord family, and you can still say your elders never had it as good as us?" his wife mocked him.

"What good did being landlords do them? They were too stingy to eat and too cheap to shit. Every fen went into more land. My parents suffered their whole lives. Mother told me once that before Liberation in '49, they would start each year with eight ounces of cooking oil, and have six left at the end of the year."

"Sounds like some kind of magic to me."

"Nope. She said that when they cooked a meal they'd wet a chopstick in water before dipping it in the oil. Then for every drop of oil that stuck to the chopstick a drop of water remained in the bottle. That's how you start out with eight ounces and end up with six."

"People knew how to get by back then."

"But their sons and daughters learned what suffering is all about," Gao Yang said. "If not for Deng Xiaoping, the landlord label would have stuck to me."

"Old Man Deng's been in power for ten years now. I hope the gods let him live a few more."

"Anyone that high-spirited is bound to live a long time." "What puzzles me is how senior officials can eat like kings, dress like princes, and have the medical care of the gods; then, when they reach their seventies or eighties and it's time to die, off they go. But take a look at our old farmers. They work all their lives, raise a couple of worthless sons, never eat good food or wear decent clothes, and in their nineties they're still out in the fields every day."

"Our leaders have to deal with all kinds of problems, while we concern ourselves with working, eating, and sleeping, period. That's why we live so long—we don't wear our brains out."

"Then tell me why everyone wants to be an official and no one wants to be a peasant."

"Being an official has its own dangers. One slip and you're worse off than any peasant could possibly imagine."

A stalk of garlic snapped in two as she yanked it out of the ground. She whimpered.

"Be careful," Gao Yang grumbled. "Each one's worth several fen."

"Why such a mean look?" His wife defended herself. "I didn't do it on purpose."

"I didn't say you did."

*

The police wagon passed through a red gateway and screeched to a halt, sending Gao Yang's head sliding into the horse-faced young man. The scent of blood persisted, but the garlic smell was gone.

CHAPTER 6

A prefecture head who exterminates clans,
A county administrator who wipes out families,
No lightheaded banter from the mouths of power:
You tell us to plant garlic, and that's what we do—
So what right have you not to buy our harvest?

– from a ballad by Zhang Kou sung in front of the home
of County Administrator Zhong after the glut

1

She drifted in and out of consciousness as she lay across Gao Ma's back, her arms wrapped tightly around his powerful neck. When they crossed Following Stream, leaving one county and entering another, she had sensed that all ties between her and the past, between her and her home, between her and her kin—if they still counted as such—had been cut with one stroke. She could no longer hear the shouts of her father and brother, but felt them on her back. Tipped with golden barbs, they danced in the air before flying across the river and snagging on the tips of jute bushes. With her eyes closed she could concentrate on the sound of Gao Ma's body crashing through the jute field, so densely packed it stopped even the wind, creating the gentle sound of ocean waves.

The jute was restless, parting like water to allow passage through it, then closing up at once. There were moments when she felt as if she were in a little boat—something she never had in real life—and when she opened her eyes, she was treated to a blindingly colorful panorama. So she shut her eyes again and experienced comfort built upon a foundation of exhaustion. Gao Ma's labored breathing sounded like the snorts of a thundering bull as he loped through the jute, an endless expanse of supple, yielding fetters against which they forged an unveering path—at least that's how she felt. In her mind, an enormous, bronze-colored sun was sinking slowly in a shrouded sky at the tip of a chaotic universe. A cluster of unfamiliar words leapt into the air—she neither understood nor recalled where she'd seen them before—and vanished as quickly as they had appeared, leaving behind the stately presence of heaven and earth. The jute bent gently in the cool dusk winds, then waved lightly before slowly righting itself; it was like a scarlet sea. She and her man had been transformed into fish that had forgotten how to swim.

Jute, all you jute bushes, you're in his way, and in mine. Your green lips pout and your crafty, ebony eyes squint; you laugh with a strange mirthfulness, and you stretch your legs—smiling faces, treacherous limbs.

Gao Ma stumbled and fell headlong to the ground, and as his body broke her fall, she felt the jute give beneath her. A sea of it swelled and crashed over them like tidal waves, swallowing them completely. Not daring to open her eyes, she tried to will herself into a state of torpor. The sounds of the world were pushed far into the distance, until all her senses were filled to bursting with the tenderness of jute.

2

The roar of waves woke her, breaking over her persistently until she opened her eyes. The first thing she saw was Gao Ma's gaunt face, framed in the rich orange rays of sunlight. His face was purple, his lips parched and cracked; there were dark circles around his eyes, and his hair looked like the wiry fur of a street mutt. Shuddering at the sight, she quickly became aware that her hand was in the tight grip of his, and as she gazed into his eyes, she felt as if a total stranger were grasping her hand. A sense of terror that swept through her was invaded by faint lurkings of guilt, the recognition of which further terrified her. She pulled her hand free and shrank from him, until her path of retreat was blocked by a tall and unyielding wall of jute. Golden slivers of sunlight seeped through the interstices of the jute wall, and the talon-shaped leaves quivered in some secret sign.

It was Father's voice, old and raspy: "Jinju . . . Jinju . . ." She sat up rigidly and grabbed Gao Ma's hand. "Jinju . . . Jinju . . ." Elder Brother's voice, shrill and flustered. Their calls glided over the tips of jute bushes and continued on toward the horizon. Gao Ma sat up, his eyes round and alert, like those of a cornered dog.

They held their breath and listened intently. The rustling of bushes and the sounds of heavy breathing at the sandbar to the north deepened the stillness of dusk. She could hear her own heartbeat.

"Jinju . . . Jinju . . . Jinju . . . Jinju! You little whore, you're doing this to ruin me!"

She could almost see her father crying. Releasing Gao Ma's hand, she stood up with tears in her eyes.

Father's shouts were, if anything, drearier than ever. She called out just before Gao Ma clamped his hand over her mouth. The hand reeked of garlic—she clawed at it, her muffled shouts oozing out between the fingers. He wrapped his other arm around her waist and began dragging her away. She clawed at his head. As he sucked in his breath, the hand covering her mouth fell. Something wet and sticky emerged from under her fingernails as they dug into his scalp, and she watched trickles of golden-red blood appear at his hairline and flow into his eyebrows.

She threw her arms around his neck. "You . . . what is it?" She was crying.

He touched his forehead with his palm. "You scraped off a scab where the stool hit me."

Laying her head on his shoulder, she sobbed softly. "Elder Brother Gao Ma, it's all my fault . . . I did this to you."

"It's not your fault. I asked for it." He paused. "Jinju, I see things more clearly now. You go back home." He squatted down and held his head in his hands.

"No . . . Elder Brother . . ." She knelt down and wrapped her arms around his knees. "My mind's made up," she said. "I'll follow you anywhere, even if we have to beg to get by."

3

Night set in as the sun sank beneath the horizon. The jute tips were capped by an ethereal green mist, through which a dozen or so fist-sized stars peeked. Jinju twisted her ankle and fell. "Gao Ma," she gasped. "I can't walk another step. . . ."

He bent down and helped her up. "We have to keep moving. Your family will send people to find us."

"But I can't walk anymore. . . ." By now she was crying.

He let go of her arms and began pacing the area. Autumn insects chirped amid the jute; a dog barked in a distant village.

Jinju lay on her back in a daze. Her ankle was swelling and her legs ached. "Get some sleep," he said. "There must be five thousand acres of jute here, and the only way they could find us would be to use police dogs. Close your eyes and get some sleep."

She awoke during the middle of the night. The sky was filled with stars, all winking mysteriously. Heavy pearl drops of dew splashed noisily on jute leaves that had fallen to the ground. Insects chirped more loudly than ever, setting up a racket like the plucking of lute strings by a bamboo pick. A sound like shifting sand rose from the floor of the jute field. This must be what it's like to sail the ocean, she thought, lying on her back. The jute had an acrid smell that scooped up the rank aroma of moist earth as it leapt from the ground. A pair of night birds circled above, the flapping of their wings and their eerie screeches penetrating the thickening mist. She tried to roll over, but her body seemed weighted down, turned to stone. A myriad of tiny, thin sounds rose from the field, as if mysterious little creatures were prancing and tiptoeing among the jute plants, from which phosphorescent eyes glimmered and winked. Her terror returned.

Mustering all her strength, Jinju staggered to her feet. The cold autumn-night air had chilled her to the bone, numbing her limbs with the dampness of the ground. She was suddenly reminded of something her mother had told her: sleeping on damp ground in misty night air is an open invitation to leprosy. Mother's face flashed before her eyes, giving rise to remorse: no heated kang to sleep on, no scurrying mice in the rafters, no crickets chirping in the corner of the wall, and none of Elder Brother's talking in his sleep or Second Brother's snores in the next room. She stood as if her body had ceased to function, her thoughts fixated on her cozy, smoky kang. Frightened by thoughts of the night around her and of the day to come, she suddenly saw herself as absurd and Gao Ma as loathsome.

Her eyes had grown accustomed to the dark, and now stars shimmered brightly, some of the light turning pale green as it reflected off of the jute leaves and stalks. She looked at Gao Ma, who was sitting up only three paces away, his hands clasped around his knees to pillow his head. He neither moved nor made a sound, like a figure carved of stone. At that moment they were separated by an immense gulf, and she felt alone as, one by one, the green eyes around drew nearer and nearer, and the crisp tramping of dry leaves by tiny paws rattled in her ears. Behind her lay a blanket of cold air, as icy snouts nuzzled the nape of her neck. A scream tore from her throat—she couldn't help herself.

Gao Ma leapt to his feet and ran in a circle; the jute crackled like burning oil, and a line of little green lights flew around him like a spinning hoop. "What's wrong? What is it?"

This was a man, not a cold, dark rock on a reef, and his panic snapped her out of her imaginings. Waves of cold air behind her drove her into his arms; into the heat from his body.

"Elder Brother Gao Ma, I'm scared, and I'm cold. . . ."

"Don't be scared, Jinju, I'm right here."

He held her tightly, and the strength of his arms rekindled long-dormant memories. Only months before he had held me like this and pressed his bristly mouth against mine. But now she had neither the will nor the strength to answer the call of his burning lips, which reeked of moldy garlic.

She twisted her stiff neck around and hugged him tightly. "I'm cold . . . numb all over. . . ."

Gao Ma loosened his grip, and her knees buckled. He picked up her coat from where she had lain, and as he shook it out, green flashes spilled into the surrounding jute, swelling and shrinking, brightening and fading.

Gao Ma draped the coat over her shoulders. Made heavy by the wet night air, it gave off the rank odor of a foul dogskin. He laid her down on the ground to massage her limbs with his callused hands. Each finger and toe, every muscle and tendon was rubbed and massaged, her joints pinched and prodded. Electric currents spread from each spot his hands touched. A warmth flowed from her feet to her head and back down to her feet. Closing her eyes to mere slits, she reached out to catch the green sparkles that floated about his naked back, which was thin and bony. But what she found most enticing were his dark, pea-sized, manly nipples, which she suddenly felt compelled to pinch.

Sometimes he kneaded her muscles with strong pressure, sometimes his hand barely brushed her skin; sometimes he pinched her joints hard, and sometimes he scarcely prodded them. Her breathing grew heavier, her heart began to race, and she purged her mind of things she had been thinking about only a moment earlier. His body felt cold and damp next to her heat. His breath came in chilled puffs, now with a slight minty odor. She was tense with anticipation.

As his fingers peeled away her skin, she reacted with a mixture of fear and curiosity, raising her arms as if wanting to protect something. But his rough hands were now caressing her breasts, sending shivers up her spine and pulling her skin taut, as jolts of electricity coursed through her body.

All around him green dots flickered; they stuck to the jute bushes, they danced, they flew, they described wobbly, dense, lovely arcs. . . . He was nearly encased in those green sparkles, which showed up even on his teeth.

She heard herself moan.

So many green sparkles, so many fireflies. They sizzled as they flew through the air. She arched her spine, grabbing at his back as if she were snaring the sparkles lighting on him. "They're not green all the time. Watch them change color: now they're a deep scarlet . . . now green . . . now scarlet . . . green again . . . and finally a shimmering blanket of gold . . ."

They didn't wake up until the dark few moments before dawn. Only nestled in his arms did she feel real; as soon as she left his embrace, everything had form, but no substance.

"You must be exhausted, Elder Brother. Are you feeling all right?"

His mouth was next to her ear, into which he breathed puffs of minty air.

The stars, tiny shards of jade green, blinked in the pale sky. The mist was getting heavier; so, too, was the rank odor of damp earth. Insects, worn out after a night of chirping, were quietly asleep. No sounds emerged from the frozen faces of jute bushes. With the rumbling of waves in her ears, her eyelids damp and sticky, she buried her head in the crook of his arm, where she fell into a deep sleep, her arms wrapped tightly around his neck.

4

Dawn was announced by the cries of birds. Dewy pearl drops draped the deep-green jute leaves, which, reenergized, pointed sharply heavenward. The stalks—deep red, occasionally light yellow—stood straight and tall. The early-morning sun sent bright-red rays slicing earthward to light up Gao Ma's face. It was a thin face, but clear and alert. An irrepressible glint of happiness shone in his eyes. At this moment he knew she couldn't be apart from him even for a minute. His strength drew her to him like a magnet, until her eyes followed his every move. Thoughts of the night that had just passed set her heart pounding and the blood rushing to her face. Once again she threw herself into his arms, unable to control her emotions, and nibbled at his neck. Greedily she swallowed her saliva mixed with his salty, sweaty grime. When she bit down on his carotid artery she felt its powerful throbbing, a sensation that transported her to a world of enchantment and wonder, where she lost control over herself. She bit, she sucked, she nuzzled his skin with her lips, and as she did, she felt her internal organs open up like new flowers. "Elder Brother Gao Ma," she said, "Elder Brother Gao Ma, nothing could make me regret any of this, not death itself!"

The dewy pearls splashed to the ground; now the branches seemed coated with a layer of oil that produced a dazzling sheen, and out of the earth rose a steamy dampness. From somewhere behind them came the cry of a spotted quail, a drawn-out, oppressive sound, as if, in some magical way, the bird had thrust its beak into the earth to muffle its cry. Another quail returned the call from somewhere in front. The early-morning air seemed to hang motionless, holding the jute bushes fast in its grip, like a coral reef standing inert in a sea of red.

He pushed her away. "We should eat something," he said.

She smiled and lay back, gazing up at the chaotic green sparkles and shards of golden-red sunlight. She was raptly concentrating on a hidden spot in the recesses of her mind where the sound of swelling tides remained, distant and mysterious. Wishing she could immerse herself forever in that realm, she lay perfectly still and held her breath; the sparkles, like tiny globules of quicksilver, froze in space and quivered briefly, as if to show they could glide away at any moment.

"Come on, get up and eat," Gao Ma said, shaking her wrist. He took some flatcakes and garlic out of his cloth bundle. After pinching the dry, withered tips and bulb ends of the stalks, leaving only the fresh-green middle parts, he rolled six of them into one of the flatcakes and handed it to Jinju.

She shook her head, for she was still immersed in the joyful feelings of a moment before and wanted to hold them for as long as possible. The pungent smell of garlic put her on edge—over time she had grown to hate its smell.

"Eat something, so we can get moving again," Gao Ma said.

Reluctantly she took the rolled flatcake, but waited until he had begun eating his before taking her first tentative bite. The thin cake was hard and resistant as a frozen rag. Gao Ma's jaw was grinding, his cheeks twitching, and she heard the raw, cold garlic crunch sickeningly in his mouth. She bit down on her garlic, which cracked coldly, like bamboo being sliced by a knife. Her mouth filled with saliva; but her heart, now raw and cold, puckered inside her.

Gao Ma wolfed down his food, grunting raspily as he chewed. He farted loudly. Turning her face away in disgust, she tossed her rolled flatcake back into the blue bundle, where it spread open to reveal its garlicky contents.

"What's wrong?" he asked anxiously, a string of garlic fiber caught between his teeth.

"Nothing. You eat," she answered softly. His garlicky breath again made her aware of the gap between them.

Once he had finished off his own flatcake, Gao Ma reached into the bundle and took hers out. "You don't have to eat this if you don't want to," he said as he rerolled it. "I'll buy you something more edible when we reach Pale Horse Township."

"Where are we going, Gao Ma?"

"When we reach Pale Horse Township we'll take a bus to Lanji and catch a train for the Northeast. I'm sure your brothers and the rest of them are waiting for us at Paradise Station." His voice took on a sinister tone as he continued: "We'll make sure their scheme fails."

"What will we do in the Northeast?" she asked, somewhat dazed.

"We'll go to Magnolia County in Heilongjiang. One of my army comrades is the deputy county administrator. He can help us find work," Gao Ma said, showing he'd thought things out. He turned his attention to the second rolled cake, which he began eating as he released another resounding fart.

She giggled, even though she didn't know what was so funny.

Gao Ma blushed. "I've lived alone too long," he said bashfully. "Don't laugh at me."

Immediately forgiving, she said as if talking to a child, "You're no different than other people. Anyone who eats grain knows what it's like to pass wind."

"Even women? I can't imagine a pretty thing like you farting."

"Women are human, too," she said.

The mist on the jute bushes evaporated. Off to the north, somewhere in the wildwoods, a donkey brayed loudly.

"We can't travel in broad daylight, can we?" she asked.

"Sure we can, since that's the last thing they'd expect us to do. We're about ten miles from Pale Horse, a three-hour walk. By the time your brothers get around to following us there, we'll already be in Lanji."

"I don't want to go," Jinju protested. "I belong to you now, so my folks might change their minds and let us be together."

"Stop dreaming, Jinju," Gao Ma said. "You'd be lucky if they didn't beat you to death."

"My mother loves me. . . ." There were tears in her eyes. "Loves you? She loves your brothers and uses you as a pawn to get them married. Spending the rest of your life with Liu Shengli, is that what you want? Use your head, Jinju, and come with me. My army comrade is a deputy county administrator. Do you hear what I'm saying? A *deputy county administrator*. Just think of the influence he has. All he has to do is give the word for us to find work. We were like brothers."

"Gao Ma, I've given you everything I have. If you call, I'll come running, just like a dog. . . ."

"Jinju," he said, draping his arm around her shoulder, "I'll make sure you have a decent life, even if I have to sell my blood to do it."

"Elder Brother, why don't we just wrap our arms around each other and end it all here? Kill me first."

"No, Jinju, we're not going to die. We'll make it, and we'll give your parents something to think about."

Seeing the cruel determination in her lover's eyes, she touched the scab on his forehead with her fingertips. "Does it still hurt?" she asked tenderly.

"It hurts here." He grabbed her hand and placed it over his heart.

She rested her head on his chest. "You've suffered because of me. My brothers are heartless wolves."

"You don't have to talk about them like that," Gao Ma objected magnanimously. "Life's not easy for them, either.

"Remember that day last year?" he continued expressively. "You know, when I was helping you in the field and told you I was going to get some fresh batteries for my cassette recorder so you could listen to it? Well, I finally did it. Here, listen to this." He took the cassette recorder out of his bundle, pushed the play button, and the scratchy sound of a woman's voice came spilling out: "Moonlight on the fifteenth cascading down on my old home and on frontier passes / In the silent night he longs for someone, and so do I."

"It's a new tape by Dong Wenhua," Gao Ma said. "She's in the army, the Shenyang Military District. Short, chubby, real cute."

"You've seen her?"

"Only on TV," he admitted. "Sun Baojia has a new color set. His family planted six acres of garlic this year and sold it for over five thousand yuan. If we weren't in such a fix, I'd stay home and make a killing on garlic, since this county is going to let us plant even more acreage next year."

He plugged the earphones into the recorder, cutting out the speaker, to Jinju's bewilderment. Then he placed the earphones over her head. "It sounds better this way," he said loudly.

She watched him take an envelope filled with ten-yuan bills out of his bundle.

"I sold off everything I could. My neighbor Yu Qiushui promised to watch my house. . . . Maybe we can come back after a few years in the Northeast."

She was listening to the woman's loud singing through the headphones: "Ali Baba, hai! Ali Baba, hai! Ali Baba is a happy young man!"

CHAPTER 7

The mid-month moon isn't round till the sixteenth—
After that the erosion begins.
Everyone is happy when the garlic is sold,
But their hearts boil over when it is not. . . .

– from a ballad sung by Zhang Kou to garlic farmers

1

Gao Yang was put into a large makeshift lockup in the county station house. At first he didn't know where he was, but the double-paneled red gate had stuck in his mind, for it was the same gate he had passed when he came to town to sell his garlic; he remembered the ditch that served as a sort of moat. The water, filthy to begin with, was a floating home for clumps of half-dead grasses. There was plenty of activity all over town, except at this spot. The polluted water in the ditch was a spawning ground for tiny red insects; the second time he came to town to sell his garlic, he had seen an old white-clad man catching with mosquito netting attached to the end of a long bamboo pole. Someone said he used them as food for goldfish.

The police removed his handcuffs, and once his hands were free, even the two ugly purple welts girding his wrists did not lessen his tearful gratitude. A comrade policeman hung the cuffs on his belt and gave Gao Yang a shove. "Inside!" he said gruffly, pointing to a cot near the window. "That's yours," he said. "From now on you're Inmate Number Nine."

One of his cellmates—a young fellow—jumped down off his cot and clapped his hands. "Welcome, comrade-in-arms. Welcome." The metal door clanged shut. The young fellow made drumrolls with his mouth and, in the cramped space, began twirling and prancing about. Gao Yang watched him nervously. His head had been shaved, but it had so many little dents that tufts of dark hair the razor missed gave his scalp an ugly, mottled look. As the young fellow twirled around the makeshift cell, Gao Yang's view of him alternated between a pale, gaunt face and a mole-spotted back. He was so skeletal he didn't seem to have any hips at all, and when he pranced around the cell he looked like one of those paper figures that turn somersaults when you squeeze the sticks they're tied between.

Someone outside banged the door with a hard object, then shouted. Almost immediately a somber, angular face appeared in the window high on the door. "Number Seven, what the hell are you up to?" the face thundered.

The young fellow stopped dancing, rolled his not-quite-white eyes, and looked at the face in the window. "Nothing, Officer."

"Then why are you hopping around?" the angular face asked sternly. "And why are you shouting?" Gao Yang saw the glinting blade of a bayonet.

"I'm exercising."

"Who said you could exercise in here, you dumb prick?"

"Aha!" The young inmate blurted out as he walked up to the door. "So, as an officer, you enjoy calling people names, is that it? Chairman Mao's instructions say: Don't beat people, and don't call them names!' I want to see the man in charge. We'll find out if you can talk to me like that!"

The guard—the so-called officer—banged the bars of the window with his rifle butt. "Hold your tongue, or I'll get the turnkey to cuff you!"

The young inmate turned and ran back to his cot, holding his head in his hands and begging shamelessly. "Officer, good Uncle, I've stopped, see, I'm sorry, please!"

"Shitty little prick!" the face grumbled as it disappeared from the window. Gao Yang heard the staccato sound of boots retreating down the corridor, which seemed endless. When Gao Yang was brought here in the police van, he was taken down the long corridor, past one steel door after another, one small window after another, behind which a parade of ashen faces appeared; they looked like white-paper cutouts, which he could have crumbled merely by blowing on them.

He dimly recalled watching two comrade policemen lift the horse-faced young man down off the van, the white tunic still wrapped around his head. A stretcher arrived then, if he wasn't mistaken, and the young man was carried away on it. He tried to imagine what happened to him after that, but those thoughts just confused him, so he gave up.

It was a murky cell, with gray flooring, gray walls, and gray cots; even the eating bowls were gray. The last few rays of light from the setting sun filtered in through the barred window, turning portions of the gray wall a reddish purple. All that was visible through the window was a blue derrick, outfitted with a glass cage that shimmered in the sunlight. A flock of doves, wings painted a golden red, swept past the cage, their mournful cries making Gao Yang tremble with fear, They flew out of sight, then changed course and returned, accompanied by the same cries.

A hunched-over old man walked up to the disoriented Gao Yang and touched him with a quaking finger. "Smoke . . . a smoke . . . new man . . . got a smoke?" he squeaked.

Gao Yang, barefoot and barechested, was wearing only a pair of baggy shorts, and his skin crawled when the old man's sticky, rank-smelling hand touched it. Somehow he kept from screaming. Rebuffed, the old man shuffled off angrily and curled up on his cot.

"What're you in for, my man?" a voice across from Gao Yang asked offhandedly.

Gao Yang couldn't make out the man's features in the murky darkness, but instinct told him that he was middle-aged. He was sitting on the concrete floor and resting his large head against a gray cot. "I . . ." Gao Yang was reluctant to answer. "I'm not sure."

"Are you saying you were framed?" the man said with hostility.

"No, that's not what I'm saying," Gao Yang defended himself.

"Don't lie to me!" the man snapped, pointing menacingly with a pudgy black finger. "You can't fool me—you're in for rape."

"Not me," Gao Yang protested bashfully. "I've got a wife and kids. How could I do something despicable like that?"

"Then you're in for robbery."

"I am not!" Gao Yang fired back angrily. "Not once in my forty years have I stolen so much as a needle!" "Then . . . then you must be a murderer."

"If anybody's a murderer, you are."

"You're close," the middle-aged man replied. "Except the fellow didn't die. I cracked his skull with a club, and they say it shook his brain loose. Who the hell ever heard of shaking a brain loose?"

A shrill whistle reverberated up and down the corridor, cutting short their conversation.

"Mealtime!" someone shouted hoarsely in the corridor. "Get your bowls out here."

The old man who had touched Gao Yang took two gray enamel basins out from under his bed and shoved them through a small rectangular opening at the base of the door. The cell was illuminated by a bright light, but only briefly, before being thrown back into a murky darkness. But it was enough for Gao Yang to see how tall and narrow the cell was: a small electric lightbulb shaped like a head of garlic hung from the ceiling—painted gray, naturally—like a single dim star in a vast sky. The high ceiling couldn't be reached even by one tall man standing on the shoulders of another. Why, he wondered, would anyone want to make a ceiling so high? It just made it hard to change the bulb. A couple of feet north of the light fixture was a small skylight covered by sheets of tin. When the light went on, a dozen or so large flies began buzzing around the room, which unsettled him. He spotted another phalanx of flies stuck to the walls.

The would-be murderer—he was indeed middle-aged, as it turned out—picked up an enamel bowl from his cot and wiped some crumbs of food from the inside with his bare hand, then held it by the edge with one hand and began drumming it with a pair of red chopsticks. The gaunt young inmate fished his bowl out from under his cot. But instead of drumming it, he flung it onto the cot, then stretched lazily and yawned, squeezing tears from his eyes and mucus from his nose.

The other inmate stopped drumming his bowl long enough to kick his younger cellmate with a rough leather shoe that looked as if it weighed several pounds; dark skin and yellow hair poked through rips in his trousers. His kick—it must have been a hard one—caught the younger man on the shin, drawing a painful screech out of him. Jumping to his feet, he hopped over to his cot and fell on it to rub his sore leg. "What was that for, killer? Do you enjoy being mean?"

The middle-aged man clenched his strong, discolored teeth and snarled, "Your old man must have died young, right?"

"*Your* old man died young!"

"Yeah, he did, the lousy bastard," the man said, to Gao Yang's puzzlement. How could he call his own father a bastard? "But I asked if *your* old man died young."

"My old man's alive and well," the young inmate said.

"Then he's a bad father, and an old bastard to boot. Didn't he teach you it's impolite to stretch and yawn in front of others?"

"What's impolite about it?"

"It brings bad luck," the middle-aged man said somberly. He spat on the floor, stomped three times on the gooey mess with his left foot, then three more with the right one.

"You've got a problem," his young cellmate said as he rubbed his leg. "You should be shot, you killer," he added under his breath.

"Not me." The middle-aged man laughed strangely. "The ones who are going to be shot are on death row."

After pushing the two enamel bowls into the corridor through the hole in the door, the old man licked his lips, like a lizard eating grease balls. Gao Yang was frightened by his rotten, misshapen teeth and weepy, festering eyes.

The stillness in the corridor was broken by the banging of a ladle against a metal pail. The sound was still quite a ways away. The stooped old man shuffled up and gripped the bars to look out, but he was too short, so he moved away from the door and began scratching his head and twitching his cheeks like a jittery monkey. Then he flopped down on his belly to peek through the hole in the bottom of the door. Most likely, the basins were all he could see, so he stood up, still licking his lips. Gao Yang turned away in disgust.

The banging sound drew closer, and the old man blinked faster. The other inmates picked up their bowls and walked to the door. Not knowing what to do, Gao Yang sat puzzled on his gray cot and stared at a centipede on the opposite wall.

The sound of the pail outside the door was joined by the voice of the guard who had screamed at them moments earlier: "Cook Han, a new man was put in here today—Number Nine."

Cook Han, or whoever it was, pounded on the door. "Listen up, Number Nine. One steamed bun and a ladleful of soup per prisoner."

The ladle banged against the pail, after which a basin slid through the hole in the door, followed by another. The first was filled with four steamed buns—gray, with a porcelain sheen—the second half-filled with soup, dark red, with globules of fat floating on the top, along with a few yellowed shreds of garlic.

The whiff of mildewed garlic thudded into Gao Yang's awareness, causing immediate anxiety and nausea. His stomach gurgled like a restive pool; it seemed still inhabited by the three bottles of cold water he'd swilled down at noon. Spasms in his belly, a swelling in his head.

Each cellmate grabbed a steamed bun, leaving one, fist-sized and gray in color, with a shiny skin. Gao Yang knew it belonged to him, but he had no appetite.

The middle-aged inmate and his younger cellmate laid their

bowls alongside the soup basin. The old man followed suit, then glanced at Gao Yang with his putrid eyes.

"Don't feel like eating, eh, my man?" the middle-aged man said. "Probably haven't digested all that rich food you had for breakfast, right?"

Gao Yang clenched his teeth to ward off the powerful feelings of nausea.

"Say, you old scoundrel, do the honors. And save some for him." The middle-aged man's voice carried the tone of authority.

The aging prisoner picked up a greasy ladle and buried it in the soup, stirring it for a moment. Then he lifted the ladle, taking care not to spill any, and with surprising deftness and balance filled the middle-aged inmate's proffered bowl. He wore an obsequious grin. But the middle-aged man's expression didn't change a bit. The second ladleful was dispatched more quickly, with no attempt at deftness or balance, straight into the bowl of the youngest inmate.

"You old hooligan!" the young man yelled. "All I got was watery broth."

"You got plenty," the old man retorted. "So what do you have to complain about?"

The young man looked at Gao Yang as if seeking an ally. "Did you know that this old bastard was caught stirring the family ashes? When his son became an official in town, he left his old lady at home like some kind of grass widow. And so this one started sleeping with his own daughter-in-law—"

Before the young prisoner could finish, his aging cellmate threw the aluminum ladle at him, hitting him with such force that he grabbed his head and howled, as soup dripped down his face. The collision had chipped the ladle, which the old inmate picked up, standing as straight as his twisted torso would allow, his neck rigid, a venomous look on his face.

The young inmate, accepting the challenge, picked up his steamed bun, looked at it long and hard, then flung it at the old hooligan's head, which was as bald as the steamed bun except for funny-looking tufts of hair along the sides. The bun landed in the middle of that broad, shiny head. The old man wobbled and stumbled backwards, wagging his head as if he were trying to shake something out of it. After careening off his bald skull, the gray bun bounced once on the floor in front of the young inmate, who snatched it out of the air and held it up to see if it had been damaged.

The entire episode made Gao Yang's hair stand on end, but it cured his nausea. The rumblings in his belly also came to an abrupt end; as if a plug had been pulled, the water seemed to empty into his intestines and from there into his bladder. Now he had to pee.

When the old prisoner was finished filling the bowls with soup and a few wispy vegetables, a bit remained at the bottom of the basin. He looked at Gao Yang, then at the middle-aged man.

"Leave it for our friend here," the latter demanded.

"Where's your bowl?" the old inmate asked Gao Yang.

With his bladder about ready to burst, Gao Yang could barely stand straight, let alone speak.

The middle-aged inmate bent over and slid a wash basin out from under Gao Yang's cot. Gray, with a red "9" stenciled on the side, it held a gray bowl for food and a pair of red chopsticks—plus the contrasting white of cobwebs and black of dirt and soot.

Gao Yang pressed his back hard against the gray wall to lessen the pressure on his bladder as much as possible. He observed that the middle-aged inmate was the only one who was confident about eating in front of him. The other two stood in separate corners, faces to the wall, bent over at the waist, necks scrunched down between their shoulders, holding their steamed buns with both hands against their abdomens, as if the buns were living objects that would scamper away if they loosened their grip. The would-be killer wolfed his food down, the young inmate chewed his food slowly and thoroughly, while the old man broke chunks off his steamed bun with trembling fingers and rolled them into doughy pellets, which he popped into his mouth and washed down with a mouthful of soup. His hands never stopped shaking, as if he were excited, or agitated, or nervous; and as he ate, a gummy liquid oozed from his festering tear ducts, under lids that no longer had any lashes.

The middle-aged inmate grunted between bites. The young one smacked his lips. By the time the middle-aged inmate had finished off the last bite of his bun, the old man was tossing the final doughy pellet into his mouth, and the young man smacked his lips for the last time. Then they exchanged hurried glances, lowered their heads, and slurped their soup.

The sounds produced a conditioned reflex in Gao Yang: the pressure against an invisible valve grew with each slurp, and the warm urine behind it seemed about to gush forth. His ears filled with garlicky soup sounds: slurping and tumbling inside his eardrums, straining against the walls of his bladder, swelling his urethra. For a brief moment he heard a fine watery spray and felt a warm liquid against his thighs.

After his cellmates had finished off their soup, the old one held his bowl in trembling hands and licked the bottom with his thick, purplish tongue, round and round. Then, still holding their bowls, all three men gaped at Gao Yang: his face was bathed in sweat—he could feel it puddling on his eyebrows—and he knew he must look like a wild man.

"Are you sick, buddy?" the middle-aged inmate asked crudely.

Gao Yang, too far gone to speak by then, concentrated every ounce of energy on an invisible valve that existed somewhere in his mind.

"There's a jailhouse doctor, you know," the man said.

Gao Yang doubled over and clutched his belly, then dragged himself to the door, where he was wracked by a urine shudder. He stood on his tiptoes, as if that could hold the valve in place, then banged the door with his fist. It clanged loudly.

Footsteps in the corridor—running—a guard. Gao Yang thought he heard the rifle butt rub against the guard's pants as he ran. He kept banging on the door.

"What's going on in there?" the guard yelled through the bars.

"We've got a sick man in here," the middle-aged man replied.

"Who is it?"

"Number Nine."

"No . . . not sick." Gao Yang looked bashfully at his cellmates. "Have to pee . . . can't hold it any longer—"

The middle-aged inmate shouted, intentionally drowning out Gao Yang's complaint. "Open up, he's at death's door!"

The rattle of keys, the bolt thrown back—*clang*—the door swung open. The guard held a rifle in his left hand and the keys in his right. "What's the matter, Number Nine?"

Gao Yang bent over. "Comrade," he said, "I have to pee . . . comrade . . ."

The guard, his face twisted in anger, kicked Gao Yang and forced him back into the cell. "Prick!" he cursed. "Who are you calling 'comrade'?"

The door clanged shut.

Gao Yang banged his head against the door. "I didn't mean 'comrade,'" he wailed. "I meant 'Officer,' Officer Officer Officer— let me out, I can't hold it back . . . can't hold it back. . . ."

"You've got a chamber pot in there, you prick!" the guard shouted from the other side of the door. "Use it."

Still holding his belly, Gao Yang spun around and, to the delight of his cellmates, flitted from one end of the cell to the other, searching for the chamber pot.

"Uncle . . . Elder Brother . . . Younger Brother . . . where is the chamber pot? Where is it?" He wept as he looked under all three cots; drops of urine oozed out each time he bent over.

His cellmates looked on and laughed.

"I can't hold it back," he sobbed. "I really can't."

The valve opened, releasing a blast of warm urine. His mind went blank as his legs began to quake and all the muscles in his body went slack. His legs felt scalded as that thing of his shuddered; he experienced the greatest sense of relief he had ever known.

The urine puddled at his feet, forming lovely patterns on the floor. "Hey, you, get the chamber pot for him, and hurry," the middle-aged inmate snapped. "There's probably more where that little bit came from."

The young man dashed over to the wall, opened a tiny gray door beneath the window, and fished out a black plastic chamber pot. A foul stench filled the cell. "Piss in that, and be quick about it," he said, giving Gao Yang a shove.

Gao Yang took it out with fumbling fingers and aimed it at the chamber pot. Revulsed by what he saw inside, he let go and made loud splashes as the stream hit. It was music to his ears. With enormous relief he closed his eyes, wishing he could listen to that sound forever.

A slap on the neck brought him rudely out of his trance. He had emptied his bladder in the chamber pot, its top now foamy.

"Go on, put it back inside," the middle-aged man commanded.

He did as he was told, depositing the chamber pot in the wall and closing the little wooden door behind it.

Now, with the cell smelling like an outhouse and his cellmates glaring at him, he nodded apologetically and meekly sat down on his cot. He felt absolutely drained. His urine-soaked pant legs stuck uncomfortably to his skin, and the injury on his urine-spattered ankle stung painfully, bringing back memories of what had happened earlier that day: as he was walking out of the house, he spotted a clay-colored rabbit streaking out of the acacia grove; it stopped and, it seemed, looked straight at him. Unnerved, he recalled an old man's assertion that if you see a wild rabbit the first thing in the morning, you're bound to have bad luck all day long. The police came for him later that day. . . . These exhausting recollections seemed years old, not hours, and were covered by layers of dust.

The old man, licking his lips and blinking his eyes, came up and asked shrilly, "You don't want to eat?"

Gao Yang shook his head.

That's all the old man needed to fall to his knees and scoop up the last steamed bun, then crawl up against the wall, his shoulders and head quaking. He purred like a cat that had just caught a mouse.

With a sign from his middle-aged cellmate, the young inmate spun and leapt onto the old man's back; his chance to avenge being hit by the ladle had arrived, and he pounded the old man's ridiculous bald head with both fists. "You want something to eat?" he shouted from his perch on the old man's back. "Here, I'll give you something!"

The two men rolled around on the floor, slugging each other and yelping and growling. That brought the guards running. A square-faced guard appeared at the window, raking his rifle butt loudly across the bars. "Are you pricks tired of living?" he snarled. "Is this what we get for feeding you? Well, if you don't break it up right now, you'll be on bread and water for three days!"

Having made his point, he stomped noisily down the corridor back to his station.

The two prisoners, one old, one young, glared at each other like combatants in a cockfight—one with hardly any feathers left, the other waiting for the first ones to grow in—trying to intimidate each other during a lull in the fighting. Still clutched in the old inmate's palsied grip was the steamed bun, his prize, and the cause of a number of cuts and bruises on his bald skull.

"Hand over that bun, you old scoundrel," the middle-aged inmate said in a controlled, authoritative voice.

The trembling in the old man's hands worsened as he pressed the steamed bun hard against his navel.

"If you don't," the middle-aged inmate said menacingly, "I'll stick your head in the chamber pot tonight and drown you!" Even in the fading light in the cell, the middle-aged inmate's eyes seemed luminous.

The old man's eyes pooled with tears; since there were no eye-lashes to control the flow, the tears fairly gushed from ducts in the festering corners. Gao Yang saw this with great clarity. The old inmate slowly stretched out his arms until they were about eight inches from his body, then opened his hands. Gao Yang counted seven old fingers buried in the steamed bun, which had long since given up its original shape. The whimpering old man suddenly went crazy, ripping off a hunk of the bun and cramming it into his mouth. Then he flung what was left into the puddle of piss Gao Yang had been unable to hold back.

"You want it? Then go get it!" he shrieked.

The middle-aged inmate curled his lip and said, "Is that the way you want it, you mongrel prick?" He walked up and grabbed the man's neck in a viselike grip. "Either you pick up that bun and eat it or I'll soak your head in the chamber pot! You choose."

The old man's eyes rolled back into his head.

"Well, what's it going to be?" the middle-aged man asked in measured tones.

"I'll eat . . . eat it," the old man wheezed.

The middle-aged inmate loosened his grip and turned to Gao Yang. "You don't look like somebody who's going to give me any trouble," he snarled. "I expect you to do as I say, and what I want you to do now is lap up the piss you deposited on the floor."

2

"Come on, let's see who can drink his own pee!" announced Wang Tai, a sixth-grader at the Gaotong Village elementary school in Paradise County's Tree Trench Commune as he stood in the lavatory. It was the summer of 1960. Wang Tai, whose father was the leader of Gaotong Production Team Number 2, had a poor-peasant background.

It was recess time. As soon as the bell rang, the students had swarmed out of the schoolhouse, merging into a single body until they reached the athletic field, where they split up by gender, with boys to the east and girls to the west. Weeds grew all over the athletic field, whose wooden basketball post sported a nice crop of edible fungus; the basket rims were rust red. A blue-eyed, bearded old billy goat tied to a wooden post on the eastern edge of the field stared at the gang of gaunt, wiry, wild children.

The lavatories were located on the southern edge of the athletic field: two open-air structures, with the boys' lavatory to the east and the girls' to the west, separated by a low wall made of brick fragments. Gao Yang recalled that the wall barely cleared his head at the time. But Wang Tai, who was the oldest boy in the class, was as tall as the wall, so by standing on bricks he could see what was happening on the other side.

Gao Yang thought back to the sight of Wang Tai standing on three bricks to peek over the wall into the girls' lavatory. He also recalled what the boys' lavatory looked like: a large brick-lined pit in the center, with boys standing on all four sides pissing at the same time. The clearing around the opening of the pit was dubbed "the precipice," the innermost portion of which was shiny from the boys' feet. Sleek black weeds and red rushes grew on the far edges, alongside purslanes, with their tiny yellow flowers.

"Hey, everybody, don't pee right away! Hold it, and we'll see who can drink his own," Wang Tai said from the precipice.

Since the boys from grades one through five couldn't squeeze up to the precipice, they watered the weeds and flowers on the outer edge, making them rustle loudly.

"Who's first?" Wang Tai asked. "Gao Yang, give it a try."

Gao Yang and Wang Tai belonged to the same production team. Wang Tai's father was the team leader, while Gao Yang's was a former landlord assigned to work under the supervision of poor and lower-middle-class peasants.

"Okay, I'll go first!" Gao Yang responded happily.

A quarter of a century later, he still recalled the incident.

Gao Yang had been only thirteen at the time, and even though their family had never had enough to eat or decent clothes to wear, by scrimping and saving, his folks kept him in school through the sixth grade. His father was a landlord, his mother a landlord's wife.

With that kind of background, all the talent in the world couldn't help Gao Yang avoid the only path open to him—straight to Gaotong Production Team Number 2 as a worker under the supervision of Wang Tai's father, and very soon. Gao Yang was pretty sure he'd never pass the middle-school entrance exam, even if he got perfect scores in every subject, which was impossible in any case. So naturally he was eager when Wang Tai gave him the chance to drink his own urine. Back then being noticed by others, for whatever reason, made him happy.

When he said he'd try, he was confident he could do it. So he aimed his taut little pecker skyward and shot a stream of yellow piss straight up, way over his head. Quickly sticking his lips into the watery column, he took a big mouthful and swallowed it. Then he did it again.

Wang Tai roared with laughter. "How'd it taste? How was it?"

"Kind of like tea," he lied.

"Who else wants to try?" Wang Tai asked. "Who's next?"

No takers.

Some of the smaller kids ran out onto the athletic field and shouted, "Come over here, quick! The sixth-graders are seeing who'll drink his own pee!"

Wang Tai turned to another of the sixth-graders. "Li Shuanzhu, go out there and take care of those little pussies." Then he lowered his voice. "Hey, guys, do you know how girls pee?"

They said they didn't.

Wang Tai spread his legs, squatted down, and made a hissing sound with his mouth. "Like that."

The sixth-graders shrieked in delight.

Then Wang Tai lined them up on the west edge of the precipice. "Now we'll see who can piss the highest," he said. "The winner gets a prize."

A dozen or more students lined up, with Wang Tai at the head, and launched that many watery columns—some yellow and some white, some clear and some murky—into the air. Most crashed down on the wall dividing the boys' and girls' lavatories, but at least two landed on the other side. By far the most turbulent stream belonged to Wang Tai himself—Gao Yang was absolutely certain of that.

A shriek erupted from the girls' lavatory, followed by curses.

Gao Yang couldn't believe it when Wang Tai put the blame on him.

The principal dragged Gao Yang into his office and smacked him in front of the teachers. "The sons of heroes are as solid as bricks, the sons of reactionaries are all little pricks," he announced, before turning to one of the younger teachers. "Liu Yaohua, go to Gaotong Village and tell Wang Tai's and Gao Yang's fathers I want to see them."

Gao Yang burst out crying, afraid his father would suffer again, all because of him.

The old inmate scooped the bun out of Gao Yang's piss and squeezed it with both hands; it made a bubbling sound as the gummy urine dripped through his gnarled, grimy fingers. After he'd squeezed it dry, he wiped his hands on his pants, then tore off a chunk and popped it into his mouth.

"See, buddy, he's eating it. Now, go on, drink up. It's your own piss, so it can't hurt you," the grinning middle-aged inmate said, softly enough so the guards wouldn't hear him.

Gao Yang glared at the would-be murderer, feeling morally superior to someone for the first time in his life. Killer! Thief! Incestuous old bastard! When the poor and lower-middle-class peasants made me drink my own piss, I did it. And when the Red Guards made me drink it, I did it. But for common criminals like you? "I won't do it!" he announced defiantly.

"Are you sure about that?" the middle-aged inmate asked with a thin laugh.

"I'm sure," Gao Yang replied as he glanced at the old man, who was gobbling up the piss-soaked bun; he felt a wave of nausea rise in his throat.

"You'd better do as he says, if you know what's good for you," the young inmate urged him.

"If the guards ordered me to drink it, I'd have no choice," Gao Yang replied. "But I've done nothing to offend any of you."

"Maybe not," the young man said sympathetically. "But rules are rules."

"Go on, drink," the old inmate added his encouragement. "People have to learn how to deal graciously with humiliation. Look at me—I'm drinking your piss, aren't I?"

"I'm not the tyrant you think I am, friend," the middle-aged inmate said earnestly. "Believe me, it's for your own good."

Beginning to waver, Gao Yang was actually touched by the man's apparent sincerity.

"Go on, Little Brother, drink it," the old man croaked, his throat filled with pieces of steamed bun.

"Do as he says, Elder Brother," the young cellmate urged him with watery eyes.

Gao Yang's nose began to ache—he was about to cry—and when he looked at the three criminals who shared his cell, he felt like a man whose loved ones were coaxing him into taking a dose of bitter medicine.

"I'll drink it . . . I'll drink it. . . ." His throat tightened until he couldn't string together a complete sentence.

"Good boy—that's what I like to hear!" the middle-aged inmate said with a friendly pat on the shoulder.

Gao Yang sank slowly to his knees on the cement floor in the middle of his own puddle of piss, which retained the enticing odor of garlic. As he closed his eyes, images of his father and mother drifted into his mind. Father wore a tattered conical rain hat, a scrawny tuft of hair peeking through the hole at the top. He was hunched over and was wheezing badly. Mother, struggling on tiny bound feet, was hauling a wagon uphill in the snow. Gao Yang quickly flattened his feverish lips against the cold cement floor. The smell of garlic—ah, the smell of garlic! He sucked up a mouthful of cool urine, and another, and a third . . . ah, the smell of garlic!

The middle-aged man grabbed him by the shoulders and lifted him up. "Little Brother," he said, "you can stop now."

After being led over to his cot, Gao Yang sat on the edge as if in a trance, not saying a word for about half as long as it takes to smoke a pipeful. A gurgle rose in his throat. Another long pause before his lips parted and he blurted out tearfully, "Father . . . Mother . . . today your son . . . drank his own piss . . . again."

Father wore his tattered conical rain hat, and wheezed badly. He held a switch in his hands as he stood in the school office, looking pitifully into the face of the nearly apoplectic principal. "Mr. Principal, sir, the boy didn't know what he was doing. . . ."

"What do you mean, he didn't know what he was doing?" the principal barked as he banged his desk. "He's a little hooligan!"

"A hoo . . . ligan?"

"He peed on the girls in his class! Was that your idea?"

"Mr. Principal . . . sir . . . I'm a lifelong reader of the classics . . . benevolence, justice, rites, knowledge, trust . . . no contact between boys and girls. . . ." Father was wailing before he finished.

"You can put away that bunch of feudalistic crap," the principal snarled.

"I had no idea he could do something as shameful as that," said Father, who was trembling from head to toe. He raised the thick willow switch in his hands. "I . . . I'll kill him. . . . I'll beat you to death. . . . You let me down, you good-for-nothing little bastard. . . . As if I didn't have enough trouble, now you do something like this. . . ."

The hunched-over old man in a tattered conical rain hat raised the willow switch in both hands . . . it arched downward toward Gao Yang's head but landed on his shoulder. . . .

"What do you think you're doing?" the principal bellowed. "Where do you think you are, pulling a stunt like that?" He yanked the switch out of Father's hands and tossed it aside. "We've decided to expel Gao Yang. Take him home with you. Once you get him home you can beat him to death for all we care."

"Mr. Principal, please don't expel me, please don't. . . ." Gao Yang felt awful.

"You expect us to keep a hooligan like you?" The principal glared at him. "Go on—go with your father!"

"Mr. Principal . . ." Father bent double, again holding the switch in both hands, quaking badly, tears running down his face. "Mr. Principal, I beg you . . . let him graduate, please."

"Button your lip!" the principal demanded. "Is Team Leader Wang out there?"

Gao Yang watched Wang Tai's father, Six-Wheels Wang, enter. Team Leader Six-Wheels would later be his superior for twenty years. For two decades Gao Yang would serve as one of his commune underlings. A tall, beefy man, he was barefoot and stripped to the waist; his skin was tanned and healthy looking. Refusing to wear a belt, he always tied his baggy white pants at the waist, his scythe tucked into the waistband. Gao Yang called him Master Six.

"Principal," Six-Wheels said in his gravelly voice, "what do you want me for?"

"Team Leader Wang," the principal said, "now don't get mad, but your son, Wang Tai, peed on some of the girls in his class. . . . Something like that, well, it's not a good idea. The heads of households share the responsibility for their children's upbringing with those of us at school."

"Where is the little asshole?" Six-Wheels Wang growled.

The principal gave the high sign to one of the teachers, who dragged Wang Tai into the office.

"You little asshole," Six-Wheels said to his son, "did you pee on girls in your class? Is that where you're supposed to pee?"

Wang Tai stood silently, his head bowed as he picked at his fingernails.

"Who told you to do something like that?" Six-Wheels asked.

Wang Tai pointed at Gao Yang. "Him," he said without a moment's hesitation.

Gao Yang was shocked. His head swirled.

"He wasn't satisfied doing a terrible thing like that himself," the principal said to Gao Yang's father. "He had to drag the son of a poor and lower-middle-class peasant into his shameful affair. Things like this don't happen by accident."

"My family is cursed . . . family is cursed . . . produce scum like this . . . scum . . ." Father was pacing.

"You've always been a bad boy," Six-Wheels Wang said to Gao Yang. "One of these days your bad nature will be the death of you." Then he turned to Gao Yang's father. "How could you sire a bad seed like this?" he asked. "Hm?"

Father picked up the switch and hit Gao Yang square in the head . . . a couple of anguished cries. . . . Gao Yang tried to recall if he had cried out. It had been twenty years, and he had no idea whether he had cried out or not. He remembered wanting to shout: "Father, all I did was drink my own piss!"

"Cheer up, Little Brother," the middle-aged inmate consoled Gao Yang. "You'll be fine now that you've passed the test. You took it like a man. You know when to stand your ground and when to give in. The best is yet to come for you. Once you leave here you'll never return."

To wash down the crumbs of his piss-soaked bun, the old inmate drank what was left in the soup bowl, reaching in to pick up a yellow sliver of garlic stuck to the bottom and shove it into his mouth. Last of all he licked the frothy, oily sides of the bowl—*slurp slurp*—like a dog.

The whistle sounded again, long and loud, followed by a tinny voice: "Attention all cells! Lights out! Bedtime! After-dark regulations: One, no talking or whispering. Two, no swapping beds. Three, no sleeping in the nude."

The yellow light went out abruptly, throwing the cell into

darkness. In the silence that ensued, Gao Yang heard his three cellmates breathing and saw six eyes flashing in the darkness as if luminous. Drained of energy, he sat on his gray blanket, which reeked of garlic; swarms of mosquitoes took to the air, filling the darkness with their buzzing.

The seemingly interminable day was finally reaching its dark conclusion. He laid his head on the blanket and closed his eyes, which gave up two meaningless tears. He sighed, so softly that no one heard him, and through the spaces between the bars he saw the blurred outline of the derrick high in the sky, the soft-yellow crescent moon hanging at its tip looking soft and inviting.

CHAPTER 8

A treacherous ape, a turncoat dog—
Ingratitude has existed since ancient times.
Little Wang, you've thrown away your scythe and hoe
To learn the tyrant's walk, just like a crab. . . .

> – from a ballad sung by Zhang Kou following the garlic glut, to curse
> roundly Wang Tai, the new deputy director of the county supply
> and marketing cooperative

1

The police van had traveled so far down the road that the dust had already settled on asphalt that was a blinding ribbon of reflected light. A squashed toad that had been there since who knows when was now no more than a dried-out flattened skin, like a decal. Jinju struggled to her feet and stumbled up to the side of the road; sweat-soaked, her knees knocking, her mind a blank, she sat down in a clump of grass, seemingly more dead than alive.

The road cut through a vast cropland, with waist-high corn and sorghum nearby and waves of golden millet in the distance. The black soil looked like a patchwork quilt in the fields, which had been prepared for a seeding of soybeans or corn. The dry air and blazing sun made the soil crack and sizzle. Everything the sun touched turned golden yellow, particularly the county government compound, where sunflowers were in bloom.

She sat lost in her thoughts until the sun sank in the west and clouds of mist climbed skyward; gloomy songs rose from the fields.

Each summer day, as night fell, cool breezes drew songs from the throats of peasants. Thick layers of dust covered their naked bodies, which seemed to grow as the sun's power faded. An ox was pulling a plow, turning the soil in a garlic field. Seen from a distance, the earth tumbled over glistening blades of the plow, rolling constantly, a shiny black wave in the wake of the plow.

Numbly, she watched the activity out in the field, and when the old man behind the plow began to sing, she wept openly.

"Sunset at West Mountain, the sky turns dark"—the old man flicked his whip, making the tip dance above the ox's head—"Second Aunt rides her mule to Yangguan . . ."

He stopped after only two lines. But a few moments later, he was at it again: "Sunset at West Mountain, the sky turns dark / Second Aunt rides her mule to Yangguan . . ."

The same two lines, then he stopped again.

Jinju stood up, brushed the dirt off her backside with her bundle, and slowly headed home.

Father was dead, Mother had been arrested. A month earlier, he had been run over by the township party secretary's car, while she had been thrown into a wagon by the police and taken away, and Jinju didn't know why.

She walked onto the river embankment, but her bulging belly made it necessary to lean backwards to keep her balance on the way down. Gingerly she stepped on the slick grass and onto the sandy stretch where weeping willows grew. The spongy soil was dotted with clumps of conch grass—green with yellow tips. Leaning against a medium-sized willow, she gazed at the glossy brown-and-green bark, on which an army of red ants was marching. Not knowing what thoughts she should force into the emptiness of her mind, she gradually became aware of a swelling in her legs and the violent, thrashing of her child. She sucked in a mouthful of cold air, leaned over, and held her breath as she wrapped her arms tightly around the tree.

Sweat beaded her forehead; tears oozed from the corners of her eyes. The child in her belly pounded and kicked as if he harbored a secret grievance against her. Feeling deeply wronged, she heard her unborn baby cry and fulminate, and she knew, with absolute certainty, that it was a boy, and that he was glaring up at her at that very moment.

Do you want to come out, my child? Is that what you want? She sat tentatively on the sandy soil and rubbed her hand lightly over the taut skin of her belly. It's not time yet, my child—don't be in such a hurry, she implored. But that infuriated the fetus, who pounded and kicked as never before, eyes wide with loathing, screeching and weeping. . . . I've never seen a baby cry with its eyes open. . . . Child, please don't be in such a hurry to come out. . . . She scraped a piece of bark off the tree . . . a stream of warm liquid ran down her legs. . . . Child, you can't come out now. . . .

Jinju's heartbreaking wails so startled the orioles above her that they squawked loudly and flew off to points unknown.

"Elder Brother Gao Ma . . . Elder Brother Gao Ma . . . come save me . . . hurry." Her loud wails shattered the silence of the willow grove.

The child in her belly would not be mollified. Cruel and relentless, his bloodshot eyes opened wide, he screeched, "Let me Out of here! Let me out, I say!"

By bracing herself against the tree and biting down hard on her lip, she was able to struggle to her feet. Every punch and kick doubled her up with pain and wrenched a tortured shout from her throat. The image of that frightful little thing floated before her eyes: skinny, dark, a high nose, big eyes, two rows of hard teeth.

Don't bite me, child . . . let loose . . . don't bite. . . .

Forcing herself into a crouch, she shuffled forward a few steps amid drooping willow branches whose leaves were covered with aphids that fell onto her face, neck, hair, and shoulders when she brushed against them. The warm liquid was seeping into her shoes, where it mixed with sand to form a gritty mud that made her feet slip and slide as if her shoes were filled with slime. She moved from one willow tree to the next, forcing them all to share the torment she endured. Hordes of aphids twinkled like fireflies, until the willow branches and leaves seemed coated with oil.

Child . . . don't glare at me like that . . . don't do that. . . . I know you're suffocating from oppression . . . not eating well, nothing good to drink . . . want to come out. . . .

Jinju stumbled and fell, wrenching a painful shout from the child in her belly, who savagely bit the wall of the womb. The stabbing pain brought her to her knees. She crawled on the ground in agony, fingers digging into the sandy soil like steel claws.

Child . . . you bit a hole in me . . . bit a hole. . . . I have to crawl like a lowly dog. . . .

Her belly scraped the sandy ground as she moved ahead on all fours, sweat and teardrops marking her passage in the dust. She cried her heart out, all because of an unruly, trouble-making, black-hearted child who was ripping her apart. She was terrified of the spiteful little brat who squirmed like a silkworm inside her, trying to stretch the limits of the space that confined him. But the walls were springy as rubber, so he no sooner stretched it in one spot than it snapped back in another. That made him so angry he flailed and kicked and bit for all he was worth. "You bitch! You lousy bitch!" he cursed.

Child . . . oh, my child . . . spare me . . . your mother. . . . I'll get down on my knees for you. . . .

Moved by her pleas, he stopped biting and kicking the wall of her womb. The pain eased up at once, and she let her tear-streaked, sweat-soaked face drop to the sandy soil, overcome with gratitude for her son's display of mercy.

The setting sun painted the tips of the willow trees gold. Jinju raised her dusty, gritty face and saw wisps of milky-white smoke rising above the village. Gingerly she stood up, fearful of rekindling the anger of her child.

By the time she made her way to Gao Ma's door, the red sun had fallen well below the willow branches. The snapping of whips above the heads of oxen on village roads and the strains of music steeped in salty water turned the evening sky a bright red.

> I think about your mother, who departed early for the Yellow
>   Springs,
> Leaving you and your sisters miserable and lonely—
> A motherless child is a horse with no reins.
> On your own at fourteen to sing in a brothel:
> Since the dawn of time harlots have been spared laughter
>   reserved for the poor . . .
> Instead of selling your body you should have a memorial arch
>   erected in your honor
> To repay this debt of blood.

2

They pushed and squeezed their way out of the jute field. The high sun had burned off the pervasive mist and cleared heaven and earth. Across the pale strip of road they saw thousands of acres of chili peppers planted by Pale Horse County farmers—a stretch of fiery red as far as the eye could see.

The moment they emerged from the field, Jinju felt as if she were standing naked in front of a crowd. Frantic with shame, she quickly retreated back into the field, followed by Gao Ma. "Keep moving," he pressed her. "Why cower in here?"

"Elder Brother Gao Ma," she said, "we can't travel in broad daylight."

"We're in Pale Horse County now. No one knows us here," Gao Ma said with mounting anxiety.

"I'm scared. What if we run into somebody we know?"

"We won't," he reassured her. "And even if we did, we have nothing to be ashamed of."

"How can you say that? Look what you've done to me. . . ." She sat down and began to cry.

"All right, my little granny," he said, exasperated. "You women are scared of wolves in front and tigers in back, changing your minds every couple of minutes."

"I can't walk anymore. My legs hurt."

"No flimsy excuses now."

"And I'm sleepy."

First scratching his head, then shaking it, Gao Ma said, "We can't live the rest of our lives in this jute field."

"I don't care, I'm not moving while the sun's out."

"Then we'll wait till tonight." He helped her to her feet. "But let's move inside a little. It's too dangerous here."

"I . . ."

"I know, you can't walk anymore." He knelt in front of her. "I'll carry you piggyback." After handing her his bundle, he reached back and wrapped his arms around the back of her knees. She glided effortlessly up onto his back.

Before long he was huffing and puffing, his dark neck thrust out at a sharp angle. Beginning to take pity on him, she prodded him with her knees. "Put me down," she said. "I can walk now."

Without a word in reply, Gao Ma slid his hands upward until they were cupped around her buttocks, which he gently squeezed. A feeling as if her organs were blossoming like fresh flowers spread through her body. She moaned and lightly pummeled Gao Ma's neck, he tripped, and they fell in a heap.

The jute plants trembled uneasily—only a few at first, but they were soon joined by the others as a wind rose, and all the sounds in the world were swallowed up by the booming yet surprisingly gentle noise of jute leaves and branches scraping against one another.

3

Early the following morning, Jinju and Gao Ma, their clothes dusty and wet with dew, walked up to the Pale Horse County long-distance bus station.

It was a tall, handsome building—on the outside, at least—whose colorfully shaded lights above the gate illuminated both the large red letters of the signboard and the pale-green plaster façade. Pushcarts that opened after dark formed two rows leading up to the gate, like a long corridor. Sleepy-eyed vendors, male and female, stood wearily behind their carts. Jinju watched a young vendor in her twenties cover up a yawn with her hand; when she was finished, tears stood in her eyes, which looked like lethargic tadpoles in the reflected blue flames from a sizzling gas lantern.

"Sweet pears . . . sweet pears . . . want some sweet pears?" a woman called to them from behind her pushcart. "Grapes . . . grapes . . . buy these fine grapes!" a man called from behind his. Apples, autumn peaches, honeyed dates: whatever you could desire, they sold. The smell of overripe fruit hung in the air, and the ground was littered with waste paper, the rotting skins of various fruits, and human excrement.

Jinju imagined something hidden behind the vendors' benign looks. Deep down they're cursing or laughing at me, she thought. They know who I am, and they know the things I've done over the past couple of days. That one over there, she can see the mud stains on my back and the crushed jute leaves on my clothes. And that old bastard over there, staring at me like I'm one of *those* women. . . . Overwhelmed by a powerful sense of degradation, Jinju shrank inward until her legs froze and her lips were tightly shut. Lowering her head in abject shame, she held on to Gao Ma's jacket. Feelings of remorse returned, and a sense that the road ahead was sealed to her. Thoughts of the future were terrifying.

Meekly she followed Gao Ma up the stairs and stood beside him on the filthy tiled floor, finally breathing a sigh of relief. The vendors, quiet now, were beginning to doze off. It was probably just my imagination, she comforted herself. They didn't see anything out of the ordinary. But then a frazzled, slovenly old woman walked out of the building and, with loathing in her dark eyes, glared at Jinju, whose heart shuddered in her chest cavity. The old woman walked down the steps, sought out a secluded corner, dropped her pants, and peed on the ground.

When Gao Ma wrapped his hand around the door handle, slick from countless thousands of greasy hands, Jinju's heart shuddered strangely again. The door creaked as he opened it a crack, releasing a blast of hot, nauseating air into Jinju's face that nearly sent her reeling. Still, she followed him into the station, where someone who looked like an attendant yawned grandly as she crossed the floor. Gao Ma dragged Jinju over to the person, who turned out to be a very pregnant woman with a faceful of moles.

"Comrade, when does the bus for Lanji leave?" he asked.

The attendant scratched her protruding belly and looked at Gao Ma and Jinju out of the corner of her eye. "Don't know. Try the ticket counter." She was nice-looking and soft-spoken. "Over there," she added, pointing with her hand.

Gao Ma nodded and said "Thank you"—three times.

The line was short, and he was at the ticket window in no time. A moment later he had their tickets in hand. Jinju, who hadn't let go of his jacket all the while he was buying the tickets, sneezed once.

As she stood in the doorway of the huge waiting room, Jinju was terrified by the thought that everyone was looking at her, studying her grimy clothes and mud-spattered shoes. Gao Ma led her into the waiting room, whose floor was carpeted with melon-seed husks, candy wrappers, fruit skins, gobs of phlegm, and standing water. The oppressively hot air carried the stink of farts and sweat and other nameless foul odors that nearly bowled her over; but within a few minutes she had gotten used to it.

Gao Ma led her in search of seats. Three rows of benches painted an unknowable color, running the length of the room, were filled with sleeping people and a few seated passengers squeezed in among them. Gao Ma and Jinju spotted an empty place on a bench next to a bulletin board for newspapers, but upon closer inspection they saw that it was all wet, as if a child had peed on it. She balked, but he just brushed the water off with his hand. "Sit down," he said. " 'Conveniences at home, trouble on the road.' You'll feel better once you get off your feet."

Gao Ma sat down first, followed by a scowling Jinju with her swollen, puffy legs. Sure enough, she soon felt much better. For now she could lean back and present a smaller target for prying eyes. When Gao Ma told her to get some sleep, since their bus wasn't due to leave for an hour and a half, she shut her eyes, even though she wasn't sleepy. Transported back to the field, she found herself surrounded by jute stalks on the sides and the sharp outlines of leaves and the cold gleam of the sky above. Sleep was out of the question.

Three of the four glass panes over the gray-green bulletin board were broken, and a couple of sheets of yellowed newspaper hung from shards of broken glass. A middle-aged man walked up and tore off a corner of one of them, all the while looking around furtively. A moment later, the pungent odor of burning tobacco drifted over, and Jinju realized that the newspaper was serving as the man's roll-your-own paper. Why didn't I think to use it to dry the bench before we sat down? she wondered, as she looked down at her shoes. The caked-on mud was dried and splitting, so she scraped it off with her finger.

Gao Ma leaned over and asked softly, "Hungry?"

She shook her head.

"I'm going to get something to eat," he said.

"Why? We'll have plenty of opportunities to spend our money from here on out."

"People are iron," he said, "and food is steel. I need to keep up my strength to find work. Save my seat."

After he laid his bundle beside her on the bench, Jinju had the sinking feeling that he was not coming back. She knew she was just being foolish—he wouldn't leave her there, he wasn't that kind of man. The image of him in the field with headphones over his ears—the first real impression he had made on her—flooded her mind. It seemed at turns to be happening right now and ages ago. She opened the bundle and took out the cassette player to listen to some music. But, afraid people might laugh at her, she shoved it back in and retied the bundle.

A woman looking like a wax figurine sat on a deck chair across from Jinju: her jet-black shoulder-length hair framed an ivory complexion and matched her thin, crescent-shaped eyebrows. She had astonishingly long lashes and lips like ripe cherries, dark red and luminous. She was wearing a skirt the color of the red flag, and her breasts jutted out so pertly they made Jinju feel bashful; reminded of talk that city girls wore padded bras, she thought about her own sagging breasts. I always knew they'd grow big and ugly, and that's exactly what happened, she thought. But city girls wait in vain for theirs to grow big and sexy. Life is full of mysteries. Her girlfriends had warned her not to let men touch her breasts, or they'd rise like leavened bread in a matter of days. They were right: that's just what had happened.

A man—also outlandish looking, of course—had lain his permed head in the lap of the woman in red, who was running her pale, tapered fingers through his hair, combing out the springy curls. She looked up and caught Jinju staring at her, so embarrassing Jinju that she lowered her head and looked away, like a thief caught in the act.

At some point during all this, the room brightened and the loudspeakers blared an announcement for Taizhen passengers to line up at Gate 10 to have their tickets punched. The heavily accented female voice on the PA system was so jarring it set Jinju's teeth on edge. Bench sleepers began to stir, and in no time a stream of passengers—bundles and baskets in hand, wives and children in tow—descended on Gate 10 like a swarm of bees. They formed a colorful mob, short and stubby.

The couple opposite her acted as if there were no one else around.

A pair of attendants walked up to the rows of benches and began nudging sleepers' buttocks and thighs with broom handles. "Get up," they insisted. "All of you get up." Most of the targets of these nudges sat up, rubbed their eyes, and fished out cigarettes; but some merely started the process, then lay back to continue their interrupted nap as soon as the attendants had moved on.

For some reason, though, the attendants were reluctant to disturb the curly-haired man. The woman in red, still running her fingers through his hair, looked up at the bedraggled attendants and asked in a loud, assured voice, "What time does the Pingdao bus leave, miss?"

Her perfect Beijing accent established her credentials, and Jinju, as if given a glimpse of Paradise, sighed appreciatively over both her good looks and her lovely way of speaking.

The attendants responded politely, "Eight-thirty."

In contrast to the well-spoken woman in red, the attendants were beneath Jinju's contempt. They began sweeping the floor, from one end of the room to the other. It seemed to Jinju that every man and half the women were puffing on cigarettes and pipes, whose smoke slowly filled the room and led to a round of coughing and spitting.

Gao Ma returned with a bulging cellophane bag. "Is everything all right?" he asked when he saw the look on her face. She said it was, so he sat down, reached into the bag, and pulled out a pear. "The local restaurants were all closed, so I bought you some fruit." He offered her the pear.

"I told you not to spend so much," she groused.

He wiped the pear on his jacket and took a noisy bite. "Here," he said, handing it to her. "I've got more."

A ragamuffin was walking up and down the rows of benches begging from anyone who was awake. Stopping in front of a young military officer, who glanced at him out of the corner of his eye, he struck a pitiful pose and said, "Officer, Colonel, could you spare a little change?"

"I don't have any money!" the moon-faced officer snapped in reply, rolling his eyes to show his displeasure.

"Anything will do," the young beggar pleaded. "Won't you take pity on me?"

"You're old enough to work. Why don't you get a job?"

"Work makes me dizzy."

The officer fished out a pack of cigarettes, opened it, removed one, and stuck it between his lips.

"If you won't give me money, Colonel, how about a smoke?"

"Do you know what kind of cigarettes these are?" The officer looked him in the eye as he whipped out a shiny cigarette lighter and— click—flipped it on. Instead of touching the flame to the tip of his cigarette right away, he just let it blaze.

"Foreign, Colonel—they're foreign cigarettes."

"Know where they came from?"

"No."

"My father-in-law brought them back from Hong Kong, that's where. And look at this lighter."

"You're lucky to have a father-in-law like that, Colonel. I can see that life has smiled on you. Your father-in-law must be a big official, and his son-in-law will be one himself one of these days. Big officials are well-heeled and generous. So how about a smoke, Colonel?"

The young officer thought it over for a moment, then said, "No, I'd rather give you money."

Jinju watched him fish out a shiny aluminum two-fen piece and hand it to the beggar, who wore a pained grin as he accepted the paltry gift with both hands and bowed deeply.

Now the beggar was walking this way, sizing up people as he came. Passing on Jinju and Gao Ma, he went up to the woman in red and her permed young man, who had just sat up. Jinju saw skin show through the beggar's worn trousers when he bowed.

"Madam, sir, take pity on a man who's down on his luck and give me some spare change."

"Aren't you ashamed of yourself?" the woman in red asked sanctimoniously. "A healthy young man like you should be out working. Don't you have any self-respect?"

"Madam, I don't understand a word you're saying. I'm only asking for a little change."

"Would you bark like a dog for it?" the permed fellow asked the beggar. "I'll give you one yuan for every bark."

"Sure. What do you prefer, a big dog or a little one?"

The permed young man turned to the woman in red and smiled. "That's up to you."

The young beggar coughed and cleared his throat, then began to bark, sounding remarkably doglike: "Arf arf—arf arf arf—arf arf arf arf arf arf arf arf arf, arf, arf, arf arf, arf arf arf arf arf arf arf arf! That was a little dog. Twenty-six barks. Ruff! Ruff ruff! Ruff ruff! Ruff ruff ruff! Ruff ruff ruff ruff ruff raff ruff raff ruff ruff! Ruff ruff ruff! Ruff ruff!! Ruff!!! That was a big dog, twenty-four barks. Big and little together comes to fifty barks, at one yuan apiece, for a total of fifty yuan, sir, madam."

The permed young man and the woman in red exchanged glances, both looking quite abashed. He took out his billfold and counted its contents, then turned to his companion and said, "Do you have any money, Yingzi?"

"Just a few coins," she replied.

"Elder Brother," the permed young man said, "we've had a long trip, and this is our last stop. All we've got left is forty-three yuan. If you'll give us an address, we'll send the seven we owe you as soon as we get home."

The young beggar took the money, wetted his finger, and carefully counted the bills—twice. Removing a red one-yuan note with a missing corner, he said, "I can't take this one, sir. You can have it back, and I'll take the forty-two. Now you owe me eight."

"Write down your address for us," the young man said.

"I don't know how to write," the beggar said. "Just send it to the President of the United States and ask him to forward it to me. He's my uncle!"

With that the beggar bowed deeply to the handsome couple and laughed until he was rocking back and forth. Then he turned and presented himself before Jinju and Gao Ma. With a bow he said, "Elder Brother, Elder Sister, how about one of those delicious-looking pears? My throat's dry from all that barking."

Jinju picked out a big one and thrust it into the beggar's hand. He acknowledged the handout with a deep bow before gobbling the pear up, one big bite after another, all the while humming a nasal tune. Then, as if there weren't another soul in sight, he turned and walked off, his head held high.

Another announcement emerged from the PA system, sending more passengers to the gates to have their tickets punched. The woman in red and the young curlyhead rose and dashed off to the gate, dragging a suitcase on rollers behind them.

"What about us?" Jinju asked Gao Ma.

He looked at his watch. "Forty minutes more," he said. "I'm getting a little impatient myself."

By this time there were no more passengers sleeping on the benches, although people continued to enter and leave the waiting room, including an old beggar who quaked from head to toe, and a woman with a child in tow, also asking for handouts. A middle-aged man in a beaked cap and a uniform tunic, holding a half-empty bottle of beer in one hand, stood in front of the bulletin board and held forth, waving the bottle in the air for effect. His sleeves were stained and greasy, and there was a piece of skin missing on his nose, exposing the pale flesh beneath. Two fountain pens were clipped in his breast pocket; Jinju assumed he was some kind of party official. He took a swig of beer, waved the bottle once or twice to watch the foam rise, and began to speak. His tongue was thick in his mouth, and his lower lip seemed not to move at all.

"The nine editorials—refuting the Open Letter of the revisionist Soviet Central Committee of the Communist Party . . . Khrushchev said, 'Stalin, you are my second father.' In Chinese it would be, 'Stalin, you are my true father'—in Paradise dialect it would be, 'Stalin, you are my big fellow.'" Another swig of beer, then he knelt down like Khrushchev the supplicant before Stalin. "But," he continued, "the heirs of perfidious people are more unbridled than their predecessors. When Khrushchev assumed power, he burned Stalin. Comrades, historical experience demands our attention. . . ." Another swig of beer. "Comrade leaders at all levels, you must give it your full attention. Do not, I repeat, do *not* be negligent. Wa—" Beer foam oozed from his mouth, which he wiped with his sleeve. "The nine editorials—refuting the open letter of the Soviet Central Committee . . ."

Mesmerized by the man, Jinju listened to him rant and rave about things she had never heard of before. The quake in his voice and the way he twisted his tongue around the name "Stalin" appealed to her the most.

Gao Ma squeezed her arm and said softly, "We've got trouble, Jinju. Here comes Deputy Yang."

She turned to look and felt as if her body had turned to ice. Deputy Yang, her lame Elder Brother, and her bull-like Second Brother stood in the waiting-room entrance.

Grabbing Gao Ma's hand in panic, she stood up.

The middle-aged official took a swig of beer, waved his arm in the air, and shouted, "Stalin . . ."

4

The long-bed Jeep bumped and jolted along the edge of the jute field, until Deputy Yang tapped the driver on the shoulder and said, "Stop here, lad."

The driver slammed on the brakes; the Jeep screeched to a halt. Deputy Yang jumped down and said, "Want to stretch your legs, Number One?"

Opening his door, Elder Brother jumped down, stumbled briefly, then stood and stretched.

Second Brother nudged Jinju. "Get out," he told her. Gao Ma was sitting on the other side of Jinju. "Get out!" Elder Brother shouted.

Gao Ma jumped down in a crouch; Second Brother nudged Jinju out of the Jeep.

The sun was directly over the chili pepper crop that lay on the Pale Horse County side of the road, a virtual sea of blood-red. On the Paradise County side, fields of jute, broad and deep, seemed to go on forever; birds noiselessly skimming the tips of the plants made Jinju feel uncommonly at peace, as if she had already dimly envisioned today's events. Now everything had fallen into place.

Her hands were bound behind her with hempen cords; her brothers had relented slightly by tying them at the wrists. With Gao Ma it was a different matter, for he had been hogtied so the ropes would dig deeply into his shoulders and force his neck out unnaturally. It broke her heart to see him like that.

Deputy Yang took a couple of steps into the jute field and relieved himself with casual immodesty. When he had finished, he turned his head and said, "Number One, Number Two, you Fangs are worthless trash!"

Elder Brother gaped at Deputy Yang with his mouth hanging slack.

"Anyone who lets his little sister get tricked into running off with some man is a dumb bastard. If it had been me . . . hmph!" He glared menacingly at Gao Ma.

Without waiting for Deputy Yang to say another word, Number Two charged Gao Ma and drove his fist straight into his nose.

With a loud protest, Gao Ma took three or four rocky steps backwards, trying to keep his balance. His shoulders lurched as if he were trying to touch his face: knocked senseless by the punch, he had apparently forgotten that his arms were bound.

"Number Two . . . don't hit him . . . hit me," Jinju pleaded as she shielded Gao Ma's body with her own.

With one kick, he sent her flying into the jute field. She took some plants with her as she tumbled head over heels. The rope around her wrists loosened as she rolled, so she immediately wrapped her arms around her knees; the sharp pain in her leg indicated a broken bone.

"Don't expect any mercy from us," Number Two shrieked, "you shameless, stinking slut!"

Trickles of blood oozed from Gao Ma's ashen nose. It flowed and flowed, black at first, then bright red. "You—against the law—to hit people," he stammered, his cheeks twitching, his mouth twisted in a grimace.

"You tricked her into running away with you, and *that's* against the law," Deputy Yang said. "Not only did you steal a man's future wife, but you destroyed the marriage prospects for three couples. They ought to put you away for twenty years."

"I did nothing illegal," Gao Ma defended himself, snapping his head to the side to launch the blood from his nose. "Jinju never registered as Liu Shengli's wife, so she's not legally married to anybody. You tried to coerce her into marrying Liu Shengli in violation of the Marriage Law. If anybody should be put away, it's you people!"

Deputy Yang curled his lip and said to the Fang brothers, "That's some sharp tongue he's got."

Second Brother drove his fist into Gao Ma's gut. *Oof!* Gao Ma grunted as he doubled over, stumbled forward a couple of steps, and crumpled to the ground.

The brothers wasted no time. Second Brother began kicking Gao Ma in the ribs and back, and since he practiced martial arts nightly on the threshing floor, every kick sent his victim rolling and screaming for dear life. Elder Brother tried to get in a few kicks of his own, but his gimp leg would barely support his weight, and by the time his good leg was cocked and ready to go, Second Brother had already sent Gao Ma rolling out of the way. Eventually he landed a kick on target, but with hardly any steam behind it; worse, he fell down, and lay on the ground for the longest time before climbing to his feet.

"Stop hitting him! I *begged* him to take me away!" Jinju pleaded as she struggled to her feet by grasping a jute stalk. But when her weight settled on the injured leg, searing pains shot up to her brain, and she fell again, dry shrieks emerging from her throat. She was finally reduced to crawling from one jute plant to the next.

Meanwhile, Gao Ma was rolling in the dirt, his face streaked with blood and mud. Second Brother kept kicking him mercilessly, as if he were a sandbag, and each kick was met with shouts of "Kick him again!" from Elder Brother, who leapt in the air as if he were on a trampoline. "Harder! Kill the jackass bastard!" Elder Brother's face was twisted; tears clouded his eyes.

After crawling to the roadside, Jinju propped herself up and took a couple of halting steps forward, only to be met with a flying drop kick in the belly, delivered by Second Brother. She groaned as she hit the ground and rolled back into the field.

Gao Ma, now bereft of the power of speech, was still able to roll, which was just fine with the sweaty Second Brother, whose kicks kept thudding into him.

"You're killing him!" Jinju had crawled back to the road.

Deputy Yang ran up, placed himself between Second Brother and Gao Ma, and said, "Okay, Number Two, that's enough!"

Gao Ma had rolled to the edge of the road, and he burrowed his face in the mud of the pepper field, his bound arms twitching above purple fingers that looked like toadstools. A worried Deputy Yang walked up, rolled him onto his back, and stuck a finger under his nose to see if he was still breathing.

They've killed Gao Ma! Jinju saw thousands of golden spots, which changed color to form a lovely green string arching in the air above her. She reached out, but couldn't catch them. Sometimes she thought she had one, but when she opened her hand it flew off. A sickening sweet taste floated up from deep in her throat, and when she opened her mouth a red clump emerged and landed on a withered branch in front of her. I'm coughing up blood! At first she was scared. I'm coughing up blood! Then she felt blessed: her fears, her worries, her troubles, all evaporated like dissipating vapor, leaving a single honeyed sorrow encircling her heart.

"You're a fucking avenger!" Deputy Yang cursed Second Brother. "You were supposed to teach him a lesson, not kill him."

"You called me and my brother worthless trash."

"Because you don't know how to watch over your own sister. I didn't mean you could kill him."

"Is he really dead? Is he?" Elder Brother asked in a panicky voice. "Deputy Yang . . . it wasn't me who kicked him."

"Just what are you saying?" Second Brother asked his brother, glaring through bloodshot eyes. "The whole idea was to get you married."

"That's not what I meant."

"Then what *did* you mean?"

"Cut out the squabbling," Deputy Yang cut in, "and move him onto the roadway."

The brothers went into the pepper field, picked Gao Ma up by the head and feet, and carried him out to the roadway. They no sooner had him laid out than Elder Brother plopped down on the ground, panting breathlessly.

"Hurry up and untie him," Deputy Yang ordered.

The brothers exchanged glances, neither saying a word, though they seemed disposed to. Second Brother rolled Gao Ma over, facedown, while Elder Brother hobbled over and tried to loosen the knot. Through the encircling green spots, Elder Brother's large hands, with their gnarled, bony fingers, looked to Jinju like ribbed fans. He was too shaky to untie the knot. "Use your teeth!" Deputy Yang screamed at Elder Brother, who looked up with a pathetic expression on his face before kneeling next to Gao Ma and trying to loosen the stubborn knot with his teeth, like a scrawny mongrel gnawing on a bone. When he finally managed to work the knot free, Deputy Yang pushed him out of the way and jerked up on the rope, as if trying to rip a tendon out of Gao Ma's body. Once the rope was removed, he rolled Gao Ma onto his back and again stuck a finger under his nose.

Jinju's heart began to shrink, and she shuddered as a breath of cold air rose inside. They've killed him—and all because of me! Elder Brother Gao Ma . . . my dear Elder Brother Gao Ma . . . Jinju's shrinking heart relaxed again and, amid her immersion in the blessing of honeyed sorrow, more sickening sweet stuff rose slowly in her throat. Jute branches and leaves rustled crisply; the sunlight was blinding bright; tens of thousands of warm red sparks danced wildly in Pale Horse County's pepper fields; and a chestnut colt bounded out of the field, flicking its tail friskily as it raced among sparks that glinted off its metal shoes like shiny precious gems. Bells around its neck played a crisp, melodic tune.

The swarthy skin on Gao Ma's swollen, puffy face shone under all that blood and mud. He lay on the ground, legs straight, arms lying stiffly at his sides. Deputy Yang laid his ear against Gao Ma's chest. Jinju heard Gao Ma's powerful, heavy heartbeat, which matched the rhythm of the colt's hoof beats: the hoof beats were the pounding of a small drum, the heartbeats the thumping of a big one.

Please don't die, Elder Brother Gao Ma. Don't leave me here alone, Jinju moaned as she watched the chestnut colt race up to the road, then lope back and forth along the edge of the pepper field, the sparks flying from its metal shoes making it appear to be prancing on water. The crisp tinkling of the bells around its neck was long and drawn-out. At the edge of the pepper field it slowed to a more hesitant gait and turned its blue eyes toward the calmly smiling face of Gao Ma.

"You boys are lucky," Deputy Yang said as he stood up. "He's still alive. If he had died, you'd be rotting in jail for a long time—and I mean both of you!"

"What now, Eighth Uncle?" Elder Brother asked helplessly.

"Now it's my turn to suffer over this business of yours," Deputy Yang grumbled, taking a small opaque vial from his pocket and waving it under the brothers' eyes. "This is Yunnan medicinal powder. We'll give it to our young friend here." He knelt down, removed the stopper from the vial, and dumped a bright red pellet into his palm. Pausing briefly for effect, he said, "Open his mouth."

Again the brothers exchanged glances. Second Brother signaled Elder Brother to stick his dark fingers into Gao Ma's mouth and pry it open. Holding the pellet between his fingers, Deputy Yang paused dramatically once more before reluctantly inserting it between Gao Ma's lips.

"Little Guo," Deputy Yang shouted to his driver, "bring the canteen."

The driver climbed lazily out of the Jeep and walked up holding an army canteen whose yellow surface was peeling. A semicircular rut etched in his cheek showed that he had been sleeping facedown on the steering wheel.

Deputy Yang poured some water into Gao Ma's mouth. It reeked of alcohol.

Then the four men stood over Gao Ma like dark pillars, all eight eyes glued to his face. The chestnut colt ran like the wind, hooves thudding loudly, sparks from its shoes crackling in the air; the circle it described was large enough to embrace Jinju, and as it passed through the field, stalks and branches bent before it like softly yielding willow twigs. Green spots careened off its glossy hide. Little colt . . . little colt . . . she wanted to wrap her arms around its satiny neck.

Gao Ma's hand twitched.

"Good," Deputy Yang exclaimed. "Excellent. That Yunnan medicinal powder deserves its reputation. Damned good stuff."

Gao Ma's eyes opened a crack. Deputy Yang bent down and said in a genial tone, "You're lucky to be alive, my boy. If not for my Yunnan medicinal powder, you'd be off meeting with Karl Marx right about now."

Gao Ma lay with a peaceful, happy smile on his face. He managed a barely perceptible nod to Deputy Yang.

"Now what, Eighth Uncle?" Elder Brother asked.

A rumble emerged from Gao Ma's chest as he pulled his arms back and rested on his elbows, slowly raising his head and body until he was in a sitting position. Frothy, blood-streaked threads oozed from the corners of his mouth. Elder Brother Gao Ma . . . dear Elder Brother Gao Ma . . . the chestnut colt is touching your face with its downy muzzle . . . it's weeping. Gao Ma's head fell back. Slowly he raised it again. The chestnut colt is licking Elder Brother Gao Ma's face with its golden tongue.

"He can take a beating," Deputy Yang said as he looked down at the now squatting Gao Ma. "Do you know why this happened?" he asked with a ring of genuine appreciation.

Gao Ma smiled and nodded. He's looking at me. There's a smile on Elder Brother Gao Ma's face. The chestnut colt is licking the traces of blood from his face.

"Are you going to try to trick our sister in going off with you again?" asked Elder Brother, limping in place.

Gao Ma smiled and nodded.

Second Brother cocked his leg to kick Gao Ma again.

"Number Two!" Deputy Yang shouted. "You stupid bastard!"

Elder Brother picked up Gao Ma's bundle and loosened the knot with his teeth, spilling the contents, including the envelope, onto the ground. He got down on his knees and held the envelope down.

"Number One, don't do it."

After wetting his finger in his mouth, Elder Brother began counting the bank notes.

"Number One, you shouldn't be doing that."

"Eighth Uncle, he corrupted our sister and used up your costly medicine. For that he must pay."

Elder Brother then dug through Gao Ma's pockets with his damp hand, fishing out some crumpled ten-fen notes and four shiny aluminum one-fen coins. The chestnut colt reared its head and knocked the coins from his hand. Elder Brother scurried after them, tears filling his eyes.

CHAPTER 9

In the old society the people paid for official lawlessness,
In the new order justice is supposed to take root and grow.
County Administrator Wang thought he was above the law;
Driver Zhang slipped through the net after a fatal accident. . . .

> – from a ballad sung at police headquarters by Zhang Kou on behalf of
> Fourth Uncle, who had been struck down on the road after trying to
> sell his garlic

1

It was noon. A dazed Fourth Aunt lay in bed, vaguely aware that
someone was tugging on her arm. She sat up, rubbed her eyes, and
was face to face with a young policewoman in a beaked cap
and white uniform.

"Why aren't you eating, Number Forty-seven?" the guard asked.
She had big brown eyes and long, fluttering lashes in a face that was
as white and round as a goose egg. Fourth Aunt was instinctively
drawn to this lovely girl, who removed her hat to fan the air. "We
expect you to behave yourself in here and own up to all the charges.
Remember, 'Leniency to those who confess, severity to those who
refuse.' Now it's mealtime, so eat."

Fourth Aunt's heart was saturated with warmth, and tears
pooled in her aging eyes. She nodded spiritedly. The guard's glossy
black hair, parted on the side, tomboylike, highlighted her soft
white complexion.

"Miss . . ." Fourth Aunt grimaced; she wanted to say something but was too choked up to get the words out.

The guard put her hat back on. "Okay, hurry up and eat. You must trust the government. A good person has nothing to worry about, and a bad person has no place to hide."

"Miss . . . I'm a good person. Let me go home," Fourth Aunt said tearfully.

"You sure talk a lot for an old lady," the frowning guard said, dimples creasing her cheeks. "It's not up to me whether you get out of here or not."

Fourth Aunt wiped her nose with her sleeve, then her tear-filled eyes. "How old are you, miss?"

The guard glared, showing a mean side. "Don't ask about things that don't concern you, Number Forty-seven!"

"I didn't mean anything by it. You're just so pretty, I thought I'd ask."

"Why do you want to know?"

"No reason."

"Twenty-two," the guard said shyly.

"About the same as my daughter, Jinju, who was born in the Year of the Dragon. I wish that useless daughter of mine could be more like—"

"I said hurry up and eat. After you're finished I want you to think about what you did, then make a clean breast of things."

"What is it you want me to think about, miss?"

"Why were you arrested?"

"I don't know." Fourth Aunt grimaced again and was soon crying. "I was home eating," she said between sobs. "Grainy flatcakes and spicy salted vegetables. Someone called at the gate. When I walked outside, they grabbed my arms. . . . I was so scared I just closed my eyes. The next thing I knew, my wrists were locked in shiny bracelets. . . . Daughter was inside crying. She's going to have her baby any day now. Laugh if you want, but I'll tell you anyway—she's not even married. I screamed, but two officers dragged me away, and another one, taller than you but not as pretty, and not nearly as nice—very mean, in fact— started kicking me—"

"That's enough," the guard broke in impatiently. "Hurry up and eat."

"Am I upsetting you, miss?" Fourth Aunt asked. "With all the criminals out there waiting to be arrested, why waste time on me?"

"You didn't help demolish the government offices?"

"Those were government offices?!" an astonished Fourth Aunt exclaimed. "I didn't know that. I had to get help somewhere. My husband—still strong and in good health—was run over by their car. . . ." She wept. "Miss . . . had to get help somewhere . . ."

"Stop that crying," the guard said. "And stop calling me 'miss.' Call me 'Guard' or 'Officer,' like the others do."

"Our sister over there said I should call you 'Officer' and not 'miss,'" Fourth Aunt admitted, pointing to her cellmate, who was lying facedown on her gray cot. "But I forgot. Getting old, memory's no good."

"Eat, I said," the guard insisted.

"Mi—Officer." Fourth Aunt pointed to the blackened steamed bun and bowl of garlic broth. "Do I have to pay for this food? Do I need ration stamps?"

Not knowing whether to laugh or cry, the guard said, "Just eat. You don't need money and you don't need ration stamps. Is that why you weren't eating, because you thought you had to pay?"

"You couldn't know, miss, but when my husband was killed, our two useless sons fought like cats and dogs over family property until there wasn't anything left . . ."

The guard turned to go, but before she was out the door, Fourth Aunt asked, "Do you have a husband picked out yet?"

"That's enough, Number Forty-seven, you crazy old hag!"

"Girls today sure have short fuses. An old lady isn't even allowed to talk."

The guard slammed the cell door shut and walked off, her high heels clicking resoundingly down the corridor, all the way to the far end.

Loud squeaks bounced off the rafters above the corridor, sounding like an old waterwheel. Crickets set up a racket in trees out in the yard. Fourth Aunt sighed and picked up the blackened bun, sniffing it before tearing off a chunk and dunking it in the now cold garlic broth; she stuffed it into her nearly toothless mouth and began munching noisily. The middle-aged woman on the opposite cot rolled over to stare at the ceiling. A long sigh escaped from her lips.

"You've hardly touched your food, Sister-in-Law," Fourth Aunt said to the woman, who opened her clouded eyes wide, shook her head, and frowned.

"I've got such a lump in the pit of my stomach I can't force another bite down," she said wearily. The uneaten half of her steamed bun lay on the gray stand beside her. Green bottleneck flies had settled on it.

"These are made from stale flour," Fourth Aunt said as she ate her bun. "They taste like mildew. But they're still better than grainy flatcakes."

Her cellmate said nothing as she lay motionless on her cot, staring at the ceiling.

After swallowing the last of her bun and slurping down the garlic broth, Fourth Aunt stared at the uneaten half of the other woman's steamed bun, which was still feeding flies on the gray table. "Sister-in-Law," she said bashfully, "I've still got some drops of oil in my bowl here, and it'd be a shame not to sop them up. What do you say I use a little of the skin from your bun?"

The woman nodded. "You can have the whole thing, Auntie."

"I can't take food out of your mouth," Fourth Aunt demurred.

"I'm not going to eat it, so you go ahead."

"Well, if you say so." She climbed down off her cot, edged over to the table, and snatched up the fly-specked bun. "It's not important who eats it," Fourth Aunt said, "so long as it isn't wasted."

The woman nodded. Then, without warning, two yellow tears slipped from the corners of her gray eyes and down her cheeks.

"What's bothering you, Sister-in-Law?" Fourth Aunt said.

No response; just more tears.

"Whatever it is, don't let it get you down." Even Fourth Aunt was crying now. "Life's hard enough already. Sometimes I think dogs are better off than we are. People feed them when they're hungry, and as a last resort, they can survive on human waste. And since they've got furry bodies, they don't have to worry about clothing. But we have to feed and clothe our families, and that keeps us hopping till we're too old to take care of ourselves. Then, if we're lucky, our children will take care of us. If not, we're abused till the day we die. . . ." Fourth Aunt reached up to dry her aging eyes.

The middle-aged woman rolled over and buried her face in her blanket, crying so bitterly her shoulders heaved. So Fourth Aunt climbed unsteadily off her cot, went over and sat down beside her. "Sister-in-Law," she said softly, patting her back, "don't do this to yourself. Try to see things as they are. The world wasn't made for people like us. We must accept our fate. Some people are born to be ministers and generals, others to be slaves and lackeys, and there's nothing anybody can do about it. The old man upstairs decided that you and I would share this cell. It's not so bad. We've got a cot and a blanket, and free food. If the window was a little bigger, maybe it wouldn't be so stuffy . . . but don't let it get you down. And if you really can't go on, then you have to find a way to end it all."

The sounds of crying intensified, drawing the attention of the guard. "Number Forty-six, stop that crying!" she ordered, banging the bars with her fist. "Did you hear me? I said stop crying!"

The order had the desired effect on the sounds but did nothing to lessen the spasms wracking the poor woman's body.

Fourth Aunt went back to her own cot, where she removed her shoes and sat with her legs under her. Swarms of flies buzzed around the cell, loud one moment, softer the next. Feeling an itch under her waistband, Fourth Aunt reached down and plucked out something fat and meaty. It was a louse, gray in color and very big. She squeezed it between her thumbnails until it was no more than a crusty shell. Since her home was louse-free, this one must have come from the bedding. She held up her gray blanket and, sure enough, the folds were teeming with the squirming insects. "Sister-in-Law," she blurted out, "there are lice in our blankets!" Gaining no response, she ignored her cellmate and brought the blanket up close to subject it to a careful search. Soon realizing that squeezing each one between her thumbnails slowed down the process, she began flipping them into her mouth and popping them with her molars—she lacked teeth up front to do the job—then spitting out the shells. They had a light syrupy taste, so addictive that she soon forgot her suffering.

2

Fourth Aunt listened with alarm to the sound of the middle-aged woman retching. She rubbed her eyes, grown tired from her louse hunt, and wiped the remnants of shells from her lips; those that stuck to the back of her hand she scraped off on the wall.

Her cellmate was doubled over with dry heaves, her mouth spread wide, so she shuffled across the cell and began patting her on the back. After wiping the spittle from the corners of her mouth, the woman lay back wearily and closed her eyes; she was gasping for breath.

"You're not . . . you know, are you?" Fourth Aunt asked.

The woman opened her dull, lifeless eyes and tried to focus on Fourth Aunt's face, not understanding the question.

"I asked if you're expecting."

The woman responded by opening her mouth and wailing, "My baby" and "My little Aiguo."

"Please, Sister-in-Law, stop. No more of that," Fourth Aunt urged. "Tell me what's bothering you. Don't keep it bottled up inside."

"Auntie . . . my little Aiguo is dead. . . . I saw it in a dream . . . head cracked open . . . blood all over his face . . . chubby little angel turned into a lifeless bag of bones . . . like when you were killing those lice. . . . I held him in my arms, called to him . . . his rosy cheeks, pretty big eyes . . . so black you could See yourself in them . . . flowers all over the riverbank, purple wild eggplants and white wither gourds and bitter fruits the color of egg yolks and pink hibiscus . . . my Aiguo, a little boy who loved flowers more than girls do, picking those flowers to make a bouquet and stick it under my nose. 'Smell these, Mommy, aren't they pretty?' 'They're like perfume,' I said. He picked a white one and said, 'Kneel down, Mommy.' I asked him why. He told me just to kneel down. My Aiguo could cry at the drop of a hat, so I knelt down, and he stuck that white flower in my hair. 'Mommy's got a flower in her hair!' I said people are supposed to wear red flowers in their hair—white flowers are unlucky, and you only wear them when someone dies. That scared Aiguo. He started crying. "Mommy, I don't want you to die. I can die, but not you. . . ."

By this time the poor woman was sobbing uncontrollably. The cell door opened with a loud clang, and an armed guard stood in the doorway with a slip of paper in his hand. "Number Forty-six, come with us!" he ordered.

The woman stopped crying, although her shoulders continued to heave, and her cheeks were still wet with tears. The guard was flanked by white-uniformed police officers. The one to the left, a man, held a pair of brass handcuffs, like golden bracelets; the other one was a short, broad-beamed woman with a pimply face and a hairy black mole at the corner of her mouth.

"Number Forty-six, come with us!"

The woman slipped her feet into her shoes and shuffled toward the door, where the policeman snapped the golden bracelets onto her wrists.

"Let's go."

She turned to look at Fourth Aunt. There was no life in her eyes, nothing. Fourth Aunt was so frightened by that look she couldn't move, and when she heard the cell door clang shut she could no longer see anything—not the guard, not the guard's shiny bayonet, not the white police officers nor the gray woman. Her eyes burned, and the cell went dark.

3

Where are they taking her? Fourth Aunt wondered, listening for signs; but all she heard were the crickets outside her steel cage and, from farther off—possibly from the public highway—the sounds of metal banging against metal. The cell was getting lighter; bottleneck flies darted around like blue-green meteors.

With the departure of her cellmate, Fourth Aunt experienced the anxieties of loneliness. She sat on Number Forty-six's cot, until she vaguely recalled being told by the pretty guard that inmates were not allowed to sit on any cot but their own. She shook open her cellmate's blanket and was hit in the face by a blast of foul air. It was coated with dark spots like droppings or dried blood, and when she scraped it with her fingernail, a horde of lice scurried out of the folds. She popped some of them into her mouth, bit down, and started to cry. She was thinking about Fourth Uncle and the way he caught lice.

Fourth Uncle sat against the wall in the sun-baked yard, stripped to the waist, his jacket draped across his knees as he picked lice out of the folds and flipped them into a chipped bowl filled with water. "Get all you can, old man," Fourth Aunt said. "When you've got a bowlful, I'll fry them to go with your wine."

Jinju, still a little girl, stuck close to her father. "How come you've got so many lice, Daddy?"

"The poor get lice, the rich get scabies," he said, flipping a particularly fat one into the bowl. As Jinju was swishing the drowning lice around with a blade of grass, a bald hen walked up, cocked its head, and scrutinized the insects.

"The hen wants to eat our lice, Daddy," she said.

"I had to work too hard for these to let you gobble them up," he said as he shooed the chicken away.

"Give her some, and she'll lay more eggs."

"I promised Mr. Wang in West Village I'd bring a thousand," Fourth Uncle said.

"What does he want them for?"

"To make medicine."

"You can make medicine out of lice?"

"You can make medicine out of just about everything."

"How many have you got so far?"

"Eight hundred and forty-seven."

"Want some help?"

"No. He said no females could touch these. He can't make medicine out of them if they've been touched by female hands."

Jinju pulled back her hand.

"It's not easy being a louse," he told her. "Did you ever hear the story of the city louse and the country louse who meet on the road? The city louse asks, 'Say, country brother, where are you off to? The country louse says, 'To the city. How about you?' 'I'm off to the country,' the city louse replies. 'What for?' 'To get something to eat.' 'Forget it. I'm going to town to find food.' When the city louse asks why, he says, 'In the countryside they scour their clothing three times a day, and if they can't find anything, they beat it with a club and pop whatever comes out into their mouths. If we're not beaten to death we're bitten to death. I barely escaped with my life.' The country louse relates its tale of woe tearfully. The city louse sighs and says, 'I assumed things had to be better in the countryside than in the city. I never thought they could be worse.' 'Things must be better in the city than in the countryside,' the country louse says. 'Like hell they are!' the city louse says. 'In the city everybody wears silks and satins, layer upon layer of them. They clean them three times a day and change them five. We never catch a glimpse of flesh. If the iron doesn't get us, the water will. I barely escaped with *my* life.' The two lice cry on each other's shoulders for a while, and when they realize they have nowhere to go, they jump down a well and drown themselves."

Jinju was in stitches. "Daddy, you made that up."

With the sound of her daughter's laughter in her ears, Fourth Aunt sniffled and bit down on a louse, saddened by thoughts of happier days. Putting aside her hunt for lice, she walked barefoot up to the barred window. But it was too high for her to see outside, so she went back and stood on the cot to get a better look. She could see a barbed-wire fence and, beyond that, fields planted with cucumbers, eggplants, and broad beans. The beans were yellowing, the eggplants blooming. A pair of pink-and-white butterflies flew around the purple flowers, moving back and forth between the bean trellises and the eggplant flowers. Fourth Aunt sat down and recommenced her hunt for lice in the blanket, and her mournful memories.

4

It was the fourth time that morning that the parakeets in the East Lane compound of Gao Zhileng had raised a din. Fourth Aunt nudged Fourth Uncle with the tip of her foot. "Hey, old man, it's time to get up. This is the fourth time I've heard the parakeets this morning."

He sat up, threw a jacket over his shoulders, and filled his pipe. Then he sat on the kang smoking as he listened to the nightmarishly shrill cries of the parakeets. "Go out and take a look at the stars," he said. "You can't rely on a bunch of pet birds. Only roosters know when it's dawn."

"Everybody says parakeets are smart," she said, her eyes flashing in the darkness. "Have you ever looked at Gao Zhileng's birds? They're so colorful—green, yellow, red—and they tuck their hooked beaks into their wing feathers, so only their bright little eyes show.

Everybody says they've got the devil in them, which means Gao Zhileng is on the devil's payroll. I never did trust him."

Fourth Uncle puffed on his pipe until the bowl glowed red, but didn't say a word. The parakeets' squawks cut through the darkness, loud one second, soft the next, and Fourth Aunt could envision the colorful birds cocking their heads and eyeing her.

She pulled the covers up over her legs, growing more fearful by the minute and wishing that her cellmate would hurry back. Guards shouted in the corridor, where she heard frequent footsteps.

Out in the yard Fourth Aunt felt chilled. A sleek cat streaked across the top of the wall and was gone. She shivered and scrunched her head down between her shoulders as she gazed into the sky, where stars twinkled brightly. The Milky Way seemed denser than last year. She sought out her three familiar stars. There they were, in the southeastern sky, beside the brilliant half-moon. It was still the middle of the night. She headed over to the new cattle shed at the foot of the eastern wall and, by groping in the dark, added some straw to the trough. Their spotted cow, bought the previous spring, lay on the ground chewing her cud, green lights emerging from her eyes. But when she heard the activity near her trough she got up and ambled over, bumping Fourth Aunt's head with her short, curved horns. "Ouch!" Fourth Aunt exclaimed as she rubbed her head. "Are you trying to kill me, you stupid animal?"

The cow was already busily munching straw, so Fourth Aunt moved up and felt her belly. Another three months and it would be time to calf.

"Well?" Fourth Uncle asked her when she returned to the kang.

"It's still the middle of the night," she replied. "Get some more sleep. I fed the cow while I was up."

"I'm awake now," he said, "so I might as well get on the road. Yesterday was a wasted trip, so I want to get there early today. It's fifteen miles to town, and the way that cow plods along, it'll be light out by the time we get there."

"Are there really that many people selling garlic?"

"Believe me, there are. The streets are jammed with farmers, trucks, oxcarts, horsecarts, tractors, bicycles, even motorbikes. The line runs from the cold-storage warehouse all the way to the railroad tracks. Garlic, nothing but garlic. They say the warehouse will be full in another day or two."

"These are bad times. It's getting harder to sell anything."

"Wake the boys and have them load the wagon and hitch up the cow," Fourth Uncle said. "I'm in no mood to do it. That tramp Jinju has me so upset the slightest thing gets my heart acting up."

"Do you know that your sons are talking about dividing up the family property and going their own way?"

"I'm not blind. Number Two's afraid his brother will ruin his own marriage prospects. Number One sees how determined Jinju is to be with Gao Ma, and with the marriage contract now a worthless piece of paper, he figures he'll take what he can get and live a bachelor's life. Damned ingrates, that's what they are!" Fourth Uncle was beside himself. "Once I sell this garlic crop we can add on three rooms, then divide everything up."

"Will Jinju stay with us?"

"She can get her ass out!"

"Where's Gao Ma going to get the ten thousand yuan we demanded?"

"He homesteaded four acres of land this year along with the two he already had, and planted it all with garlic. I passed his field the other day, and I can tell you he's going to have a bumper crop, six thousand pounds at least, which he'll sell for five thousand yuan. I'll take that and tell him he can give me the other half next year. The little tramp's getting off cheap, but I won't let her raise some bastard kid here at home."

"After she's gone and we have Gao Ma's money, she'll really suffer."

"Are you starting to feel sorry for her?" He tapped his pipe on the kang. "I don't care if the little slut starves."

He turned and went out to the cow shed, where Fourth Aunt heard him tap on the west-wing window. "Number One, Number Two—time to get up, load the garlic." She got down off the kang, lit the lamp, and hung it beside the door, then poured a ladleful of water from the vat into the pot.

"What's that for?" Fourth Uncle asked her when he returned.

"To make some broth," she replied. "You'll be walking half the night."

"Don't worry about me," he snapped back. "I'm not going to walk. I'll ride the whole way. Go water the cow if you want to make yourself useful."

The brothers emerged from their room and stood in the middle of the yard, shivering in the cold night air and not saying a word.

Meanwhile Fourth Aunt dumped three ladlefuls of water into a basin, spread a layer of bran husks over the top, and stirred it with a poker. Then she carried it outside and laid it on the path as Fourth Uncle led the cow out of the shed. But it just stood there smacking its lips stupidly without taking a sip.

"Drink, drink," she urged the animal. "Drink some water."

The cow stood there without moving, a heated stench rising from its hide. The parakeets were at it again, their squawks rising like shifting clouds. The half-moon, a bit higher in the sky now, flooded the yard with golden rays. The stars had lost some of their glitter.

"Throw in some more bran husks," Fourth Uncle said.

Fourth Aunt did as she was told.

"Come on, girl," he said, patting the cow gently. "Drink up."

The cow lowered her head, snorted into the basin, then began lapping up the water.

"What are you standing around for?" Fourth Uncle snapped at his sons. "Hitch up the wagon and load the garlic!"

After fetching the wagon bed, they rolled out the wheels and axles and assembled the vehicle. There were too many thieves in the village to leave it outside the gate. All the garlic had been stacked in bundles by the southern wall, under sheets of plastic.

"Sprinkle some water on it to keep it from drying out," Fourth Uncle said. His eldest son did as he was told.

"Why not take Number Two along?" his wife asked him.

"No," he said curtly.

"Stubborn ass," she groused. "At least get something decent to eat in town, since I don't have anything to send with you."

"I thought there was still half a grainy flatcake," Fourth Uncle said.

"That's all you've eaten for days."

"Get it for me." He led the cow out the gate and hitched it to the wagon. Then he walked back into the yard, threw a tattered coat over his shoulders, stuffed the cold flatcake down the front of his shirt, picked up a switch, and headed out the gate.

"The older you are, the more mule-headed you get," she complained. "I don't know what else to call someone who won't let his own son help him sell his harvest."

"He's afraid I'll skim off all the profits," Number Two said sarcastically.

"Father's just thinking about our well-being," his elder brother rebuked him.

"Who asked him to?" Number Two grumbled on his way inside to go back to bed.

Fourth Aunt heaved a sigh as she stood in the yard listening to the creaking axles of the wagon slowly taper off in the murky darkness. Gao Zhileng's parakeets set up a frenzy of squawks, and poor Fourth Aunt was a bundle of nerves as she faltered in the yard, which was now draped in dull yellow moonlight.

The cell door swung open and the policemen removed Number Forty-six's handcuffs. She took a couple of jerky steps before flopping onto her cot, where she lay as if dead.

"Officers," Fourth Aunt implored as they were closing the door, "please let me go home. My husband's fifth-week memorial service is coming up. . . ."

The clanging door was her only answer.

CHAPTER 10

County Boss Thong, put your hand over your heart and think:
As government protector, where is the kindness in your soul?
If you are a benighted official, go home and stay in bed;
If you are an upright steward, take charge and do some good. ...

> – from a lament by Zhang Kou, sung standing on the steps of the
> government office after a glut in garlic had driven thousands
> of villagers to seek aid from the county administrator, who
> refused to get out of bed

1

Jinju had nearly made it to Gao Ma's yard when, with an anguished yelp, she collapsed. The fetus raised his fists and thundered, "Let me out! God damn it, let me out of here!"

"Gao Ma ... come here ... help me ... come mind your son. ..."

She crawled across the yard, then stood up by holding on to the door jamb. Four bare walls, a rusted pot, puddles of black water, and some rats that jumped out from behind the pot were all she saw inside. It looked as if a bull had been turned loose, and a sense of impending doom gripped her. As the child in her belly struck out with fists and feet, she wailed, "Gao Ma ... Gao Ma ..."

The baby punched her. "Stop shouting! Gao Ma's a fugitive, a criminal! How did I wind up with parents like you?" He kicked her, sending shivers up her spine; again she yelped, and everything turned black. As she fell, she banged her head against the one table not smashed by her brothers.

*

Father, worn out from the beating he had administered, sat on the doorstep smoking his pipe. Mother, equally tired, sat on the bellows to catch her breath and wipe her tear-filled eyes. Jinju lay curled atop a pile of grass and weeds, neither crying nor complaining, a grin frozen on her face.

Her brothers returned, the older one carrying a couple of metal pails and a string of dried peppers, the younger one pushing a nearly new bicycle with some military uniforms on the rack. They were breathless. "He didn't have much worth taking," the younger one said. "I had to stop this one from smashing the pot," chided his older brother, "so we could leave him something."

"Tell me, do you still plan to run away with Gao Ma?" Father's anger was rekindled.

The sound of music from Gao Ma's cassette recorder filled her ears. Father's words, out there somewhere, were irrelevant.

"Are you deaf? Your father asked if you still plan to run away with him!" Mother shouted, jumping down off the bellows and tapping her daughter on the forehead with a poker.

She closed her eyes. "Yes," she replied softly.

"Beat her! Beat her! Beat her!" Father jumped up from the doorstep and stomped his feet. "String her up! I'll show this little whore what it means to defy me!"

"I can't, Father," the older son dissented. "She's my sister. She doesn't know what she's doing right now, that's all. Go ahead, yell at her, that'll do it. Jinju, you're smart enough to know you're bringing shame to the family by what you're doing. People will be laughing at us for generations. Admit you're wrong and start living a normal life. Mistakes are part of growing up. Be a good girl and say you're sorry."

"No," she said softly.

"String her up!" Father repeated. "What's the matter with you?" he railed at his sons. "Are you dead, or deaf, or what?"

"Father, we . . ." The older son was full of misgivings.

"She's my daughter, and if I say she dies, she dies! Who's going to stop me?" He stuck his pipe into his waistband and gave his wife a malignant look. "Go out and bolt the gate!"

She was quaking. "Let her do what she wants, all right?"

"Are you looking for a beating, too?" He slapped her. "Get out there and bolt the gate, I said."

Mother backed up a couple of steps, her eyes starting to glaze over, then turned, like a marionette, and staggered out toward the gate. Jinju felt sorry for her.

Father took a coil of new rope down from the wall, shook it out, and ordered his sons, "Strip her!"

The older brother turned white as a sheet. "Don't beat her, Father. I don't need to get married."

Father lashed out with the rope, wrapping it around his son's waist. That straightened him up in a hurry. He and his brother went up to Jinju and looked away as they groped for her buttons. But she jerked their hands away and removed her own jacket, then her trousers, and stood before them in a tattered undershirt and red underpants.

Father tossed one end of the rope to Elder Brother. "Tie her arms," he commanded.

Holding the rope in his hand, Elder Brother begged Jinju, "Please, ask Father's forgiveness."

She shook her head. "No."

Second Brother pushed Elder Brother away, then jerked Jinju's arms behind her and tied them at the wrists. "The fact that this family has produced a Communist Party member who'd actually rather die than surrender amazes me."

She laughed in his face. He tossed the loose end of the rope over the roof beam and looked over at his father.

"String her up!"

Jinju felt her arms jerk out and up. Her tendons went taut; her shoulders popped. All the slack went out of the skin on her arms, and sweat oozed from her pores. She bit down on her lip, but too late to hold back the pitiful wails that burst from her throat.

"Now what do you say—still plan to run away?"

She strained to raise her head. "Yes!"

"Pull, pull harder—pull her up!"

Green sparks flew past her eyes; the sound of crackling flames exploded around her ears; jute plants swayed in front of her. The chestnut colt was standing beside Gao Ma, licking his face clean of dried blood and grime with its purplish tongue as golden layers of fog rose from the roadside, from thousands of acres of jute plants, and from the pepper crop in Pale Horse County. The colt disappeared, then reappeared in the golden fog. . . . Elder Brother's face was ashen, Second Brother's was blue, Father's was green, and Mother's was black; Elder Brother's eyes were white, Second Brother's were red, Father's were yellow, and Mother's were purple. As she hung in the air, she looked down at them and felt enormously gratified. Another shout from Father. She stared into his green face and yellow eyes; with a grin she shook her head. He ran into the yard, fetched the whip from the oxcart, and lashed her with it; wherever the tip landed, her skin erupted in flames.

She regained consciousness in a corner of the wall; people were talking, including, it seemed to her, Deputy Yang. She struggled to her feet; light-headed and leg-weary, she collapsed at the foot of her parents' kang. A hand reached out to help her up; she didn't know whose it was. She found her parents' faces. "You can beat me to death if you want, but even then I'll belong to Gao Ma, because I slept with him and I'm carrying his baby." With that she dissolved in tears and loud wails.

"I give up," she heard Father say. "Tell Gao Ma to bring me ten thousand yuan. We'll hand over the girl when he gives us the cash."

Jinju smiled.

2

Gao Ma's scowling son roared, "Let me out of here! Let me out this minute! What kind of mother wouldn't even let her own son out?"

Her eyes bled. Pushing away the cool head of the chestnut colt, she said, "Don't come out, child. Mother knows what's best for you. What do you plan to do out here? Do you have any idea how tough life is?"

He stopped struggling. "What's it like out there? Tell me."

The chestnut colt tried to lick her face with its warm, purplish tongue. "Can you hear the cries of the parakeets, child?" she asked. "Listen carefully."

His ears stood straight up as he concentrated on the sound.

"Those are parakeets in Gao Zhileng's yard—yellow ones, red ones, blue ones, every imaginable color. They've got curved beaks and topknots on their crowns. They eat meat, drink blood, and suck brains. Do you still have the nerve to come out, child?"

This struck fear into the boy, who drew into himself.

"Look, child, see how that broad expanse of garlic looks like a nest of poisonous serpents, all intertwined? They're also meat eaters, blood drinkers, and brain suckers. Do you still have the nerve to come out, child?"

His hands and feet curled inward; his eyes frosted over.

"I wanted to come out and see the world when I was like you, child, but once I got here, I ate pig slops and dog food, I worked like an ox and a horse, I was beaten and kicked, I was even strung up and whipped by your grandfather. Do you still want to come out, child?"

He scrunched his neck down between his shoulders, becoming a virtual ball with staring, pathetic eyes.

"Child, your father's a fugitive from justice, and his family is so poor they can't even raise rats. Your grandfather was struck down by a car, your grandmother has been arrested, and your uncles have divided up all our property. The family no longer exists—some members are gone, others are dead, and there's no one to turn to. Do you still want to come out, child?"

The boy closed his eyes.

The chestnut colt stuck its head in through the open window to lick her hand with its warm tongue. The bell around its neck clanged loudly. She stroked its smooth head and sunken eyes with her free hand. The colt's hide had the cool sheen of costly satin. Tears welled up in her eyes; there were also tears in the colt's eyes.

The boy began to squirm again. "Mother," he said, squinting, "I want to come out and look around. I saw a spinning fireball."

"That's the sun, child."

"I want to look at the sun."

"You can't do that, child—its flames burn your mother's flesh and skin."

"I saw flowers in the fields, and smelled their perfume."

"Those flowers are poisonous, child, and their perfume is a miasma. They will cause your mother's death!"

"Mother, I want to come out and stroke the red colt's head."

She reached up and slapped the horse, momentarily stunning it before it withdrew its head from the window and galloped away.

"There's no colt, child—it's an apparition."

The boy squeezed his eyes shut and stopped moving.

She found some rope in the corner, tossed it over a beam, and made a noose in the other end. Then she fetched a stool and stood on it. The coarse fibers of the rope pricked her fingers. Maybe she should rub some oil on it. She was beginning to waver. Then she heard the colt whinny outside the window, and to protect the boy from any further shocks, she thrust her head through the noose and kicked the stool away. The colt stuck its head through the window again. She wanted to reach out and stroke its cool, glossy forehead, but she couldn't lift her arms.

CHAPTER 11

Paradise County once produced bold, heroic men.
Now we see nothing but flaccid, weak-kneed cowards
With furrowed brows and scowling faces:
They sigh and fret before their rotting garlic. . . .

– from a ballad by Zhang Kou urging garlic farmers
to storm the county government offices

1

As Gao Ma scrambled over the wall, two shots rang out, raising puffs of smoke and sending tiny shards of the mud wall down on him. He stumbled into a pigpen, scattering muck in all directions and causing a couple of startled pigs to squeal and run around in panic. Not knowing which way to turn, he quickly crawled into the covered area. A loud buzz erupted above his head, and sharp pains tore at his cheeks and scalp. He jerked his head up and saw that he had disturbed a hornets' nest hanging from the sorghum-stalk covering. With hundreds of agitated hornets descending on him like a yellow cloud, he flattened out in the muck, afraid to move. But, reminded that the police were right on his heels, he wrapped his arms around his head, wriggled back outside, grabbed the enclosure fence, and leapt over it, landing behind a woodpile. He quickly rolled out into the yard, jumped to his feet, and turned to head east, when someone grabbed him by the arm and held him fast. Panic-stricken, he looked up into the face of a fair-skinned man. Recognition set in almost at once: it was Schoolmaster Zhu from the local elementary school. Having suffered a broken pelvis at the hands of the Red Guards, Zhu could no longer stand straight; the frames of his glasses were held together with tape.

Gao Ma fell to his knees, like an actor in a soap opera, and pleaded for Schoolmaster Zhu to save him from the police, who were trying to arrest him in connection with the garlic incident.

Zhu grabbed his hand and led him into a dark room where chicken feathers and garlic leaves nearly covered the floor and a pickling vat filled with sweet-potato slops stood in the corner. "Climb in," Zhu said.

Undeterred by the stench, Gao Ma climbed into the vat and squatted down, raising the level of slops to the rim, where it frothed noisily. He was up to his neck in the stuff, but Schoolmaster Zhu pushed him until it covered his mouth. "Don't make a sound," Zhu said, "and hold your breath." He covered Gao Ma's head with a well-used gourd, then slid a battered lid over the vat, leaving just a crack.

Footsteps sounded in the yard. Gao Ma raised his head to listen. He could tell the police had reached the sty. "You . . . you're hiding in the p-pigpen, don't think I won't f-find you. C-come out of there."

"Come out or we'll shoot!"

"Comrades, what's going on out here?" Zhu asked them.

"C-catching a c-counter-revolutionary!"

"In my pigpen?"

"Stay out of the way. We'll get to you after we've caught him," the policeman demanded. "Come out of there, or we'll shoot! We can use deadly force if you resist arrest."

"Comrades, is this a joke or something?"

"W-who's joking?" the stammerer said. "I'm going in to see for myself."

With his hands on the low wall, he leapfrogged into the pigpen, then waded into the covered area and stuck his head in, where he was greeted by a couple of hornets that stung him on the mouth.

"Comrades," Schoolmaster Zhu said, "what do you take me for, a Nationalist spy? Do you really think I'd try to put something over on you? I heard shots, and when my pigs started to squeal, I came out to see what was going on, just in time to spot a dark figure running like hell toward the southern wall."

"Aiding a fugitive is a felony," the policeman said. "I want you to be clear on that score."

"I know," Zhu replied.

"W-what's your name?" the stammerer asked.

"Zhu Santian."

"Y-you say you spotted a dark figure running toward the southern wall?"

"That's right."

"What do you do?"

"I'm a teacher."

"A p-party member?"

"I was in the Nationalist Party before Liberation."

"The Nationalist Party? That must have been the life. I'm t-telling you, if you're l-lying, you'll be up on charges, no matter what party you belong to."

"I understand."

Both policemen jumped out of the pigpen and ran toward the southern wall in search of the dark figure. Gao Ma knew that the lane beyond the southern wall dead-ended at a noodle mill alongside a ditch of putrid stagnant water.

Schoolmaster Zhu removed the beat-up gourd from Gao Ma's head and said urgently, "Get moving. Head east down the lane."

Gao Ma pulled himself out of the gooey slops. He was covered with rotting sweet-potato leaves, and a dark-red liquid dripped from his arms and legs. The room was filled with the stink. Again he bent over as if wanting to kneel in front of Schoolmaster Zhu to show his gratitude. "None of that," Zhu said. "Get moving!"

Dripping wet, Gao Ma was greeted in the yard by a chilling wind as he tore through Schoolmaster Zhu's gate and headed east down a narrow lane that opened into a wider north-south lane after about fifty paces. He paused at the intersection, fearful that a hard leather boot was waiting for him no matter which way he ran. The wide lane appeared to be deserted. He stood for a moment in front of a waist-high bamboo fence, then took a step backward for leverage and shot forward, clearing the fence and landing in a field of coriander about two hands high, emerald green in color, and sweetly redolent. It was wonderful. But this was no time to sightsee, so he jumped up and headed east down a field dike as fast as his legs would carry him. White-haired old Gao Pingchuan, unseeing, crouched on his hands and knees, tending some cabbages. Another bamboo fence blocked his way, so once again he leapt over it. This time he wasn't so lucky. The handcuff dangling from his wrist caught on a sorghum stalk, which snapped in two. "Who's there?" Gao Pingchuan called out.

Gao Ma didn't linger, but entered another broad north-south lane, where a group of women sitting under a shade tree at the southern end were enjoying a noisy visit. Since a row of linked houses blocked his way east, he headed north, reaching the sandy riverbank in a minute or so; after stumbling into a grove of red willows, he turned east instinctively. The untended grove was like a maze, with branches growing every which way, their limbs serving as home for millions of light-brown poisonous caterpillars the locals called "scar creepers." Just touching their little bristles turned the skin all red and puffy and made it itch horribly. Gao Ma didn't realize he'd encountered the scar creepers until he was well past them, and far too busy trampling over the puncture vines that grew in wild profusion on the sandbar to notice their stings; even now, running barefoot over the vines, he felt no pain.

His sudden passage startled jackrabbits out of their hiding places in the willow grove, and even though they ran beside him, he quickly outdistanced them all. As he reached the end of the willow grove, a tottering cobblestone bridge resting on wooden stanchions appeared on his left. Built for horse carts, it linked the eastern edge of the village with the fields. Fearful of being seen, he cut across a patch of ground dotted with holes dug by village thieves and rushed into a woods where mulberry and acacia trees grew side by side. The acacias were just blooming, and the air was stiflingly heavy with their fragrance. He kept running, his legs feeling more and more like lead weights, his vision blurring, his skin stinging painfully, his breath coming in pants. The gnarled tree trunks—white mulberry and rich brown acacia—formed a perilous and nearly impenetrable net. As soon as a path opened up, it was closed off by the next tree, and in one of his sudden lurches he crashed headlong to the ground.

2

Gao Ma regained consciousness sometime around dusk, and his first sensation was a parched thirst that made even his belly burn, followed by an awareness of painful itches all over—wherever he pressed the skin with his finger, a gloomy breath of cool air seeped into the pores. His eyes were nearly swollen shut, but it wasn't until he actually touched the puffy skin that he vaguely recalled diving into Schoolmaster Zhu's pigpen and banging a hornets' nest with his head.

The sun, a red wheel, was sinking slowly in the west. Besides being spectacularly beautiful, the early-summer sunset was exceedingly soft and gentle: black mulberry leaves turned as red as roses; pristine white acacia petals shed an enshrouding pale-green aura. Mild evening breezes made both the mulberry leaves and the acacia petals dance and whirl, filling the woods with a soft rustle.

He stood up by holding on to a mulberry branch, even though every joint in his body cried out in pain. His legs were swollen, as were his feet, and his sinuses felt as if they might explode. He desperately needed some water. For a moment he wrestled with his thoughts to determine whether the events of that afternoon had actually happened or were just a bad dream. Dried bits of pig slops sticking to him and the glistening bracelets dangling from his left wrist were all the proof he needed that he was in fact a fugitive from justice. And he knew the crime for which they wanted to arrest him. He had been nervously expecting it to happen for over a month, which was why he had stopped securing the latch on his window. Debilitating thirst and the painful tautness of his skin made calm thought impossible, so he continued through the stand of mulberry and acacia trees heading north toward the dry riverbed where, he recalled, Gao Qunjia and his son had dug a well that spring.

In order to avoid stepping on more puncture vines growing in the sandy soil, he was forced to walk among prickly reed-grass that was only slightly less painful to the soles of his feet. Bright red ribbons of light filtering through the acacia flowers and mulberry leaves settled on his bare skin, and as he examined his nakedness, especially his arms and chest, he saw that he was a mass of angry red blisters: mementos bestowed upon him by the scar creepers.

The gleaming sand of the dry riverbed nearly blinded him as he emerged from the wooded area; the descending fireball crackled as it picked up speed, painting the sky to look like a celestial flower garden. But Gao Ma was too busy scanning the area for a sign of the well to notice. Finally, amid the seemingly endless red-and-yellow sand of the riverbed, he spotted some mounds of chocolate-colored earth and staggered toward them.

Water, water. He fell to his knees and greedily sucked up the water like a thirsty horse. Within seconds his mouth, throat, and stomach shared the relief of the craved-for water. But the walls of his stomach cramped up with the sudden flood, and he heard the crackling sounds of bone-dry organs being irrigated. After another minute of frenzied drinking, he raised his head for about ten seconds to catch his breath, then leaned over and started in again, more leisurely this time, in order to savor the water's taste and warmth.

The water was brackish, salty, and hot. But he buried his face in it one last time before slowly getting to his feet and letting it drip onto his neck and shoulders, then down to his abdomen, reaching the blisters left by the scar creepers, which popped open and released their poison; the killing pain tightened his rectum.

"Oh, Mother!" he moaned weakly, and lowered his head until his glance fell on the well's crumbling walls and some tender green moss floating on the surface that was home to schools of tiny tadpoles. Three large speckled frogs crouched at the edge of the well, their opaque croaking sacs expanding and retracting rhythmically as six emerald eyes stared greedily at him. He jumped to his feet. A dry belch rose in his throat; his stomach and intestines felt as if hundreds of tadpoles were squirming around in them. Water erupted like a geyser out his mouth. Having seen all he could bear of the well, he turned and returned to the mulberry and acacia woods, rocking back and forth as he walked.

Even though the sun had fallen beneath the horizon, the sky had not yet turned dark; a heavy mist settled around multitudes of silkworms as they raised their strangely contoured metallic heads and gnawed through tinplatelike mulberry leaves, each crunch penetrating Gao Ma's chest and sawing at his heart. He sat down against a mulberry tree and stared at the filmy waves of acacia blossoms peeking out through the enshrouding mist; the fragrance deepened at dusk, and a saffron powder soared on the wind currents as silkworm droppings like iron filings landed on his legs, which stretched out in front of him.

The moon rose in the deep-blue canopy of heaven, accompanied by a smattering of golden stars; the dew-laden silkworm droppings falling on his legs seemed to him to be the excrement of heavenly constellations. Every so often he felt compelled to jump to his feet in reaction to a powerful stimulus, which evaporated as soon as he tried to bend his knees. At other times he wanted to remove the manacles dangling from his wrist; but that resolve, too, vanished when he tried to raise his arm.

The silence was broken by the flapping wings of night birds; he thought he saw them deposit traces of phosphorescence on the tips of mulberry branches as they flew by. But when he strained to get a closer look, he realized it was just his imagination, and he couldn't be sure he had even seen any birds.

It was past midnight, and he was getting cold; as his stomach growled, he felt an immense buildup of gas, which he couldn't pass, no matter how he tried. He spotted Jinju moving past mulberry trees and skirting acacias, a red bundle over her arm, her belly sticking way out in front. She cringed as she walked up to him, stopping about five paces away. She held a quivering jute plant in one hand and was scraping its surface with her fingernails. "Come here, Jinju," he said. Her face changed color—from red to yellow, from yellow to light green, then to dark green, and finally to a terrifying gray. "Elder Brother Gao Ma," she said, "I've come to say goodbye." The ominous tone of her words hit him full in the face; he struggled to go to her, but his legs were tied to the tree, and he couldn't move. So he stuck out his arms, which began to grow, longer and longer. Just as his fingers were about to touch her face, when he could detect the chill of her body on his nails—at that critical point between the right length and not quite long enough—his arms stopped growing. "Jinju," he called out anxiously, "you can't leave—not before we have spent even a single happy day together! I'll marry you as soon as I've sold my garlic, and I promise you'll never again be buffeted by the wind, baked by the sun, soaked by the rain, or frozen by the snow! You'll stay home to mind the children and work in the kitchen!"

"Stop dreaming, Elder Brother Gao Ma. You'll never sell your garlic. It's rotted away. You broke the law when you demolished the county offices. The police have a Wanted poster out on you. . . . I have no choice but to take our son and leave."

She opened her red bundle and took out a small cassette recorder. "This is yours," she said. "I took it when my second brother wasn't looking. You'll be alone after I'm gone, and this will ease some of the loneliness."

She turned and walked off, her red clothes dissolving into a white shadow.

"Jinju!" His own shout woke him.

He watched the pale half-moon climb into the southeastern sky; disappointment and loss glazed over his eyes. With mounting fear, he relived what had just happened in his mind. Over and over he counted the days, and it came out the same each time: the baby was due either yesterday or today.

Finally he stood up, just as he had less than a year before in Pale Horse County, on that piece of land between the jute field and the pepper crop. It was dusk then, and after getting to his feet he had spat out at least a dozen mouthfuls of blood. The Fang brothers had beaten him so badly they had nearly sent him to see Yama, the King of the Underworld—and would have if not for Deputy Yang's life-saving powder, or if the wife of his neighbor Yu hadn't looked after him, or if she hadn't come to him with a message from the Fangs that he could marry Jinju for the sum of ten thousand yuan— cash money for her freedom. He recalled the immense joy the news had brought him, and how he had wept openly and bitterly. Mrs. Yu had remarked that they were selling their daughter like livestock, and he recalled saying to her, "Dear Sister-in-Law, I'm crying because I'm so happy. I'll scrape the ten thousand together somehow. I'll keep planting garlic, and I'll sell it. Jinju will be my bride within two years."

Garlic! All because of that damned garlic. He ripped at mulberry branches, bent acacia trees, crashed into mulberry trunks, tore acacia bark—north, south, east, west, he circled in and out among the stand of trees. A sudden cloud formation of birds was swallowed up by the moon, and he was just as suddenly penned in by four walls—the demons' pen. Men prosper for a decade, and demons dare not draw near! Gao Ma, from the day you met Jinju, from the first time you held her hand, you were fated to learn a lesson in blood.

3

Gao Ma spent the night among the mulberries and acacias, not emerging from the world of ghosts and goblins until dawn broke, and then feeling chilled all over—except for deep down in his chest, where a breath of warmth remained. The puffiness had abated around his eyes, and that brought him comfort. The red sun warmed him as it rose in the sky, and that brought him pleasure. His stomach growled; that was followed by the release of dozens of cold farts, proof that his digestive system and his internal organs were still in good working order; that restored hope. Regaining his clear-headedness squelched the desire to go into the village to see Jinju, for he guessed that the police were probably armed and hiding in his house, waiting for him to walk into a trap. Only a fool would enter the village in broad daylight, so he decided to go after nightfall. Even if Jinju was due today, her mother would be with her, so there was nothing to worry about. The cruelest mother in the world is still a mother.

But what about the days to follow? He stopped to ponder the question. He couldn't show his face anywhere in Paradise County, not with handcuffs dangling from his wrist. He'd go see Jinju after dark, then leave for the Northeast. Once he was back on his feet he'd send for her and the baby.

The stand of trees came to life with the arrival of brightly colored birds. Feeling hungry, he searched out a young eight-foot acacia whose branches were covered with blossoms. He jumped up, grabbed the tip of the tree, and bent it over with all his might. It arched, cracked loudly, and snapped in two. The exposed portions of pale wood oozed a yellow sap, but he was already reaping a two-handed harvest of acacia flowers—fully opened, partially opened, even unopened buds, it didn't matter—and stuffing them into his mouth. The first few entered his stomach whole, but they were followed by petals that released their unique flavor—an overripe, somewhat bitter tang to the older blossoms and a slight puckery bite to the buds—as he chewed. The newly opened blossoms with their delicious nectar were the best. It took him most of the morning to devour three trees' worth.

After Gao Ma couldn't eat another acacia flower, he detected a sweet, slightly tart aroma in the hot, humid midday air; looking closely, he found purple, red, and off-white thorn-tipped balls in the crotches of mulberry branches. "Mulberries!" he shouted joyously. He attacked them just as he had the acacia petals: at first he closed his eyes and gobbled them down, green, red, black, white. But after a while, he grew more selective. Off-white mulberries: hard, semi-sweet, tart, somewhat puckery. Red mulberries: more yielding, sweeter, only slightly tart. Purple mulberries: soft, very sweet, with a strong, pleasant aftertaste. He hunted for the purple ones, soon learning that if he shook a mulberry tree, only the ripe ones fell to the ground. By the afternoon he knew his lips were stained purple by looking at his fingers.

The bellyache hit at sunset. After rolling on the sand in excruciating pain until stars lit up the sky, he relieved himself for a good half-hour. The pain vanished. He could only guess at the time.

4

He would check things out that night, no matter what. He was already feeling the pangs of alienation from other people, even though he had heard women talking as they gathered mulberries, and had watched farmers in the field from a hiding place on the riverbank. A southern wind carried the smell of ripened millet, a sign that tomorrow the harvest would begin. "Silkworms emerge without warning, and millet ripens overnight." That increased his anxiety: having planted two acres of millet, he had been looking forward to a good harvest. Now that his garlic crop was a total loss, how would he make it through the year if he lost his millet? As he wearily rubbed his face, he noted that his forehead and the corners of his mouth were becoming lined.

He made plans to sneak into the village under the cover of darkness, doubting that the police would subject themselves to the discomfort of spending two nights in his house waiting for him to show up. The first order of business would be to get some clothes and, more importantly, shoes. A pair of new sneakers from his army days lay in a cardboard box in the corner—one of the few items that had survived the Fang brothers' ransacking. There was also the 470 yuan from the initial sale of garlic—he had been one of the few lucky villagers who had managed to sell any in the glut—which he had stuffed in a crack in the eastern wall. He would retrieve this hidden cache, giving Jinju four hundred to buy food and baby clothes. The remaining seventy would be enough to get him to the Northeast, where he would look up his old army buddy the deputy county head and ask him to write to Paradise County for a formal pardon.

The dangling handcuffs gleamed darkly in the murky air. They had to go, that's all there was to it. He rubbed the thin metal ring digging into his wrist, and knew he could eventually free himself with a hammer and chisel. One more time—he needed to go home just one more time.

As he retraced his steps of the past day, avoiding streets and roads, he stayed alert to the sounds around him. Proceeding step by cautious step, he comforted himself with the thought that the police were on unfamiliar turf and did not enjoy the support of the masses; so even if he came face to face with them, he still had a good chance of getting away. Their revolvers gave him pause—they had fired a couple of shots the day before—but even if they shot him dead, so what? And if they were such bad shots that they'd missed him in broad daylight, he felt even safer at night.

His nerves were on edge as he turned into the lane, but his heart was warmed by the familiar shapes of houses and trees on either side. From the nearby stand of acacias he surveyed his yard, which was quiet, except for the bats flying around his window. He picked up a dirt clod and flung it toward the window. There was a loud thump when it hit the overturned pot on the ground. Nothing stirred in the house or in the yard. He threw another dirt clod, with no result, but skirted the yard just in case, and went to the back of the house, hugging the wall as he crept up to the rear window. He could hear nothing but scurrying rats.

Feeling secure at last, he remembered seeing clusters of bright parakeets darting in and out among the acacia trees, and he assumed that Gao Zhileng's cages must have sprung a leak, releasing the birds into the night sky. The chestnut colt, which seemingly would never grow to adulthood, was galloping up and down the lane, its sleek hide smelling like bath soap.

The door stood open; that made the hair on his arms stand up. His eyes were already used to the dark, and he spotted the figure in the doorway of the east room the moment he entered. His first impulse was to turn and run; but his feet seemed to take root. He detected the faint smell of blood just before the familiar but oddly stagnant odor of Jinju came rushing toward him. The scene from last night's nightmare flashed through his mind like a bolt of lightning, and he had to grab the doorframe to keep from falling.

With trembling hands he picked up a match from the stove; it took three tries to light it. In the flickering matchlight he saw Jinju's purple face as she hung in the opening of the door, bulging eyeballs, lolling tongue, and sagging belly.

Reaching up as if to hold her in his arms, he crumpled heavily to the floor like a toppled wall.

CHAPTER 12

Townsfolk, stick out your chests, show what you're made of –
Hand in hand we will advance to the seat of power!
Township County Administrator Thong is no heavenly constellation,
And the commonfolk are not dumb farm animals. . . .

> – from a ballad sung by Zhang Kou inciting the masses to storm the
> county compound on the seventh day after the glut, when garlic
> lay rotting on the streets, sending a foul miasma skyward

1

Gao Yang stretched out on the prison cot and was asleep before he'd pulled up the covers. Then came the nightmares, one after the other. First he dreamed of a dog gnawing leisurely on his ankle, chewing and licking as if it wanted to bleed him dry and consume the marrow in his bones. He tried to kick the dog away, but his leg wouldn't move; he tried to reach out and punch it, but he couldn't lift his arm. Then he dreamed he was locked in an empty room at the production brigade for burying his mother instead of delivering her to the crematorium. Two members of the "four bad categories"—landlords, counter-revolutionaries, rich peasants, and criminals—carried her into the house at ten o'clock at night. Her head was shiny as a gourd, her front teeth missing, her mouth bloodied. When he lit a lamp and asked what had happened, they just looked at him pitifully before turning and walking silently out the door. He laid her on the kang, wailing and gnashing his teeth. She opened her eyes, and her lips quivered, as if she wanted to speak; but before she could say a word, her head lolled to the side and she was dead. Grief-stricken, he threw himself on her. . . .

A large hand clamped down over his mouth. He wrenched his head free, spitting saliva in all directions. The hand fell away.

"What's all the screaming about, my boy?" The question, in a low, somber voice, emerged from beneath two phosphorescent dots.

He was awake now, and he knew what had happened. A light from the sentry box lit up the corridor, where a guard paced nervously.

He sobbed. "I dreamed about my mother."

Chuckles emerged from beneath the dots. "You'd have been better off dreaming about your wife," came the voice.

The dots went out, returning the cell to darkness. But the old inmate's sputtering snores, the young one's greedy lip-smacking, and the middle-aged one's demonic gasps kept him awake.

The mosquitoes, having sucked up all the blood they could handle, were resting on the walls, and at some time after midnight the buzzing stopped altogether. He covered himself with a blanket that suddenly seemed to move on its own—an army of insects began crawling over his skin. Gasping from fear and disgust, he flung the blanket away; but that only brought back the cold air, and the blanket was the lesser of the two evils. The middle-aged inmate giggled in his sleep.

Mother's head lolled to the side and she was dead. No last words. It was July, the stifling dog days of summer. But that night it rained, creating puddles that attracted croaking frogs. Water dripped noisily from the straw roof long after the rain had stopped. Shortly after dawn he rummaged around until he found a tattered blanket to wrap his mother in; then, laying her over his shoulder, he picked up a shovel and slipped out of the village. He had already decided not to bury her in the local cemetery, since that was where poor and lower-middle-class peasants wound up—he couldn't bury her among people like that, for fear that their ghosts would harass her—and he couldn't afford to take her to the county crematorium.

On and on he walked, his dead mother over his shoulder, until he reached a plot of land between Paradise and Pale Horse counties that belonged to no one he knew of. Weeds and other wild vegetation were the only signs of life. After wading across Following Stream, whose rapid, chest-deep waters nearly claimed him and his mother, he laid the rolled blanket containing her body on the other side of the stream. Her head poked out. Lightly falling raindrops splashed into her open mouth and eyes, skittering across her taut, shiny face. Her feet stuck out the other side. One of her badly worn shoes had fallen off along the way; the bare foot, ghostly pale and shaped like the horn of an ox, was coated with mud. As Gao Yang fell to his knees, dry wails split his throat, but he shed no tears even though a knife seemed to be gouging out his heart.

After scouting the area and choosing a spot on a rise, he picked up his shovel and began to prepare the grave site. First he cleared away the weeds, with dirt clods still stuck to the roots, and placed them carefully to the side. Then he started digging. When the hole was chest-deep, water began seeping up through the gray sandy soil. So he carried the body over next to the new grave, laid it on the ground, and fell to his knees. "Mother," he said loudly, after kowtowing three times, "it's raining, and water is seeping into the hole. I can't afford a coffin, so this worn blanket will have to do. Mother, you . . . you'll have to make do."

With great care he laid her in the hole, then gathered up some fresh green grass to cover her face. That done, he began shoveling dirt into the hole, stopping occasionally to tap it down so as not to leave telltale signs. Still, the idea of jumping on his mother's body brought tears to his eyes and a buzzing to his ears. Finally he retrieved the weeds and wild grasses and replanted them where they'd been, just as rain clouds gathered overhead and bolts of blood-red lightning split the dark clouds. A cold wind swept past the wildwood and into fields planted with sorghum and corn, setting the leaves dancing in the air like snapping banners of silk. Standing beside the grave, Gao Yang looked around one last time: a river to the north, a large canal to the east, a seemingly endless broad plain to the west, and misty Little Mount Zhou to the south. The surroundings put him at ease. Again he knelt down, kowtowed three times, and said softly, "Mother, you have a good spot here."

By the time he was on his feet, his sadness was gone, except for an occasional pang in his chest. Shovel in hand, he forded the river, heading back; the water, which had risen precipitously, was now above his chin.

The young inmate groped his way over to the window, yanked open the tiny door in the wall, and pissed into the plastic pail, his splashing urine adding to the cell's rank odor. Fortunately, the window glass had long since been smashed and cleared away; there was a small opening at the bottom of the door where the food was passed in, and the ceiling had a small skylight, all of which admitted some cool night breezes from the outside, making the air inside tolerable.

Wiping his mind clean of all extraneous thoughts, he concentrated on his reveries.

Heaven and earth had turned a misty gray, and the wet pounding noise of rain falling violently on branch and trunk rose from the wild-wood. Once he was safely home, he stripped naked, wrung most of the water out of his tattered clothes, and hung them up to dry. The room leaked terribly—water was everywhere, especially at the junction of eaves and mud walls, where rivulets of dirty scarlet ran down to the muddy floor. He tried to catch the drips with an array of pots and pans, but resigned himself to sitting on the edge of the kang and letting the water go where it wanted.

Stretching out on his back, he gazed through the barred window at a faint strip of sky.

*

This is the unluckiest time of my life, he mused. Father is dead, Mother has joined him, and my roof leaks.

He stared up at the grimy, greasy roof beam until his attention was caught by a mouse crouching on the stove after being driven out of hiding by the rain. He thought about hanging himself from the roof beam, but lacked the resolve.

When the rain stopped and the sun came out, he put on his damp clothes and, expecting the worst, went outside to see how his roof, pitted and weakened by the rain, was holding up. Gao Jinglong, the local police chief, came charging into the yard just then, leading seven militiamen armed with .38-caliber rifles. They wore black rain boots and conical hats woven of sorghum stalks, and had draped fertilizer sacks over their shoulders; they advanced like a moving wall.

"Gao Yang," the police chief said, "Secretary Huang wants to know if you secretly buried your mother, that ancient member of the landlord class."

Gao Yang was stunned by how quickly the news had spread and amazed that the production brigade would be so concerned about one of their deceased members. "In rainy weather like this," he said, "she'd have started to stink if I'd waited. . . . How was I supposed to get her to town in pouring rain like that?"

"I didn't come here to argue," the police chief said. "You can plead your case with Secretary Huang."

"Uncle . . ." Gao Yang clasped his hands, lowered his head, and bowed at the waist. "Uncle . . . can't you just let me go?"

"Get moving. Doing what you're told is your only chance of staying out of trouble," Gao Jinglong said.

A beefy man walked up and prodded him with his rifle butt. "Get moving, my boy."

Gao Yang turned to the man. "Anping, we're like brothers. . . ."

Anping prodded him again. "I said get going. The ugly bride has to meet her in-laws sooner or later."

A table had been set up in the brigade office. Secretary Huang sat behind it smoking a cigarette. The glaring red of posters and slogans papering the walls terrified Gao Yang. His teeth chattered as he stood in front of the table.

Secretary Huang smiled genially. "Gao Yang, you've sure got nerve."

"Master . . . I . . ." His legs buckled, and he was on his knees.

"Get up!" Secretary Huang demanded. "Who's your master?"

"Get your ass up!" ordered the police chief, who kicked him.

He stood up.

"Are you aware of the regulation to send all bodies to the crematorium ?"

"Yes."

"Then you knowingly broke the law?"

"Secretary Huang," Gao Yang defended himself, "it was pouring out there. . . . I live so far from town, and can't afford the cremation fee . . . or an urn for the ashes. I figured I'd have to bury them when I got home, anyway. That takes up space in the field, too."

"Well, aren't you a paragon of reason!" Secretary Huang said sarcastically. "The Communist Party is no match for you."

"No, Secretary Huang. What I meant was—"

"I don't want to hear another word from you!" Secretary Huang banged the table and jumped to his feet. "Go dig up your mother and take her straight to the crematorium."

"Secretary Huang, I beg you, please don't . . ." He was back on his knees, crying and pleading. "My mother suffered her whole life. Death was a release for her. Now that she's in the ground, let her lie there in peace—"

Secretary Huang cut him off. "Gao Yang, you'd better straighten out your thinking! Your mother enjoyed a life of leisure and luxury by exploiting others. It was only proper that she be reeducated and reformed through labor after Liberation. Now that she's dead, cremation is just as proper. That's what will happen to me when I die."

"But Secretary Huang, she told me that before Liberation she wouldn't even allow herself a single meal of stuffed dumplings, and that she'd get up before dawn, whether she'd had enough sleep or not, to earn money to buy land."

"Are you asking to have the party's verdict overturned?" an enraged Secretary Huang demanded. "Are you saying that land reform was a mistake?"

A rifle butt thudded into the back of Gao Yang's head. Golden flowers danced before his eyes as he fell forward, his face banging the brick floor.

A militiaman jerked him to his feet by his hair so the police chief could smack him across both cheeks with a shiny wooden switch. *Crack! Crack!*—loud and crisp.

"Lock him up in the west wing," the police chief said. "Dai Zijin, call an immediate meeting of the branch-committee members here in the office—use the PA system."

Gao Yang was locked in an empty room in the west wing of the brigade headquarters, under the watchful eye of two armed militiamen sitting on a bench across from him. Thunder rolled outside, and the skies sent buckets of rain thudding into the leaves of parasol trees in the compound and onto the red-tiled roof in a deafening cadence.

The loudspeakers crackled for a moment, then sent forth the voice of Dai Zijin. Gao Yang knew the names released into the air.

"Gao Yang," one of the militiamen said, "you're in big trouble this time."

"Little Uncle," replied Gao Yang, "I didn't bury my mother on brigade land."

"What you did with her body isn't what this is all about."

"What *is* it all about?" he asked fearfully.

"Aren't you trying to get the verdict on her reversed?"

"I only told the truth. Everybody knows that. My father was a famous skinflint who only cared about saving up money to buy land. He'd beat my mother if she bought an extra turnip."

"You're wasting your time telling me," the militiaman said indifferently.

That evening, in spite of the heavy rainfall, a meeting of all brigade members was held, and although Gao Yang eventually forgot most of the particulars, he would always remember the sound of the rain and the shouted slogans, which continued without let-up from early evening to late at night.

The following morning a squad of militiamen tied Gao Yang to a bench and placed four bricks strung together with hemp around his neck; it felt like a piece of garroting wire that would lop off his head if he so much as moved. Then in the afternoon the police chief tied his thumbs together with a piece of wire and strung him up from a steel overhead beam. He didn't feel much pain, but the moment his feet left the ground, sweat seemed to squirt from every pore in his body.

"Now tell us, where's the landlord's wife buried?"

He shook his head, which swelled with images of a weed-covered plot of land and a swollen stream. The clumps of grass he had dug up and replanted had been soaking up rain all this time, until they must look as if they had never been moved. His footprints, too, would have been washed away by the rain; so long as he kept his mouth shut, Mother could rest in peace. He vowed never to reveal his secret, not if it cost him his life.

Not that his determination remained rock-solid the whole time: he screamed in agony when the police chief rammed a thorny branch several inches up his ass: "Uncle, spare me, please ... I'll take you there. . . ."

The bloody branch was removed and he was lowered from the steel beam. "Where's she buried?"

He looked into the police chief's dark face, then peeked down at his own body, and finally gazed out the window at the misty sky. "Mother," he said, "wait for me, I'll be there soon. . . ." Lowering his head, he made a mad dash for the wall, but was restrained by two militiamen.

Indignation filled his heart. "Brothers," he shouted hoarsely, "I—Gao Yang—have always done what's right, ever since I was a little boy. There's no bad blood between us, so why are you doing this to me?"

The police chief stopped hitting him, but then the traces of sympathy in his eyes were driven out by his stern response: "We're talking about class struggle here!"

Since Gao Yang was to be detained that night, the militiamen carried two benches into the room. The plan was to sleep in turns, but before the night was very far gone, they were both snoring.

The window frame in the otherwise vacant room was made of wood, so if he wanted to run away, a well-placed kick would do the trick. But he neither felt like escaping nor had the leg strength to smash the window frame. The police chief's branch had so swollen his rectum that he couldn't pass the gas that was making his belly bulge and his guts swell. A kerosene lamp hung from the roof beam, its shade turned black by an accumulation of smoke that dimmed the light and cast a shadow the size of a millstone on the brick floor. When he looked at the two militiamen, clutching their rifles to their chests as they slept, fully dressed, he felt guilty for putting them to all this trouble. Once or twice he thought about snatching one of the rifles from its owner, smashing the window with the butt, and making his getaway into the yard. But it was a fleeting thought at most, replaced each time with a conviction that his punishment was simply the price he must pay to keep his mother from the flames of the crematorium. He'd just have to grit his teeth and bear whatever came along. Otherwise, she'd have suffered in vain.

The militiamen had slept like babies, but not him. Just like tonight—his cellmates were fast asleep, but he wasn't the least bit drowsy after awaking from his nightmares.

Stars blazed beyond the barred window above parasol-tree leaves and roof tiles that found their voices under a light drizzle. But there was another sound, too, a distant roar that could only mean a floodtide in Following Stream to the south and Sandy River, north of the village. Inexplicably, he grew anxious for farmers in fields that would turn into swampland if the rivers overflowed their banks. Taller stalks might hold out for a few days, but the shorter ones were doomed.

He curled up in the corner, his back pressed against the damp wall. Someone darted past the window, and a small paper bundle landed at his feet. He picked it up, unwrapped it, and was treated to a wonderful smell. It was a fried onion roll—still warm—and he had to fight to keep from bawling like a baby. Taking care not to disturb the sleeping militiamen, he nibbled at the onion roll, carefully chewing and swallowing each tasty bite. He had never before realized how noisy people are when they eat; heaven looked after him, he thought, since he managed to finish the roll without waking his guards.

After finishing the onion roll, Gao Yang again felt that life was worth living. So he closed his eyes and slept for a couple of hours, until he had to piss. Then, neither daring nor caring to awaken the militiamen, he searched for a mouse hole in which he could quietly relieve himself. Unfortunately, the brigade buildings all had brick floors, and he couldn't find even a good-sized crack, let alone a mouse hole. To his surprise he found an empty wine bottle, which served his purpose just fine. But he hadn't figured on the noise—like tossing rocks into a canyon— and he held back as much as possible to keep from disturbing his guards. Froth spilled over the neck of the bottle long before it was full, so he stopped the flow to let it subside before continuing; he repeated the process—three times in all— until the bottle was brimming. Then, holding it by its neck, he placed it in the corner, where it caught the dim light of dawn just enough to highlight the label. Quickly realizing that the militiamen couldn't miss it there, he moved it to another corner. Just as noticeable. So he put it on the windowsill. Even worse.

Just then one of them woke up. "What are you doing?"

His cheeks burned from embarrassment.

"Where'd you get that wine?"

"It's not wine. . . . I . . . my . . ."

The militiaman laughed. "What a character!"

The police chief opened the door. When the guards told him about the wine bottle, he laughed.

"Go ahead, drink up," the police chief said.

"Chief, I didn't want to wake them up. . . . I wouldn't have . . . I'll dump it." An embarrassed Gao Yang tried to talk and beg his way out of a bad situation.

"No need for that," the smiling police chief said. "A man's piss can clean the poisons out of his body. Go on, drink it."

Suddenly exhilarated by a strangely wonderful emotion, he blurted out, "Uncle, it's really a bottle of fine wine."

The police chief grinned and exchanged looks with the two militiamen. "If it's a fucking bottle of fine wine," he said, "then drink it!"

Without another word, Gao Yang picked up the bottle and took a mighty swig. It was still warm, and on the salty side, but not bad, all in all. Tipping the bottle back a second time, he gulped about half of the remaining urine, then wiped his mouth with his sleeve as hot tears gushed from his eyes. With a smile frozen on his face, he said, "Gao Yang, oh Gao Yang, you bastard, how could you be so lucky? Who else could have the good fortune to feast on a delicious onion roll and wash it down with fine wine?"

He finished off the bottle, then sprawled out on the brick floor and cried his eyes out.

Later that day Party Secretary Huang came to tell him that the police had to deal with containing the floodwaters of the Sandy River, and hadn't time to waste looking for the body of his mother, anyway. So he was fined two hundred yuan and released.

The roads were already a sea of mud when he trudged home at dawn, and it was raining again; large drops pelting him on the head felt wonderful. "Mother," he thought aloud, "I wasn't a filial son while you were alive, but at least I managed to give you a decent burial. The poor and lower-middle-class peasants go to the crematorium when they die, but not you. That makes it all worth it."

As he turned into his yard he witnessed the roof of the three-room hut he called home slowly caving in, sending pockets of water and mud splashing in all directions. Then the whole thing collapsed with a roar, and there in front of him, all of a sudden, was the acacia grove and the roiling yellow water of the river that flowed behind his house.

He cried out for his mother and fell to his knees in the mud.

2

Dawn came. He had, apparently, gotten a little sleep, but now he was sore all over. Fire seemed to shoot from his nose and mouth, both of which nearly ignited spontaneously from the superheated air. He shivered so violently that the metal springs of the cot creaked. Why do people shiver? That's what I want to know—why do people shiver? A covey of little red girls ran and jumped and screeched and yelled on the ceiling, so flimsy that swirling gusts of wind easily bent them this way and that. One of them—naked, holding a bamboo staff—stood off by herself. "Isn't that Xinghua?" he asked out loud. "Xinghua, get down from there this minute! If you fall, you'll kill yourself!"

"I can't get down, Daddy." She began to cry. Large crystalline tears hung suspended in midair on the tips of her hair instead of falling to the floor.

A strong gust of wind swept the children away, and a gray-haired old woman slogged unsteadily through the roadside muck, a tattered blanket thrown over her shoulders, one shoe missing. She was mud-spattered from head to toe.

"Mother!" he screamed. "I thought you were dead!"

As he ran toward her, he felt his body grow lighter, until he was as insubstantial as the cluster of little girls. Buffeted by gusty winds, his body was stretched to several times its original length, and he had to hold on to the rails around him to keep his balance as he stood before his mother. She rolled her muddy eyes and gaped at him.

"Mother!" he exclaimed excitedly. "Where have you been all these years? I thought you were dead."

She shook her head lightly.

"Mother, eight years ago all the landlords, rich peasants, counter-revolutionaries, bad elements, and rightists had their labels removed, and land was parceled out to people who work the fields. I married a woman with a crippled arm and a good heart. She bore you a granddaughter and a grandson, so our line won't die out. We have a surplus of food, and if this year's garlic crop hadn't rotted before it could be sold, we'd even have some money saved up."

Mother's face underwent a metamorphosis, and a pair of wormy maggots slithered out of her muddy eye sockets. Once the initial shock had worn off, he reached over to pluck out the maggots; but when he touched her skin, a clammy chill streaked from the tip of his finger all the way to the core of his heart. At the same time a yellow fluid oozed from Mother's body, and her flesh and sinews flew off in chunks in the wind, until only a bare skeleton stood before him. A fearful scream tore from his throat.

Shouts came from far away: "Hey, pal . . . say, pal . . . wake up! Are you possessed or something?"

Six blazing green eyes were fixed on him. A clawlike hand, covered with green fur, reached out, utterly terrifying him. The icy hand recoiled when it brushed his forehead, as if scalded.

The green claw-hand returned to cover his forehead, bringing terror and contentment at the same time.

"You're sick, pal," the middle-aged inmate said loudly. "You're burning up with fever." He covered Gao Yang with a blanket—almost tenderly—this same man who had forced him to drink his own piss. "I'd say it's the flu, so you'll have to sweat it out."

His mind was in an upheaval, and he was shivering

uncontrollably. Why do people shiver? he asked himself. Why do they have to do that? His cellmates came up and added the weight of their blankets to his. He was still shivering, setting the four blankets in sympathetic motion. One rode up until it covered his face and blocked out the light. The stench made him gasp. Sweat oozing from his pores had the lice squirming and leaping. He sensed the imminence of his own death, if not from the illness that gripped him, then from the stifling oppressiveness of piled-on blankets that felt like moth-eaten cowhides. Straining with all his might, he managed to lift the errant blanket from his face, and immediately felt like a man whose head has bobbed to the surface of a swamp. "Help me, you people—save me!" he screamed.

He struggled to grab an invisible handle that was the only thing keeping him from falling into a stupor—like a man grasping a drooping willow branch as he sinks into a quagmire. The space before his eyes was light one minute, dark the next. In the darkness, all the demons danced; his dead parents and the cluster of red children leaped and spun, giggling as they circled him, tickling him under the arms or tweaking his ears or nipping him on the buttocks. Father wandered a glass-strewn street, willow switch in hand, frequently stumbling for no apparent reason—sometimes intentionally, it seemed, and sometimes as if an invisible behemoth had pushed him. But every time he fell, either by design or by accident, he rose with shards of glass inlaid in his face, which sparkled and shone.

When Gao Yang reached out to grab the spirits, the darkness vanished, leaving only the giggles of spirits to reverberate near the ceiling. The emerging sun lit up the sky, but not his cell, even though he could make out the shapes of objects in it. The towering middle-aged inmate pounded angrily on the creaky door with both fists, while the other cellmates—one old and one young—raised their voices like wolves baying at the moon.

Thudding footsteps in the corridor signaled the approach of the guards. A face appeared at the opening. "Is this a rebellion or something?"

"It's no rebellion. Number Nine's so sick I think he's dying."

"This cell's more trouble than all the others combined! I'll tell the watch officer when he comes on duty."

"He'll be dead before then."

The guard shone his flashlight on Gao Yang, who squeezed his eyes shut to keep out the blinding light.

"His color looks pretty rosy to me."

"Because he's got a fever."

"Why all the fuss over a common cold?" The guard walked off.

Gao Yang returned to an agonizing realm of alternating light and darkness, where Father and Mother led little demons up to torment him. He could feel their breath and smell their odor. But, as before, when he reached out, they vanished, taking the darkness with them and leaving behind only the anxious faces of his cellmates.

Breakfast was slid in through the slot at the bottom of the door. He overheard his cellmates talking in hushed voices.

"Try to eat something, buddy," the middle-aged inmate said as he held him by the shoulders.

He didn't even have the strength to shake his head.

Some time later he heard the door open and felt a rush of fresh air fill the cell, which helped clear his head. One blanket after another was peeled away like layers of skin.

"What's wrong?" It was a gentle, feminine voice. A simple question, so earnest and so warm. Dimly he saw the once-kindly face of his mother. Opening his eyes to gaze through strata of mist, he discerned the shape of a large white face atop a long white gown. The gown had an antiseptic smell; the wearer, the clean, soapy smell of an aristocratic woman.

It *was* an aristocratic woman, husky and thick-waisted, who held his wrist in icy fingers that moved up to his forehead, drawing the welcome antiseptic smell more powerfully to his nostrils. As he breathed it in greedily, the stuffiness of his chest began to dissolve. The scent of the woman gave him a powerful sense of well-being; an airy feeling of sadness, beauty, and blessedness all rolled into one cradled him. His nose ached—he was about to cry.

"Hold this down." He watched her shake a glittering glass tube, then slip it under his armpit. "Hold it tight."

A dark, gaunt, uniformed man wearing an unsure, uneasy expression stood behind the woman, hiding like a bashful child in front of strangers.

"You should be dressed," the woman said.

He tried to say something in reply, but was unable to.

"That's how you people brought him in," the middle-aged inmate said. "Stripped to the waist and barefoot."

"Warden Sun." The woman turned to address the gaunt man behind her. "Can you have his family bring him some clothes?"

The warden nodded, then disappeared behind her.

"What's it like, being in here?" he heard the warden ask.

"Great!" the young inmate boomed. "Cool, comfortable, a touch of Paradise! If not for those damned lice, that is."

"Lice, you say?"

"No—at least none that can speak."

"Officer, how about dispensing some of that revolutionary humanism by getting rid of the lice in here?"

"That's a reasonable request," the warden said. "Dr. Song, have the infirmary make up some pesticide."

"All together there are three of us in the infirmary. Where are we supposed to find the time to mix pesticide for every cell in the place?" Dr. Song grumbled as she removed the thermometer from under Gao Yang's armpit. He heard her suck in her breath when she held it up to the light.

From her leather bag she removed an instrument, draped it around her neck, and stuck the ends in her ears. Then she lifted a shiny, round metal object dangling from the end of a quivering rubber tube and bent over until her large white face was directly over his. The smell of her skin nearly sent him into another world, as the metal object moved heavily from spot to spot on his chest—a most pleasurable pressure.

If my life ends right now, in this cell, I'll die fulfilled, he thought hazily. An aristocratic woman has touched my forehead and put her face next to mine, so close I can smell her natural fragrance and see the skin, fair as powder, below her neck when she bends over. It doesn't get any better than this.

She tapped him. "Roll over," she said gently, then held up a glass tube with dark rings around its surface. It was filled with a golden fluid and tipped with a long silvery needle. He rolled over as he was told. Her fingers, so soft and gentle, so cool and refreshing, so wonderful, grabbed the band of his underpants and jerked them down, exposing his buttocks to the cold air, which touched his anus; every muscle tensed. Something even colder touched his left cheek and began spreading outward.

"Relax!" This time her voice was stern. "Relax your muscles. What are you afraid of? Haven't you ever had a shot before?"

She smacked him on the rear. "How am I supposed to stick a needle in something this tight?"

What more could I ask of life? An aristocratic woman like this doesn't even care how dirty I am. She smacked my grimy ass with her clean hand! I could die here and now with no regrets.

Gently she rubbed the spot with two fingers. "What happened to your foot?" she asked. "Why is it so swollen?"

His thoughts turned to his ankle and the kicks rained on it by the policemen, and he was so overwhelmed by the pressure of the well-being he felt now that he was incapable of answering.

Again she smacked him on the rear, but this time that was followed by a bee sting. He heard her breathe heavily as she pushed the needle in, and felt her pinkie make painless little nicks in his skin. Never before had such tenderness settled upon him. Feeling as if his very soul were in suspended animation, he shook with sobs.

The doctor pulled the needle out. As she put her instruments into her medical kit, she said, "What are you crying for? It didn't hurt that much."

He said nothing, for all he could think was, she'll be leaving now that she's given me the shot.

"Doctor," the young inmate said, "I'm constipated. Would you check me out while you're at it?"

"Why get rid of it? Let it stay put," she told him.

"That's no way for a doctor to talk."

"How am I supposed to talk to a little hooligan like you?"

"You have no right to call me a little hooligan. Your daughter and I were schoolmates. We even considered marriage."

"Watch your mouth, Number Seven!" the warden threatened.

The dialogue between the young inmate and the doctor pained Gao Yang. He hoped she'd have more to say to him. But it wasn't to be, for she picked up her bag, slung it over her shoulder, and walked out with the warden, who returned a half-hour later. "We have prepared a special meal for you, Number Nine," he said from the corridor. "Try to eat it."

A gray bowl slid under the door, flooding the cell with a delicious fragrance. Green lights shot from his cellmates' eyes. The middle-aged inmate personally carried the bowl of noodles over to him, and when Gao Yang sat up he saw a pair of golden eggs nestled in the noodles and a layer of green onions and oil floating in the broth.

"Warden, Officer, I'm sick, too!" the young prisoner yelled. "I've got a bellyache!"

"Little Li," the warden called to one of the soldiers pacing the corridor. "Make sure they don't steal his food."

Rattled, the middle-aged inmate quickly set the bowl down on Gao Yang's cot and returned reluctantly to his own cot.

The sight of the noodles and eggs triggered Gao Yang's appetite. Picking up his chopsticks with a trembling hand, he stirred the slippery white noodles—the thinnest and whitest he'd ever seen—then lifted the bowl to his lips and delivered a mouthful of the warm broth to his stomach and intestines, which rumbled pleasurably. As tears brimmed in his eyes, he faced the door and muttered to the soldier, "Thank you, Officer, for your great kindness."

Gao Yang, you're a lucky man. An aristocratic woman you could only gaze at from afar before actually touched your head, and noodles the likes of which you never saw before now rest in your stomach. Gao Yang, people are never content with their lot. Well, it's time for you to be content with yours. . . .

He ate every noodle in the bowl, and slurped up every drop of broth. With some embarrassment, he noticed that the old and young inmates' eyes were glued to his bowl. He was still hungry.

"Still sick?" the guard asked through the bars. "You could probably polish off a bucketful if you weren't."

"Officer, I'm sick, too," his young cellmate wailed. "I've got a bellyache . . . ow! Dear Mother, it's killing me!"

3

A shrill whistle signaled the exercise period, a time for prisoners to stretch their legs and get some fresh air. Two guards unlocked the cells, and as Gao Yang's older cellmates stepped into the corridor, the younger one removed the plastic pail, which was brim-full of the inhabitants' waste. An idea hit him. "Hey, new man," he said to Gao Yang, "since you ate a big bowl of noodles, you should be the one to dump this."

Without waiting for a response, he darted into the corridor.

Feeling a bit sheepish about being treated to a bowl of noodles and an injection by an aristocratic woman, Gao Yang strained to sit up. After stepping barefoot onto the cold, damp cement floor, his head swimming, he stood wobbily, his injured foot so numb it felt as if he were stepping on cotton. He picked up the plastic pail, which wasn't particularly heavy but stank horribly, and tried to hold it at arm's length. Unfortunately, he wasn't up to the task, and each time it bumped against him it splashed its stinking contents onto his bare leg.

The sun's rays were blinding, his eyes ached unbelievably, and his face was awash with tears. After a moment, his eyes stopped hurting, but he still couldn't get his arms and legs to stop quaking; so he halted, put down the pail, and grasped a post to steady himself and catch his breath. His respite was short-lived: a guard at the end of the corridor screamed at him, "No pails on the floor!" Frantically he picked it up and fell in line behind other prisoners carrying similar pails. At the end of the corridor they turned southwest, toward a little room with walls of corrugated metal and wormy planks, one of which sported the word "Men" in a red circle. Dozens of pail-toting prisoners lined up in single file waiting to enter the room. One came out, another went in, over and over.

When it was his turn, he walked inside, barefoot, and was immediately ankle-deep in a sickening mixture of mud and human waste. An open pit filled the center of the outhouse, and it was all he could do to keep from falling dizzily into it as he dumped his load. The other prisoners lined up beside a rusty water tap near the outhouse to clean their pails. The water came out weakly, like the stream of a little boy pissing into the air. The prisoners swabbed their pails with a balding short-handled broom, as if reaming out their own entrails. He felt like puking, and could nearly see the stringy noodles squirm around his stomach, chased by golden fried eggs. Clenching his teeth, he forced back the soggy lump that had risen to his throat. I can't throw up. I mustn't waste good food like that.

Before swabbing out his pail when he reached the tap, Gao Yang stuck his injured foot under the water to remove an accumulation of filth he didn't dare look at. The man behind thumped him in the rear with his pail. "What the hell are you so picky about?" he growled. "This is no bathhouse!"

He turned and was face to face with a clean-shaven middle-aged inmate with large, jaundiced eyes and crinkled skin—a shriveled face that looked like a soybean soaked in water, then set out to dry. Frightened and chastened, Gao Yang excused himself pathetically:

"Elder Brother, I'm new here . . . don't know the rules . . . injured foot—"

The jaundiced-eyed inmate cut him short. "Speed it up, damn it! Exercise period's almost over."

Gao Yang hastily rinsed off his feet—the skin on his injured left foot was a ghostly white—then hastily scrubbed the inside of his pail.

Exhausted by the time he returned the refuse pail to its place in the wall, he could scarcely believe that in the space of twenty-four hours a vigorous man like him had been turned into a worthless, panting shell of a human being. The brief stay outside his cell made him aware of how foul the air was inside. He heard a rattle deep down in his chest and was confronted with thoughts of death. I can't die now, he thought. He steadied himself and moved out through the still-open door into the light of the corridor, a vantage point that gave him a better sense of the prison layout.

Each end of the long, narrow corridor featured a steel cage manned by an armed guard. He spotted two small doors in the gray southern wall of the now-empty corridor, and wondered where the other prisoners were.

"Number Nine," the guard at the western station called to him, "through that door."

Doing as he was told, he emerged into the glorious outdoors, or, more exactly, an open-air cage around a concrete slab whose length corresponded to the corridor, but was some thirty feet wide and a good ten or fifteen feet high. Thick bluish steel ribs strung between rust-spotted steel posts formed the barrier between the prisoners and the land beyond the cage, which was planted with greens, potatoes, cucumbers, and tomatoes. Female guards were out picking cucumbers. Beyond the garden area rose an imposing gray wall topped with barbed wire, which reminded him of what he'd heard as a child, that prison walls are equipped with high-voltage wires that electrocute anything that comes into contact with them, even a bird.

Most of the prisoners gripped the steel ribs and gazed outside the enclosure; the spaces between the ribs were about the size of a small bowl, nowhere big enough to accommodate even the smallest head. A few men sat on the ground against the northern wall, sunning themselves, while others paced the outer edges of the cage, which was divided into two sections: the western half for male prisoners, the eastern half for women.

Gao Yang spotted Fourth Aunt Fang holding on to the bars in the women's side. He barely recognized her, she had changed so much in the day since he'd last seen her. He chose not to hail her.

Under the watchful eyes of silent prisoners holding on to the bars, the guards carried a large bamboo basket over to the tomato patch. They were giggling and having a grand time, especially a short, freckle-faced girl of about twenty, who was laughing the loudest.

Gao Yang heard his young cellmate call out playfully, "Officer, be a good girl and toss one of those tomatoes this way, all right?"

The woman just gaped at the cage.

"Come on, be a good girl, and toss me one," he tried again.

"Call me 'Great-Aunt,'" the freckle-faced guard said, "and maybe I will."

"Great-Aunt!" the young prisoner shouted without hesitation.

Shocked at first, she then doubled over with laughter.

"Little Liu, you'd better give your great-nephew a tomato," her companions teased her.

So she straightened up, pulled a half-ripe tomato out of the bamboo basket, took careful aim, and flung it with all her might. It rebounded off a bar and landed a couple of feet from the cage.

"Is that the best you can do, Little Liu?" one of her companions, who was skinny as fishbone, mocked her.

The freckle-faced guard picked up another tomato, aimed it at the young inmate, and let fly again. This one made it through the bars and landed on the cement floor, where it was pounced on by a swarm of prisoners. Gao Yang couldn't see who wound up with the tomato, but he heard strange, piteous wails.

"Damn it!" the young inmate cursed. "That was a gift from my great-aunt! Damn it to hell! The tiger kills the prey just so the bear can eat."

By now the tomato was in someone else's stomach, so the prisoners went back to holding the bars and gazing outside.

"Great-Aunt, one more, please!" the young inmate pleaded.

He was joined by a chorus of shouts—"Great-Aunt" by some prisoners, "Big Sister" by others—and the unmistakable voice of his middle-aged cellmate: "Fuck your great-aunt!" By then the guards were pelting the cage with tomatoes, over which the prisoners fought like a pack of mad dogs, snarling and growling and forming tight little clusters.

Guards came rushing up from both ends of the corridor, rifles at the ready, followed by turnkeys, who ran into the cage. Rifle bolts clicked as the cloth-shod turnkeys kicked the array of legs and buttocks in front of them. The shriek of a police whistle split the air.

"Get your asses back inside, all of you!" the turnkeys shouted.

Like a tightly packed school of fish, the inmates slipped through the little metal door. It clanged shut and was bolted behind Gao Yang, the last man in. The exercise period was over.

The cage, the garden, the barbed wire—all of it gone. For the first time, Gao Yang realized how narrow the corridor was. He heard a man arguing with the female guards outside. The high-pitched voice of the freckle-faced officer was easy to distinguish from all the others.

4

Reentering the cell felt like crawling into a cave, one so dark it dulled Gao Yang's sight and hearing—but not, unfortunately, his sense of smell. The stench of mildew and rot nearly bowled him over.

In a low voice the middle-aged inmate said, "You there, new man, stand up."

"Elder B-Brother," he stammered, "what do you want from me?"

The man grinned conspiratorily. "How were those noodles?"

"They were good," he replied shyly.

"Did you hear that? He said they were good."

"Good, but hard to digest," the young inmate said.

"You got special food," the old prisoner spat out as he rushed Gao Yang and began scratching his head and face.

The middle-aged inmate pulled the old man away and forced Gao Yang to back up. When his back was against the wall, he gazed fearfully at the opening in the door. "Don't shout, or I'll strangle you," the inmate threatened. "An ass-licking, tail-wagging dog is what you are!"

"Elder Brother . . . please don't."

"Tell us what kind of noodles they were."

He shook his head.

"I know, they were hollow-core noodles. Now we'll see how hollow your core is!" The inmate signaled the others. "Come on, men, three punches apiece, until we get him to puke!"

The young inmate clenched his fist, took aim at Gao Yang's breastbone, and delivered three quick, hard punches.

Gao Yang wailed piteously, and while his mouth was open, the mass of noodles came tumbling out. When he was through vomiting, he lay sprawled on the cement floor.

"Okay, thief," the middle-aged inmate said, "I heard you yell for your great-aunt out there, but you didn't get a single tomato. So now I'm going to reward you."

"Uncle, I don't want—"

"Keep your voice down. I'm going to let you lap up the noodles he just deposited on the floor."

Down on his knees, the young inmate begged softly, "Uncle, good Uncle, dear Uncle, I promise I'll never again—"

The sudden rattle of keys at the door sent the three men scurrying to their cots.

The door opened with a blaze of light, and an officer standing in the doorway held up a sheet of paper. "Number Nine, out!"

Crawling over to the door as fast as he could, leaving a trail of tears and snot, Gao Yang pleaded, "Officer, please, please save me!"

"What's wrong with you, Number Nine?" the officer asked him.

"He's sick," the middle-aged inmate said. "All feverish, talks jibberish. They brought him some food from the infirmary, but he threw everything up."

"Should we still take him out?" the man asked his partner.

"Let's try it and see what happens."

"On your feet!" the guard ordered.

As soon as Gao Yang was standing, the nearest officer snapped a pair of golden handcuffs over his wrists.

CHAPTER 13

A panicky County Administrator Thong made the walls higher,
Added a topping of broken glass and rings of barbed wire.
But no wall can stop the masses' shouts, no matter how high,
And barbed wire cannot hold back the people's fury....

> – from a ballad sung by Zhang Kou at the County Building wall, made
> scale-proof on orders of County Administrator Zhong Weimin
> following an incident in which the people broke into the county
> administrator's office and trounced some long-resented officials

1

After clambering unsteadily to his feet, Gao Ma toppled over again, just as seven or eight gaily colored parakeets flew in through the open window, made passes above and below the roof beams, then playfully hugged the walls, brushing past Jinju's hanging corpse. The silkiness of their feathers made them appear bare-skinned. Jinju's body swung gracefully, causing the doorframe to creak. In the late-night silence even the faintest sounds thudded against his eardrum. Although no pain disturbed his numbed heart, the sickeningly sweet taste in his mouth told him he was about to cough up blood again. "Gao Ma!" He shouted his own name. Gao Ma, you were fated to take a bloody fall from the moment Jinju became yours. You have coughed up blood, vomited blood, spat blood, pissed blood—you are blood-spattered from head to toe.

Clutching the doorframe, he straightened up slowly, like a bent tree reaching for the sky. It was hard, but he managed to stand on his own two feet. It's all my fault, Jinju. The sight of her sagging belly made the sickeningly sweet taste in his throat stronger than ever. Mounting a bench, he fumbled with the knot in the rope—shaky hands, feeble fingers. The strong, acrid, and garlicky smell of her body hit him full-force; so did the sickeningly sweet taste in his throat. He could discern a slight difference between the smell of her blood and his. A man's blood is blazing hot, a woman's icy cold. A woman's blood is clean and pure, a man's dirty and polluted. Parakeets flitted under his armpits and between his legs, their malicious squawks making his heart skip a beat. He lacked the strength to loosen the knot. The rope was so thick, and was stretched so taut, that he knew he could never untie it.

He found a match and lit the kerosene lamp; as light flooded the vacant room and cast shadows of flying parakeets on the wall, he seethed with sudden hostility toward those lovely birds. The shadow of Jinju's body spread out across the wall and the floor.

He brushed against her as he went into the kitchen for the cleaver. In his gropings his hand touched the chimney brush and the spatula, but not his cleaver.

"Have you forgotten that my brothers took your cleaver, Gao Ma?" It was Jinju's voice. With her face backed by the lamplight, she appeared to be smiling, although he couldn't be sure. "Elder Brother Gao Ma," she said with a smile, "I'm sure it's a son."

"I'd be just as happy with a daughter. I've never favored boys over girls."

"No, a daughter won't do. We have to make sure he gets a good education, high school and college, so he can find work in town and not have to suffer the miserable life of a farmer."

"Jinju, going away with me brought you nothing but misery." He stroked her head.

"You shared my misery." She rubbed his bony chest. "My parents shouldn't have demanded so much money from you," she said sadly.

"That's okay, I'll scrape it together," he said confidently. "I'll get at least five thousand for the garlic. And since all the villagers will

have plenty of money, I can borrow the rest—I'm sure they'll help—
so we can get married before the baby arrives."

"Marry me now," she said. "I can't live in that house any longer."
Little green dots played on her face, and he wondered if they were
parakeet feathers that had stuck to it.

That was when he remembered the saber, a family relic. He'd been
caught handling it when he was a child. "Put it down!" Grandpa had
said. Grandpa was still alive then. "It's rusty. I'm going to sharpen
it," Gao Ma had retorted. "This is no toy!" Grandpa had said, and
snatched it out of his hand. "This saber has killed a man," Mother
had said. She was still alive then, too. "Don't you dare play with it."
And so they had hidden it on a roof beam to keep it away from him.

He moved the stool over, reached up to the beam, and felt around
until his hand bumped into something long and hard. He brought it
into the light. As he slipped the saber out of its wooden scabbard, the
faces of Grandpa and Mother appeared before him.

The blade was dotted with red rust but still plenty sharp. And even
though the tip had snapped off, it was made of good steel. Gao Ma's
hand moved through the air until saber met rope. But the saber
inexplicably bounced back, sending him crashing to the floor. He
scrambled to his feet just as the rope parted and Jinju fell to the
floor—toes first, then heels, then the rest of her body, face up: a
crumbling mountain of silver, a collapsed jade pillar, raising a pitiful
ill wind that made the kerosene lamp flicker. He knelt down and
loosened the noose around her neck. A breathy sigh escaping from
her mouth drew a shriek of joy from his. But she didn't make
another sound. Her body was cold and stiff, as a touch of his hand
proved. He tried to stuff her tongue back into her mouth, but it had
puffed up to such an extraordinary thickness that it no longer fit. Yet
even then a bewitching smile was visible on her face.

"Have you already scraped the money together, Elder Brother
Gao Ma? When can we get married?"

He covered her face and upper body with a blanket.

After wailing piteously for some minutes, he realized how weary he was. Picking up the pitted, rusty saber, he staggered into the yard, the wind in his face and the taste of blood in his mouth. As he gazed up at the moon and the stars in the cloudless sky, the gaily colored parakeets emerged from the house en masse through the open window and front door, slipping through the air with such ease you'd have thought their wings were greased.

He swung at one with his saber. The bird veered, shot past him, and reentered the house. I'll slaughter you all! Wait till I hone my saber, and I'll slaughter you all!

He knelt beside a huge whetstone brought down from Little Mount Zhou and began working on his saber. First he scraped it dry to remove the rust; then he fetched a chipped ceramic bowl, filled it half-full with water, and began honing it wet. Through the rest of the night he kept at it. At cockcrow he wiped the blade clean with a handful of weeds, then held it up to the light. The icy glint of steel sent shivers up his spine. When he moved the blade lightly against his face, he heard a crackle and felt even the softest whiskers, which always bow beneath a dull knife, fall away.

The heft of the saber made him feel like a night-stalking swordsman; his palm itched around the handle. First he bounded into the township compound, quickly decapitating several tall sunflowers around him and leveling others nearer the ground. The razor-sharp saber seemed to cut and slash of its own volition, guiding his hand through the beds of sunflowers. Nothing could stop it. The stems remained suspended in place long after his saber had passed through them; then he watched them shudder once before falling noiselessly to the ground of their own weight, dim starlight falling lightly on the large fanlike leaves. Consumed by murderous intent, he turned his attention to the nearby pine trees. White chips of virgin wood flew, while in the branches above him swarms of frantic parakeets scattered in the sky, then formed a cloud of living color that whirled above the township compound, depositing pale droppings onto the blue roof tiles below until, wing-weary, they fell like stones, thudding like heavy raindrops. After felling three pine trees, Gao Ma watched four scarlet moons climb into the uncommonly expansive sky, one at each point of the compass, lighting up the land as if it were daytime. Parakeet feathers shimmered in many colors; birds' eyes sparkled gemlike in the blinding light.

He raised the saber in his right hand, then his left. He was a giant. He slashed at the contemptible parakeets who'd risen up to circle him; cold blood from their dismembered bodies splashed onto his face, and as he reached up to wipe it away with his free hand, the stench of parakeet blood filled his nostrils.

Undaunted, the birds entered the house through the windows and door, then flew back out. The moons had long since fallen out of the sky above the gray courtyard, which was dotted by blurred woodpiles. He stood in the doorway, saber in hand, waiting. A parakeet flew up near him, mischievously, rolling its colorful wing feathers. His saber described an arc as it sliced through the bird; half fell at his feet, the other half landed a yard or so away. With a single kick he sent the half-bird at his feet sailing over the wall; then he skewered the other half with the tip of his saber and brought it up close to get a better look. The muscles were still twitching, the exposed innards quivering; a breath of hot air hit him full in the face. Cold, sticky blood slid down the blade and onto the brass guard over the hilt. A flick of the wrist, and the second half of the parakeet sailed over the wall.

The surviving parakeets, enraged by what he had done, raised a terrifying screech of protest. Assuming a fighting stance, he accepted the challenge: "Come on, you bastards, here I am!" He then rushed headlong into the thick flock of birds, swinging the saber over his head. A shower of parakeets thudded earthward, some dead when they hit the ground, others mortally wounded, hopping in the dirt like frogs. But the birds, having a numerical advantage, launched a counterattack. Now he was fighting for his own survival.

Finally he collapsed wearily onto a heap of small, bloody corpses, as the surviving parakeets circled above, screeching piteously, the fight taken out of them.

Hoof beats sounded in the lane. Summoning up what little energy he had left, Gao Ma gripped his saber tightly and stood up, just in time to see his beloved chestnut colt poke its head over the broken wall. It seemed thinner; its eyes, larger now, and filled with compassion, were fixed on him. Tears gushed from his eyes: "Dearest . . . don't leave me, please don't leave me . . . I miss you . . . I need you . . ."

The horse slowly drew its head back into the surrounding darkness. He heard hoof beats, heading south, away from him: loud and crisp at first, then softer and dull-edged, and finally, nothing.

2

He handed a wad of bank notes to his neighbors Mr. and Mrs. Yu. "Elder Brother, Sister-in-Law, this is all I have. See what you can do. If it's not enough, consider it a down payment. I'll pay you back someday, I promise."

He sat leaning against the wall beneath the window, saber in hand.

The Yus exchanged glances. "Should we inform her brothers?" she asked. "Your mother-in-law was arrested yesterday, along with Gao Yang."

"Do what you can, folks, that's all I ask."

"Cremation or burial?" the man asked.

The idea of flames lapping the skin of Jinju and the infant in her belly nearly broke his heart. "Burial," he said firmly.

The Yus hurried off, just as curious neighbors swooped down on the place. Some wept, others looked on dry-eyed and expressionless. The village boss, Gao Jinjiao, prowled the area, nosing around and sighing conspicuously. "Worthy Nephew," he said as he approached Gao Ma, "You . . . um . . ."

Gao Ma flashed his saber. "Village Boss, don't push me!"

Gao Jinjiao scooted out of the way without even bothering to stand up straight.

Mrs. Yu returned with two yards of red satin, which she laid out in the yard after calling some women over. One of them, a seamstress, went inside to take Jinju's measurements. Then she went to work with her scissors.

More curious villagers streamed into the yard, trampling the mangled parakeets, whose colorful feathers, swept up by breezes, stuck to their legs, clothing, and faces—but no one noticed.

Jinju's body was laid out on the kang, in plain view of Gao Ma. The sun, directly overhead now, shone down through the red and yellow jute branches and talon-shaped leaves to light up her face and turn it into a golden chrysanthemum—a *jinju*—whose petals were coaxed open by autumn sunlight. He touched her face. It had the sleek resilience of costly velvet.

Then the Fang brothers showed up. First came Number Two, who marched sullenly across the yard, kicking parakeet feathers into the air; they floated down onto the red satin. As he strode through the door, a parakeet flew straight at him, as if wanting to peck out his eye. A swipe of his hand sent the bird crashing into the wall. He walked up to the kang and lifted a corner of the blanket, exposing Jinju's face. She smiled up at him.

Disgusted, he let the blanket fall and walked into the yard. "Gao Ma," he snarled, "you've ruined our family, you fucking bastard!" Rolling up his sleeves as he went, he headed straight for the wall, where Gao Ma was banging the dull side of the saber with the dangling manacle chain—*clang clang clang.* He glared at Fang Two through bloodshot eyes, stopping him in his tracks. Fang Two paused only to growl, "I'm charging you with the death of my sister!"

He had barely stormed off when Fang One came into the crowded yard, limping more noticeably than ever. His hair was streaked with gray, his eyes were clouded; he had become an old man almost overnight. He announced his arrival with loud wails that swirled through the yard—just like an old woman. Inside the house he pounded the kang and wept. "Sister—my poor baby sister—you shouldn't have died like this!"

Fang One's persistent wailing infected a gaggle of old women, who dabbed their teary eyes as they led the men into the room to carry him outside. "Elder Brother Fang," they tried to console him, "there's nothing you can do for her now except arrange for the funeral. That's a brother's responsibility."

It worked; he stopped wailing, wiped his runny nose, and said, "Marrying off a daughter is the same as dumping water on the ground. She stopped being a member of the Fang family long ago. Whether she's buried in a crypt or tossed into a ditch is no concern of ours." He began to limp off, crying as he went.

Gao Ma stood up and halted him with a shout. "See if there's anything left inside that you want to take with you."

Fang One paused, but said nothing, then continued on out of the yard.

The women carried Jinju's red satin funeral clothes inside, where they stripped her naked, washed her, and dressed her for her final trip. When they were finished, she wore bright red from head to toe, just like a new bride.

Gao Zhileng's feet nearly flew as he charged into Gao Ma's yard, where the corpses of his parakeets were strewn. He cursed and wept as he picked up the mangled bodies and laid them in a basket he'd brought along. "Gao Ma, Gao Ma, what did these birds ever do to you? Do what you want with people, but why kill my birds? They were my wealth. Now I've got nothing. . . ."

Seven or eight surviving parakeets perched precariously on the tips of jute plants, rumpled feathers covered with blood. Their squawks were cries of desolation. Even Gao Ma felt sorry for them. Gao Zhileng puckered up and summoned them with a strange whistle.

"I'm from the provincial TV station. We heard about the tragic love affair between you and the girl Jinju. Would you mind telling our viewers exactly what happened?" The reporter, a man in his thirties who wore owl-shaped glasses, had a large mouth and terrible breath.

"I'm with the county league of women, in charge of investigating the three-family marriage contract, and would like your views on the subject." She was young and heavily powdered. Her mouth had the smell of urine, and it was all Gao Ma could do to keep from lopping off her head with his saber.

"Get out of here, all of you!" he snarled as he got to his feet, saber in hand. "I have nothing to say to any of you!"

"Elder Brother Gao Ma, it's too hot to worry about a coffin. Besides, the price of wood has soared since the Manchurian forest fire," Yu Qiushui said as he took another look at Jinju's swollen belly. "I bought a couple of rush mats and two yards of plastic. Wrapping her in plastic, then covering her with rush mats is as good as a coffin. That way we can get her peacefully into the ground without delay. What do you think?" "Whatever you say, Elder Brother," Gao Ma replied. Meanwhile the TV reporter was all over the place, squatting and kneeling to get the best shots, including one of the parakeets perched on jute plants. It was a genre painting: yellow jute stalks, red jute stalks, green jute stalks . . . golden sunbeams on jute leaves . . . brightly colored parakeets . . . a distraught Gao Zhileng, lips puckered in a whistle. The birds' necks were drawn in as they made mournful cries that brought tears to their owner's eyes.

"I sent six men to the graveyard east of the village to dig a hole. It's time to start out," Mr. Yu announced.

So the two new rush mats were laid out in the yard and covered with the sheet of pale blue plastic. Then four women carried out Jinju, in her new red satin clothes, and laid her on the plastic. *Click! Pop!* The reporter's camera kept snapping pictures, while the powdered young woman ostentatiously filled a notebook with whatever she was writing. The yellow skin of her neck clashed with her white face powder, and again Gao Ma had to force back the urge to lop her head off where the two colors met.

"Elder Brother, come see if there's anything else we need to do," Mrs. Yu said to Gao Ma.

He took a last, close look at Jinju. Jute stalks and leaves rustled in the wind, and the eerie fragrance of indigo saturated his heart; the sunlight was bright and beautiful, the outline of the pale daytime moon sharp and clean. He was breathing hard and sweating profusely as he gazed down into Jinju's smiling face. Jinju, Jinju, your scent fills my nostrils. . . .

Dimly he watched them roll her body up in the pale blue plastic and wrap it with the golden rush mats, which a couple of men then secured with new cords made of jute, using their feet on the mats as leverage to lash them as tightly as possible. He heard bits of rush fiber snap as the cords tightened and watched the men's feet step on Jinju's bulging belly.

Flinging his saber to the ground, he fell to his knees and coughed up a mouthful of blood, some of it dribbling down his chest. The parakeets rose from the jute plants and flew as fast as their wings would take them, then swooped earthward like swallows skimming the surface of water, their bellies nearly scraping the tips of the jute plants. The reporter couldn't take pictures fast enough. The birds flew like shuttles on a loom, weaving a kaleiodoscopic design over Gao Ma's and Jinju's faces.

He raised his arms high in front of him. The stammering policeman removed the broken handcuffs and replaced them with a new pair that gleamed bright yellow—both wrists this time.

"Y-you think you can r-run away again? You might make it past the f-first of the month, but n-never past the fifteenth!"

CHAPTER 14

Anyone not afraid of being hacked to pieces
Can unseat a party secretary or county administrator.
Inciting a mob may be against the law,
But what about hiding behind closed doors, shunning duties, and letting
  subordinates exploit peasants?

> – from a ballad sung by Zhang Kou following mass interrogations at
> the police station

1

Gao Yang drove his donkey cart, loaded with garlic, down the
county road under a starlit sky. The load was so heavy, the cart so
rickety, that creaks accompanied him the whole trip, and each time
the cart hit a pothole, he was fearful it might shake apart. As he
crossed the little stone bridge over the Sandy River, he tightened the
donkey's bridle and used his body weight to steady the cart for
the sake of the spindly animal, which looked more like an oversized
billy goat than a donkey. Uneven stones made the wheels creak and
groan. The trickle of water beneath them reflected cold stars.
Negotiating the rise, he slipped a rope over his shoulder to help the
donkey pull. The paved road leading to the county town began at
the top of the rise; level and smooth, and unaffected by the elements,
it had been built after the Third Plenum of the Central Committee.
He thought back to his complaints at the time: "Why spend all that
money? How many trips to town will any of us take in a lifetime?"
But now he realized his error. Peasants always take the short view,

never seeing beyond petty personal gains. The government is wise; you will never go wrong by heeding its advice, was what he told people these days.

As he set out on the new road, he heard the rumbling of another cart twenty or thirty yards ahead, and an old man's coughs. It was very late and very quiet. The strains of a song reverberated above the surrounding fields, and Gao Yang could tell it was Fourth Uncle Fang. In his youth, Fourth Uncle had been a dashing young man who sang duets with a woman from the traveling opera troupe.

"Sister, Sister, such a fetching sight / Ushered into the bridal chamber late at night / A golden needle pierces the lotus blossom / Stains of precious juice greet the morning light."

Dirty old man! Gao Yang swore under his breath as he urged his donkey on. But it would be a long night, and there was a great distance to travel, so the thought of having someone to talk to was appealing. When the silhouette of the cart came into view, he hailed, "Is that you, Fourth Uncle? It's me, Gao Yang."

Fourth Uncle kept his silence.

Katydids chirped in roadside foliage, Gao Yang's donkey clip-clopped loudly on the paved road, and the air was heavy with the smell of garlic as the moon rose behind tall trees, its pale rays falling onto the road. Filled with hope, he caught up with the cart in front. "Is that you, Fourth Uncle?" he repeated.

Fourth Uncle grunted in reply.

"Keep singing, Fourth Uncle."

Fourth Uncle sighed. "Sing? At this point I can't even cry."

"I started out so early this morning, I never figured to be behind you, Fourth Uncle."

"There are others ahead of us. Haven't you seen all the animal droppings?"

"Didn't you sell your crop yesterday, Fourth Uncle?"

"Did you?"

"Didn't go. My wife just had a baby, and it was such a difficult delivery I was too busy to leave the house."

"What did she have?" Fourth Uncle asked.

"A boy." Gao Yang could not conceal his excitement. His wife had given him a son, and there had been a bumper crop of garlic. Gao Yang, your fortunes have changed. He thought about his mother's grave. It was an auspicious site. What he had suffered over not divulging the location to the authorities all those years before had been worth it.

Fourth Uncle, who was sitting on the cart railing, lit his pipe, the match flame briefly illuminating his face. The bowl glowed as the acrid smell of burning tobacco was carried off on the chilled night air.

Gao Yang guessed why Fourth Uncle was so melancholy. "People's lives are controlled by fate, Fourth Uncle. Marriage and wealth are determined before we're born, so it's useless to worry about them." Trying to comfort Fourth Uncle, he discovered, lifted his own spirits, and he took no pleasure in Fourth Uncle's problems. There was enough joy in his heart for him to hope that Fourth Uncle's sons would also find wives soon. "Peasants like us can't hold a candle to the well-to-do. Some folks' lives aren't worth living, and some stuff isn't worth having. It could be worse for us—we could all be out begging. We know where our next meal is coming from, and tattered clothes are better than walking around bare-assed naked. Sure, life's tough, but we've got our health, and a game leg or withered arm is better than leprosy. Don't you agree, Fourth Uncle?"

Another grunted response as Fourth Uncle sucked on his pipe. Silvery moonlight bathed the shafts of his cart, the horns of the cow pulling it, the ears of Gao Yang's donkey, and the thin plastic tarpaulin covering the garlic.

"My mother's death helped to convince me that we should be content with our lot and no harder on ourselves than we have to. If everyone was on top, who would hold them up at the bottom? If everybody went to town for a good time, who would stay home to plant the crops? When the old man up there made people, he used different raw materials. The good stuff went for officials, the so-so stuff for workers, and whatever was left for us peasants. You and me, we're made of scraps, and we're lucky just to be alive. Isn't that right, Fourth Uncle? Like that cow of yours, for example. She pulls your garlic, and has to give you a ride in the bargain. If she slows down, she gets a taste of your whip. The same rules govern all living creatures. That's why you have to endure, Fourth Uncle. If you make it, you're a man, and if you don't, you're a ghost. Some years ago, Wang Tai and his bunch made me drink my own piss— that was before Wang Tai's heyday—so I gritted my teeth and did it. It was just a little piss, that's all. The things we worry about are all in our heads. We fool ourselves into believing we're clean. Those doctors in their white smocks, are they clean? Then why do they eat afterbirth? Just think, it comes out of a woman's you-know-what, all bloody and everything, and without even washing it, they cover it with chopped garlic, salt, soy sauce, and other stuff, then fry it medium rare and gobble it up. Dr. Wu took my wife's afterbirth with him, and when I asked him how it tasted, he said it was just like jellyfish. Imagine that—jellyfish! Have you ever heard anything so disgusting? So when they told me to drink my own piss, I slurped it down, a big bottle of it. And what about afterwards? I was still the same old me, everything still in place. Secretary Huang didn't drink his own piss back then, but when he got cancer later, he ate raw vipers, centipedes, toads, scorpions, and wasps—fighting fire with fire, they said—but he only managed to keep up the fight for six months before breathing his last!"

Their carts rounded a bend where the road crossed the wasteland behind Sand Roost Village. The area was dotted with sandy hillocks on which red willows, indigo bushes, wax reeds, and maples grew. Branches and leaves twinkled in the moonlight. A dung beetle flew through the air, buzzing loudly until it crash-landed on the road. Fourth Uncle smacked the cow's rump with a willow switch and relit his pipe. At an incline the donkey lowered its head and strained in silence as it pulled its load. A sympathetic Gao Yang slung the rope over his shoulder and helped pull. It was a long, gradual climb, and when they made the top, he looked back to see where they'd been; he was surprised to see flickering lanterns in what seemed to be a deep pit. On the way down he tried sitting, but when he saw how the donkey arched its back and how its hooves were bouncing all over the place, he jumped down and walked alongside the cart to forestall disaster.

"We'll be halfway there at the bottom of this slope, won't we?" Gao Yang asked.

"Just about," Fourth Uncle replied dispiritedly.

Insects in the trees and bushes along the way heralded their passage with dull, dreary chirps. Fourth Uncle's cow tripped and nearly lost its footing. A light mist rose from the road. Rumblings were audible in the distance, due south, and the ground shook slightly.

"There goes a train," Fourth Uncle commented.

"Have you ever ridden one, Fourth Uncle?"

"Trains aren't meant for people like us, to use your words," Fourth Uncle said. "Maybe the next time around I'll be born into an official's family. Then I'll ride one. Meanwhile I have to be content with watching them from a distance."

"I've never been on one, either," Gao Yang said. "If the old man up there smiles down on me with five good harvests, I'll splurge a hundred or so to ride a train. Trying something new might make up for having to drag myself through life like a beast in human garb."

"You're young yet," Fourth Uncle said. "There's still hope."

"Hope for what? At thirty you're middle-aged, at fifty they plant you in the ground. I'm forty-one, a year older than your first son. The dirt's already up to my armpits."

"People survive a generation; plants make it till autumn. Climbing trees to snare sparrows, and wading in water to catch fish, it seems like only yesterday. But before you know it, it's time to die."

"How old are you this year, Fourth Uncle?"

"Sixty-four," he replied. "Seventy-three and sixty-four, the critical years. If the King of the Underworld doesn't come get you,

you go on your own. There's little chance I'll be around to eat any of this year's millet crop."

"Come, now, you're strong and healthy enough to live another eight or ten years at least," Gao Yang said to perk him up.

"You don't need to try to raise my spirits. I'm not afraid of dying. It can't be worse than living. And just think of the food I'll save the nation," Fourth Uncle added wryly.

"You wouldn't save the nation any food by dying, since you only eat what you grow. You're not one of those elite parasites."

The moon burrowed into a gray cloud, blurring the outlines of roadside trees and increasing the resonance of the insects inhabiting them.

"Fourth Uncle, Gao Ma's not bad. You were right to give him permission to marry Jinju." It just slipped out, and he regretted it at once, especially when he heard Fourth Uncle suck in his breath. Moving quickly to change the subject, he said, "Did you hear what happened to the third son of the Xiong family in Sheep's Pen Village, the one who went off to study in America? He wasn't there a year before he went and married a blond, blue-eyed American girl. He sent a picture home, and now Old Man Xiong shows her off to everybody he sees."

"His ancestral graves are located on auspicious land."

That reminded Gao Yang of his mother's grave: it was on high land, with a river to the north and a canal to the east; off to the south you could see Little Mount Zhou, and to the west a seemingly endless broad plain. Then he thought of his two-day-old son, his big-headed son. All my life I've been a brick right from the kiln, and I can't change now. But Mother's final resting place might work to the advantage of her grandson and give him a decent life when he grows up.

A tractor chugged past, headlight blazings, a mountain of garlic stacked on its bed. Realizing that their small-talk was slowing them down, they prodded the animals to pick up the pace.

2

They approached the railroad tracks under a red morning sun. Even at that hour dozens of tractors were lined up ahead of them, all loaded down with garlic.

Their way was blocked by a zebra-striped guard rail on the north side of the tracks. A long line of carts pulled by oxen, donkeys, horses, and humans, plus the tractors and trucks, snaked behind them, as the entire garlic crop from four townships was drawn like a magnet to the county town. The sun showed half of its red face, outlined in black, as it climbed above the horizon and fell under the canopy of a white cloud whose lower half was dyed pale red. Four shiny east-west tracks lay before them. A green eastbound loco-motive, belching white smoke and splitting the sky with whistle shrieks, shot past, followed by a procession of passenger cars and the bloated faces of the elite at the windows.

A middle-aged man holding a red-and-green warning flag stood by the lowered guard rail. His face was also round and heavy. Did all the elite people who worked for the railroad have bloated faces? The ground was still shaking after the train passed, and his donkey quaked from the terrifying shrieks of the train whistle. Gao Yang, who had been covering the animal's eyes, let his hands drop and gazed at the flag-holding crossing guard as he raised the guard rail with his free hand. Vehicles poured across the tracks before the rail was all the way up. The narrow road could only accommodate double file, and Gao Yang stood wide-eyed as more maneuverable hand-pulled carts and bicycles squeezed past him and Fourth Uncle and shot ahead. The land rose quickly on the other side of the tracks, where their way was further hampered by the rocky surface of the road, which was undergoing repairs. Carts struggling to make the climb shook and rattled in agony, forcing drivers to jump down and carefully lead the animals along by their bridles to steady the carts amid the clay and yellow sand.

As before, Fourth Uncle led the way. Gao Yang watched steam rise from his body and noticed that his face was black as the business end of a skillet as he strained to lead his cow, the rope in his left hand and a willow switch in his right. "Hee-ya, giddap!" he hollered, waving his switch over the animal's rump without actually touching it. Frothy bubbles formed at the corners of the cow's raised mouth; her breathing was loud and raspy; her flanks twisted and wriggled, probably because of stones cutting into her hooves.

The red ball of a sun and a few ragged clouds were all the scenery the sky could offer; a chewed-up highway and lots of garlic-laden carts comprised the earthly sights. Gao Yang had never been part of such a vast undertaking before, and was so flustered he kept his eyes glued to the back of Fourth Uncle's head, not letting his gaze wander an inch. His little donkey seemed to be doing a jig on hooves gouged mercilessly by sharp stones; its left hoof was already leaving a dark bloody trail on the white stones. The poor animal was pulled from side to side by the lurching motions of the axle, but Gao Yang was too intent on moving forward to feel much sympathy. No one dared to even slow down, fearing that the subhuman creature behind them might try to take advantage.

An explosion, as from a hand grenade, went off to his left, scaring the hell out of man and beast. He shuddered. Jerking his head toward the sound, he saw that a handcart had blown a tire, whose red inner tube was fanned out over the black rubber. Two young women, about the same age, had been pulling the cart. The slightly older one's head was shaped like the bole of a tree and covered with the bark of acne scars. Her fair-skinned companion had an attractive oval face, with— lamentably—one blind eye. He sighed. Blind old Zhang Kou said it best: even a famous beauty like Diao Zhan had pockmarks, which proves that perfect beauty simply doesn't exist. The two women stared down at the flat tire and wrung their hands, as people behind them shouted and swore to get them moving again. So, stumbling and straining, they wrestled their cart over to the muddy roadside, as the others quickly closed up ranks.

That started an epidemic of blow outs; a fifty-horsepower tractor lost several in one deafening explosion that drove the metal wheels deep into the roadway and nearly tipped the tractor over. A cluster of officials stood helplessly alongside a mass of ruined rubber, while the driver—a young man whose sweaty face was black with mud— stood by holding a large wrench and heaping insults on the mothers of everyone who worked for the transportation department.

Up a gradual incline they went, then down the other side. Both the climb and the descent were hindered by the same stony roadbed— jagged teeth and wolfish fangs nipping at their heels. More and more blow outs caused a succession of traffic jams, and Gao Yang prayed silently: Old man up there, please look after my tires and don't let them pop.

At the bottom of the last hill they moved onto an east-west highway, where a gang of men in gray uniforms and broad-billed caps stood waiting at a traffic light. Garlic-laden carts filling the highway were joined by a stream of latecomers emerging from the south. Fourth Uncle informed him that they and everyone else were headed toward the county's new cold-storage warehouses east of them.

After they had traveled several hundred yards on the highway, their way was blocked by the carts ahead of them. That was when the gray-uniformed men, little black plastic satchels in hand, moved into action. Their badges identified them as employees of the traffic control station.

From experience Gao Yang knew that traffic controllers dealt with motor vehicles; so when one of them, an imposing young fellow in gray, blocked his way, black satchel in hand, he was unconcerned, even flashing him a friendly, if foolish, grin.

The stony-faced young man wrote out a slip of paper, handed it to him, and said, "That'll be one yuan."

Taken by surprise, and not sure what was going on, Gao Yang could only stare. The man in gray waved the slip of paper in front of him. "Give me one yuan," he said icily.

"What for?" Gao Yang asked anxiously.

"Highway toll."

"For a donkey cart?"

"It wouldn't matter if it was a handcart."

"I don't have any money, comrade. My wife just had a baby, and that cost me every penny I owned."

"I'm telling you to hand it over. Without one of these," he said, waving the slip of paper in the air, "without one of these, the marketing co-op won't buy your garlic."

"Honest, I don't have any money," Gao Yang insisted as he turned his pockets inside-out. "See—nothing!"

"Then I'll take some of your garlic. Three pounds."

"Three pounds is worth three yuan, comrade."

"If you don't think that's fair, then hand over the money."

"That's blackmail!"

"Are you calling me a blackmailer? You think I like doing this? It's state-mandated."

"Oh, well . . . if it's state-mandated, then go ahead."

The man scooped up a bundle of garlic and tossed it into a basket behind him—attended by two boys—and stuffed the white slip of paper with the official red seal into Gao Yang's hand.

The traffic controller then turned to Fourth Uncle, who handed over two fifty-fen notes. He was also given a white slip of paper with a red seal for his troubles.

The boys picked up the nearly full basket and staggered under its weight toward the traffic control station, where a truck was parked. Two men in white, who appeared to be loaders, leaned against the rear bumper with their arms crossed.

At least twenty gray-uniformed men were busy handing out slips of paper from their black satchels. An argument erupted between one of them and a young fellow in a red vest who spoke his mind: "You bunch of cunt babies are worse than any son of a bitch I can think of!" The traffic controller calmly slapped him across the face without batting an eye.

"Who do you think you are, hitting me like that?" the young man in the red vest shrieked.

"That was a love tap," the traffic controller replied in a level voice. "Let's hear what else you have to say."

The young man rushed the controller but was held back by two middle-aged men. "Stop it—stop it this minute! Give him what he wants, and keep your mouth shut." Two white-uniformed policemen taking a smoke break under a nearby poplar tree ignored this completely. What was that all about? Gao Yang was thinking. Of course they're cunt babies. What did he think they were, asshole babies? Facts may not sound elegant, but they're still the facts. He congratulated himself for not pulling a stunt like that, but the thought of losing all that juicy garlic nearly broke his heart. He breathed a heavy sigh.

By this time it was late morning, and Gao Yang's donkey cart had barely moved an inch. The road was black with vehicles in both directions. From Fourth Uncle he learned that the cold-storage warehouse— where the garlic was bought—was a mile or so east of them. He was itching to see for himself, drawn by the shouts, whinnies, and other signs of frantic activity, but didn't dare budge from where he was standing.

Noticing the first pangs of hunger, Gao Yang took a cloth bundle down from his cart and opened it to remove a flatcake and half a chunk of pickled vegetable, first offering some to Fourth Uncle as a courtesy, then digging in when his offer was refused. When it was about half-gone, Gao Yang plucked five stalks of garlic from his load, thinking, I'll count these as part of the highway toll. Crisp and sweet, they complemented his meal perfectly.

He was still eating when another man in a uniform and broad-billed cap came up and blocked his way, scaring the wits out of him. Quickly taking out his slip of paper, he waved it in front of the man and said, "I already paid, comrade."

"This is from the controller station," the man said after giving the slip a cursory glance. "I need to collect a two-yuan commodity tax."

Gao Yang's first emotion this time was anger. "I haven't sold a single stalk of garlic yet," he said.

"You won't stick around to pay once you have," the commodity-exchange official said.

"I don't have any money!" Gao Yang said testily. "Now you listen to me," the man said. "The co-op won't buy your garlic without seeing a tax receipt."

"Comrade," Gao Yang said, softening his attitude, "I mean it, I don't have any money."

"Then give me five pounds of garlic."

This dizzying turn of events had Gao Yang on the verge of tears. "Comrade, this little bit of garlic is all I've got. Three pounds here and five pounds there, and before long I won't have anything left. I've got a wife and kids, and this is all the garlic I could harvest, working day and night. Please, comrade."

"Government policy," the man said sympathetically. "You have to pay a tax when you deal with the commodity exchange."

"If it's government policy, then go ahead and take what you want," Gao Yang mumbled. "Imperial grain levies, national taxes . . . they're killing me, and I can't raise a hand in my own defense. . . ."

The commodity-exchange official picked up a bundle of garlic and flipped it into the basket behind him. Again, two young boys who looked like puppets on a string were in charge of the basket. As Gao Yang watched his garlic flip end-over-end into the basket, his nose began to ache, and two large teardrops slid out of the corners of his eyes.

At high noon the blazing sun drained the energy out of Gao Yang and his donkey; the latter listlessly raised its tail and released a dozen or so road apples. That brought over a gray-uniformed man in a broad-billed cap who wrote out a slip of paper and handed it to Gao Yang. "A two-yuan fine for littering," he said. Another man, this one in a white uniform and broad-billed cap, strolled up, wrote out a slip, and handed it to Gao Yang. "As sanitation inspector I'm fining you two yuan."

He just stared at the environment and sanitation inspectors. "I don't have any money," he said weakly. "Take some garlic."

3

Night was falling when Gao Yang and Fourth Uncle finally reached the purchasing station in front of the cold-storage warehouse. The scales were manned by two operators whose faces had all the radiance of dead embers. After stiffly announcing the weights, the scale operators entered figures on their receipt pads with ballpoint pens. Gao Yang broke out in a cold sweat when he saw all the uniformed men patrolling the area.

"Well, we made it," a relieved Fourth Uncle commented.

"Yeah, we made it," he echoed.

Fourth Uncle was next in line, ahead of Gao Yang, and the look of anxious anticipation on his face made Gao Yang's heart race, only to beat even faster and harder when he noticed the inspector standing next to the scale.

A uniformed man with a bullhorn climbed onto a red table. "Attention, farmers," he announced. "The warehouse is temporarily suspending the purchase of garlic. We'll notify local co-ops when we're ready to open again, and they'll get the word out to you."

Gao Yang felt as if he had been clubbed. His head spun, and he had to clutch the donkey's back to keep from falling.

"That's it?" Fourth Uncle cried. "You stop buying just when I reach the scale? I've been on the road since midnight, almost twenty-four hours!"

"Go home, garlic farmers. Once we've cleared some space in the warehouse we'll let you know."

"I live fifteen miles away!" Fourth Uncle complained, his voice cracking.

The scale operator stood up, abacus in hand.

"Comrade, I paid a highway toll and a commodity tax . . ." said Fourth Uncle.

"Keep your receipts. They'll still be valid the next time. Now go home, all of you. We're working day and night. As soon as this load is safely stored, we'll open for business again."

People at the rear surged forward, screaming, shouting, bawling, swearing.

Still gripping his bullhorn, the man jumped down off the table and ran like mad, bent at the waist. The steel gate slammed shut just as a swarthy young man hopped onto the red table and shouted at the top of his lungs, "Shit! You have to go through back doors to get anything done—even at a crematorium! What chance does our garlic have?" He jumped down and disappeared amid the piles of garlic.

His place was taken by a pimply-faced youngster who shouted, "You inside the warehouse, I'll impale your old lady on my dick!"

Roars of laughter.

Someone removed a scale hook and flung it at the galvanized-steel warehouse door. *Clang!* When the surging crowd knocked over the scales and smashed the table, an old man stormed out of the warehouse. "What is this, an uprising?"

"Grab the old bastard! Beat him! His son, Pocky Liu from the Commerce Department, gives the old bastard a hundred a month to be a gatekeeper!"

"Beat him—*beat him*—BEAT HIM!" Men rushed the gate and began pounding it with their fists.

"Let's get out of here, Fourth Uncle," Gao Yang urged. "Not selling our garlic is one thing. Getting into trouble is another."

"I'd like to go up there and get my licks in!"

"Come on, Fourth Uncle, let's get out of here. If we head due east, we'll come out on the north side of the tracks."

So Fourth Uncle turned his cart around and set out to the east, followed closely by Gao Yang, who was leading his donkey.

After a few hundred yards they looked back and saw that a fire had been set in front of the warehouse gate. A man whose skin showed up red ripped down the signboard and consigned it to the flames. "The cold-storage warehouse is actually called a 'temperature-controlled warehouse,'" Gao Yang informed Fourth Uncle. "That's what the sign said."

"Who gives a shit what it's called?" Fourth Uncle replied. "I hope they burn the fucker down!"

They were still watching when the gate fell and the crowd swarmed into the compound. Flickering light from the flames danced on people's faces, even from that distance. Thunderous shouts carried over to Gao Yang and Fourth Uncle, that and the sound of glass splintering.

A black sedan drove up from the east. "The authorities!" Gao Yang said with alarm as the car screeched to a halt near the fire and the occupants jumped out. They were immediately pushed into the gutter as the mob began pounding the roof of the car with clubs, filling the air with dull thuds. Then someone dragged a burning log from the fire and crammed it into the besieged sedan.

"Let's get out of here, Fourth Uncle!" Gao Yang insisted.

Fourth Uncle, beginning to share Gao Yang's fear, smacked his cow on the rump with his switch.

As they headed down the road they heard a massive explosion behind them, and when they turned to look, they saw a fiery column rise into the air, higher than the building, lighting up the area for miles around. Not sure what he was feeling, ecstasy or terror, Gao Yang heard his own heartbeat and felt a clammy sweat on his palms.

4

The two men skirted the county town and crossed the railroad tracks before Gao Yang breathed a sigh of relief, feeling like a man who has escaped from a wolves' den. He couldn't tell if Fourth Uncle shared his relief. If he listened carefully, he could still hear the din back at the warehouse.

After heading north for a mile or so, they heard the putt-putt of a diesel engine and the splashing of water a little east of the road, where a ring of pale lamplight was visible. The sound of water reminded Gao Yang how thirsty he was; Fourth Uncle must be just as thirsty, he figured, since he hadn't eaten or drunk anything all day. "Watch my cart, Fourth Uncle, while I get us some water. The animals need to be fed and watered, since we still have a long ways to go."

Reining in his cow in silent assent, Fourth Uncle edged his cart over to the side of the road, as Gao Yang took down a metal pail and headed toward the light, soon locating a narrow footpath amid some knee-high cornstalks whose leaves brushed his legs and pail. The lamplight was dim, yet he could tell that its source was probably no more than a couple of arrow shots from the road, although getting to it would not be easy. The sound of the diesel engine and splashing water remained constant, as if forever beyond his reach. At one point the path simply vanished, forcing him to thread his way through the field, careful not to trample any stalks. He couldn't help noticing the difference between the rich soil beneath his feet and the mineral-poor dirt back home, far from town. Then the footpath reappeared, and a few steps later widened enough to accommodate a small cart. Shallow ditches separated it from rolling farmland that gave off an aromatic mixture of cotton, peanuts, corn, and sorghum, each odor quite distinct.

Suddenly the lamplight brightened considerably, and the sounds of the diesel motor and gurgling water grew louder and clearer. Seeing his own shadow made Gao Yang bashfully aware of his own timidity, even as he walked up to the lamp. It hung from a wooden pole beside a red, twelve-horsepower diesel motor mounted on four wooden posts above the path. The fan belt didn't appear to be turning, but he knew that was an illusion, since the shiny metal clip kept flashing past and making a clicking noise. Clear water gurgled up through a thick plastic hose inserted deep into a well and gushed out of the pump. A pair of sneakers on a sheet of plastic was the only sign of life, even when he squinted to get a better look. The air was heavy with the smell of young corn.

"Who's there?" came a voice out of the darkness.

"Just a passer-by in need of a little water," he replied.

Rustling cornstalks preceded the appearance of a tall, husky man with a hoe over his shoulder. He walked up to the pump and washed his muddy feet in the gushing water, then rinsed off the hoe. Lamplight shimmered in the water dripping from the blade.

After jumping across the irrigation ditch, the man leaned against his hoe and said, "Go ahead, drink as much as you want."

Gao Yang ran over, knelt down, and thrust his mouth into the powerful stream of water, which numbed his lips and nearly choked him. When he couldn't drink another drop, he washed his face, filled his pail, and carried it over to the lantern.

The man was observing him closely, so he returned the favor. He was a poised young man in a short-sleeved shirt and a pair of uniform trousers. He reached down to unfasten a shiny watch that hung from his belt, and slipped it over his wrist. He checked the time. "What are you doing out so late?"

"Selling my garlic. I haven't had a drop to drink all day long. The sound of your water was music to my ears."

"What township are you from?"

"Gaotong."

"That's a long ways from here. Didn't your local co-op set up a purchasing station?"

"They're too busy selling fertilizer to worry about things like that."

The young man laughed. "That's normal. Everybody wants to get rich these days. How did the sale go?"

"Not good. When our turn came, we were told that the warehouse was full and no more garlic would be bought for the time being. If they were going to reopen tomorrow, I'd hang around all night instead of going home. But who the devil knows if the scales will be back in business this month or even this year!"

Out came the rest—he couldn't help himself. "It was a near riot," he said. "The scales were smashed, the table set on fire, windows broke—they even torched an official sedan."

"Do you mean to say the masses rose up in revolt?" the young man asked excitedly.

"I don't know about a revolt," Gao Yang replied with a sigh, "but it was a riot for sure. Some didn't seem to care what happened to them."

"My father and one of my brothers went to town to sell our garlic. I wonder if they're okay."

Gao Yang's gaze fell on the young man's white, even teeth, and he could tell he was trying to disguise his northern accent. "There's something special about you, Elder Brother," he commented. "I can tell."

"I'm in the army, nothing special," the young man said.

"I can see you're a decent man. No matter how well life is treating you, you still come home to help your father. That tells me you're bound to have a bright future."

The young man took out a pack of cigarettes, which looked like a fresh flower in the lamplight. He offered one to Gao Yang. "I don't smoke," Gao Yang said, "but a friend of mine is waiting for me back on the road. I'm sure he's never smoked a cigarette this good before." He tucked it behind his ear, picked up his pail, and retraced his steps back to the road.

"Where'd you go for that water, the East Ocean?" Fourth Uncle grumbled. The donkey stood there stupidly. Fourth Uncle's cow was lying on the road beside the cart.

"Here, have some water," Gao Yang said. "I'll take care of the animals."

Burying his face in the pail, Fourth Uncle drank his fill, then stood up and belched several times. Gao Yang removed the cigarette from behind his ear and handed it to him. "I met someone special," he said. "He said he was just a soldier, but I could see right off he was an officer. When he offered me a cigarette, I said I don't smoke, but I brought it back for you."

Fourth Uncle accepted it and held it up under his nose. "It smells pretty ordinary."

"He came home to help his father in the field, even though he's an officer. Not bad, hm? Most people nowadays can't wait to throw away their beggar's staff and beat up on the next person with one. Look at our own Wang Tai. He pretends he doesn't even know us.

"Had enough?" Gao Yang asked. "I'll water the cow."

"Start with the donkey. This cow of mine won't chew her cud. I'm afraid she might be sick. She's pregnant, and if I lose her on top of not selling my garlic, I'm in bad shape."

The donkey, having gotten wind of the water, began to snort, but Gao Yang walked up to the cow. She tried to get to her feet, but couldn't manage without Fourth Uncles help. A bluish light emerged from her large, sad eyes. Gao Yang held the pail under her nose, but she only lapped up a swallow or two before raising her head and licking her lips and nose with her long tongue.

"Is that all she's going to drink?" Gao Yang asked.

"She's picky. The only way Fourth Aunt can get her to drink is by spreading bran on top of the water."

"A life of ease, even the cow you please," Gao Yang quipped. "Not many years ago *people* went without bran, let alone cows."

"Quit dawdling and water your donkey."

The donkey strained at the bit as it lapped up every last drop in the pail, then shook its head to show it wanted more.

"Let's get moving," Fourth Uncle said. "The animals will get sick if they don't work up a sweat after that cold water."

"How much did she cost you, Fourth Uncle?"

"Nine hundred thirty, not counting the tax."

"That much?" Gao Yang clicked his tongue. "You could cover her from head to hoof with that many bills."

"Money's worthless these days," Fourth Uncle said. "Pork has gone up ninety fen in six months—ninety fen a pound! We can't afford more than a few pounds a year."

"But you make out okay, Fourth Uncle, since you can count on a calf every year. If the first one's a female, you break even right there. Raising cows is a lot better than planting garlic."

"You only see one side of things," Fourth Uncle protested. "Do you suppose all a cow needs is the northwest wind? Where do you think the hay and mash come from?"

Their conversation waned as the night deepened. Both carts rocked lightly from side to side. A weary Gao Yang jumped onto his cart—donkey be damned—and sat down, leaning against the rail. His eyelids felt weighted down, but he forced himself to stay awake. By then they were on sandy soil; the roadside foliage was unchanged from the night before, except that the absence of moonlight kept the leaves from shining. Also unchanged, and interminable, were the chirps of katydids and crickets.

Another incline placed an even greater strain on the donkey, which began to sound like an asthmatic old man. Gao Yang got off the cart and walked on the road, lessening the animal's wheezing a bit. Fourth Uncle stayed on his cart and let his pregnant cow pull him up the incline, whatever the strain; that did not go unnoticed by Gao Yang. I thought he had a kinder heart than that, he mused, reminding himself to have as little as possible to do with people like him from now on.

About halfway up the slope, the moon made an appearance in the eastern sky, barely clearing the lowland way off in the distance. Gao Yang was familiar enough with the laws of nature to know that tonight's moonrise was a tad later than last night's, and that tonight's moon was a tad smaller. It was sallow, with a hint of pink: there it was, a chewed-up, sallow, slightly pink, flimsy, turbid, feeble, sleepy half-moon, a tad smaller than the night before, and a tad larger than it would be tomorrow. Its beams were so frail they seemed to fall short of the sandy hill, the foliage, and the highway. He slapped the donkey on the sweaty ridge of its back; the wheels turned slowly on axles that squealed and protested from a lack of grease. Every once in a while Fourth Uncle sang a snatch of some bawdy popular tune, then just as abruptly stopped, with no discernible pattern. In reality, the moonbeams did reach them—what was dancing on the leaves around them if not moonlight? If that wasn't moonlight shimmering on the crickets' wings like slivers of glass, what was it? Who would deny that the warm scent of moonlight was mixed with the cold odor of garlic? A heavy mist hung over the lowland; light breezes swept over the outcroppings.

Fourth Uncle began swearing—hard to say if he was swearing at something or someone: "You child of a whore—dog spawn—as soon as you pull up your pants, you think you're so respectable!" Gao Yang didn't know whether to laugh or to cry.

Just then two blinding rays of light came at them from the top of the hill—high one moment, low the next; now left, now right, like a pair of pinking shears moving across fabric—followed by the urgent roar of an engine. Gao Yang wrapped his arms around his donkey's cold, sweaty head and nudged it and the cart over to the side of the road. Framed in the light beams, Fourth Uncle's cow looked like a scrawny rabbit. He jumped off his cart, grabbed the harness, and guided her to the side of the road. They both seemed to disintegrate in the light beams.

What happened next was a joke, a dream, a common shit, a leisurely piss.

Gao Yang would later recall that the car barreled down on them like an avalanche, making violent, crunching noises, as the darkness swallowed up Fourth Uncle's cow, his cart, his garlic, and him. Standing there wide-eyed, Gao Yang saw two middle-aged faces frozen behind a windshield: one fat, puffy, and smiling; the other skinny and twisted in a grimace. Gao Yang and his donkey were nearly smothered by the car's heat.

He would recall watching the car surge toward them, hearing Fourth Uncle's cow bellow, and seeing Fourth Uncle wrap his arms around the animal's neck. Fourth Uncle's head shrank in size until it looked like a tiny metallic bead reflecting yellow and blue light. Fourth Uncle, his eyes mere slits, his mouth a gaping hole, looked terrified and pathetic. The white light shone right through his protruding ears. With unhurried inevitability the car's bumper smashed into the legs of Fourth Uncle and his cow, driving his torso forward for an instant before he was airborne, his arms outstretched like wings, his shirt flapping behind him like tailfeathers. He landed in a clump of wax reeds. As her neck twisted, his cow fell to the ground on her belly. The car kept coming. After pushing the cow and the cart ahead of it a short distance, it ran up over them.

And then? Then the fat man shouted, "Let's get out of here!" The skinny man tried to back the car up but couldn't. Jamming the pedal to the floor, he lurched backwards. Then he spun the car around, skirted the spot where Gao Yang was standing with his donkey, and sped down the hill, leaving puddles of water from a punctured radiator—a wet, leaky, short trip.

With his arms still wrapped around his donkey's head, Gao Yang tried to figure out what had happened. He reached up and felt his own head. It was still whole. Nose, eyes, ears, mouth: all right where they should be. Then he examined the donkey's head; it was also in fine shape, except for its ears, which were icy cold. He broke down and cried like a baby.

CHAPTER 15

Pluck the two-stringed erhu and bring me great joy,
Sing of the brilliant Party Central Committee.
The Third Plenary Session has taken the proper road—
Elders and brothers, get rich on garlic, remake yourselves!

> – a song of congratulation sung by Zhang Kou in the first lunar month
> of 1987, at the wildly jubilant wedding party for Wang Mingniu's
> third son at Qingyang Bazaar (Zhang Kou, drunk as a lord, slept for
> three straight days at the Wang home)

1

On the second night of her incarceration, Fourth Aunt dreamed that a blood-spattered Fourth Uncle stood at the foot of her bed. "Why aren't you trying to clear your husband's name and avenge his death instead of sitting around eating prepared food and enjoying a life of leisure?" "Husband," she replied, "I cannot clear your name or avenge your death, for I have become a criminal." "Then there's nothing to be done, I guess," Fourth Uncle said with a sigh. "I stashed two hundred yuan in a crack between the second row of bricks under the window. When you get out of jail, use a hundred of it to buy me a replica of the National Treasury and fill it with all manner of riches. The world of darkness is the same as the world of light—to get anything done you have to find a back door somewhere, and everything takes money." Reaching up to wipe his bloody face, Fourth Uncle turned and walked slowly away.

The specter frightened Fourth Aunt awake; her bedding, hard and rough as armor plating, was soaked with cold sweat. The tragic, bloody image of Fourth Uncle swayed before her eyes, terrifying and saddening her at the same time. Is there really a nether world? she wondered. When I get home, I'll knock out the second row of bricks under the window, and if there's two hundred yuan there, that means there is a nether world. I mustn't divulge any of this to my sons, since those two bastards seem to be trying to outdo each other in the pursuit of evil.

The mere thought of her sons made Fourth Aunt sigh. Her cellmate, whose thoughts were on her own son, also sighed. She had been taken out for more questioning that evening, and when they brought her back, she flopped down on her cot and cried awhile, then lay there as if in a trance. Asleep now, she was snoring loudly— fast one moment, slow the next, as if dreaming.

For Fourth Aunt sleep was out of the question. Her husband still had not returned from selling the garlic. A bat flew in through the window, circled the room a time or two, then flew back out. The boundless darkness of night harbored scattered dreamlike mutter-ings and the ominous squawks of parakeets. She got up, threw her jacket over her shoulders, and walked into the yard. Amid the eerie squawks of her neighbor's parakeets, she gazed up at the stars and the waxing half-moon. It was past midnight, and she was worried.

"Yixiang," she had said to her son after dinner, "aren't you going out to meet your father?"

"What for?" he replied. "If he's not coming home, what good would going out to meet him do? And if he is, what harm would not going out to meet him do?"

Fourth Aunt was speechless. "I wonder why we ever took the trouble to raise you," she said after a while.

"I didn't ask you to. You should have stuffed me down the septic tank when I was born and let me drown. That way you could have spared me years of grief."

Choked with sobs, Fourth Aunt sat on the edge of the kang and let her tears flow. Her shadow spread across the floor, painted by yellow moonlight.

A frantic pounding at the door.

Fourth Aunt rushed to open it. Gao Yang stumbled into the room.

"Fourth Aunt," he muttered through his sobs, "Fourth Uncle was killed by a car. . . ."

Fourth Aunt crumpled to the floor, where she lay without twitching. Gao Yang picked her up and thumped her back and shoulders until she spat out a mouthful of phlegm. "Number One, Number Two, Jinju . . . get up, all of you. Your father's been killed by a car. . . ."

Jinju, far along in her pregnancy, came running into the room, followed by her brothers.

2

Two horse-drawn wagons entered the lane at dawn and stopped in front of the threshing floor. Fourth Aunt ran outside, shouting for her husband. The area was packed with people, including even the village boss, Gao Jinjiao. Elder and Younger Brother stood impassively beside the wagon.

"Your father, where's your father?" Fourth Aunt demanded, her hands spread out questioningly in front of her.

Elder Brother squatted down and held his head in his hands as he wept softly. "Father . . . my dear father . . ."

His younger brother, dry-eyed, flung back the sheet of plastic covering the bed of the wagon to reveal the rigid corpse of Fourth Uncle. His mouth was open, his eyes staring, his cheeks spattered with mud.

Husband, my husband, such a cruel way to die! Let me touch your face, your hands. Your face is cold as ice; so are your hands. Last night you were full of life, this morning just a cold cadaver! Fourth

Aunt rubbed Fourth Uncle's bald pate, then his ears. Through rips in his thin jacket she glimpsed his dark, sunken abdomen. Shredded pant legs revealed a gory mess of skin and blood.

Husband, bringing down a farmer is supposed to be so hard. A bump on the leg shouldn't do it. She felt his cold scalp for wounds. And found one: a dent the size of an egg in the center of his cranium. Here it is, the spot where they cracked your skull and drove bone splinters into your brain—this is how they killed you.

Two of the villagers dragged Fourth Aunt away, teeth clenched and gasping for breath. Fearful that she was about to follow her husband in death, a couple of the bystanders forced her mouth open with a chop-stick; Jinju's tearful, pathetic cries sounded in the background. "Take it easy, not so hard! Don't gouge her teeth out," the one holding her head cautioned the one holding the chopstick. Once they had her lips parted, a mouthful of cold water brought her to her senses.

The dead cow lay on its side in the second wagon, its stiff legs poking over the side of the wagon like gun barrels. Inside its belly an unborn calf squirmed and wriggled.

A burst of weeping, followed by one of wailing. When the people next looked up, they saw that the sun was high in the sky. "Fang Yijun," the village boss, Gao Jinjiao, said, "your father's dead, and no amount of tears can bring him back. In this heat he'll start to stink pretty soon, so dress him up in the newest clothing you can find, then hire a truck and take him to the county crematorium. As for the cow, skin it and sell the meat—tomorrow's market day, and the price of beef has gone through the ceiling. What you get for the hide and meat will be more than enough for your father's funeral expenses."

"Uncle," Fang Yijun said to the village boss, "do you expect us to accept our father's death without a murmur? Gao Yang says they were parked by the side of the road, and that the car swerved into them."

"Oh?" Gao Jinjiao commented. "Is that how it happened? Then

the driver should go to jail, and the owner should pay restitution. Whose car was it?"

"The township government. Party Secretary Wang Jiaxiu was in the car when it happened," Gao Yang said.

Gao Jinjiao blanched. "Gao Yang," he said sternly, "I want the truth. Are you sure?"

"That *is* the truth, Uncle. The car sprung a leak and broke down a few seconds later. I was holding Fourth Uncle in my arms and crying when Secretary Wang and his driver came running back. Little Zhang was shaking like a leaf, and he reeked of alcohol. 'You don't have anything to be scared of as long as I'm around, Little Zhang,' Secretary Wang assured him. Then he asked what village I was from, and when I told him, he breathed a sigh of relief. 'Little Zhang,' he said, 'there's nothing to be afraid of. They're peasants from our township. That's easy. A little cash for the family will take care of everything.' "

"Enough of that crazy talk, Gao Yang!" Gao Jinjiao said. "What about the license number?"

"It's a black car, with no license plate. The only time they dare drive it is at night," Gao Zhileng, the neighbor who raised parakeets, remarked angrily. "The driver's a cousin of Secretary Wang's wife. Used to be a tractor driver, and doesn't have a passenger-car license."

"Gao Zhileng!" Gao Jinjiao shouted.

"What?" Gao Zhileng asked, glaring defiantly. "You want me to keep my mouth shut, is that it? Well, you may be afraid of him, but I'm not! My uncle is deputy director of the Municipal Committee Organization Department, and that makes our Wang Jiaxiu look like a cunt hair!"

"Okay, do what you want," Gao Jinjiao said. "As long as it includes cremating the body and paying the village committee an administrative fee of ten yuan from the sale of the cow."

"If you Fang boys weren't such worthless garbage you'd carry your father over to the township compound and force Wang Jiaxiu's hand," Gao Zhileng said.

The older one stood there shilly-shallying, but his brother's eyes blazed. "Let's go, Brother!" he said resolutely. "Jinju, watch the house. Mother, you come with us."

Well, the boys lifted their father's body off the wagon and lay it facedown on the ground like a dead dog. "Hold on, Number Two," I said. "Dress your father up first. He's got a new lined jacket in the house. He needs to look good if he's going to see an official." "To hell with looking good!" Number Two said. "He's dead." He took down a door and laid his father on it, still facedown. "Turn him face-up, Number Two," I said. So he rolled my husband over, to let him stare blindly at the sky. Good old Gao Zhileng went home to fetch a couple of ropes to tie the body down. Then the boys carried their father off to the township compound, the older one limping along up front, the younger one behind, and me bringing up the rear. Villagers crowded around me, and even that bastard Gao Ma showed up. But no matter what anyone says about him, he still would have been our son-in-law. Well, he walked up and grabbed the pole out of my oldest son's hands. Since Gao Ma and my second son are the same height, the door leveled out and the old man's head stopped lolling from side to side.

But when we reached the compound, the gatekeeper tried to stop us from entering, so Gao Ma shouldered him aside. The place was deserted except for a big barking dog that was squatting by the kitchen door. The car that killed my husband was parked there. The top was almost covered by a wagonload of green garlic, and the hood was all bloody.

The three of us waited in the compound with my husband's body. We waited and we waited, all the way to high noon, but nobody came up to ask what we wanted. Flies were crawling all over my husband's face, trying to find their way into his eye sockets and mouth and nostrils and ears to put their gunk inside. What's gunk? You know, maggots. It didn't take them long to start squirming all over the place. They were everywhere. When one swarm of flies left, another took its place. Then it flew off. I tried to cover the old man's face with a sheet of newspaper, but the flies kept finding their way under it. Villagers from all over came to gawk—East Village, West Hamlet, Northville, and Southburg— everyone but the officials who should have been there.

My younger son went to the local café and bought a bunch of oil fritters, brought them back wrapped in newspaper, and tried to get me to eat. But I just couldn't, not with my husband lying dead in front of me. He'd been there all morning and was starting to smell. My oldest son couldn't eat, either. In fact, his brother was the only one who could. He scraped a handful of garlic off the car, then stood there with garlic in one hand and fritters in the other, taking a bite out of the left hand, then the right, back and forth, over and over. His eyes were wide and his cheeks puffed way out, and I could tell that deep down he felt bad.

Finally our waiting paid off. An official turned up, though by then the sun was good and red. It was Deputy Yang, a distant relative until he disowned us for letting our daughter go off with Gao Ma. But at least he's no stranger. In fact my older son calls him Eighth Uncle, and my younger one does chores for him, like helping him build his house, put up walls, deliver manure, stuff like that. He's almost one of his hired hands.

Well, he rode his bicycle through the gate. At last, I thought. After waiting for the stars and the moon, our savior from heaven had arrived! My sons ran up to greet him, with me right on their heels. But what was I supposed to call him? "Eighth Uncle" seemed the safest, I figured. "Eighth Uncle, we need your help. Here, I'll get down on my knees and beg. As the saying goes, 'Kneeling is the weightiest form of respect.'" Well, that was more than Deputy Yang could bear, and he quickly helped me to my feet. I didn't realize it was all for show until later on. He even took out a handkerchief and wiped his eyes. Then he lifted up the sheet of newspaper and looked into my husband's face. The flies took off with a buzz, and he jumped back in fright. "Fourth Aunt," he said to me, "you can't leave him here. That won't solve anything."

My second son said, "Since Secretary Wang killed my father, the least he could do was show up and admit it. My father may have been a poor man, low on the social ladder, but he was a living, breathing human being. If you run over a dog, at least you offer your apologies to its owner!"

With a squint, Deputy Yang said, "Number Two, when your sister ran off with another man and broke the marriage contract, my poor nephew was an emotional wreck. Now all day long he cries like a baby or laughs like a madman. But even that doesn't alter the fact that we're family. Like they say, a deal gone sour doesn't affect justice and humanity. Now don't take me wrong, but what you say proves you're not using your head. Secretary Wang wasn't driving the car, so how could he have killed your father? The driver was wrong to run into your father, and the courts will deal with him. But by bringing the body to the township compound and attracting hundreds of curious bystanders, you're obstructing township work. By 'township' I mean the government, so obstructing the township is obstructing the government, and that's illegal. You were on the right side of the law at first, but keep this up and you'll wind up on the wrong side. Am I right or not?"

Unswayed by the argument, Number Two replied, "I don't care. Secretary Wang is responsible for what happened, since he was riding in an official car and making deals for garlic when it ran my father down. Now he won't even show his face. That kind of behavior is unacceptable anywhere."

"Number Two, you get farther off the track every time you open your mouth," Deputy Yang said. "Who told you Secretary Wang was making garlic deals? That's slander! Secretary Wang is at an emergency meeting on public security at the county seat. What's more important, an emergency meeting on public security or this affair with your father? When he returns from his meeting, he'll announce measures to deal with criminal behavior that disrupts social order. What you're doing here is a perfect example."

That shut the boy up. So it was his elder brother's turn. "Eighth

Uncle, our father's dead, which isn't uncommon for a man in his sixties. It must have been fate. Otherwise, how come out of all the millions of people walking this earth, he was the one who got hit by the car? Fate had this tragic end planned for him all along. If King Yama of the Underworld wants to claim somebody during the third watch, who would dare hold on till the fifth? I reckon the Underworld has its rules and regulations, just like any other place. So tell us what to do, Eighth Uncle."

"If you ask me," Deputy Yang said, "you should take him home and have him cremated as soon as possible, like the first thing tomorrow, since it's too late today. You can have the crematorium send a hearse for forty yuan. The price of everything else keeps going up, but they still only charge forty yuan for the hearse. A real bargain. If you agree to do it tomorrow, I'll make arrangements for the hearse. I think you should wash him, give him a shave, and dress him in some decent funeral clothes, then stay up with the body tonight, like good filial sons and daughters. The hearse will show up at your door first thing in the morning. Your father never rode in a car while he was alive, so you might as well splurge a bit now that he's gone. Meanwhile I'll talk to the man in charge of the crematorium and get him to fill the urn more than usual with your father's ashes. Then after you take him home, call your friends and relatives together for a wake. That should bring in some needed cash. The head of the household may be gone, but the rest of you have to go on living, don't you? But if you go on like this, not only will you ruin your reputation, you'll make things tough on yourselves for the rest of your lives. Am I right or aren't I, Fourth Aunt?"

Well I told him I was only a woman, so what did I know? I said I'd leave it up to him.

"What worries me," Number Two said, "is that once Father's been cremated, Secretary Wang won't admit to anything."

"Don't talk like a fool, Number Two," Deputy Yang scolded him. "Secretary Wang is a party secretary, after all. More wealth passes through his fingers every day than you can count. As long as you don't make things difficult for him, you won't have to worry about being taken care of. The township government may be small, but it's still government, and the money that slips through the cracks would be enough for you folks to get by on from here on out."

Number One said, "Eighth Uncle, people say we should report this to the county. What do you think?"

"It's your father who's dead, not mine," Deputy Yang replied, "so it's up to you. But I wouldn't, if it were me. It's too late to do anything for him now, so it's time to think about yourselves—in other words, money. I say get it any way you can. If you take your case to the county, even if the driver goes to jail, what good does that do you? Once a case gets into the courts, things have to be done by the book. The most you can hope for then is a few hundred for funeral expenses. With Secretary Wang's connections at the county level, even if the driver is sent to jail, he'll be out in a couple of months and back on the street, doing whatever it is he does. And by offending Secretary Wang, you'll have marked yourselves as undesirables. In that case, you boys can forget about ever seeing a wedding day. On the other hand, if you forget about reporting it, and worry about taking care of the funeral arrangements instead, people will call you just plain folks, and with the reputation of a good family, Secretary Wang will be happy to settle things amicably, to your advantage. Now go do what you think is right."

"Is money the only thing people live for?" Gao Ma asked.

"Aha!" Deputy Yang said. "So you're here, too, are you? What are you up to? First you entice their daughter away, then you get her pregnant without marrying her, and wedding plans for three families—Cao, Fang, and Liu—are scrapped, all because of you. You ruined everything, so what does that make you? Boys, do what you want. There's nothing in it for me, anyway. I don't have to worry about people talking behind my back."

The older Fang boy spoke up: "Gao Ma, you've done enough harm for one person. Go scrape up the ten thousand and take Jinju with you. We don't want a sister like that, and we sure as hell don't want a brother-in-law like you!"

Gao Ma, his face scarlet, walked off without another word.

3

As she lay in her jail cell, Fourth Aunt relived the events surrounding the return of Fourth Uncle from the government compound. Once again it was the lame elder brother in front and the younger brother in the rear, which caused the door to rock and Fourth Uncle's head to loll from side to side. The sound of his head thumping against the door wasn't nearly as crisp as it had been on the way over. No sooner had they emerged onto the street than the gate was closed behind them. Troubled by feelings of emptiness, Fourth Aunt turned to take a last look inside, where she saw a group of administrative types stream into the yard as if popping out of the ground, to gather around Deputy Yang; there were sneers and grins on their faces, Deputy Yang's included.

The passage of Fourth Uncle's corpse attracted far less attention than it had on the way over, when anyone who could walk fell in behind the grisly procession. Now the cortege comprised only a few yapping dogs.

Back home, the brothers laid their poles in front of the gate, making the door thud against the ground and raising clouds of noise from Gao Zhileng's parakeets. Jinju, a blank look in her eyes, opened the gate. "Carry your father inside and lay him on the kang," Fourth Aunt said. Neither son spoke or budged.

"Mother," Number One broke the silence, "people say you shouldn't lay the corpse of someone who's died a violent death on the kang—"

Fourth Aunt cut him off. "Your father worked like a dog all his life, and now that he's dead is he to be denied the comfort of a warm kang? That would be more than I could stand."

Number Two remarked, "He is dead, after all, so a regular bed is just as good. 'Death is like extinguishing a light,' as the saying goes. 'Breath becomes a spring breeze, flesh and bones turn to mud.' If you put him on a heated kang, he'll turn bad even faster."

"In other words, do you plan to let your own father lie outside?"

"It's as good a place as any," Number Two replied. "The cool winds will cut down on the smell, and we'll be spared the trouble of having to carry him outside tomorrow morning."

"And let the dogs get at him?"

"Mother," Number One spoke up, "we'll be skinning the cow and carving up the meat to take to market tomorrow. What Deputy Yang said made sense, especially the part about how the dead are gone, but the survivors have to keep on living."

Poor Fourth Aunt had no choice. Between sobs she said, "Husband, since your sons won't let you sleep on the kang, you'll have to lie out here tonight."

"Don't make yourself feel worse, Mother," the older son said. "Go in and lie down. We'll take care of things out here." He then lit the lantern and set it on a stone roller alongside the threshing floor, while his brother brought out a pair of stools and placed them several feet apart on the ground. They picked up the door on which Fourth Uncle's corpse lay and rested it on the stools.

"Go inside and get some rest, Mother," her older son urged. "We'll watch the body. Say what you want, but Father was fated to die like this, so there's no reason to be so sad."

But she sat down beside the raised door and cleaned maggots out of Fourth Uncle's various openings with a twig while her sons spread a beat-up old tarp out on the threshing floor and rolled the dead cow up onto it until its belly was facing skyward. Then they propped the animal in that position by placing bricks on either side of its backbone. Four legs, stiff as boards, stuck straight up in the air.

Number One picked up a carving knife, Number Two a cleaver. Beginning in the center of the abdomen, they sliced the animal open, then began skinning it, Number One to the east, Number Two to the west. Fourth Aunt's nostrils picked up the powerful stench of the dead cow and of Fourth Uncle.

Sister-in-Law, the murky light from that lantern fell on my husband's face, and his black eyes bored into me until blasts of cold air shot out of every joint in my body. No matter how hard I tried I couldn't dig those maggots out of him. I know it sounds disgusting, but it didn't seem so to me at the time. I hated those maggots, and I squashed every one I got my hands on. And my sons, all they cared about was skinning that cow. Not a thought for their own father. But my daughter carried a basin of water outside to clean his face with damp cotton. And since we didn't have another knife, she trimmed the gray stubble on his chin with a pair of scissors, and even cut back his nose hairs. He cut quite a figure when he was young, but got all shriveled up when he was old, and was a real sight. Then she brought out his dark-green jacket, and the two of us put it on him. I know it doesn't seem right for a couple of women to be dressing a man, but right after I asked my sons to help, I noticed their bloody hands and told them to forget it. Jinju, I said, this is your own father, not some strange man, so let's you and me do it. He was skin and bones, and the clothes helped a lot. All this time, my sons were struggling with that cowhide, until their faces were all sweaty. That reminded me of a joke. An old man calls his three sons to his deathbed. "I'm going to die soon. How do you boys plan to dispose of my body?" The eldest son says, "Dad, we're so poor we can't afford a decent coffin, so I say we buy a cheap pine box, put you in it, and bury you. How does that sound?" "No good," his father says, shaking his head, "no good at all." "Dad," the second son says, "I think we ought to wrap you in an old straw mat and bury you that way. How's that?" "No good," his father says, "no good at all." The third son says, "Dad, here's what I recommend: we chop you into three pieces, skin you, and take everything to market, where we palm you off as dogmeat, beef, and donkey. What do you think of that?" Their father smiles and says, "Number Three knows his father's mind. Now don't forget to add a little water to the meat to keep the weight up." Are you asleep, Sister-in-Law?

Her sons' hands were so coated with blood and gore that the knives kept slipping, so they wiped them off on the ground; the yellow grains of sand that stuck to their hands looked like little gold nuggets. Flies from the government compound, having picked up the smell, came flitting over and landed on the cow's carcass, crawling all over it. Number Two smashed them with the side of his cleaver. Meanwhile, Fourth Aunt told Jinju to get her well-used fan so she could keep the flies from landing on Fourth Uncle's face and producing more maggots.

The sound of birds on the wing broke the silence above them. Dark recesses in the wall were home to the green eyes and urgent pantings of wild creatures.

Around midnight the brothers finally finished skinning the cow. Now the animal was in the raw, except for its four hooves—sort of like a naked man wearing only a pair of shoes. Number Two dumped a bucket of water on the skinned animal; then the boys squatted alongside it and smoked cigarettes. When they finished their smokes, they began the butchering process. "Easy, now," Number One said. "Don't damage the organs." Number Two made an incision in the abdomen, and the animal's guts tumbled out, along with the unborn calf. A hot, rank odor assailed Fourth Aunt's nostrils. The shrieks of birds rent the sky above them.

After evacuating the long coils of intestines, Number Two was about to throw them away when Number One said they went well with wine if you cleaned them up. As for the calf, he said that an unborn bovine fetus had medicinal properties, and that people got rich palming it off as balm of deer uterus.

Don't be so sad, Sister-in-Law. You say they gave you five years? Well, those years will just fly by, and by the time you get out, your son will be a useful member of society.

4

"Better to be a military advisor than a property divider," the village boss, Gao Jinjiao, said. "Why me? 'Officials who don't bail people out of jams should stay home and plant their yams.' Okay, let's hear what each of you has to say, and confine it to the here and now."

"Director," Number One said, "we want you to divide it up."

So Gao Jinjiao began. "You have a four-room house. One for each brother, two for Fourth Aunt. When she dies—I don't mean to make you feel bad, Fourth Aunt, but the truth isn't always pleasant—each of you gets one of her rooms. Since one is larger than the other, the smaller one includes the gate and the arch above it. The kitchen utensils will be divided into three portions; then you'll draw lots to see who gets which portion. Damages for Fourth Uncle and the cow came to three thousand six hundred yuan, which divides out to twelve hundred apiece. There is thirteen hundred yuan in the bank, so each son gets four hundred, Fourth Aunt gets five. When Gao Ma hands over the ten thousand, half will go to Fourth Aunt, the other half will be divided equally between the two brothers. When Jinju marries, Fourth Aunt will be responsible for the dowry. You boys are welcome to help out, but no one's forcing you to. Your grain stores will be divided into three and a half portions, with Jinju getting the half-portion. When Fourth Aunt gets to the age where she can't take care of herself, you boys will take turns caring for her, alternating every month or every year, however you want to work it out. That's about it. Have I forgotten anything?"

"What about the garlic?" Elder Brother asked.

"Divide that into three portions as well," Gao Jinjiao replied. "But is Fourth Aunt able to go to market and sell her share of the garlic at her age? Number One, why not add her share to yours, and you sell it at the market, then divide the profits?"

"Director, with this leg of mine . . ."

"Okay, then, how about you, Number Two?"

"If he won't do it, I'll be damned if I will!"

"This is your mother we're talking about, not some total stranger."

"I don't need their help. I'll sell it myself!" Fourth Aunt proclaimed.

"That settles it," Number Two said.

"Anything else?" Gao Jinjiao asked.

Number One said, "I recall he had a new jacket."

"Nothing gets past you, does it, you little bastard?" Fourth Aunt snapped at her son. "That jacket's for me."

"Remember the saying," Number One protested. "'Father's jacket, Mother's bindings, next generation riches finding.' Why do you want to keep his jacket?"

"Since we're dividing things up, let's do it right," Number Two remarked.

"Majority rules," Gao Jinjiao declared. "You'd better bring it out, Fourth Aunt."

She opened the beat-up old chest and took out the jacket.

"Brother," Number One said, "now that we've divided up all the family property, my bachelorhood is settled once and for all. Since you can easily find a wife, I should get the jacket."

"Dear Brother," Number Two replied, "I can eat shit, I just don't like the taste. Since we're dividing the family property, we have to be fair. No one should do better than anyone else."

"One jacket, and both of you want it," Gao Jinjiao commented. "Any ideas? Except for cutting it in two, that is."

"Then cut it in two if that's the only way," Number Two demanded. Picking the jacket up, he draped it over a wood stump, went inside for his cleaver, and split the jacket right down the middle seam, as Fourth Aunt looked on and cried her eyes out. Then, gritting his teeth with the fire of determination in his eyes, he picked up the two halves and tossed one to his brother. "Half for you and half for me," he said. "We're even." A sneering Jinju picked up a pair of worn-out shoes. "These were Father's. One for you and one for you!"—and she flung a single shoe at each of her brothers.

CHAPTER 16

Arrest me if that's what you want . . .
Someone read the Criminal Code aloud for me—
Blind lawbreakers get lenient treatment—
I won't shut my mouth just because you put me in jail. . . .

> – from a ballad by Zhang Kou sung after being touched on the mouth
> with a policeman's electric prod. The incident occurred in a tiny
> lane around the corner from the county government compound on
> the twenty-ninth of May, 1987

1

A jailer led him down the long corridor while another walked behind him to the right, pressing a rifle muzzle up against his ribs. An identical gray metal door with an identical small opening fronted each cell, the only differences being the Arabic numbers above the doors and the faces looking out through the tiny openings. They were bloated, grotesquely enlarged, the faces of living ghosts. He shuddered. Every step was torture. Behind one of the windows a female convict giggled. "Jailer, here's twenty cents, buy me some sanitary napkins, okay?" The jailer responded with an angry curse: "Slut!" But when Gao Yang turned to see what the woman looked like, he felt a nudge from the rifle. "Keep moving!"

Reaching the end of the corridor, they passed through a steel door and climbed a narrow, rickety staircase. The jailer's leather shoes clacked loudly on the wooden, steps, while the slaps of Gao Yang's bare feet were barely audible. The warm, dry wood felt so much better on his feet than the damp, slippery concrete corridor floor. Up and up he climbed, with no end in sight; he was soon panting, and as the staircase wound steeply round, he began to get dizzy. If not for the jailer behind him, silently nudging him along with his rifle, he'd have lain down like a dying dog, spread out over as many steps as were required to support him. His injured ankle throbbed like a pulsating heart; the surrounding skin was so puffy his anklebone all but disappeared. It burned and ached. Old man in heaven, please don't let it get infected, he uttered in silent prayer. Would that aristocratic woman be willing to lance it and release the pus? That thought reminded him of how she had smelled.

A large room with a wooden floor painted red. White plaster shows through the peeling green paint on the walls. Bright daylight shines down from the ceiling on four crackling electric prods. Desks line the northern wall. A male and two female jailers sit behind the desks. One of the women has a face like a persimmon fresh from the garden. He recognizes the words painted on the wall behind them.

A jailer orders him to sit on the floor, for which he is immensely grateful. He is then told to stretch his legs out in front and rest his manacled hands on his knees. He does as he's told.

"Is your name Gao Yang?"

"Yes."

"Age?"

"Forty-one."

"Occupation?"

"Farmer."

"Family background?"

"Um . . . my, uh, parents were landlords. . . ."

"Are you familiar with government policy?"

"Yes. Leniency to those who confess, severity to those who refuse to do so. Not coming clean brings severe punishment."

"Good. Now tell us about your criminal activities of May twenty-eighth."

2

Dark clouds filled the sky on May 28 as Gao Yang drove his donkey; it was scrawnier than ever, after exhausting itself day after day lugging eighty bundles of wilting garlic to town so Gao Yang could try his luck again. Nine days since Fourth Uncle had met his tragic end, but it seemed like an eternity. During that period Gao Yang had made four trips to town, selling fifty bundles of garlic for a total of a hundred twenty yuan, minus eighteen yuan for the various fees and taxes, which left him a profit of one hundred and two. The eighty bundles he was hauling now should have been sold two days earlier at a purchasing station set up north of the tracks by the South Counties Supply and Marketing Cooperative, which was buying garlic at fifty fen a pound. But just as Gao Yang reached the scales with his load, a gang of men in gray uniforms and wide-brimmed hats showed up, led by Wang Tai.

Gao Yang nodded obsequiously to Wang Tai, who, ignoring him, went up and began arguing with the co-op representatives, eventually knocking over their scales. "No one's going to walk off with a single stalk of Paradise garlic until *my* storehouse is filled," Wang Tai insisted. The dejected representatives of the South Counties Supply and Marketing Cooperative climbed into their trucks and drove off.

So Gao Yang packed up his garlic. But before he left, he tried again to get the attention of Wang Tai as he walked off with his men.

Dark clouds filled the sky two days later, on May 28. It looked like rain. Gao Yang had just crossed the tracks when someone up ahead passed word down: "The supply and marketing co-op's storehouses are full, so now we can sell our garlic anywhere we want."

"But where? The locals have already squeezed out us farmers from outlying districts. They don't care if we live or die."

As the talk heated up, feelings of helplessness began to grip the farmers, but none turned his cart around and headed home. It was as if their only hope lay up ahead somewhere.

The line of wagons pressed forward, so Gao Yang fell in behind them, gradually realizing that instead of heading toward the cold-storage area, they were rolling down the renowned May First Boulevard on their way to May First Square, directly in front of the county government compound.

As the number of garlic farmers increased, the air above the square grew increasingly pungent. Dark clouds roiled above the downcast farmers, who began to grumble and swear. Zhang Kou, the blind minstrel, stood atop a rickety oxcart, strumming his *erhu* and chanting loudly in his raspy voice, froth bubbling at the corners of his mouth. His song plucked the heartstrings of everyone within earshot; Gao Yang couldn't speak for the others, but he felt sad one moment and angry the next, with a measure of hidden fear mixed in. He had a premonition that trouble was brewing that day, for there, in a nearby lane, some people—he couldn't tell who—were taking pictures of the square. He wanted to turn his wagon around and put some distance between him and this dangerous spot, but was hemmed in.

The county government compound was on the northern side of the boulevard, running past the public square. Pines and poplars grew tall and green behind the wall; fresh flowers bloomed everywhere; and a column of water rose in the center of the compound, only to fan out and rain down on the fountain below. The government offices were housed in a handsome three-story building with glass-inlaid arched eaves and yellow ceramic tiles set in the walls. A bright red flag billowed atop a flagpole. The place was as grand as an imperial palace. Traffic on May First Boulevard was blocked by the carts and wagons and their loads of garlic. Impatient drivers honked their horns, but their sonorous complaints were ignored. Noticing the carefree looks on others' faces, Gao Yang relaxed. Why worry? he thought. The worst that can happen is I lose my load of garlic.

Zhang Kou, the blind minstrel, sang: ". . . Hand baby to Mother to stem its grief. / If you can't sell your garlic, look up the county administrator. . . ."

The heavy wrought-iron gate was shut tight. Well-dressed office workers peeked through windows to watch the goings-on in the square, where hundreds of people were massed before the gate. A cry went up: "Come out, County Administrator! Come out here, Zhong Weimin! If your name really means 'Serve the People,' then do it!"

Fists and clubs pounded the gate, but the compound remained still as death—not a person in sight, until an old caretaker came out to secure the gate with a huge padlock. While he was about his business, phlegm and spittle rained down on his clothes and face. Not daring to say a word, he turned and darted inside.

"Hey, you old dog, you old watchdog, come back and open this gate!" the crowd bellowed.

By now the horns of the jammed-up cars were silent. Drivers leaned out their windows to see what was going on.

"Get the county administrator or the party secretary out here to give us an explanation!"

"Get out here, Zhong Weimin!"

Gao Yang saw a horse-faced young man perched on a cart, like a crane standing amid a flock of chickens. "Fellow townsmen," he shouted, "don't just yell anything that comes to mind! The county administrator won't hear you that way. F-follow my lead!" He had a slight stammer. The crowd roared its approval.

"His name is 'Serve the People,' but he should change it to 'Serve Myself!" The horse-faced young man shook his fist.

The shout was repeated by the crowd, including Gao Yang, who was so caught up in the heat of the moment he too shook his fist.

"County Administrator, Master 'Serve the People' Zhong, come out and face your people!" The horse-faced young man had a strange look on his face; his lips hardly moved.

The crowd echoed his shout, a deafening roar to which Gao Yang contributed.

"Officials who don't bail people out of jams should stay home and plant their yams!" Everyone knew that slogan, so they shouted it over and over.

Finally two men in Western suits emerged from the building and walked up to the gate. "Garlic farmers, quiet down! Quiet down, I said!"

The crowd held its collective tongue to observe the newcomers on the other side of the gate. The gaunt-faced one pointed to the middle-aged man beside him, who wore tinted sunglasses, and said, "Garlic farmers, this is Deputy Director Pang of the County Government Administrative Office. He has instructions."

"Garlic farmers, I am here on behalf of the county administrator, who wants you all to go home and stop this unlawful and potentially explosive demonstration. Don't let a few rabble-rousers lead you astray!"

"What about our garlic?" someone shouted.

"The county administrator says that since the co-op cold-storage storehouse is filled to capacity, take your garlic home with you. What you do with it is your business. If you can sell it, well and good. If not, eat it yourselves!"

"Go fuck yourself! You're the ones who told us to plant the stuff, and now you refuse to take it off our hands. Is this some sick joke?"

"To keep us from selling our crops, you confiscated or smashed the scales!'

"We can't give the stuff away now!"

"Come out here, Zhong Weimin! Officials who don't bail people out of jams should fuck off and plant their yams!"

"Back off, garlic farmers!" Deputy Director Pang screamed angrily, his face sweaty. "The county administrator can't come out now. He has important business to attend to. Don't you understand that he's in charge of an entire county? His hands are full just taking care of really important matters. You don't expect him to sell your garlic for you, too, do you?"

Gao Yang felt his heart go thump as he listened to Deputy Director Pang's harangue. That's right, he's in charge of the whole county, and we can't expect him to sell our garlic for us, can we? Of course not, even if we have to let it rot. He wished he could quietly leave and go home, but he was boxed in by wagons and farmers. He was nearly in tears.

"Tell him to come out and talk to us!"

"Right! Bring out the county administrator! Bring out the county administrator!"

"Garlic farmers," Deputy Director Pang shouted, "I'm warning you—turn around and go home, right now, or we'll call the police and let them teach you some manners!"

"Fellow townsmen," the horse-faced young man raised his voice, "don't fall for their scare tactics! We're not breaking any law. Who says it's illegal for the people to ask to see the county administrator? He's an elected public servant, and we're within our rights to see him."

"Who the fuck elected him? I couldn't tell you if his face was black or white! How did he get elected?"

"Zhong Weimin, get out here! Zhong Weimin, get out here!"

"Now you've gone too far!" Deputy Director Pang thundered.

"Down with corrupt officials! Down with bureaucrats!" Gao Yang saw Gao Ma climb onto the oxcart and shake his fist.

Gao Ma picked up a bundle of garlic and flung it into the compound. "We don't want this stuff. Put it on the old masters' dinner tables!"

"Right, we don't want it. It's worthless, anyhow! Get rid of it! Throw it into the county compound to feed the old masters!"

Frenzy gripped the crowd, as thousands of bundles of garlic sprouted wings and flew across the wall, landing in heaps inside the government compound.

Deputy Director Pang turned to make a dash for the building. "Stop him!" someone shouted. "He's going to call the police!"

The heavy gate shuddered violently as the people up front crashed into it. Clubs, fists, feet, shoulders, bricks, and tiles all became weapons as the gate began to yield to the assault.

"Storm the compound! If the county administrator won't come talk to us, we'll go find him!"

Emitting one last gasp, the lock snapped, and the gate flew open in the face of a surging tide of people. Poor Gao Yang was swept along, powerless to resist. He hadn't thrown a single bundle of his precious garlic, and was worried that his donkey might get trampled. But he was not even able to look behind him.

The crowd carried him along, his feet barely touching the octagonal slabs of cement covering the ground; his face was moistened by an icy spray as he passed the fountain. The crowd surged into the office building, where a grand clatter echoed across the tiled floor, compounded by the crisp tinkle of shattering glass, the thud of splintering cabinets, and the shrieks of terrified women. A sense of ecstasy crept into Gao Yang's mounting anxiety as he saw the destruction of luxurious trappings that induced in him feelings of envy and hatred. As an initial probe, he picked up a flowering cactus in a shallow red-and-pink vase and flung it at a window whose glass was polished until it shone. It parted without a murmur, allowing the vase and its contents to pass slowly through. He ran to the window in time to see the red-and-pink vase, the green cactus, and shards of window glass dance and skitter across the concrete ground. The vase broke, the detached petals scattered in all directions. A gratifying sight. Then he went back, picked up an oval aquarium, and admired the plump black and orange goldfish for a moment. The sloshing water and filthy debris rising from the bottom alarmed the aquarium's denizens, which began splashing frantically, releasing a fishy odor that he found extremely disagreeable. He flung it against another window, which also disintegrated slowly as he ran up to watch the aquarium float downward, followed by glistening drops of water and sparkling shards of glass. The black and orange goldfish swam in midair. When it hit the concrete below, the aquarium shattered without a sound.

Unsettled by the sight of goldfish flapping around on the concrete below, he looked up and saw that the square was alive with people and animals, all in motion. His donkey and wagon were nowhere in sight, he noted with chagrin. Throngs of people poured into the compound, as a phalanx of armed policemen in white uniforms emerged from a lane east of the square and swarmed over it like tigers on a flock of sheep, swinging their batons to clear a path to the compound. He turned away from the window, concentrating on getting out of there as fast as his legs would carry him. But his way was blocked by dozens of people who by then had flocked into the office. He could hardly believe his eyes when he spotted Fourth Aunt Fang, who had hobbled in on tiny bound feet. A youngster in a white vest with an anchor logo shouted, "This is the county administrator's office. Let's hunt him down!" Oh my God! Gao Yang thought, the young man's shout hitting him like a thunderbolt. The county administrator's office! It was his vase, his aquarium, his windows. He would have fled if he could, but there were too many sticks and clubs fanning the air between him and the door. Vases with exotic plants came off the floor and began flying out the windows like so many artillery shells. One of them must have hit someone, if the string of screams and curses below were any indication.

Scrolls were ripped off the walls, and one young fellow even smashed a filing cabinet with a dumbbell, sending files, documents, and books tumbling out into a pile. He then used the same dumbbell to smash two telephones on the desk.

Meanwhile, Fourth Aunt was grabbing everything in sight, including some green satin curtains, which she pulled down and began tearing to shreds, as if ripping a rival's hair. "Give me back my husband!" she screamed through her tears. "I want my husband back!"

While farmers rifled desk drawers, the young fellow put his dumbbell to work smashing the glass top and metal ashtray. The county administrator had cleared out so fast that his cigarette was still smoldering in the ashtray. Spotting a tin of ginseng cigarettes and a box of matches on the desk, the young fellow stuck one of the former between his lips and announced, "I'm going to try out the old magistrate's throne." With that he sat down in the county administrator's rattan chair, leaned back, lit up, and crossed his feet on the desk, looking mighty pleased with himself, as the other farmers rushed up to fight over the remaining cigarettes. Fourth Aunt, who had made a pile of the torn curtains, scrolls, and files, lit a match from the box on the desk and touched it to the satin curtains, which began to burn at once. Amid puffs of smoke, the paper then caught fire, sending tongues of flames snaking up the smashed cabinets by the wall. Falling to her knees, she banged her head on the floor in a kowtow and muttered, "Husband, I've avenged your death!"

The fire quickly spread, forcing the farmers into the hallway. On his way out the door, Gao Yang grabbed Fourth Aunt and yelled, "Run for your life!"

Dense smoke swirling up and down the hallway indicated that more than one office had been torched. Everything was shaking—the ceiling above and the stairs below. People ran and clawed for their lives. As Gao Yang dragged Fourth Aunt out the entrance, he thought about the black and orange goldfish, but only for a fleeting moment, since with a thousand heads and twice that many legs fighting over limited space, anyone who stumbled was sure to be trampled—already you could hear the screams. Holding Fourth Aunt's hand in a deathlike grip, he virtually flew out of the compound, past the blurred faces of seven or eight armed policemen.

3

"Was it you who led the mob that demolished the county administrator's office?"

"Mr. Jailer, I didn't know it was his office. . . . I stopped as soon as I found out." He was on his knees.

"Sit down like you're supposed to!" the policeman demanded roughly. "Do you mean to say if it had been somebody else's office it would have been okay?"

"Mr. Jailer, I didn't know what I was doing. I got swept along with the crowd. . . . I've been a model citizen all my life. I've never done anything bad."

"If you weren't such a model citizen you'd have torched the State Council Headquarters, I suppose," the policeman said derisively.

"I didn't start the fire. Fourth Aunt did that."

A policewoman handed a sheet of paper to the policeman in the center, who read it aloud. "Is this an accurate statement of what you said, Gao Yang?" he asked.

"Yes."

"Come over here and sign it."

One of the policemen dragged him over to the desk, where the policewoman handed him a pen. His hand shook as he held it. Were there two vertical strokes in "Yang," or three? "Three," the police-woman told him.

"Take him back to his cell."

"Mr. Jailer," Gao Yang fell to his knees again and begged, "I'm afraid to go back there. . . ."

"Why?"

"Because they gang up on me. Please, Mr. Jailer, put me in another cell!"

"Let him bunk with the condemned prisoner," the policeman in the center said to his colleagues.

"Want to bunk with a condemned man, Number Nine?"

"Anything, just so you don't put me back with them!"

"Okay, but make sure he doesn't try to kill himself. That'll be your job, for which you'll get an extra bun at each meal."

4

The condemned man, sallow-faced, clean-shaven, with green eyes that rolled around his sunken sockets, terrified Gao Yang, who was in his new cell only a few seconds before realizing what a terrible mistake he'd made. Except for a single cot, the cell was furnished only with a rotting straw mat. The condemned man, manacled hand and foot, hunkered in the corner and glared menacingly at Gao Yang, who nodded and bowed slightly. "Elder Brother, they sent me to keep you company."

The condemned man's lips split into what passed for a smile. His face was the color of gold foil, and so were his teeth. "Come over here," he said with a nod.

Gao Yang was wary, but the manacles were reassuring—how much damage could he do all trussed up like that? Cautiously he approached the condemned man, who smiled and nodded, urging him to come closer, and closer, and closer.

"Elder Brother, is there something you want?"

The words were barely out of Gao Yang's mouth when the condemned man reached out and banged Gao Yang's head with the handcuff chain. With a cry of pain, Gao Yang crawled and rolled over to the cell door, followed by the condemned man, who hopped in pursuit, murder in his eyes, his manacles scraping the floor. Gao Yang slipped under the outstretched arms and darted over to the bed, only to be driven back to the door when the man came after him again. That went on another dozen times or so, until the condemned man plopped down on the bed and said through clenched teeth, "Don't come near me or I'll bite your head off. Since I'm going to die, I want somebody to lead the way."

An exhausted Gao Yang forced himself to stay away that night. The overhead light, which was left on twenty-four hours a day, allowed a measure of well-being as he curled up on the floor alongside the door, putting as much distance between him and his cellmate as possible.

The condemned man's greenish eyes stayed open all night long, and whenever Gao Yang started to doze off, he stood up. Gradually the threat of danger sharpened Gao Yang's senses: at the first sign of a rattle he sprang to his feet and readied himself for another confrontation.

At dawn the condemned man finally rested his head against the wall and closed his eyes. He looked dead already. Gao Yang recalled hearing people talk when he was just a boy about the scary business of spending the night with a corpse. They said that late at night, when everyone's asleep, the dead rise to haunt the living, chasing them round and round until cockcrow, when they finally lie down again. The night just past was pretty much like that, except that spending the night with a corpse could earn you a tidy sum, while all he'd get for watching his condemned cellmate was an extra bun at mealtime.

At this rate, he thought, I'll be dead in a month.

He could kick himself.

Old man upstairs, get me out of here. If you do, I'll never complain, never fight, never ask for help, even if someone dumps a load of shit on my head.

CHAPTER 17

Townsfolk, hard work and sweat never hurt anyone.
Dig wells, lug water, fight the drought:
Watering the garlic makes it grow an inch a night—
Each inch is the gold you turn into cash. . . .

– from a ballad by Zhang Kou urging the townsfolk
to fight the April drought

1

A bright full moon rose slowly like a voluptuous flower, its beams carrying a strong bouquet of new posies that settled over the vast wild-woods. Dry, warm breezes, unique to April, swept across the fields. No rain had fallen in months, leaving the land as parched and chapped as the farmers' lips. Crops were coated with rust; newly emerged garlic shoots hung their heads in dejection.

Glimmers of lantern light dotted the fields where farmers irrigated their garlic crops by hand. Gao Ma was one of them. Well water was at a premium—no more than twenty bucketfuls came up before the dry bottom reappeared—so he trotted more than a hundred yards to a piece of land farmed by the old graybeard Wang Changli to pass the time while he waited for the next buildup.

Old Man Wang's well was outfitted with a windlass, but the water level was no higher than anyone else's. It had just gone dry when Gao Ma ran up.

"Take a break, Grandpa Three, and have a smoke," Gao Ma said.

"Sure, why not?" the old man said, edging his wooden bucket over to the rim of the well with his foot.

"How about a story?" Gao Ma rolled a cigarette and handed it to Old Man Wang.

"Now, where would I get a story?" the old man said as he puffed on the cigarette, the glow turning his lips bright red.

The crisp gurgle of water flowing into the well rose to merge with the sputtering of a diesel engine in the distance. Leaves of irrigated garlic plants reached out to catch the dimmed moonbeams. A raven flying near the moon sent loud caws earthward.

"Ever been to Zhang Family Bay?" Old Man Wang asked.

"No."

"The frogs there never croak."

"How come?"

"Listen, and I'll tell you."

Moonbeams streamed through the barred window of the solitary confinement cell reserved for serious offenders like Gao Ma.

A mother and her son once lived in Zhang Family Bay. Her name was Zhang née Liu; her son's name was Nine-five. Little Nine-five was smarter than the other boys, so his mother went out begging to earn his tuition. But Nine-five, a mischievous little boy, was forever getting into trouble. His teacher always left the room after passing out the homework assignments. Why? Since that's a story in itself, I'll start with it.

The mother of one of the students, a boy named Winter-born, was a real beauty, so the story goes. Everyone called her Teapot Lid. One day the teacher asked Winter-born, "Does your mother ever think about me, Winter-born?" When he went home that day, Winter-born said to his mother, "Mother, the teacher wants to know if you ever think about him." His mother smiled but said nothing. One day led to another, and each time the teacher saw Winter-born he asked the same question. And Winter-born dutifully went home and told his mother. One day, after the teacher asked, as always, and his student went home and told his mother, as always, she said, "Tell your teacher that I do think about him, and invite him to drop by tomorrow." The next day, after the student had carried out his mother's wishes, the teacher hurriedly passed out the assignment, turned, and bolted out of the classroom. Where was he headed? To Winter-born's house, where the boy's mother was sitting on the kang, face powdered and hair oiled. The moment he laid eyes on her, he rushed up like a cat pouncing on a mouse and began fondling her breasts and kissing her on the mouth. She let his hands roam freely until he tried to undo her waistband. Yet he persisted until the waistband was loosened. But then came a knock at the door. "Oh-oh," she exclaimed, "it's Winter-born's father!" The teacher was scared silly. What to do? The knocking at the door grew more urgent. "Teacher," Winter-born's mother said, "there's a millstone in the back room. Pretend you're a donkey turning the millstone." Caring only about his own skin, the teacher jumped at the idea. A millstone stood in the center of the room, just as she had said. Two pecks of raw wheat had been spread over it, waiting to be ground. So, grabbing the handle, he began turning the millstone; neither too large nor too small, it was just the right size for a grown man. Through the door he heard Winter-born's mother climb slowly off the kang and open the door for her husband, who demanded, "What were you doing in here—committing adultery?" "How dare you!" she replied indignantly. "I borrowed a donkey to turn the millstone, since we're out of flour, as you very well know." 'An obedient animal?" he asked. "No, it took forever to hitch it up to the millstone," she said with a pout. "That's why it took me so long to answer the door." She continued: "And for that I get accused of committing adultery!" "Wait here," Winter-born's father said, "while I go give that bastard of a donkey a good beating. That should make you feel better." The teacher, nearly filling his shorts and peeing his pants, turned the millstone with renewed vigor. "Hear that?" Winter-born's mother said. "The donkey heard you and started pulling even harder." "Warm me a pot of wine," Winter-born's father said, after which the teacher overheard the couple drink and whisper and giggle on the kang. How to describe the feeling that flooded his heart—sweet, sour, bitter, spicy? He couldn't say for sure, but as he pondered these thoughts, his movements slowed. "You borrowed a lazy donkey," Winter-born's father said. "I'm going in there to give the bastard a good beating!" That got the teacher moving again—he nearly flew around that millstone. "No need," Winter-born's mother said. "It speeds up every time it hears your voice." The sweaty-faced teacher turned the mill for all he was worth. "Teapot Lid, since the boy isn't home, let's have some fun," Winter-born's father said. "Why, you greedy thing!" she said. "What if the donkey hears us?" "I'll go stop up its ears," Winter-born's father said. The rattled teacher nearly flew around that millstone. "No need for that," Winter-born's mother said. "All it cares about is turning the millstone. It's not interested in what we do." So the teacher listened to them have their fun, getting a taste of how the mute feels when he eats bitter herbs and can tell no one. Their frolicking ended, Winter-born's father said, "I have to go till the field on the southern slope." "Go ahead," Winter-born's mother said. And he did, shutting the door behind him. The teacher crumpled into the rut around the millstone as Winter-born's mother rushed into the room. "Teacher, get out of here, fast, while Winter-born's father is out in the field!" And he did. Several days later, Winter-born said to the teacher, "Master, my mother says she's been thinking about you again." The teacher grabbed the boy's hand and smacked it with his pointer. "You little bastard!" he cursed. "Have you run out of flour again?"

Gao Ma laughed loud and long. "Now there's a teacher who knows what it means to suffer!"

"There's truth to the saying that warmth and comfort give rise to lurid desires, but hunger and cold produce thoughts of larceny," Old Man Wang said. "Thieves and robbers ran wild a few years back, but there aren't as many now as there once were. Adultery cases, on the other hand, are way up. If you'd been good and hungry, my boy, Jinju wouldn't have a big belly today."

An embarrassed Gao Ma said, "Grandpa Three, with us it's love. Sooner or later we'll get married."

The old-timer shook his head. "My boy, there's a dark cloud over your head. Blood will be spilled within a hundred days. Be careful, and stay indoors whenever possible."

"I don't believe in that mumbo-jumbo," Gao Ma said.

"You must believe," Old Man Wang said cryptically. "Two suns appeared in the sky this spring. A bad sign. Over New Year's I watched some TV at Gao Zhileng's, and the man—or maybe it was a woman—on the screen sang a song that went, 'A great fire, a great fire, a great fire burns a corner of the Northeast.' That was a bad sign, too."

Gao Ma rolled over. Everything the old man said has come true, Gao Ma reflected. I got into trouble, and there was a forest fire in the Northeast. With someone sick at home, it's easy to become a believer. There's more to Old Man Wang than I thought.

"Well, back to the crops," Old Man Wang said. "We can talk some more the next time the well dries up."

I was happy back then, Gao Ma recalled, and when he thought about the teacher turning the millstone, he nearly laughed all over again. There was half a meter of water at the bottom of the well. I scooped it up for my garlic crop. The young shoots were green under the full moon, which seemed smaller and brighter. The air was fresh and clean, the garlic shoots sparkled like quicksilver, and silvery water slithered down the irrigation troughs. I had confidence back then. I placed my hopes on the crop. To me that garlic was everything. Now it's all gone. I have nothing.

"That dog whelp at the weights and measures office took my scale."

"No cursing allowed," the policeman demanded.

"He said my scale wasn't accurate, and when I opened my mouth to protest, he crushed the thing under his heel. Then he fined me ten yuan. All I could think was, the price of garlic dropped from sixty fen a pound to twenty, and finally all the way down to three. The agreements we signed with other counties to purchase our garlic were canceled, and when buyers came, they were turned back by the supply and marketing co-op. All to make things hard on garlic farmers. The more I thought about it, the angrier I got, and that's when I jumped up on the wagon and started shouting slogans. The first was 'Down with corrupt officials!' and the other was 'Down with bureaucrats!' Find me guilty of whatever you want. It's up to you. I'm all alone, so it doesn't matter one way or the other. Cut off my head or put a bullet in it, even bury me alive if you want. It's all the same to me. I hate you dog-bastard officials! All you know how to do is trample the people! I hate you!"

"Time for a smoke break, Grandpa Three," Gao Ma said.

Old Man Wang edged the pail up alongside the well with his foot and squatted down.

The moon was so bright and clear the whole world seemed lighted up.

"Got your garlic crop fertilized, Grandpa Three?"

"Not this time. To hell with it," Old Man Wang said bluntly. "I don't trust those money grubbers at the supply and marketing co-op. How do I know what they put in their fertilizer?"

"You're being too cautious. They can't adulterate chemical fertilizers."

"Like they say, there's never been an honest merchant. You don't think they get rich by being legitimate, do you?" Old Man Wang said spitefully. "It's an imperial edict."

"Just because it's an imperial edict doesn't mean it has to be that way forever, does it?"

"Forever and ever," Old Man Wang said. "The frogs at Zhang Family Bay still don't croak."

"Was that an imperial edict, too? Which Emperor?"

"Let me pick up where I left off last time."

Gao Ma drew his shoulders in. He felt a chill.

When the teacher slipped out of the classroom, Zhang Nine-five went up to the teacher's desk, sat down, and took charge of the class, ordering all the little mischief makers to form two teams and fight it out. When that was done, he dispensed honors and punishments, just like an emperor. After several days of this, the teacher happened to observe Nine-five's little game from his vantage point outside the door. He coughed to announce his presence before entering the room, where the students had quickly returned to their seats and were noisily reciting their lessons. Quickly bringing the class to order, the teacher asked, "Have you prepared your lesson Nine-five?" Zhang Nine-five rose to his feet, leafed through his book, and replied, "Yes. I have." "You little bastard," the teacher muttered under his breath, "you call that preparing? . . . All right," he said aloud, "let's hear it." Snapping his book shut, Zhang Nine-five looked up. *Blah blah blah*—he recited the entire lesson, every single word of it. The teacher nodded and said, "Take your seat, Nine-five." But from that day on he treated Zhang Nine-five differently, spending far more time instructing him than he did any of the other students. And Zhang Nine-five took to his lessons like a cow takes to grass. In less than six months, the teacher had poured all his meager knowledge into his student's head. It was time to move on, and on the eve of his departure he left a note for Zhang Nine-five: "Nine-five, Nine-five, with the heavenly constellations as my witness, you will have a meteoric rise in your career. I hope you don't forget your old teacher." Well, the next person on the scene was a teacher of vast learning who was also a remarkable judge of talent; he immediately waived Zhang Nine-five's tuition. This act set in motion a series of frequent heart-to-heart talks between teacher and student, whose relationship could not have been closer. After one late-night talk, the teacher crawled into bed under the mosquito netting, leaving Nine-five to sleep on his desk. It was a summer night, the kind mosquitoes dearly love. Again and again they stung the teacher through the netting. But Nine-five slept through the onslaught, his breathing calm and even. The bewildered teacher sat up and asked loudly, 'Aren't the mosquitoes biting you, Nine-five?" Nine-five replied, "There are no mosquitoes." "No mosquitoes?" His teacher was amazed. "Aren't you hot?" "Not at all," Zhang Nine-five replied. "Let's change places, Nine-five," the teacher said. "You sleep under the netting and I'll take the desk. What do you say?" "All right," Nine-five agreed. And that's what they did. When the teacher stretched out on top of the desk, cool breezes swept over him. Not a mosquito anywhere. He could not explain the mystery, though not for lack of trying. But then his thoughts were interrupted by a voice in the air: "Damned idiots! The Emperor's gone, so stop wasting your time fanning the air above this poor pedant!" As the sound of the voice faded way, the swarm of mosquitoes regrouped overhead, united in their buzzing. The stifling heat returned with a vengeance, and the teacher jumped to his feet, a silent prayer on his lips: Save me, gods and spirits, and forgive me!

"That's a sad excuse for a story," Gao Ma complained. "A pack of lies to protect the interests of the feudal class. They assume for themselves the role of genius and superman to keep the masses under their thumbs."

"You can recite your lessons or you can accept the truth. The frogs in Zhang Family Bay still don't croak. What do you say to that?"

Grandpa Three picked up where he had left off.

The teacher had known that Zhang Nine-five was not going to grow up to be a flash-in-the-pan scholar, but the true Son of Heaven. Just think, the Son of Heaven! He with the golden mouth and teeth of jade! The teacher rejoiced inwardly. Just think, you, the Emperor's mentor, a great man in his own right! From that point on, not only did the teacher waive Zhang Nine-five's tuition, he even assumed personal responsibility for mother and son's living expenses, down to the last copper. Needless to say, Nine-five and his mother were immensely grateful. Now, the teacher had a sixteen-year-old daughter at home, a girl of unsurpassed beauty and great literary potential. Struck with an inspiration, he sought out Nine-five's mother. "Elder Sister-in-Law, may I be so bold as to discuss Nine-five's marital situation with you? I have a humble daughter at home, and would like to propose that she look after your esteemed son." A startled Madame Zhang née Liu replied, "Dear Teacher, how can we, a lowly widow and fatherless child, aspire to kinship with you?" "Elder Sister-in-Law, you honor me. I shall bring my daughter over tomorrow, and we can hold the ceremony then." Mother Zhang shed tears of gratitude, then went home and told Nine-five, who had already seen his teacher's spectacularly beautiful daughter. He couldn't agree fast enough. The very next day they were wed—a gifted scholar and a talented beauty. The romantic prospects were endless. I'll leave it to you to imagine what went on that night, but from then on, Zhang Nine-five threw himself into his studies. Then one day he took his bride to burn incense at the City God Temple, where he spotted a writing brush and paper on the altar. Itching to put them to use, he picked up the brush and wrote: "City God, City God, hie thee to Luoyang. Leave this very night, return on the morrow." Then, laying down the brush, he left the temple and returned home with his wife. That night his teacher dreamed he saw the City God carrying a bottle of Maotai spirits. (Come on, now, where would he get a bottle of Maotai? I'm just using that as an example for the story!) He also carried a meaty pig's head. "Esteemed Minister," he said, "I beg you to plead the case of this insignificant City God with the Emperor. Get him to retract the imperial edict commanding me to go to Luoyang tonight and return tomorrow night. Tell me, sir, how can I manage a trip of a thousand miles in a single day?" The teacher was jolted awake by this startling development. Ah, it was only a dream. He rubbed his eyes and sat up. But, after lighting the lamp, he walked into the next room, where he saw a bottle of Maotai spirits on the stove alongside a debristled pig's head. He pinched his thigh and bit his finger. Both smarted. So he reached out to feel the pig's head and shake the bottle of spirits. Both real. Figuring he was still dreaming, he woke his wife and told her to See if the spirits and pig's head were real. "Husband," she said, "since you knew we had barely enough rice to get us through tomorrow, what possessed you to buy these luxuries?" Unable to contain his delight, he told her everything, forgetting that the mysteries of heaven must not be divulged.

Once again, the gurgling sound of water rose from the well. "Time to irrigate the crops again, my boy," Old Man Wang said. "The water's back."

"Finish your story, Grandpa Three," Gao Ma pleaded. "Don't keep me in suspense."

"Take it easy, my boy. Be patient. Never finish good food in one meal, or tell a good story in one sitting."

"Do you really hate socialism that much?" the policeman asked.

"It's not socialism I hate, it's you. To you socialism is a mere signboard, but to me it's a social formation—concrete, not abstract. It's embodied in public ownership of the means of production and in a system of distribution. Unfortunately it's also embodied in corrupt officials like you. Isn't that right?" Gao Ma demanded.

The policeman, hardly less irate than he, pounded the table and said, "Gao Ma, I'm interrogating you as an officer of the court. This is no debating contest! We're waiting for you to confess how you incited the masses to beat, smash, and loot, and how you joined them in this criminal activity. You were a soldier once, then a veteran. But you became a common criminal who resisted arrest and fled, only to ultimately fall into our grasp!"

"I already told you, you can shoot me or cut off my head or bury me alive, it doesn't matter to me. I hate corrupt officials like you who, under the guise of unfurling the flag of the Communist Party, destroy its reputation. I hate you all!"

It was after midnight. Farmers irrigating their crops under an even brighter, even clearer moon grew increasingly spectral. Lanterns faded and darkened under the luminous moonbeams.

Gao Ma handed a cigarette to Old Man Wang, who picked up the thread of his tale.

The teacher did what he never ever should have done: he revealed to his wife Zhang Nine-five's imperial future. So many of the world's great events have come a cropper because of women, who, like dogs, can eat butter but can't keep it down. Just imagine the thoughts that ran through her head when she heard that her son-in-law was fated to become the Son of Heaven. Her daughter would be Empress, making her Empress Mother—a relationship with royalty that could never be broken: more riches and honors than she could ever fully appreciate, more silks and satins than she could ever possibly wear, and more delicacies and rich foods than she could ever eat. She lost touch with reality. But that's another story. The next day the teacher went to the City God Temple, where he walked straight to the altar, picked up the slip of paper Zhang Nine-five had written, and, without a word to anyone, slipped it up his sleeve and took it home. "Did you write this, worthy son-in-law?" he confronted Zhang Nine-five. "Yes, I did," Nine-five replied bashfully. "It's at least five hundred miles from here to Luoyang," the teacher said, "a round trip of a thousand li. How is he to travel that distance in a single day?" "I was just having some fun," Nine-five protested. "Well, you'd better write another slip to spare him the trip," the teacher said. So Nine-five picked up the brush and wrote on a torn slip of paper, "City God, City God, you need not go to Luoyang. Off to bed after a hearty meal, and stay in good health." That night the City God returned to the teacher in a dream. "My heartfelt thanks for interceding on my behalf," he said, "for which I want to give you this

roast lamb and fine wine." As before, when the teacher awoke and
went into the next room, there on the stove awaited a roast lamb
and a bottle of fine wine.

A meteor streaked earthward, dragging its fiery tail behind it. Old
Man Wang continued the tale: Nine-five's mother-in-law had a
dispute with a neighbor that day, and in the heat of the argument
forgot her husband's admonition to keep this secret. "For your
information," she said, "my son-in-law is a future Son of Heaven,
and after he mounts the Dragon Throne, I'll have him lop off all
your heads, one after the other." Treating it as an idle threat, the
neighbor said, "Everybody knows that scrawny monkey of a son-in-
law doesn't have a bone in his body worthy of an Emperor. Even if
he did, with a black-hearted, ham-handed mother-in-law like you,
Old Man Heaven would replace those bones!" A passing spirit,
overhearing the angry comment, reported it to the Jade Emperor,
who was so incensed he ordered Heavenly Prince Li and his son
Nuozha to go down and replace Zhang Nine-five's bones. That
afternoon Heavenly Prince Li and his son arrived at the City God
Temple, where they were fêted with a banquet, at which Heavenly
Prince Li had a bit too much to drink and let slip their reason for
coming. Recalling with gratitude Zhang Nine-five's retraction of the
imperial edict, the City God quickly appeared in a dream to the
teacher, saying, "Dear teacher, your wife repeated something that
angered the Jade Emperor, who sent Heavenly Prince Li and his son
to remove your worthy son-in-law's imperial bones and replace
them with turtle bones during the third watch tonight. Tell your
worthy son-in-law that he must grit his teeth and bear up under any
pain, no matter how great, and not to scream under any circum-
stances. That way he retains his golden mouth and teeth of jade. One
scream, and even his teeth will become those of a turtle. The
mysteries of heaven cannot be divulged. Please inform your worthy
son-in-law that he must watch what he says." After ensuring that his
message was understood, the City God mounted the wind and rode

off. This time the teacher awoke covered with sweat. Knowing this was no false alarm, he immediately informed Nine-five that later that night, no matter how much pain he experienced, he was to grit his teeth and not cry out. Nine-five, who was smarter than most, understood at once. Later that night, as expected, his body was racked with unbearable pain; but, remembering his teacher's admonition, he gritted his teeth and didn't utter a sound. The teacher, angered over his wife's dreams of imperial favor, was tempted to throttle her, but didn't dare let on. As for Zhang Nine-five, he retained his golden mouth and teeth of jade. Then one summer day, as he sat under a tree reading a book, his peace was shattered by croaking frogs in the bay. "Stop your croaking," he said, "or I'll turn you all belly-up!" The frogs in Zhang Family Bay haven't croaked since that day, and every time one of them gets the urge to break its silence, the croak no sooner leaves its mouth than the frog goes belly-up.

"I guess a golden mouth and teeth of jade are as potent as they say." Gao Ma giggled. "Grandpa Three, being Emperor isn't as easy as it sounds. You're not free to say what you want, like we are."

"True enough," Grandpa Three agreed. "The Son of Heaven isn't permitted light banter."

"But I don't really believe that if the Emperor ordered horses to grow horns, or cows to grow scales, or roosters to lay eggs, or hens to crow, that those things would happen."

"In such matters some speak, others obey," Grandpa Three insisted. "Since no nonsense ever passes the Emperor's lips, if he says to grow horns, no horse would dare disobey. If you want an example closer to home, take our Secretary Wang. A township party secretary isn't even a rank-seven official, but the way he swaggers around, if he said he only had seven teeth, who would dare pry open his mouth to check it out?"

After a thoughtful pause, Gao Ma said, "You've got a point."

2

"Elder Brother Gao Ma," Jinju said petulantly, "tell me about your relationship with the chief of staff's concubine."

"It wasn't the chief of staff's concubine, it was the regiment commander's concubine."

"Then tell me about your relationship with her."

"She wanted to get married, but I never got used to her foul breath or her pouting. I didn't love her." He cringed at the word "love." "I figured she was my ticket to officer rank. I hated them, but I was no better than them, and didn't deserve a promotion."

"How about your love for me? Is it real or phony?"

"You can actually ask that after all we've been through together?"

"If you'd become an officer in the army, you probably wouldn't have fallen in love with me."

"If I'd become an officer, I'd have turned bad."

"Would you have married the regiment commander's concubine?"

"Now listen to me. My promotion order was in the works, so I dropped the regiment commander's concubine—after all, I was going to get what I wanted. So what happened? The regiment commander tore up the promotion order."

"Good for him!" Jinju said through clenched teeth.

"If he hadn't, I wouldn't have become your man."

"Oh, I see, I'm a last-ditch rebound!" Jinju blurted out as she dissolved in tears, feeling terribly wronged.

Gao Ma rubbed her shoulders in an attempt to console her. "Don't cry. Who hasn't been guilty of a youthful indiscretion at one time or another? I just want to sell my crop as fast as possible and give your blackhearted parents the money they demand for your hand, so we can live in peace together. Become an officer? What for? To sell my conscience? That's what you have to do."

"Number Fifty-one, we've heard that you and the girl Fang Jinju from this village had an illicit love affair. Is that right?" The question came from a pale-faced interrogator sitting on Gao Ma's cot. Gao Ma sat in the corner glaring daggers at the man, who grinned and said, "Apparently you hate me, too. Young man, you're too extreme in your judgments. There are plenty of good officials in the party and the government."

"Crows are black wherever you go."

"Try to be a little more level-headed, my boy. I'm not here to argue with you. To tell the truth, I'm on your side. Trust me. I advise you not to smash your own water jug."

"Half a lifetime of being a slug is enough," Gao Ma said.

The interrogator fished out a pack of cigarettes. "Smoke?" Gao Ma shook his head. The interrogator lit one and let it dangle between his lips as he flipped through some papers filled with penciled notes. "I've studied your case thoroughly," he said. "Even went on a fact-finding visit to your home village. I want you to understand that what you did at the county government compound on May 28th— destroying two telephones, setting fire to a stack of dossiers, and injuring a typist—was criminal, so your arrest was justified. And before the incident you incited the crowd to riot. Some call that counter-revolutionary activity intended to destroy social order, for which you must be punished."

"Is it serious enough for you to shoot me?"

"No. I want a detailed account of your relationship with Fang Jinju. In my view, the tragic love affair was a major factor in your criminalization."

"You're wrong! I hate you all! If I could I'd skin every single corrupt official!"

"You don't want my help?"

"I want you to shoot me!"

The interrogator walked out shaking his head. Gao Ma heard him say to someone, "There's a man whose head is screwed on wrong."

CHAPTER 18

Calling me a counter-revolutionary is a slanderous lie:
I, Zhang Kou, have always been a law-abiding citizen.
The Communist Party, which didn't fear the Jap devils—
Is it now afraid to listen to its own people?

> – from a ballad sung by Zhang Kou following his interrogation

1

Morning. A rail-thin cook was led into the cell. "Tell old Sun here what you want for your last meal, Number One," the jailer said.

The prisoner was momentarily speechless. "I'm not giving up yet," he said finally.

"Your appeal was denied. The sentence will be carried out."

The condemned prisoner's head slumped forward.

"Come on, now," the jailer said, "be reasonable, and tell us what you'd like. This is the last village on your trip. Let us dispense a little revolutionary humanism."

"Tell me," the cook urged. "We don't want you leaving as a hungry ghost. It's a long trip down to the Yellow Springs, and you'll need a full stomach to make it."

The condemned man breathed a long sigh and raised his head. There was a faraway look in his eyes, but a glow in his cheeks.

"Braised pork," he said.

"Okay, braised pork it is," Cook Sun agreed.

"With potatoes. And I want the meat nice and fatty."

"Okay, braised pork and potatoes. Fatty meat. What else?"

The man's eyes narrowed into slits as he strained to expand the menu.

"Don't be afraid to ask," Cook Sun said. "Whatever you want. It's on the house."

He scrunched up his mouth as tears slipped down his cheeks. "I'd like some wafer cakes, fried on a griddle and stuffed with green onions, and, let's see . . . some bean paste."

"That's it?"

"That's enough," the condemned prisoner said, adding warmly, "Sorry to put you to all this trouble."

"It's my job," Cook Sun remarked. "I'll be back in a little while."

The two men left the cell.

The condemned prisoner lay facedown on his cot and sobbed piteously, nearly drawing tears of sympathy from Gao Yang, who walked up quietly and tapped him on the shoulder. "Don't cry like that," he whispered. "It won't help."

The condemned man rolled over and grabbed his hand. But when the frightened Gao Yang tried to pull it back, he said, "Don't be scared, I won't hurt you. I wish I hadn't waited until my dying day to appreciate what it means to have a friend. You'll be getting out someday, won't you? Would you go see my father and make sure he doesn't grieve over me? Tell him I had braised pork, potatoes, and wafer cakes made from bleached flour, with green onions and bean paste, for my last meal. I'm from Song Family Village. My father's name is Song Shuangyang."

"I give you my word," Gao Yang promised.

A short while later, the cook returned with the braised pork and potatoes, some peeled green onions, a bowl of bean paste, a stack of wafer cakes, plus half a bottle of rice wine.

The guard removed the condemned prisoner's manacles, then sat across from him, his revolver drawn, as the prisoner knelt before the food and wine. His hand shook as he poured the wine into a cup, then tipped his head back and tossed it down, managing a single "Father!" before he was choked up by a flood of tears.

2

As the condemned man was taken out, he turned to give Gao Yang a smile, which plunged into his heart like a knife.

"Outside, Number Nine!" a jailer ordered through the open door. Gao Yang nearly jumped out of his skin. A stream of warm urine dampened his shorts.

"I've got a wife and kids at home, Officer! Make me eat shit or drink my own piss, but please don't shoot me!"

"Who said anything about shooting you?" the shocked jailer replied.

"You're not going to shoot me?"

"What makes you think China's got so many bullets we can waste them on the likes of you? Let's go. You'll be happy to know your wife's here to visit you."

A weight fell from Gao Yang's heart, and he nearly leaped through the cell door. As a pair of brass handcuffs was snapped on his wrists, he said, "Please don't cuff me, Officer. I promise I won't run. Seeing them will just make my wife feel worse."

"Rules are rules."

"Look at my ankle. I couldn't run on that if I wanted to."

"Button your lip," the jailer barked, "and be grateful we're letting her visit you at all. Normally we don't allow that before sentencing."

He was led to a seemingly unoccupied room. "Go on, you've got twenty minutes."

Hesitantly he pushed open the door. There, sitting on a stool cradling the baby, was his wife; his daughter, Xinghua, stood so close to her their legs were touching. His wife stood up abruptly, and he watched her face scrunch up and her mouth pucker as she began to cry.

With his hands frozen to the doorframe, he tried to speak, but something hot and sticky stopped up his throat. It was the same feeling he'd had several days before as he watched his daughter in the acacia grove from the tree to which he was tied.

"Daddy!" Xinghua spread her hands to feel where he was standing. "Is that you, Daddy?"

3

As his wife tossed a bundle of garlic onto the bed of the wagon, she clutched her belly and doubled over.

"Is it time?" an anxious, almost panicky Gao Yang asked.

"I tried," she said, "but I think this is it."

"Can't you hold back for another day or two? At least until I've sold the garlic?" There was a grudging edge to his voice. "If not a day or two late, a day or two earlier would have been fine. Why does it have to be now?"

"It's not my fault. . . . I didn't will it to come now. . . . If it was a bowel movement, I could hold off a little longer, but . . ." She gripped the railing, beads of sweat bathing her face.

"Okay, have your baby now," he said with resignation. "Shall I go get Qingyun?"

"Not her," she replied. "She charges too much, and she's not very good. I'll go to the clinic. I think it's a boy."

"Give me a son and I'll buy you a nice, plump hen. I'll even carry you on my back if you want."

"I can walk. Just let me lean on you." By then she was lying facedown on the ground.

"We'll use the wagon." After unloading the garlic, Gao Yang pulled the wagon through the gate, hitched up the donkey, then went back to get a comforter for the wagon bed.

"What else do we need?"

"A couple of wads of paper . . . everything's ready . . . blue cloth bundle at the head of the kang."

Gao Yang went inside, fetched the bundle, then carried his wife piggyback out the gate and laid her gently in the wagon. Xinghua, awakened by the commotion, was screaming. Gao Yang walked back inside. "Xinghua," he said, "your mother and I are going to fetch you a baby brother. Go back to sleep."

"Where are you going to get him?"

"In a burrow in the field."

"I want to go with you."

"Children aren't allowed. We have to be alone to get one."

The moon still hadn't risen as he drove his rickety wagon across the bumpy bridge, his wife moaning behind him. "What are you groaning about?" he asked, irritated by the sight of garlic-laden carts on the paved road. "You're having a baby, not dying!"

The moans stopped. The wagon smelled of garlic mixed with his wife's sweat.

The health clinic was located in a clearing by a graveyard. A cornfield lay to the east, a field of yams to the west, and a recently harvested field of garlic to the south. After reining in his wagon, Gao Yang went to locate the delivery room. He was stopped from knocking by a hand attached to a man whose features were unclear in the dark. "Someone's having a baby in there," the man said hoarsely. The glow of a cigarette dangling from his lips flickered on his face. The smoke smelled good.

"My wife's having a baby, too," Gao Yang said.

"Get in line," the man said.

"Even to have a baby?"

"You stand in line for everything," the man replied icily.

That was when Gao Yang noticed the other carts parked outside the delivery room: two ox-drawn, one horse-drawn, and a pushcart over which a blanket was draped.

"Is it your wife inside?"

"Yes."

"Why's it so quiet?"

"The noisy part's over."

"Boy or girl?"

"Don't know yet." The man walked up and put his ear to a crack in the door.

Gao Yang moved his wagon up closer.

The dark red, blurry moon had risen above the yard, where datura plants bloomed at the base of the wall, their flowers looking like ethereal white moths in the murky moonlight. Their pleasant medicinal odor vied with the stench from the outhouse, neither able to overpower the other. Gao Yang moved his wagon up next to the three carts: pregnant women lay in each, either faceup or facedown, their men standing nearby.

As the moonlight brightened, the other carts and their occupants became increasingly visible. The two oxen were chewing their cuds, glistening threads of spittle suspended from their lips like spun silk. Two of the men were smoking; the third was waving his whip idly. Sure that he'd seen them somewhere, Gao Yang assumed they were farmers from villages in his township whom he'd met up with at one time or another. The expectant mothers were a fright: grimy faces, ratty hair, scarcely human. The one in the westernmost cart filled the air with hideous wails that had her husband storming around the area and grumbling, "Stop that crying—stop it! You'll have people laughing at us."

The delivery-room door opened and a light beneath the eaves snapped on. A doctor in white, a woman, stood in the doorway, her hands encased in elbow-length rubber globes that were dripping wet— blood, most likely. The man pacing the area ran up to her. "What is it, Doctor?" he asked anxiously.

"A little girl," the doctor mumbled.

Hearing that he was the father of a little girl, the man rocked a time or two, then fell over backwards, cracking his head resoundingly on tile, which he apparently smashed.

"What's *that* all about?" the doctor remarked. "Times have changed, and girls are every bit as good as boys. Where would you males come from if not for us females? Out from under a rock?"

Slowly the man sat up, trancelike. Then he began to wail and weep, like a crazy man, punctuating his cries with reproachful shouts of "Zhou Jinhua, you worthless woman, my life's over, thanks to you!"

His shouts were joined by sounds of crying from inside: Zhou Jinhua, Gao Yang assumed. The absence of infant sounds puzzled him. Jinhua hadn't smothered her own baby, had she?

"Get up right this minute," the doctor demanded, "and take care of your wife and baby. Other people are waiting."

Rising unsteadily to his feet, the man staggered inside, emerging a few moments later carrying a bundle. "Doctor," he said as he paused in the doorway, "do you know anyone who'd like a little girl? Could you help us find her a home?"

"Do you have a stone for a heart?" the doctor asked angrily. "Take your baby home and treat her well. When she's eighteen you can get at least ten thousand for her."

A middle-aged woman shuffled out the door, her rumpled hair looking like a bird's nest, her clothing torn and tattered, and a grimy face that looked anything but human. The man handed her the bundled-up baby as he went to fetch his pushcart, in which she sat opposite a dung basket filled with black dirt. After slipping the harness around his neck, he took a few faltering steps before the cart flipped over, dumping his wife and the baby in her arms onto the ground. She was wailing, the baby was bawling, he was weeping.

Gao Yang heaved a sigh; so did the man standing beside him.

The doctor walked up. "Where'd that other cart come from?"

"Doctor," a flustered Gao Yang replied, "my wife's going to have a baby."

The doctor raised her arm, peeled back a rubber glove, and looked at her watch. "No sleep for me tonight," she muttered.

"When did the contractions start?"

"About . . . maybe as long as it takes to eat a meal."

"Then there's plenty of time. Wait your turn."

The lightbulb and moonlight illuminated the area. The fair-skinned doctor, who had large features on a round face, went from one cart to the next, poking and probing distended abdomens. To the woman lying in the westernmost cart, a little horse-drawn affair, she said, "Screaming like that only makes it worse. Look at the others. You don't see them carrying on like that, do you? Is this your first?"

The little man standing beside the wagon answered for his wife: "Her third."

"Your third?" the doctor replied, obviously displeased. "How can you scream like that? And what's that awful smell? Have you soiled yourself? Body odor shouldn't stink *that* bad!"

The woman, properly chastised, stopped screaming.

"You should have washed up before coming," the doctor said.

"We're sorry, Doctor," the little man said apologetically, "but we've been too busy harvesting garlic the past few days . . . plus there are the kids to worry about."

"And here you are, having another?"

"The other two are girls,' he explained. "Farmers need sons to help in the fields. Girls grow up and marry out of the family. What good's a child who can't do hard work? Besides, people laugh if you don't have a son."

"If you brought up a daughter like the famous Dowager Empress, you'd have something far better than ten thousand of your precious sons," the doctor countered.

"You're making fun of me, aren't you?" the little man said. "Any child born to parents as ugly as us is lucky if it's not crippled, blind, deaf, or dumb. All this talk of having a child with a pedigree is just that—talk."

"Maybe, maybe not," the doctor replied. "A plain chrysalis brings forth a lovely butterfly, so what's to stop a couple like you from producing a future party chairman?"

"With a mother who looks like her? I'd fall to my knees and kowtow till the end of time if she gave me a son whose features managed to be in the right places," the little man said.

From the bed of the wagon, the woman strained to sit up. "What makes you think *you're* so goddamned desirable? Look at yourself in a puddle of piss if you want to see what I see: rat eyes, a toad's mouth, the ears of a jackass, all stooped over like a turtle. I must have been blind to marry someone like you!"

He giggled. "I wasn't bad looking in my youth."

"Dog fart! You looked more animal than human. As bad as the hideous Wu Dalang, maybe worse!"

That got a laugh out of the others, including the doctor, whose gaping mouth could have accommodated a whole apple. Nearby fields were suffused with joyous airs, as the fragrance of datura plants finally won out over the outhouse stench. A pale green moth flitted in the air around the lightbulb, and the ugly couple's white pony pawed the ground happily.

"Okay, it's your turn," the doctor said to the woman.

The little man lifted his wife down off the wagon. You'd have thought he was killing her, the way she groaned. "Stop that!" he demanded, giving her a rap on the head. "The first time it hurts, the second time it goes smoothly, and the third's like taking a shit."

She scratched his face. "Your mother's burning hemorrhoids! How do you know what it's like—ow, Mother, it's killing me!"

"You're a couple of real gems," the doctor commented, "a match made in heaven."

"The scar-faced woman marries a harelipped man. That way nobody has any complaints," the little man said.

"Screw your mother! After this one's born, I'm starting divorce proceedings . . . ow, Mother!"

The doctor led the woman inside. "Wait here," she said to the husband, who paused in the doorway for a moment, then walked back to his wagon and picked up his feedbag. The white pony snorted loudly as it began munching the feed.

The other three expectant fathers clustered around the little man, who handed cigarettes around. Gao Yang, not used to smoking, had a fit of coughing. "Where are you from?" the little man asked him.

"The village south of here."

"Where the Fang family lives?"

"Yes."

"They've got a slut for a daughter!" he said indignantly.

"You mean Jinju? She's as innocent as the day is long," Gao Yang defended her.

"Who asked you?" Gao Yang's wife demanded.

"Innocent, you say?" the little man's lip curled. "She changes her mind, and three weddings are called off. My fellow villager Cao Wen had a nervous breakdown because of it."

"It hasn't been easy for her," Gao Yang said defensively, "what with all those beatings and stuff. She and Gao Ma were made for each other."

The little man muttered sorrowfully, "What are the times coming to when a girl can decide who she marries?"

A prematurely gray man standing next to his oxcart said, "It's those movies. Young people nowadays learn all the wrong things from movies."

"Cao Wen's a fool," one of the others commented. "Why is someone like him, with a powerful official for an uncle behind him, mooning over not having a wife, anyway? It's not worth losing your mind over."

"Not enough girls is the problem," the gray-haired man said. "They get engaged when they're still teenagers. I'd like to know where all the girls went. There are plenty of young bachelors, but you never seen an unmarried woman. It's gotten to the point where young men fight over them like warm beancurd, even if they're crippled or blind."

Gao Yang coughed. The gray-haired fellow angered him. "Where do you get off laughing at others?" he said. "No one knows what's in a mother's belly till it's out. One head or two, who can say?"

The gray-haired man, missing Gao Yang's point completely, continued, although he could have been talking to himself for all anyone knew. "Where did the girls go? Into town? City boys aren't interested in girls off the farm. A real puzzle. Take a steer or a horse: when it's time to raise their tails and drop a young one, if it's female people jump for joy; but if it's a male, nothing but long faces all around. With people it's just the opposite. Rejoicing follows the birth of a boy, but long faces greet the birth of a girl. Then when the boy grows up and can't find a wife, out come the long faces again."

A baby's cry interrupted their conversation. The little man stopped feeding his horse and walked toward the delivery room tentatively, as if his legs were lead weights.

"You there, little man," the doctor called to him as she opened the delivery-room door, "your wife's given you a son."

He grew two inches on the spot. Striding into the clinic, he emerged moments later with his newborn son, whom he placed in the bed of the wagon. "Say, friend," he said to the gray-haired man, "watch my horse for me while I go fetch the mother of my son, would you? Don't spook him."

"He's sure feeling potent all of a sudden," Gao Yang heard one of the women comment.

"He'll be able to stand tall around other men now."

He emerged all stooped over, carrying his wife on his back, her feet dragging in the dirt; one of her shoes fell off, but the gray-haired man retrieved it.

"I'm holding you to your word," she said to her husband once she was lying in the wagon bed.

"I mean it. I did!"

"You'll buy me a nylon jacket."

"One with two rows of metal snaps."

"And a pair of nylon stockings."

"Two pairs. One red, one green."

The little man put the feed basket away, picked up his whip, and turned the wagon around until it was perpendicular to the other carts. The pony's hide glistened like silver. After reining the animal in, he passed more cigarettes around. "I don't smoke," Gao Yang said. "I'll just waste a good cigarette."

"Give it a try," the little man encouraged him. "It's only a cigarette. Can't you see how happy I am? Aren't you glad for me?"

"Sure, sure I am." Gao Yang accepted the cigarette.

The gray-haired man's wife was next. "Brothers," the little man said, "you'll all have sons. Kids are like yellow fish in schools. Since our sons will all have the same birthday, they'll be like brothers when they grow up!"

He cracked his whip, shouted at his horse, and rode out of the compound in high spirits, the clicking of his horses's hooves quickly swallowed up in the murky moonlight.

The gray-haired man's wife had a baby girl.

The other man's wife delivered a stillborn, misshapen fetus.

After taking his wife into the delivery room, Gao Yang paced the compound, which he now had all to himself. By this time the moon shone directly down on the datura plants. His wife was toughing it out, since not a sound came from the delivery room. Outside, all alone with his donkey, he felt emotionally drained, so he walked over to the flower bed, where, in the grip of his private terror, he sniffed the strange fragrance and studied the fluttering petals. He bent down and poked one of the plump white leaves. It felt cool as dewdrops rolled off it. His heart fluttered. Before he knew it, his nose was buried in the flower, his nostrils filled with its strange fragrance. With a grimace he gazed at the moon and sneezed violently.

At daybreak his wife bore him a son. Shit! he muttered amid his joy. Why? Because his darling son had six toes on each foot.

His wife's heart knotted up, but Gao Yang consoled her, "You're the mother of my children, so you should be happy. 'Special people have special features.' Who knows, he might grow up to be a big official. And when that happens, you and I will get a taste of the good life."

4

Gao Yang said, "I broke the law. How can I make it up to you?"

His wife sighed. "You weren't alone. Even Fourth Aunt Fang was arrested, at her age. Compared to her we're in fine shape."

The baby started crying, so she stuffed a nipple into his mouth. Gao Yang leaned over to study the face of his son, whose eyes were closed. He flicked some flaky white skin off the face. "He's getting so big," he said. "He keeps growing out of his skin." The baby kicked his mother's breast with his six-toed right foot. She pushed it away. "You have to name him," she said.

"Let's call him Shoufa—Law Abider," he said after a thoughtful pause. "I don't expect him to become a high official, and I'll be happy if he's a farmer who abides by the laws."

Xinghua felt her father's arm, from his shoulder all the way down to the handcuffs. "What are these, Daddy?"

Gao Yang stood up. "Nothing."

The baby slept at his mother's breast, so when she stood up she gently removed the nipple, then laid him on the table and hurriedly opened her bundle. She fished out a pair of plastic sandals (new), a blue workshirt (also new), and a pair of black gabardine pants (brand new). "Put these on," she said. "I was worried sick when they dragged you off half-naked. I wanted to bring you some clothes, but didn't know where you were until a couple of days ago. I spent last night outside. Then this morning a kind woman opened all the right doors for me to see you."

"Did you walk the whole way?" Gao Yang asked her.

"After a mile or two somebody happened by. Guess who it was. Remember that little man at the clinic the night I had the baby? He was heading to town with some ammonia, so he gave us a ride."

"Who bought these new clothes? Where'd the money come from?"

"I sold the garlic. Don't worry about us. We've broken the law and we'll take our punishment, whatever it is. I can manage things at home, and Xinghua can watch the baby for me. The neighbors have been so helpful it's embarrassing."

"What about Gao Ma? What happened after he scaled the wall and took off?"

"I'll tell you, but don't breathe a word of this to Fourth Aunt. Jinju's dead."

"How'd she die?"

"Hanged herself. The poor girl's legs were covered with blood. It was nearly time, but the baby never saw the light of day."

"Does Gao Ma know?"

"They arrested him when he was making funeral arrangements."

"A waste of a good woman," Gao Yang lamented. "She brought a melon to Fourth Aunt the afternoon we were arrested."

"Let's not talk about other people. I brought some food." She dumped the contents of a plastic bag—some dark-skinned hard-boiled eggs dyed red—onto the table.

He stuffed two of them into Xinghua's hands. "You eat them, Daddy, they're for you," his daughter said.

His wife peeled one for him. He jammed it whole into his mouth, but tears were running down his face before it was gone.

CHAPTER 19

County Chief, your hands aren't big enough to cover heaven!
Party Secretary, your power isn't as weighty as the mountain!
You cannot hide the ugly events of Paradise County,
For the people have eyes—

> — At this point in Zhang Kou's ballad a ferocious policeman jumped to his feet and cursed, "You blind bastard, you're the prime suspect in the Paradise County garlic case! We've got you dead to rights!" He kicked Zhang Kou in the mouth, cutting off the final note. Blood spurted from Zhang Kou's mouth; several white teeth hit the floor. Zhang Kou climbed back into the chair; the policeman sent him back to the floor with another kick. Garbled speech spilled from Zhang Kou's lips, scaring the interrogators, even though they hadn't understood a word of it. The chief interrogator stopped the policeman from kicking him a third time, as another man bent down and sealed Zhang Kou's mouth with a plastic gag.

1

Shouting erupted in the corridor, followed by the clanging of cell doors being thrown open. Gao Yang's was one of them. A gaunt, sharp-featured policeman stood in the doorway; he smiled and nodded. Realizing that he was being summoned, Gao Yang slipped on his shoes and tied the laces, noticing the opaque skin around his injured ankle, and the green-tinted, shifting pus lying just below the surface. He limped to the doorway, where the mysterious smile frozen on the policeman's face had an ominous effect on him. He smiled foolishly in return, as if to ingratiate himself and lessen the psychological pressures at the same time.

The policeman no sooner raised his hand than Gao Yang stuck out his arms, wrists together. The policeman retreated a step in the face of such immediate cooperation before separating Gao Yang's hands slightly and snapping on the cuffs. Then, with a slight jerk of the head, he signaled Gao Yang out into the corridor, where policemen were putting handcuffs on other prisoners. Gao Yang glanced bashfully at his escort, recalling seeing him in the government compound. With a nudge from behind he fell in alongside other prisoners, who filed into the prison yard, where they were told to form a line and count off. There were ten in all. Someone grabbed Gao Yang's arms. By cocking his head to the left he saw the sharp-featured policeman who had handcuffed him, and by twisting to look behind him he saw another policeman—fat, with pinched lips and puffy cheeks, clearly someone who would brook no nonsense. For some strange reason, Gao Yang tried to look up at the electrified wire atop the wall, but his neck stiffened up on him.

He was last in line, in a column so straight that all he could see were the three backs in front of him, a black one sandwiched between two white ones.

As they filed through the prison gate it dawned on him why he wanted to look at the electrified wire: during the previous day's exercise period a piece of red cloth hung from the wire, and the old hooligan with whom he had first shared a cell was staring up at it. The malicious middle-aged convict walked up and winked at Gao Yang. "You're being questioned tomorrow," he said, "and your wife came to visit you." Gao Yang stood there, mouth agape, unable to say a word. The other man changed the subject. "The old bastard's lost his mind. That's his daughter-in-law's waistband hanging up there. Know what the old bastard does? Know his name? Know how the old bastard tricked his daughter-in-law? Know who his son is?" Gao Yang shook his head in response to each question. "Well, I can't tell you," the man said. "The shock would kill you."

He squirmed in the grip of the two policemen as they walked, which only made them grip him more tightly. "Keep moving," one of them whispered into his left ear, "and don't try anything funny."

Crowds lined the road, eyes staring and mouth slack, as if waiting to snap at some floating object.

They shuffled down the street, birds following their progress overhead and sending a foul rain down on prisoners and guards alike. But no one made a sound, as if oblivious to the assault, and no one raised a hand to wipe the black and white bird droppings from his head or shoulders.

The road seemed endless as Gao Yang passed an occasional cluster of buildings with slogans painted on the sides, or a construction site with pale yellow derricks reaching the clouds; but always there were crowds of gawkers, including one hideous-looking, bare-assed juvenile who flung a cow chip at them, although it was impossible to tell if he was trying to hit a prisoner, or a policeman, or both, or was just moved to throw something. Whatever his intent, the missile caused a brief disruption in the procession, but not enough to stop it.

They entered a wooded area and headed down a footpath barely wide enough for three people shoulder to shoulder. The policemen brushed against the mossy bark of trees, making soft scraping sounds. Sometimes the path was strewn with golden leaves, at others covered with pools of foul green water in which tiny red insects snapped and flipped like miniature shrimp; the surface was alive with red insects taking off or landing.

A heavy rain began to fall as they crossed some railroad tracks, raindrops thudding onto shaved heads like pebbles. As Gao Yang tucked his head down between his shoulders, he carelessly banged his injured ankle on a railroad tie, sending sharp pains from the outside of his foot all the way up to the hollow of his knee. The skin above his ankle ruptured, releasing a pool of pus that ran into his shoe. My brand-new shoes, he thought sadly. "Officers, can I stop to squeeze the pus out of my foot?" he pleaded with his police escorts.

They ignored his request, like deaf-mutes. No wonder: they cleared the tracks just as a freight train chugged by, its wheels sending clouds of dust into the air and passing so close it nearly separated Gao Yang from the seat of his pants. It also seemed to take the rain with it.

A rooster with immature wing feathers came flapping out of some bushes across the road, cocked its head, and sized up a puzzled Gao Yang. What's a rooster doing out here in the middle of nowhere? While he was caught up in this question, the rooster rushed him from behind, its neck bobbing with each step, and pecked his injured, pus-filled ankle, causing such intense pain that he nearly broke the iron grip of the policemen on either side of him. Startled by the sudden, violent movement, they dug their fingers into his upper arms.

The little rooster stuck like glue, pecking at him every couple of steps, while the policemen, ignoring his screams of pain, kept propelling him forward. Then, as they negotiated the down slope of a hill, the rooster actually plucked a white tendon out of the open sore on Gao Yang's ankle. Digging in with its claws, its tail feathers touching the ground, its neck feathers fanned out, and its comb turning bright red, it tugged on the tendon with all its might, pulling it a foot or more until it snapped in two. Gao Yang, reeling, turned to see the little rooster swallowing it like one big noodle. The gaunt policeman leaned over and stuck his pointy mouth up to Gao Yang's ear. "Okay," he whispered, "he's plucked out the root of your problem." The stubble around his mouth brushed against Gao Yang, who involuntarily drew in his neck. The man's garlic breath nearly bowled Gao Yang over.

Having crossed the tracks, they turned west, then north. Shortly after that they headed east, then doubled back to the south—or so it seemed to Gao Yang. They were walking through fields with waist-high plants on whose branches objects like Ping-Pong balls grew. Green in color, the pods were covered with a pale fuzz. Gao Yang had no idea what they were. But the fat policeman bent down, picked one, popped it into his mouth, and chewed until frothy green slobber dribbled down his chin. Then he spat a sticky gob into the palm of his hand. It looked like something scraped out of a cow's stomach.

The fat policeman held him fast while his gaunt companion kept tugging forward. Gao Yang's arms twisted as he lurched sideways, snapping the handcuff chain taut. The stalemate held for a moment, until the gaunt policeman stood still, breathing hard. Yet even though he was no longer pulling Gao Yang forward, his iron grip intensified. The fat policeman bent down and stuck the gooey mass onto Gao Yang's injured ankle, then covered it with a bristly white leaf. A coolness spread upward. "An old folk remedy for injuries," the policeman said. "Your sore will heal within three days."

The procession had left them far enough behind that all they could see was an expanse of that strange crop. Not a soul anywhere, but there were unmistakable signs of people passing through the foliage. The white underbellies of large green leaves showed the path the procession had taken. Lifting Gao Yang up until his feet left the ground, the policemen began trotting with their prisoner.

Eventually they caught up with the others at a railroad crossing, which, for all they knew, could have been the same one as a while ago. Nine prisoners and eighteen policemen, standing in three rows, were waiting for them on the elevated track bed. A half-turn, and the procession trebled its length, one black sandwiched between two whites, like a stiff black-and-white snake. Fourth Aunt was the only female prisoner, her escorts the only policewomen. They were shouting, the sound loud and lingering, the words indistinguishable.

After rejoining the procession and forming up again into three columns, the procession entered an unlighted tunnel, where the water was ankle deep and dripped from the overhead arch, making a hollow sound in the inky darkness. Some wagons shot past, the horses' hooves splashing loudly.

They emerged from the tunnel onto May First Boulevard, to their surprise, and five minutes later were in May First Square, walking on a layer of rotting, disgustingly slippery garlic. Gao Yang felt miserable about his new shoes.

Throngs of peasants lined the square. The frost on their faces, dusted with grime, didn't look as if it would ever melt. Tears streamed down the cheeks of the few who were looking up into the sun, nearly blinded by its rays. One of them looked like an ape man, the kind he'd seen in a schoolbook—narrow, jutting forehead, wide mouth, long, apelike arms. Anyway, this strange creature leaped out of the crowd, raised one of his long arms, opened his mouth wide, and bellowed, "Hua-lala, hua-lala, one hand on a nice big tit, add soy sauce and vinegar . . ." Gao Yang had no idea what he meant, but he heard his gaunt police escort mutter angrily, "A loony, a real loony!"

After passing through the square, they turned into a narrow lane, where a boy in a nylon jacket had a pigtailed girl pinned up against a hollow in the wall and was nibbling at her face. She was trying her best to push him away. Mud-spattered geese strutted back and forth behind them. The procession passed so close behind the boy that the girl wrapped her arms around his waist and drew him to her so the column could squeeze by.

They emerged from the lane, and there in front of them, amazingly, was May First Boulevard—again. Across the street a multistoried building was going up behind a rumbling cement mixer tended by a boy and a girl no more than eleven or twelve years old. He was shoveling sand and pouring lime and cement into the funnel, while she squirted water into the funnel with a black plastic hose that shook so violently from the high pressure that she could barely hold it. The mixing oar scraped loudly against the funnel. Then the pale-yellow derrick slowly lifted a prefab concrete slab with airholes. Four men in hard hats sat on it playing poker, shocking observers by their nonchalance.

After another turn around the square, the prison wall was in front of him once again. The electrified wire crackled and gave off blue sparks. The piece of red cloth still hung from it. "Team Leader Xing," one of the policemen shouted, "shouldn't we be heading back to rest?"

A tall, heavyset fellow with a dark face glanced at his wristwatch, then looked up at the sky. "Half an hour," he shouted back.

The prison gate opened with a clang, and the police herded the prisoners inside the yard. Rather than put them back into their cells, they had them sit in a circle on the lush green grass, where they were told to stretch their legs out in front of them, hands on their knees. The police walked off lazily, their place taken by an armed guard who kept watch over the prisoners. Some of the policemen went to the toilet, others did stretching exercises on a horizontal bar.

After ten minutes or so, Fourth Aunt's escorts emerged with red lacquer trays holding soft drinks in opened bottles with drinking straws. There were two kinds. "The colors are different, but they taste exactly the same," they announced. "One bottle apiece." One of them bent down in front of Gao Yang. "Which do you want?"

He looked uncertainly at the bottles on her tray. Some were the color of blood; others appeared to be filled with ink.

"Hurry up, choose one. And no changing your mind later."

"I'll take a red one," he said firmly.

She handed him a bottle filled with the red liquid, which he accepted with both hands, then held, not daring to start right away.

After all the drinks were distributed, Gao Yang noticed that everyone but Gao Ma had chosen red.

"Go on, drink," one of the policewomen said.

But the prisoners just looked at each other, not daring to take a drink.

"You can't repair a wall with dog shit!" the policewoman complained angrily. "Drink up, I said. On three: one, two, three, drink!"

Gao Yang took a timid sip; a liquid tasting like garlic slid tickling down his throat.

When the soft drinks were finished, the police regrouped, taking up their positions alongside the prisoners to form three ranks. After proceeding out the prison gate, they turned north, crossed the street, and climbed the steps of a large building with a spacious hall. It was packed with spectators, and you could have heard a pin drop. Solemn airs.

A booming voice broke the silence: "Bring up the prisoners associated with the Paradise County garlic incident!"

Two policemen removed Gao Yang's handcuffs, pulled his shoulders back and forced his head down, then dragged and carried him to the defendants' dock.

2

The first thing Gao Yang saw when he looked past the railing was a large, shiny replica of the national seal. He was pinned uncomfortably between his two escorts, one fat, one skinny. A cultured-looking uniformed official with sagging jowls sat beneath the seal; seven or eight additional uniformed men were fanned out beside him, all looking like characters in a movie.

The man in the middle, who was older than the others, cleared his throat and spoke into a microphone wrapped in red: "The first session of the Paradise County garlic incident proceedings will come to order!" He stood up—the guards on either side of him remained seated—and began reading names from a list. When his name was read out, Gao Yang didn't know what to do. "Say 'Present,'" his skinny escort said, nudging him.

"All defendants are present," the officer announced. "Now the charges. On the twenty-eighth of May, defendants Gao Ma, Gao Yang, the woman Fang née Wu, Zheng Changnian . . ." he droned on, ". . . smashed, looted, and demolished the county government offices, beating and injuring a number of civil servants in the process. The People's Tribunal of Paradise County, agreeing to hear the case in accordance with Article 105, Section 1, Book 3 of the Criminal Code, has decreed a public trial before a panel of judges."

Gao Yang heard the spectators behind him buzz excitedly. "Order in the court!" the officer demanded, banging the table with his fist. He then took a sip of tea and said, "Three judges make up the panel, headed by me, Kang Botao, presiding judge of the Paradise County People's Tribunal. My associates are Yu Ya, member of the Standing Committee of the People's Consultative Congress of Paradise County, and Jiang Xiwang, director of the General Office of the Paradise County Branch of the People's Congress. Miss Song Xiufen serves as clerk. The prosecutor is Liu Feng, Deputy Chief Procurator of the Paradise County People's Procuratorate."

The presiding judge sat down, as if thoroughly exhausted, took another sip of tea, and said hoarsely, "In accordance with Article 113, Subsection 1, Section 2 of the Criminal Code, the defendants have the right to challenge any member of the panel of judges, the court clerk, or the prosecutor. They also have the right to argue on their own behalf."

Gao Yang understood the presiding judge's words but little of his meaning. He was so nervous his heart raced one moment and seemed to stop the next. His bladder felt as if it were about to burst, even though he knew it was empty. When he squirmed to ease the pressure, his police escorts told him to sit still.

"Do I hear any challenges? Hm?" the presiding judge asked listlessly. "No? Fine. The prosecutor will read the formal charges."

The prosecutor rose. He had a pinched, tinny voice, and Gao Yang could tell by the accent that he wasn't local. With his eyes glued to the prosecutor's flapping lips and tightly knit brow, he gradually forgot about having to pee. Unsure of what the man was saying, he sensed vaguely that the events being chronicled had little to do with him.

The presiding judge laid down his tea. "The court will now entertain pleas. Defendant Gao Ma, did you or did you not shout reactionary slogans, inciting the masses to smash and loot the county offices on the morning of May twenty-eighth?"

Gao Yang turned to look at Gao Ma, who stood in a separate dock some distance away staring at a slowly moving ceiling fan.

"Defendant Gao Ma, did you understand the question?" The presiding judge sounded sterner this time.

Gao Ma lowered his head until he was staring straight at the presiding judge. "I despise you people!"

"You despise us? What on earth for?" the presiding judge said sarcastically. "We are proceeding on the basis of facts and by the authority of the law. We will not punish an innocent person nor let a single guilty one go free. Whether or not you accept that is irrelevant. Call the first witness."

The first witness was a fair-skinned youngster who fiddled with his shirt the whole time he was on the, stand.

"What is your name and where do you work?",

"My name is Wang Jinshan. I'm a driver for the county."

"Wang Jinshan, you must tell the truth, the whole truth, and nothing but the truth, subject to the laws of perjury. Do you understand?"

The witness nodded. "On the morning of May twenty-eighth I drove one of County Administrator Zhong's guests to the station, and on the way back I was caught in a traffic jam about a hundred yards east of the county office building. There I saw the prisoner Gao Ma shout from the top of an oxcart, 'Down with corrupt officials! Down with bureaucrats!'"

"The witness is excused," the presiding judge said. "Do you have anything to say to that, Gao Ma?"

"I despise you people!" Gao Ma replied coldly.

As the trial proceeded, Gao Yang's knees began to knock and he grew light-headed. When the presiding judge addressed him, he said, "Sir, I've already told everything. Please don't ask me any more questions."

"This is a court of law, and you will behave accordingly," the judge replied, releasing a spray of spittle. But soon even he seemed to weary of the questioning, which hardly varied, so he announced, "That's all I have. Now we'll hear final arguments by the prosecutor."

The prosecutor stood up, made some brief comments, then sat back down.

"Now we'll hear from the injured parties."

Three individuals whose hands were wrapped in gauze came forward.

Blah blah blah, yak yak yak, went the injured parties.

"Do the defendants have anything to say?" the presiding judge asked.

"Sir, my poor husband was killed. Altogether I lost him, two cows, and a wagon, and all Party Secretary Wang gave me was thirty-five hundred yuan. Sir, I've been victimized. . . ." By the time she finished, Fourth Aunt was pounding the railing in front of her and wailing.

The presiding judge frowned. "Defendant Fang née Wu, that has nothing to do with the case before us."

"Sir, you officials aren't supposed to protect each other like that!" she complained.

"Defendant Fang née Wu, you are out of order. Any more outbursts like that and I'll hold you in contempt of court!" The presiding judge was clearly irritated. "Defense counsel may now present its case."

Among the representatives for the defendants was a young military officer. Gao Yang had seen him before but couldn't recall where.

"I am an instructor in the Marxist-Leninist Teaching and Research Section at the Artillery Academy. In accordance with Section 3, Article 26 of the Criminal Code, I am entitled to defend my father, defendant Zheng Changnian."

His statement breathed life into the proceedings. A buzzing echoed off of the domed ceiling. Even the prisoners looked around until they spotted the white-haired old man seated in the center dock.

"Order in the court!" the presiding judge demanded.

The spectators quieted down to hear what the young officer had to say.

Looking straight at the presiding judge, he began, "Your Honor, before I begin my fathers defense, I request permission to make an opening statement related to the trial."

"Permission granted," the presiding judge said.

He turned to face the spectators, speaking with a passion that touched everyone who heard him. "Your Honors, ladies and gentlemen, the situation in our farming villages has changed drastically in the wake of the Party's Third Plenary Session of the Eleventh Central Committee, including those here in Paradise County. The peasants are much better off than they were during the Cultural Revolution. This is obvious to everyone. But the benefits they enjoyed as a result of rural economic reforms are gradually disappearing."

"Please don't stray too far from the subject," the presiding judge broke in.

"Thank you for reminding me, Your Honor. I'll get right to the point. In recent years the peasants have been called upon to shoulder ever heavier burdens: fees, taxes, fines, and inflated prices for just about everything they need. No wonder you hear them talk about plucking the wild goose's tail feathers as it flies by. Over the past couple of years these trends have gotten out of control, which is why, I believe, the Paradise County garlic incident should have come as no surprise."

The presiding judge glanced down at his wristwatch.

"Not being able to sell their crops was the spark that ignited this explosive incident, but the root cause was the unenlightened policies of the Paradise County government!" the officer continued. "Before Liberation only about a dozen people were employed by the district government, and things worked fine. Now even a township government in charge of the affairs of a mere thirty thousand people employs more than sixty people! And when you add those in the communes it's nearly a hundred, seventy percent of whose salaries are paid by peasants through township fees and taxes. Put in the bluntest possible terms, they are feudal parasites on the body of society! So in my view, the slogans 'Down with corrupt officials!' and

'Down with bureaucrats!' comprise a progressive call for the awakening of the peasants, and the defendant Gao Ma is innocent of counterrevolutionary behavior! But since I was not asked to speak on his behalf, my comments cannot be construed as arguments in his defense."

"If you continue this line of propaganda I will revoke your right to defend anyone in this court!" the presiding judge announced sternly.

"Let him talk!" came a voice from the rear of the courtroom. Gao Yang turned to look. Even the corridor was packed with spectators.

"Order in the court!" the presiding judge shouted.

"My father smashed a TV set, set fire to official documents, and struck a civil servant. As his son, his criminal acts pain me, and it is not my intent to absolve him of his guilt. But what puzzles me is: how did someone like him, a decorated stretcher bearer during the War of Liberation who followed the Liberation Army all the way to Jiangxi, become a common criminal? His love for the Communist Party is deep, so why did he defy the government over a few bunches of garlic?"

"The Communist Party has changed! It isn't the Communist Party we once knew!" came a shout from the defendants' dock.

Pandemonium broke out. The presiding judge rose and pounded the table frantically. "Order! Order in the court!" he bellowed. When the uproar died down, he announced, "Defendant Zheng Changnian, you may not speak without the express permission of the court!"

"I'd like to continue," the young military officer said.

"You have another five minutes."

"I'll take as long as I need," the young officer insisted. "The Criminal Code places no time limits on defense arguments. Nor does it give a panel of judges the authority to set them!"

"In the opinion of this court, your comments have strayed beyond the scope of this case!" the presiding judge replied.

"My comments are becoming increasingly relevant to the defense of my father."

"Let him speak!" a spectator shouted. "Let him speak!"

Gao Yang saw the young officer wipe his eyes with a white handkerchief.

"All right, go ahead and speak," the judge relented. "But the clerk is recording everything you say, for which you are solely responsible."

"Of course I accept responsibility for anything I say," he replied with a slight stammer. "In my view, the Paradise County garlic incident has sounded an alarm: any political party or government that disregards the well-being of its people is just asking to be overthrown by them!"

A hush fell over the courtroom; the air seemed to vibrate with electricity. The pressure on Gao Yang's eardrums was nearly unbearable. The presiding judge, face bathed in sweat, literally shook. In reaching for his tea, he knocked it over, soaking the white tablecloth with the rust-colored liquid, some of which dripped to the floor.

"What . . . what do you think you're doing?" the aghast judge shouted. "Clerk, make sure you take down every word!"

Don't say any more, young fellow, Gao Yang prayed silently. A light flashed in his head. Now he remembered: this was the young officer who was helping his father irrigate his corn that night Fourth Uncle was killed.

"What I want to say is this," the young officer continued. "The people have the right to overthrow any party or government that disregards their well-being. If an official assumes the role of public master rather than public servant, the people have the right to throw him out! In my view this conforms in all respects to the Four Cardinal Principles of Socialism. Of course, I'm talking about possibilities—*if* that were the case. In point of fact, things have improved in the wake of the party rectification, and most of Paradise County's responsible party members are doing a fine job. But one rat turd can spoil a whole pot of porridge, and the unprincipled behavior of a single party member adversely affects the party's reputation and the government's prestige. The people aren't always fair and discerning, and can be forgiven if their dissatisfaction with a particular official carries over into their attitudes toward officials in general. But shouldn't that be a reminder to officials to act in such a way as to best represent the party and the government?

"I further believe that the actions of the Paradise County administrator, Zhong Weimin, can be seen as dereliction of duty. As events unfolded, he refused to show his face, choosing instead to make the compound walls higher and top them with broken glass to ensure his own personal safety. When trouble came, he refused to meet with the masses, despite the entreaties of his own civil servants. That made the ensuing chaos inevitable. If we endorse the proposition that all people are equal under the law, then we must demand that the Paradise County People's Procuratorate indict Paradise County administrator Zhong Weimin on charges of official misconduct! I have nothing more to say."

The young officer remained standing for a moment before wearily taking a seat behind the defense table. Thunderous applause erupted from the spectator section behind him.

The presiding judge rose to his feet and patiently waited for the applause to die down. "Do the other defendants have anything to say in their defense? No? Then this court stands in recess while the panel of judges deliberates the case, based upon the evidence, arguments, and provisions of the law. We will return in thirty minutes to announce our verdict."

CHAPTER 20

I sing of May in the year 1987,
Of a criminal case in Paradise:
Police converged from all directions,
Arresting ninety-three of their fellow citizens.
Some died, others went to jail—
When will the common folk see the blue sky of justice?

– from a ballad sung by Zhang Kou on a side street
west of the government office building

1

After finishing the verse he felt the ground beside him for his
canteen. A gulp of cool water moistened his parched, raspy throat,
All around him he heard applause and an occasional roar from one
of the young voices: "Bravo, Zhang Kou! More, more, more!"
Hearing their voices, he could nearly see their dusty bodies and
blazing eyes. By then it was late autumn, and the tumult surrounding the Paradise garlic incident had subsided. A couple of
dozen peasants, including Gao Ma, who was seen as the ringleader,
had been sentenced to labor-reform camps; County Head Zhong
"Serve the People" Weimin, and the county party secretary, Ji
Nancheng, had been reassigned elsewhere. Their replacements, after
delivering a series of reports to local dignitaries, organized a
compulsory program for county workers to rake up the garlic
rotting on city streets and haul it over to White Water Stream, which
flowed through town. Baked by the midsummer sun, the garlic

emitted a stench that lay like a pall over town until a couple of summery rainstorms eased the torment. At first the incident was all the people talked about; but farm duties and a creeping awareness that the topic was growing stale had the same effect on their conversations that the rain had on the smell of garlic. Zhang Kou, whose blindness had gained him leniency at court, proved to be the exception. Ensconced on a side street alongside the government office building, he tirelessly strummed his *erhu* and sang a ballad of garlic in Paradise, each version building upon the one that went before.

> . . . *They say officials love to serve the people,*
> *so why do they treat the common folk as enemies?*
> *Heavy taxes and under-the-table levies, like ravenous beasts,*
> *force the farmers to head for the hills.*
> *The common folk have a bellyful of grievances,*
> *but they dare not let them out.*
> *For the moment they open their mouths, electric prods close*
> *them fast. . . .*

At this point in his song something hot stung his blind eyes, as if tears had materialized from somewhere, and he remembered all he had suffered in the county lockup.

The policeman held the hot electric prod up to his mouth until he could hear it crackle. "Shut your trap, you blind fuck!" the policeman spat out venomously. Then the sparking prod touched his lips, and lightning hit him like a thousand needles. His teeth, his gums, his tongue, and his throat—bursts of pain shot to the top of his head and down to the rest of his body. A scream tore from his throat, sending chills up his spine. Blood gushed from his withered eye sockets. "You can make me eat shit," he said, "but I couldn't keep my mouth shut if I wanted to. There are things inside me that must be said. I, Zhang Kou, am linked forever to the townspeople. . . ."

"Good for you, Great-Uncle Zhang Kou!" a couple of young fellows shouted. "There are half a million people in Paradise County, and yours is the only mouth that dares to speak out!"

"Zhang Kou, you might be elected county head!" someone jeered.

Everyone says our local leaders are chosen by the masses.
But why do the servants keep spending all their masters' money?
We common folk sweat blood like beasts of burden,
Just so corrupt, greedy officials can grow fat and lazy!

At this point in his song, Zhang Kou bit off each word, loud and crisp, whipping his audience into a frenzy of wild talk.

"Shit! They call themselves public servants, do they? Blood-sucking demons is what they are!"

"They say you can become a county leader for fifty thousand yuan a year!"

"The guest house lays out a fancy spread every day, with enough food to last us a year."

"Rotten to the core!"

An old man's voice joined the discussion: "You young people better watch what you're saying. You, too, Brother Zhang Kou. Remember what happened to the people who trashed the government offices!"

Zhang Kou sang his response: "Good brother, stand there quietly and listen to my story. . . ."

The words were barely out of his mouth when several raucous men elbowed their way into the crowd. "What are you people doing here? You're blocking traffic and disrupting order. Break it up, move on!"

Realizing at once that the voices belonged to the policemen who had dealt with him in the lockup, Zhang Kou recommenced plucking his *erhu*:

I sing of a sexy young girl with nice big tits and a willowy

waist Sashaying down the street, turning the heads of single young
men. . . .

"Zhang Kou, are you still singing those dirty rhymes?" one of the
policemen asked.

"Officer, don't be too quick to judge me," Zhang Kou replied. "As
a blind man, I have to rely on this mouth of mine for a living. I'm
no criminal."

A young fellow in the crowd spoke up: "Uncle Zhang Kou must
be tired after singing all afternoon. He deserves a rest. Come on,
folks, dig into your pockets. If you can't spare ten yuan, a single
copper is better than nothing. If everybody pitches in, he can treat
himself to some good meaty buns."

Coins clanked and paper notes rustled on the ground in front of
him. "Thank you," he said repeatedly, "thank you, one and all,
young and old."

"Officers, good Uncles, your rations come from the national
treasury, and you make a good enough wage that you'll never miss
the few coins that drop between your fingers. Show some pity for a
blind old man."

"Shit! What makes you think we've got any money?" one of the
policemen retorted angrily. "You earn more from one acre of garlic
than we do from working our asses off all year long!"

"More talk about garlic? Maybe your grandsons will be stupid
enough to plant garlic next year!" a young man jeered.

"You there," the policeman demanded, "what did you mean
by that?"

"What did I mean? Nothing. All I'm saying is no more garlic for
me. From now on I'm going to plant beans and maybe a little
opium," the young man grumbled.

"Opium? How many heads do you have on your shoulders, you
little punk?" the policeman demanded.

"Just one. But you'll see me begging on the street before I'll plant
another stalk of garlic!" The young man walked off.

"Stop right there! What's your name? What village?" The policeman ran after him.

"Everybody, run! The police are at it again!" someone shouted. With yells and shrieks, the crowd dispersed in all directions, leaving Zhang Kou in a blanket of silence. He cocked his ear to determine what was going on, but his rapt audience had slipped away like fish in the depths of the ocean, leaving behind a pall of silence and the stink of their sweat. From somewhere off in the distance came the sound of a bugle, followed by the noise of children on their way into a schoolhouse. He felt the warmth of the late-autumn afternoon sun on his back. After picking up his *erhu*, he groped around on the ground for the coins and paper money the people had thrown at his feet. Gratitude flooded his heart when he picked up an oversized ten-yuan bill; his hand began to quake. The depth of feeling toward his anonymous benefactor was unfathomable.

Back on his feet again, he negotiated the bumpy road, staff in hand, heading toward the train station and abandoned warehouse he and several other old vagrants called home. Ever since his release from the lockup, where he had been subjected to a barrage of physical abuse, he had earned the veneration of local thieves, beggars, and fortunetellers—the so-called dregs of society. The thieves stole a rush sleeping mat and enough cotton wadding to make him a nice soft bed, and the beggars shared their meager bounty with him. Over the long days and weeks he was on the mend, these were the people who cared for him, restoring in his mind a long-dormant faith in human nature. So, subordinating his own safety to a love for his outcast companions, he sang a ballad of garlic loud and long to protest the mistreatment of the common people.

About midway home, along with the smell of withered leaves on a familiar old tree, he also picked up the biting, metallic scent of rust-resistant oil. He barely had time to react before a hand clamped down on his shoulder. Instinctively, he drew his head down between his shoulders and squeezed his lips shut, fully expecting to be roundly cuffed. But whoever it was merely laughed amiably and said in a soft voice, "What are you flinching for? I won't hurt you."

"What do you want?" he asked in a quaking voice.

"Zhang Kou," the man said softly, "you haven't forgotten what an electric prod does to the mouth, have you?"

"I didn't say anything."

"Really?"

"I'm just a blind old man who sings tales to get by. That's how I keep from starving."

"I'm only thinking about your well-being," the man said. "No more songs about garlic, do you hear me? Which do you think will give out first, your mouth or the electric prod?"

"Thanks for the warning. I understand."

"That's good. Now don't do anything foolish. A big mouth is the cause of most problems."

The man turned and walked off, and a moment later Zhang Kou heard a motorbike start up and go putt-putting down the road. He stood beneath the old tree without moving for a long, long time. The woman who ran a snack shop near the big old tree saw him. "Is that you, Great-Uncle Zhang?" she called out warmly. "What are you standing there for? Come on over for some nice meaty buns, fresh from the oven. My treat."

A wry laugh escaped from him as he banged the tree trunk with his staff; then he exploded in furious shrieks: "You black-hearted hyenas, do you really think you can shut me up so easily? Sixty-six years is long enough for any man to live!"

The poor woman gasped in alarm. "Great-Uncle, who got you so angry? Is anything worth getting hysterical over?"

"Blind and poor, my life's never been worth more than a few coppers. Anyone who thinks he can shut Zhang Kou's mouth better be prepared to overturn the verdicts in the garlic case!" Back on the street again, he began singing at the top of his lungs.

The proprietress heaved a long sigh as she watched the blind old man's gaunt silhouette lurch down the street.

Three days later the autumn rains turned the side street into a sea of mud. As the snack-shop proprietress stood in her doorway gazing at the street lamp at the far end of the street, with raindrops dancing in its pale yellow light, she experienced a sense of desperate loneliness and paralyzing boredom. Before shutting the door and going to bed, she thought she heard the strains of Zhang Kou's dreary song hover around her. She jerked the door open and looked up and down the street, but the music died out. It returned when she shut the door again, more intimate and moving than ever.

The next morning they found Zhang Kou's body sprawled in the side street, his mouth crammed full of sticky mud. Lying beside him was the headless corpse of a cat.

Rain clouds brought with them the nauseating stench of rotting garlic, pressing it down over the town. Thieves, beggars, and other undesirables carried Zhang Kou's body up and down the side street, wailing and lamenting from dawn to dusk, when they dug a hole next to the big old tree and buried Zhang Kou in it.

From that day onward the proprietress of the snack shop heard Zhang Kou sing every night. Soon the little side street turned into a street of ghosts. One by one the local residents moved away, except for the proprietress, who one day hanged herself on the big tree, joining the area's spectral population.

2

All night long Fourth Aunt wheezed and coughed and fussed, robbing her cellmates of their sleep. The one they called Wild Mule cursed angrily, "If you're dying, damn you, be quick about it!"

"I'm not *trying* to cough, girl," Fourth Aunt said apologetically, "and I'd surely stop wheezing if I could. . . ."

The girl with long, pretty brows who slept on the bunk above Fourth Aunt grumbled, "It's criminal the way they make an old woman like her serve time."

Wounded by the reminder of injustice, Fourth Aunt felt tears well up in her eyes and spill out. And the more she thought about it, the worse she felt, until an agonizing groan swelled in her throat.

Her cellmates—about a dozen in all—sat up. The tender-hearted ones threw their coats over their shoulders and came up to see what was wrong, while those not so easily moved just grumbled and cursed. "Knock that off!" Wild Mule demanded. "I knew this would happen. I thought you were supposed to be hard as nails. You got off easy—five years for burning down a government building!"

Between sobs and wheezes Fourth Aunt moaned, "Girl, I know I'll die in this camp. . . ."

A sleepy-eyed guard appeared at the window and rapped on the bars. "What's going on? Who's making all that noise in the middle of the night?"

"Reporting, Officer," the long-browed girl said. "Number Thirty-eight is sick."

"What's she got?"

"She can't stop coughing and wheezing."

"That's nothing new. Now knock it off and get some sleep. Calisthenics first thing in the morning, don't forget."

After the guard left, the long-browed girl poured some water into a mug and held it up to Fourth Aunt's lips, then reached under her pillow for some tablets. "Here, Auntie," she said, "these are for pain and inflammation. Take a couple, they might just help."

"I can't use up your medicine, dear," Fourth Aunt demurred.

"We're all in the same boat," the girl replied, "so why worry about niceties like that now?"

The girl helped Fourth Aunt take the tablets. "Young lady," a tearful Fourth Aunt said, "how can I repay you for this?"

"Try her out as a daughter-in-law," Wild Mule volunteered.

"With those sons of mine?" Fourth Aunt remarked. "They're not worthy of somebody like this."

"And you, while you're selling a mule up front, the head of a turtle sneaks up from behind," the girl snapped.

Wild Mule sat up angrily and glared at her. "Who are you talking to?"

"You," the girl replied defiantly. "I'm calling you a stinking whore who sells her pussy!"

Mortified, then enraged, Wild Mule picked up a scuffed leather shoe and flung it at her antagonist. "*I* sell pussy?" she snarled. "And you don't? Stop acting so high and mighty around me. Nice little virgins don't wind up in a place like this!"

The long-browed girl ducked just in time for the shoe to sail by and hit the shrewish woman in bed three, who was serving time for drowning her own child; she picked it up off the floor and hit the long-browed girl on the head.

All hell broke loose then, with the long-browed girl and Wild Mule clawing and scratching each other, the shrew cursing up a storm, and Fourth Aunt shrieking tearfully. The other prisoners joined in by banging on the bars, howling, or getting in a few cheap shots of their own.

Two jailers armed with nightsticks burst into the cell and quickly subdued the combatants without worrying about sorting things out first.

"The next person who makes a sound," one of them threatened, "goes hungry for three days!"

The other said, "Numbers Twenty-nine and Forty, outside! You're coming with us."

"I didn't do anything," the long-browed girl whined.

"Shut up," said the jailer, underscoring her command with a well-placed thump with her nightstick.

Wild Mule smiled shyly. "Officers, I admit I was wrong, but I promise I won't do it again. I just want to get some sleep."

"Don't give me that! Now get dressed and come with me."

Fourth Aunt, bent at the waist, pleaded for her cellmates. "Don't blame them, Officers, it's all my fault. I'm just an old woman who can't stop wheezing and coughing. The other girls couldn't take it."

"That's enough," the jailer said. "Don't pull that saintly mother act on us!"

As the jailers led the long-browed girl and Wild Mule out of the cell, Fourth Aunt had to cover her mouth to keep from crying out loud.

That night she had a succession of nightmares. First she dreamt that Jinju came to see her, but when Fourth Aunt stepped forward, her pregnant daughter's tongue shot out and her eyes bulged. Fourth Aunt woke with a scream, her skin cold and clammy. Telephone wires strung outside the prison wall sang in the autumn winds. Moonbeams slanting in through the window landed on the face of the thief in bed four. Hardly a grown woman yet, the girl slept with her nose scrunched up and ground her teeth to one of her many dreams.

Fourth Aunt had barely closed her eyes again when Fourth Uncle stood at the foot of her bed, his head bloodied, and said, "Mother of my children, why are you still here? I want you with me." He reached out to Fourth Aunt, who once again was startled out of her sleep. Her heart was thumping wildly. Out beyond the camp's kitchen a rooster crowed. One more time and it would be daybreak.

Reveille was sounded. Fourth Aunt scrambled out of bed, reeled briefly, and collapsed like a rag doll. The shouts of her cellmates, who were making their beds, brought a jailer running. Fourth Aunt was sprawled facedown when she opened the door.

"Pick her up off the floor!" the jailer commanded.

Fourth Aunt's cellmates did as they were told, quickly if not very efficiently. Then the jailer called for the camp doctor, who gave Fourth Aunt an injection. Her mouth twitched, and murky tears spilled out of her eyes as the doctor bandaged a cut on her head. Right after breakfast, the jailer said, "You can take the day off, Number Thirty-eight."

Fourth Aunt was speechless with gratitude.

After the other inmates had formed ranks in the compound and marched into the fields to begin the day's labors, a hush fell over the cellblock, amplifying the sound of huge rats scurrying about the prison yard and chasing hungry sparrows away from food crumbs in the dirt. Some of the birds took refuge on the window ledge, where they cocked their heads and fixed their black, beady eyes on Fourth Aunt. All alone, and overcome by sadness, she wept; then, once the need to cry had passed, she murmured, "It's time to join you, Husband. . . ."

She removed her trousers, slipped the waistband around the metal frame of the bunk above her and rehooked the top button. Another sob, a final thought—Husband, I can't take any more of this—before slipping the loop of trouser cloth over her head and falling forward. . . .

But Fourth Aunt did not die, not then. She was saved by a passing jailer, who, with a resounding slap across the face, cursed, "What the hell were you thinking, you old skunk?"

With a loud wail, Fourth Aunt fell to her knees. "Be a good girl and let me die, please. . . ."

The jailer hesitated for a moment, her face transformed by a gentle femininity, and as she helped Fourth Aunt to her feet she said softly, "Old Mother, don't tell a soul what happened here today. It'll be our secret. If you'll stop carrying on all the time and work at being a model prisoner, I'll try to get you released early."

This time, as Fourth Aunt fell to her knees again, the jailer stopped her. "You're a good girl," Fourth Aunt said. "But someone has to pay for the death of my husband."

"Now stop saying things like that," the jailer counseled. "Leading a mob to destroy government offices is a serious crime."

"I lost my head. I promise I will never do it again. . . ."

A month later, Fourth Aunt was released for medical treatment, and not long afterwards she was back in her own home.

3

New Year's Day, 1988, was a holiday for the several hundred inmates in the labor-reform camp. Some observed it by sleeping in, others wrote letters home, and still others packed the yard outside the dayroom window to watch a variety show on a black-and-white TV set.

Gao Ma and Gao Yang sat on a large marble slab in the yard, stripped to the waist as they deloused their jackets. Sunbeams warming the dirt around them fell on their tanned skin. Here and there other small groups of prisoners sat in the sun conversing in hushed voices. Armed guards manned the towers beyond the inner gate, keeping a wary eye on the men below. The main gate, covered with steel mesh, was securely locked. Some camp officers were giving the inmates haircuts, bantering lightheartedly.

Gigantic rats scurried in and out of the open-air latrine. In the area between the two gates, a large black cat had been treed by a swarm of rodents.

"When the rats get this big, even cats stay out of their way," Gao Yang remarked.

Gao Ma smiled.

"I told my wife to bring you a pair of shoes after the first of the year," Gao Yang said.

"Don't go to all that trouble on my account," Gao Ma said, obviously touched. "She has her hands full with the two children. A bachelor like me doesn't need much."

"Bear up, Cousin, and make it through the coming year the best you can. Then when you get out, find yourself a wife and settle down."

Gao Ma smiled wanly but said nothing.

"You're a veteran, after all," Gao Yang went on. "The camp leaders have their eye on you. I know you can get an early release if you do what you're told. You could be out of here before me."

"Early or late, what difference does it make?" Gao Ma replied.

"What I'd rather do is serve your time for you, so you could go home and provide for your family again."

"Cousin," Gao Yang said, "we were fated to have bad luck. For men to suffer like this is no big deal, but think of poor Fourth Aunt. . . ."

Anxiously, Gao Ma asked, "Didn't they release her for medical reasons?"

Suddenly hesitant, Gao Yang said, "My wife said not to tell you . . ."

"Tell me what?" Gao Ma demanded anxiously, grabbing Gao Yang's hand.

Gao Yang sighed. "She was your mother-in-law, after all, so it wouldn't be right to keep it from you."

"Tell me, Cousin. Don't keep me in suspense."

"Remember when my wife visited me?" Gao Yang said. "That's when she told me."

"Told you what?"

"The Fang brothers are no-good bastards. They don't deserve to be called human!"

Gao Ma's patience was wearing thin. "Cousin Gao Yang, it's time to pour the beans out of the basket. Get it all out. You're driving me crazy the way you ramble."

Gao Yang sighed again. "Okay, here it is. Deputy Yang is no good either. Remember his nephew Cao Wen? Well, he jumped down a well, and his family decided to arrange an underworld marriage."

"A what?"

"You don't even know what an underworld marriage is?"

Gao Ma shook his head.

"It's where two dead people are united in marriage. So after Cao Wen died, his family thought first of Jinju."

Gao Ma jumped to his feet.

"Let me finish, Cousin," Gao Yang said. "The Caos wanted Jinju's ghost to be the wife of their dead son, so they asked Deputy Yang to act as matchmaker."

Gao Ma gnashed his teeth and cursed, "Fuck his lousy ancestors! Jinju belongs to me!"

"That's what makes me so angry," Gao Yang said. "Everybody in the village knows that Jinju belonged to you. She was carrying your child. But the Fang boys jumped at Deputy Yang's proposal and sold Jinju's remains to the Cao family for eight hundred yuan, which they split between them. Then the Caos sent people to open Jinju's grave and deliver her remains to them."

Gao Ma, his face the color of cold iron, didn't make a sound.

Gao Yang continued: "My wife said that the ceremony outdid any regular wedding she'd ever seen. They hired musicians from somewhere outside the county, who played while the guests enjoyed a huge spread. Then Jinju's and Cao Wen's remains were placed in a bright red coffin and buried together. Villagers who came to watch the festivities cursed the Cao family, and Deputy Yang, and the Fang brothers. Everyone agreed that the whole affair was an insult to heaven and a crime against reason!"

Gao Ma remained absolutely silent.

Gao Yang looked at Gao Ma. "Cousin," he quickly went on, "it won't help to brood over this. They committed this crime against heaven, and the old man up there will punish them. . . . It's all my fault. My wife told me to keep quiet, but this stinking mouth of mine can't keep a secret."

A chilling smile spread across Gao Ma's face.

"Cousin," Gao Yang blurted out fearfully, "don't get any wild ideas. You're a veteran, so you can't believe in ghosts and things like that."

"What about Fourth Aunt?" Gao Ma asked softly.

Gao Yang hemmed and hawed for a moment, then reluctantly said, "The day the Caos came for Jinju's remains she . . . hanged herself."

An anguished roar tore from Gao Ma's throat, followed by a mouthful of bright red blood.

4

A major snowstorm fell shortly after New Year's Day.

Prisoners shoveled the snow into piles and loaded it onto handcarts to be deposited in a nearby millet field.

Gao Ma, the first to volunteer, pulled a snow-laden handcart out the main gate. Extra guards had not been posted, since only a few prisoners were let out the gate. Instead, one of the camp officers stood watch at the gate, his arms folded as he chatted with a tower guard.

"Old Li," the guard said, "has your wife had the baby yet?"

The officer, worry written all over his face, replied, "Not yet. She's a month overdue."

"Don't worry," the guard comforted him. "As the saying goes, A melon drops when it's ripe.'"

"Don't worry? How would you like it if your old lady was a month overdue? Talk's cheap."

Gao Ma, sweat-soaked, returned with an empty cart.

The officer looked at him sympathetically. "Take a break, Number Eighty-eight. Somebody else can wrestle with the cart for a while."

"I'm not tired," Gao Ma said as he passed through the gate.

"That Number Eighty-eight's a pretty good guy," the guard remarked.

"A veteran," the officer said. "A little too high-spirited is all. Well, nothing surprises me these days."

"Those shitty Paradise County officials went too far, if you want my opinion," the guard said. "The common folk don't deserve all the blame for what happened."

"That's why I recommended that this one's sentence be trimmed. They came down too hard on him, if you ask me."

"But that's how things go these days."

Gao Ma approached the gate with another load of snow.

"Didn't I tell you to take a break?" the officer asked him.

"After this load." He headed toward the millet field.

"I hear Deputy Commissar Yu is being reassigned," the guard said.

"I'd like to be reassigned," the officer said wistfully. "This job stinks. No holidays, not even New Year's, and miserable wages. I'd get out in a minute if I had someplace else to go."

"You can always quit, if it's that bad," the guard noted. "Me, I've decided to become an entrepreneur."

"In times like these, if you're smart you're an official. But if you can't manage that, make some money any way you can."

"Hey, where's Number Eighty-eight?" the guard asked with alarm.

The officer turned toward the field, where the sunshine made the snow sparkle with extraordinary beauty.

The watchtower siren wailed loudly.

"Number Eighty-eight," the guard shouted, "halt or I'll shoot!"

Gao Ma was running straight into the sun, nearly blinded by its brightness. The fresh air of freedom rolled like waves over the snowy fields. He ran like a man possessed, oblivious to his surroundings, hellbent on revenge. He rose into the air as if riding the clouds and soaring through the mist, until he realized with wonder that he was sprawled in the icy snow, facedown. He sensed something hot and sticky spurting out of his back. With a soft "Jinju . . ." on his lips, he buried his face in the wet snow.

TRANSLATOR'S NOTE

The translator is grateful to William Tay for bringing this novel to his attention soon after its appearance in a Chinese magazine; to Joseph Lau and Xiaobing Tang for ideas and encouragements; and to Courtney Hodell for her editorial insights and unflagging enthusiasm. The Taiwan Hung-fan 1989 edition was used, while other versions were consulted. Parts of Chapter Nineteen and all of Chapter Twenty have been revised, in conjunction with the author.

CHARACTER AND PRONUNCIATION GUIDE

Surnames (family names) always precede given names and titles (our author is Mr. Mo, not Mr. Yan). It is common in rural villages for a single surname to predominate; it is also common for rural and urban Chinese alike to address one another not by name but by family hierarchical title—Elder Brother, Aunt, Cousin—even in the absence of blood relationships. The major characters in the novel are:

GAO YANG ("Sheep" Gao): a garlic farmer
HIS WIFE
XINGHUA: his blind daughter
GAO MA ("Horse" Gao): a garlic farmer
GAO ZHILENG: a parakeet raiser
GAO JINJIAO: the village boss (formally "director")

The FANG family:

FANG YUNQIU (Fourth Uncle): head of the household
FOURTH AUNT: his wife
FANG YIJUN (also Number One, Elder Brother): his son
FANG YIXIANG (also Number Two, Second Brother): his son
FANG JINJU (Golden Chrysanthemum): his daughter

DEPUTY YANG (Eighth Uncle): a local dignitary
SECRETARY WANG (Wang Jiaxiu): the local party boss
YU QIUSHUI: a peasant
ZHANG KOU: a blind minstrel

The proximate pronunciation of modern Chinese has not been materially aided by the pinyin ("spell-sound") system. For the most part, the key is in the vowels:

a as in father (except after *y*, when it is the same as *e*)
e as in met
i as in see (*in* and *ing* are the same as in English)
o as in pork
u as in mood
ao as in cow
ei as in hay
iu as in use
ou as in old
u after *j, q, x,* and *y*, as the German ü? (über)
c is pronounced as *ts* (i*ts*)
q is pronounced as *ch* (*ch*ill)
x is pronounced as *sh* (*sh*e)
z is pronounced as *ds* (yar*ds*)
zh is pronounced as *j*

methuen

For more information on all Methuen titles,
visit our website at

www.methuen.co.uk

For sales enquiries about Methuen books
please contact

The Sales Department
Methuen Publishing Ltd
11–12 Buckingham Gate
London SW1E 6LB
Tel: 020 7798 1609
Fax: 020 7828 2098
sales@methuen.co.uk

Prices are subject to change without notice